General Editor: David Stuart Davies

DOCTOR NIKOLA,
MASTER CRIMINAL

Doctor Nikola, Master Criminal

A BID FOR FORTUNE
DOCTOR NIKOLA

Guy Boothby

with an introduction by
Mark Valentine

WORDSWORTH EDITIONS

In loving memory of
MICHAEL TRAYLER
the founder of Wordsworth Editions

1

Readers who are interested in other titles from
Wordsworth Editions are invited to visit our website at
www.wordsworth-editions.com

For our latest list and a full mail-order service contact
Bibliophile Books, Unit 5 Datapoint,
South Crescent, London E16 4TL
Tel: +44 020 74 74 24 74
Fax: +44 020 74 74 85 89
orders@bibliophilebooks.com
www.bibliophilebooks.com

This edition published 2009 by
Wordsworth Editions Limited
8B East Street, Ware, Hertfordshire SG12 9HJ

ISBN 978 1 84022 165 7

Typeset in Great Britain by Roperford Editorial
Printed by Clays Ltd, St Ives plc

CONTENTS

INTRODUCTION

As well as having all the best tunes, it might be said the devil has all the best books. No sooner had the thriller, or shocker as it was then called, taken hold of the Victorian imagination, than shrewd authors realised their readers loved a good – or rather, far from good – villain. Arthur Conan Doyle obliged, with his criminal mastermind Professor Moriarty, arch-enemy of Sherlock Holmes. E. W. Hornung went one step further and made his hero a villain, with the gentleman cricketer and crook, A. J. Raffles. Oscar Wilde's vice-ridden aesthete Dorian Gray, and Bram Stoker's sleek, cloaked Count Dracula are equally demonic figures.

But perhaps none lured late nineteenth century readers into his grasp more surely than Dr Nikola, the mysterious and saturnine creation of Guy Boothby. When he appeared on the literary scene, in *A Bid for Fortune* (1895), there was certainly no shortage of strange and striking fiction. In that year, H. G. Wells startled readers with his classic scientific romance, *The Time Machine*. Veteran fantasist George Macdonald published *Lilith*, which relates a journey in an otherworld, in the company of a bookish raven. And Arthur Machen, the master of supernatural horror, issued *The Three Impostors*, the labyrinthine tale of a satanic conspiracy, led by his own arch-villain, Dr Lipsius.

So Dr Nikola had many rivals for readers' attention. The character was launched on the reading public gently enough. In the opening scenes, private rooms in the Imperial Restaurant, London, are being prepared for a very particular dinner party. A few guests, each somewhat strange, arrive. Then, in strides . . . Dr Nikola. And with him, there is a perennial companion. Huge, baleful, gleaming-eyed, it is the black cat Apollyon, named after a dark angel. He is often to be found haughtily perched upon Nikola's shoulders, directing his sardonic green gaze upon the unfortunates who find themselves in the Doctor's power.

Yet, despite his feline familiar, Nikola is no stock-in-trade villain. His ways are inscrutable. If his methods are direct and ruthless, he has no time for needless violence and is courteous and even considerate towards his enemies. As he pursues his strange schemes across the world, he appears sometimes as a force for evil and on occasion in support of virtue and desperate causes. The adventures started in *A Bid for Fortune*, which is sometimes entitled *Enter, Dr Nikola!*, and continued just a year later in the next book in the series, *Dr Nikola* (1896), also known as *Dr Nikola Returns*. The two books really make up one great, complete, global tale, so we have brought them together in this edition. There were three further books in the series, all separate adventures: *The Lust of Hate* (1898), *Dr Nikola's Experiment* (1899) and *Farewell, Nikola* (1901).

Such was their confidence in its stirring qualities, that the opening episode of that first Dr Nikola adventure, *A Bid for Fortune*, was used by Boothby's publisher to launch their new periodical, *The Windsor Magazine* (a rival to *The Strand Magazine*) in January 1895, and they even had a little swipe at the penchant for minute scrutiny that was the hallmark of the Holmes stories. The journal's foreword said: 'In our first number begins a serial story, "A Bid for Fortune", by Mr. Guy Boothby, a writer who has given proof of his capacity to keep alight in fiction the campfires of adventure. Though despised [by a contemporary critic], the adventure story has an abiding fascination for households in which nothing eventful ever happens, for the world is not yet so completely cured of marvels that every novelist is reduced to evolving analytic significance from the buttons of the heroine's shoe!"

Boothby's publisher also made sure that the design of the Nikola books would seize readers' attention. A portrait of Dr Nikola, in white cravat and fur coat, with Apollyon on his shoulder, stares compellingly from the covers. Inside, Stanley L. Woods provided numerous illustrations capturing the most exciting scenes. But this alone was not the reason for the books' success. The author knew how to keep the pace going, moving swiftly from incident to incident, never letting the reader stop to reflect (perhaps fortunately in view of some of the implausibilities which Boothby blithely carries through in a glorious cavalier fashion).

No wonder that even that staid old chronicler *The Times* exclaimed, 'He never allows the interest to drop from first page to last . . . The plot is highly ingenious, and . . . exciting to a degree', while the cautious *Scotsman* also kicked up its heels: 'One hair-breadth escape succeeds another with a rapidity that scarce leaves the reader breathing space . . . a story ingeniously and inventively told.' Another paper conceded, 'Guy Boothby's books are not literature – but they certainly make the blood tingle.'

It was the sheer range and reach of Dr Nikola, the vast ambitions of his plans, which marked him out as something new and exciting in crime and adventure fiction. A character exclaims, 'Dr Nikola! Well, he's Nikola, and that's all I can tell you. If you're a wise man you'll want to know no more . . . Ask the Japanese, ask the Malays, the Hindoos, the Burmese, the coal porter in Port Said, the Buddhist priests of Ceylon; ask the King of Corea, the men up in Tibet, the Spanish priests in Manila or the Sultans of Borneo, the Ministers of Siam, or the French in Saigon. They'll all know Dr. Nikola and his cat, and take my word for it, they fear him.'

Indeed, we may justly call Nikola the first real master villain. He is no less predominant than Conan Doyle's Moriarty, described by Sherlock Holmes in 'The Final Problem' (1893) in this way: 'He is the Napoleon of crime, Watson. He is the organiser of half that is evil and of nearly all that is undetected in this great city. He is a genius, a philosopher, an abstract thinker. He has a brain of the first order. He sits motionless, like a spider in the centre of its web, but that web has a thousand radiations, and he knows well every quiver of each of them.'

This is all true of Nikola, too. Unlike Moriarty, though, there are frequent hints throughout the books that Dr Nikola has subtle occult powers. He is a mesmerist, certainly, and can cause his victims to see visions. He pitches his heightened mind into unknown realms and undertakes astral journeys that allow him to see scenes distant in space and time. He has a strong sense of his own destiny, which forces him on in his remorseless quest for hidden knowledge. None of these powers are used to excess, however, for they evidently require great concentration and will.

The first two books, presented here, are usually regarded as the strongest in the series, and in them Nikola exercises all his powers in the quest for a sacred relic that will allow him to win influence over certain sects practising Tibetan magic. He believes that they will gain him access to a remote Himalayan monastery which holds the secret of how to raise the dead and secure immortality; and he is determined to possess this.

The reading public would already be familiar with the idea of holy secrets in the Himalayas. This was a key belief in Theosophy, the occult teachings founded by Madame Blavatsky in 1880, which were said to be derived from 'Secret Masters' located in those mountains. It is difficult to grasp now just how popular Theosophy was at the time – a worldwide organisation with a membership numbered in the hundreds of thousands, with many associated societies.

Helena Blavatsky, the daughter of a Russian imperial governor, fled from a marriage to a much older man, and in her subsequent wanderings claimed to have spent seven years in Tibet, where she studied under the 'Himalayan Masters' in their temples hidden in the unexplored mountains, perhaps in the 1850s. These great supernatural figures, guiding the esoteric future of the world, were advanced both in wisdom and age. As a recent historian of Theosophy has observed, 'Whether real or imagined, Blavatsky's trips to Tibet were to take on considerable significance as the romantic and religious symbolism of that country increased in the late nineteenth century, in direct proportion to its perceived remoteness.' (Peter Washington, *Madame Blavatsky's Baboon*, 1993). It was not until the British military mission to Lhassa, led by Francis Younghusband in 1903-4, that some understanding of Tibet and its religion began to arise in the West. Until then, it was a blank on the physical and spiritual map, and one which authors were intent in exploring in fiction.

Dr Nikola and all his works were the inspiration of Guy Newell Boothby (1867-1905), who packed into less than a dozen years of writing life a torrent of over thirty novels. He was born in Adelaide, South Australia on 12 October 1867 but sent to school in England at an early age: he attended the Christ's Hospital public school, an ancient foundation, in London. He only returned to his native country when he was sixteen, in 1883. His grandfather had been a High Court judge in his home state, and his father was a local politician, and, no doubt through these connections, for a while Guy Boothby held the responsible position of secretary to the mayor of his home town. This brought him into contact with the polite society that he gently mocks in his books, but it was clear that his restless temperament would soon lead him elsewhere. Perhaps wanting to get to know the country of his birth better, he went on a trek across the continent from North to South, and later wrote up his adventures in his first book, *On the Wallaby: or, Through the East and Across Australia* (1894). Young wanderers are the chief characters in many of his books: they find their way around South America, the East Indies, the Far East, and bohemian Europe: almost anywhere on the globe, in fact, where fortunes might be found – or lost.

Guy Boothby himself left Australia again for England in his early twenties and this time remained there, as he pursued his literary career. At first, he wrote tales of the South Seas and the Australian outback, sure to win favour with a British audience interested in the *outré* ways of the far-flung colonies. In this, his career was quite similar to that of E. W. Hornung, who had worked in Australia as a young man and whose own first books used this as a setting. Like Hornung and his breakthrough creation of Raffles, though, it took a different sort of character, the cosmopolitan and cultivated Nikola, to really win Boothby acclaim. Another intriguing similarity is that both men wrote of gentleman crooks: for in Guy Boothby's *The Duchess of Wiltshire's Diamonds* (1897) a detective is so bored with a lack of cases that he commits a sensational crime himself. It's interesting that both men, not quite rooted in either British or colonial society, wrote most vividly and persuasively of figures who were renegades: perhaps this was the way they felt about themselves.

Next to Tibet, the other great source of mystic power and strangeness for the British reader was Egypt. And, after the Nikola books, Guy Boothby's other notable success was with *Pharos, the Egyptian* (1899), a tale of Egyptian magic, a sinister mummy, and the modern day sorcerer of the title, who holds sway over a beautiful young Hungarian woman, and an English artist in love with her. As in the Dr Nikola tales, it is the villain who is the most vivid portrayal in the book. Boothby's romance may have been one of the inspirations for Bram Stoker's story of Egypt and the occult, *The Jewel of the Seven Stars* (1903). Macabre powers were also to the fore in Boothby's *The Curse of the Snake* (1902), in which the malefic serpent possesses its victims and drains their vitality – a theme Stoker also deployed in *The Lair of the White Worm* (1911).

None of Boothby's other books was quite as popular as the Nikola titles, but there was still a large readership for many. His friend and mentor Rudyard Kipling observed that 'he has come to great honours . . . his name is large upon the hoardings, his books sell like hot cakes.' Amongst many other successful titles, we should note *The Maker of Nations* (1900), in which the hero leads a South American revolution but changes sides when he falls in love with the dictator's daughter, and *A Prince of Swindlers* in the same year, featuring another charming genteel rogue. Just as Nikola is a character for whom expediency is a virtue, and idealism an unknown quantity, one senses that Boothby had no great allegiances or causes at heart. An extravagant gusto for his books does, however, clearly come across. *The Times* rightly described his work in 1905 as 'frank sensationalism carried to its furthest limits', and he would scarcely have disagreed.

Guy Boothby died at his home in Boscombe, near Bournemouth, from complications arising from influenza, on 26 February 1905, and his grave is in the town's Wimborne Road cemetery. Tributes at the time called him 'one of the leading novelists of his generation', if only in popularity, and reported that fellow writers jocularly claimed to believe he had perfected a sinister machine, to be able to produce his books at such a bewildering rate. Yet his work ensured his name endured. The Nikola books, especially, continued to be reprinted for many years afterwards, often adorned with that sinister portrait of the great man and his cat.

Nor was Kipling the only champion of Guy Boothby. His books were remembered with affection by George Orwell, who noted: 'The books one reads in childhood, and perhaps most of all the bad and good bad books, create in one's mind a sort of false map of the world, a series of fabulous countries into which one can retreat at odd moments throughout the rest of life, and which in some cases can even survive a visit to the real countries which they are supposed to represent. The pampas, the Amazon, the coral islands of the Pacific, Russia, land of birch-tree and samovar, Transylvania with its boyars and vampires, the China of Guy Boothby, the Paris of du Maurier – one could continue the list for a long time . . . '

In the final Nikola book, the great mastermind and mage, somewhat redeemed, retires to his own fabulous world, that remote Himalayan monastery, to perfect his fate. But the name of Dr Nikola had a strange after-life. In the early part of the last century, there was an itinerant atheist who used to harangue crowds in the West Yorkshire mill town of Keighley with satirical attacks upon biblical passages, emphasising the more absurd aspects. Such was his virulence – and popularity – that eventually the authorities had to silence him, which they achieved by imprisoning him for blasphemy. The vagrant pagan called himself – Dr Nikola. It is a curious tribute to a figure that had obviously fully seized the popular imagination.

And now . . . it is London, in the eighteen-nineties, at the Imperial Restaurant. The tables are laid, and an elegant host, whose invitation you cannot refuse, awaits your presence. Make your peace with the purring Apollyon. Dare now, if you will, to enter the lair of Dr Nikola . . .

MARK VALENTINE

A BID FOR FORTUNE

Doctor Nikola's Vendetta

PART ONE

PROLOGUE

Dr Nikola

The manager of the new Imperial Restaurant on the Thames Embankment went into his luxurious private office and shut the door. Having done so, he first scratched his chin reflectively, and then took a letter from the drawer in which it had reposed for more than two months and perused it carefully. Though he was not aware of it, this was the thirtieth time he had read it since breakfast that morning. And yet he was not a whit nearer understanding it than he had been at the beginning. He turned it over and scrutinised the back, where not a sign of writing was to be seen; he held it up to the window, as if he might hope to discover something from the watermark; but there was evidently nothing in either of these places of a nature calculated to set his troubled mind at rest. Then, though he had a clock upon his mantelpiece in good working order, he took a magnificent repeater watch from his waistcoat pocket and glanced at the dial; the hands stood at half-past seven. He immediately threw the letter on the table, and as he did so his anxiety found relief in words.

'It's really the most extraordinary affair I ever had to do with,' he remarked to the placid face of the clock above mentioned. 'And as I've been in the business just three-and-thirty years at eleven a.m. next Monday morning, I ought to know something about it. I only hope I've done right, that's all.'

As he spoke, the chief bookkeeper, who had the treble advantage of being tall, pretty, and just eight-and-twenty years of age, entered the room. She noticed the open letter and the look upon her chief's face, and her curiosity was proportionately excited.

'You seem worried, Mr McPherson,' she said tenderly, as she put down the papers she had brought in for his signature.

'You have just hit it, Miss O'Sullivan,' he answered, pushing them farther on to the table. 'I am worried about many things, but particularly about this letter.'

He handed the epistle to her, and she, being desirous of impressing him with her business capabilities, read it with ostentatious care. But it was noticeable that when she reached the signature she too turned back to the beginning, and then deliberately read it over again. The manager rose, crossed to the mantelpiece, and rang for the head waiter. Having relieved his feelings in this way, he seated himself again at his writing-table, put on his glasses, and stared at his companion, while waiting for her to speak.

'It's very funny,' she said at length, seeing that she was expected to say something. 'Very funny indeed!'

'It's the most extraordinary communication I have ever received,' he replied with conviction. 'You see it is written from Cuyaba, Brazil. The date is three months ago to a day. Now I have taken the trouble to find out where and what Cuyaba is.'

He made this confession with an air of conscious pride, and having done so, laid himself back in his chair, stuck his thumbs into the armholes of his waistcoat, and looked at his fair subordinate for approval.

Nor was he destined to be disappointed. He was a bachelor in possession of a snug income, and she, besides being a pretty woman, was a lady with a keen eye to the main chance.

'And where is Cuyaba?' she asked humbly.

'Cuyaba,' he replied, rolling his tongue with considerable relish round his unconscious mispronunciation of the name, 'is a town almost on the western or Bolivian border of Brazil. It is of moderate size, is situated on the banks of the river Cuyaba, and is considerably connected with the famous Brazilian Diamond Fields.'

'And does the writer of this letter live there?'

'I cannot say. He writes from there – that is enough for us.'

'And he orders dinner for four – here, in a private room overlooking the river, three months ahead – punctually at eight o'clock, gives you a list of the things he wants, and even arranges the decoration of the table. Says he has never seen either of his three friends before; that one of them hails from (here she consulted the letter again) Hang-chow, another from Bloemfontein, while the third resides, at present, in England. Each one is to present an ordinary visiting card with a red dot on it to the porter in the hall, and to be shown to the room at once. I don't understand it at all.'

The manager paused for a moment, and then said deliberately: 'Hang-chow is in China, Bloemfontein is in South Africa.'

'What a wonderful man you are, to be sure, Mr McPherson! I never can *think* how you manage to carry so much in your head.'

There spoke the true woman. And it was a move in the right direction, for the manager was susceptible to her gentle influence, as she had occasion to know.

At this juncture the head waiter appeared upon the scene, and took up a position just inside the doorway, as if he were afraid of injuring the carpet by coming further.

'Is No 22 ready, Williams?'

'Quite ready, sir. The wine is on the ice, and cook tells me he'll be ready to dish punctual to the moment.'

'The letter says, "no electric light; candles with red shades". Have you put on those shades I got this morning?'

'Just seen it done this very minute, sir.'

'And let me see, there was one other thing.' He took the letter from the chief bookkeeper's hand and glanced at it.

'Ah, yes, a porcelain saucer, and a small jug of new milk upon the mantelpiece. An extraordinary request, but has it been attended to?'

'I put it there myself, sir.'

'Who wait?'

'Jones, Edmunds, Brooks, and Tomkins.'

'Very good. Then I think that will do. Stay! You had better tell the hall porter to look out for three gentlemen presenting plain visiting cards with a little red spot on them. Let Brooks wait in the hall, and when they arrive tell him to show them straight up to the room.'

'It shall be done, sir.'

The head waiter left the room, and the manager stretched himself in his chair, yawned by way of showing his importance, and then said solemnly: 'I don't believe they'll any of them turn up; but if they do, this Dr Nikola, whoever he may be, won't be able to find fault with my arrangements.'

Then, leaving the dusty high road of Business, he and his companion wandered in the shady bridle-paths of Love to the end that when the chief bookkeeper returned to her own department she had forgotten the strange dinner party about to take place upstairs, and was busily engaged upon a calculation as to how she would look in white satin and orange blossoms, and, that settled, fell to wondering whether it was true, as Miss Joyce, a subordinate, had been heard to declare, that the manager had once shown himself partial to a certain widow with reputed savings and a share in an extensive egg and dairy business.

At ten minutes to eight precisely a hansom drew up at the steps of the hotel. As soon as it stopped, an undersized gentleman, with a clean-shaven countenance, a canonical corporation, and bow legs, dressed in a decidedly clerical garb, alighted. He paid and discharged his cabman, and then took from his ticket pocket an ordinary white visiting card, which he presented to the gold-laced individual who had opened the apron. The latter, having noted the red spot, called a waiter, and the reverend gentleman was immediately escorted upstairs.

Hardly had the attendant time to return to his station in the hall, before a second cab made its appearance, closely followed by a third. Out of the second jumped a tall, active, well-built man of about thirty years of age. He was dressed in evening dress of the latest fashion, and to conceal it from the vulgar gaze, wore a large Inverness cape of heavy texture. He also in his turn handed a white card to the porter, and, having done so, proceeded into the hall, followed by the occupant of the last cab, who had closely copied his example. This individual was also in evening dress, but it was of a different stamp. It was old-fashioned and had seen much use. The wearer, too, was taller than the ordinary run of men, while it was noticeable that his hair was snow-white, and that his face was deeply pitted with smallpox. After disposing of their hats and coats in an ante-room, they reached room No 22, where they found the gentleman in clerical costume pacing impatiently up and down.

Left alone, the tallest of the trio, who for want of a better title we may call the Best Dressed Man, took out his watch, and having glanced at it, looked at his companions.

'Gentlemen,' he said, with a slight American accent, 'it is three minutes to eight o'clock. My name is Eastover!'

'I'm glad to hear it, for I'm most uncommonly hungry,' said the next tallest, whom I have already described as being so marked by disease. 'My name is Prendergast!'

'We only wait for our friend and host,' remarked the clerical gentleman, as if he felt he ought to take a share in the conversation, and then, as if an afterthought had struck him, he continued, 'My name is Baxter!'

They shook hands all round with marked cordiality, seated themselves again, and took it in turns to examine the clock.

'Have you ever had the pleasure of meeting our host before?' asked Mr Baxter of Mr Prendergast.

'Never,' replied that gentleman, with a shake of his head. 'Perhaps Mr Eastover has been more fortunate?'

'Not I,' was the brief rejoinder. 'I've had to do with him off and on for longer than I care to reckon, but I've never set eyes on him up to date.'

'And where may he have been the first time you heard from him?'

'In Nashville, Tennessee,' said Eastover. 'After that, Tahupapa, New Zealand; after that, Papeete, in the Society Islands; then Pekin, China. And you?'

'First time, Brussels; second, Monte Video; third, Mandalay, and then the Gold Coast, Africa. It's your turn, Mr Baxter.'

The clergyman glanced at the timepiece. It was exactly eight o'clock.

'First time, Cabul, Afghanistan; second, Nijni Novgorod, Russia; third, Wilcannia, Darling River, Australia; fourth, Valparaiso, Chile; fifth, Nagasaki, Japan.'

'He is evidently a great traveller and a most mysterious person.'

'He is more than that,' said Eastover with conviction; 'he is late for dinner!'

Prendergast looked at his watch.

'That clock is two minutes fast. Hark, there goes Big Ben! Eight exactly.'

As he spoke the door was thrown open and a voice announced 'Dr Nikola.'

The three men sprang to their feet simultaneously, with exclamations of astonishment, as the man they had been discussing made his appearance.

It would take more time than I can spare the subject to give you an adequate and inclusive description of the person who entered the room at that moment. In stature he was slightly above the ordinary, his shoulders were broad, his limbs perfectly shaped and plainly muscular, but very slim. His head, which was magnificently set upon his shoulders, was adorned with a profusion of glossy black hair; his face was destitute of beard or moustache, and was of oval shape and handsome moulding; while his skin was of a dark olive hue, a colour which harmonised well with his piercing black eyes and pearly teeth. His hands and feet were small, and the greatest dandy must have admitted that he was irreproachably dressed, with a neatness that bordered on the puritanical. In age he might have been anything from eight-and-twenty to forty; in reality he was thirty-three. He advanced into the room and walked with out-stretched hand directly across to where Eastover was standing by the fireplace.

'Mr Eastover, I feel certain,' he said, fixing his glittering eyes upon the man he addressed, and allowing a curious smile to play upon his face.

'That is my name, Dr Nikola,' the other answered with evident surprise. 'But how on earth can you distinguish me from your other guests?'

'Ah! it would surprise you if you knew. And Mr Prendergast, and Mr Baxter. This is delightful; I hope I am not late. We had a collision in the Channel this morning, and I was almost afraid I might not be up to time. Dinner seems ready; shall we sit down to it?'

They seated themselves, and the meal commenced. The Imperial Restaurant has earned an enviable reputation for doing things well, and the dinner that night did not in any way detract from its lustre. But delightful as it all was, it was noticeable that the three guests paid more attention to their host than to his excellent menu. As they had said before his arrival, they had all had dealings with him for several years, but what those dealings were they were careful not to describe. It was more than possible that they hardly liked to remember them themselves.

When coffee had been served and the servants had withdrawn, Dr Nikola rose from the table, and went across to the massive sideboard. On it stood a basket of very curious shape and workmanship. This he opened, and as he did so, to the astonishment of his guests, an enormous cat, as black as his master's coat, leaped out on to the floor. The reason for the saucer and jug of milk became evident.

Seating himself at the table again, the host followed the example of his guests and lit a cigar, blowing a cloud of smoke luxuriously through his delicately chiselled nostrils. His eyes wandered round the cornice of the room, took in the pictures and decorations, and then came down to meet the faces of his companions. As they did so, the black cat, having finished its meal, sprang on to his shoulder to crouch there, watching the three men through the curling smoke drift with its green, blinking, fiendish eyes.

Dr Nikola smiled as he noticed the effect the animal had upon his guests.

'Now shall we get to business?' he said briskly.

The others almost simultaneously knocked the ashes off their cigars and brought themselves to attention. Dr Nikola's dainty, languid manner seemed to drop from him like a cloak, his eyes brightened, and his voice, when he spoke, was clean cut as chiselled silver.

'You are doubtless anxious to be informed why I summoned you from all parts of the globe to meet me here tonight? And it is very natural you should be. But then from what you know of me you should not be surprised at anything I do.'

His voice gradually dropped back into its old tone of gentle languor. He drew in a great breath of smoke and then sent it slowly out from his lips again. His eyes were half closed, and he drummed with one finger on the table edge.

The cat looked through the smoke at the three men, and it seemed to them that he grew every moment larger and more ferocious. Presently his owner took him from his perch and seating him on his knee fell to stroking his fur, from head to tail, with his long slim fingers. It was as if he were drawing inspiration for some deadly mischief from the uncanny beast.

'To preface what I have to say to you, let me tell you that this is by far the most important business for which I have ever required your help. (Three slow strokes down the centre of the back and one round each ear.) When it first came into my mind I was at a loss who to trust in the matter. I thought of Vendon, but I found Vendon was dead. I thought of Brownlow, but Brownlow was no longer faithful. (Two strokes down the back and two on the throat.) Then bit by bit I remembered you. I was in Brazil at the time. So I sent for you. You came, and we meet here. So far so good.'

He rose and crossed over to the fireplace. As he went the cat crawled back to its original position on his shoulder. Then his voice changed once more to its former business-like tone.

'I am not going to tell you very much about it. But from what I do tell you, you will be able to gather a great deal and imagine the rest. To begin with, there is a man living in this world today who has done me a great and lasting injury. What that injury is is no concern of yours. You would not understand if I told you. So we'll leave that out of the question. He is immensely rich. His cheque for 300,000 pounds would be honoured by his bank at any minute. Obviously he is a power. He has had reason to know that I am pitting my wits against his, and he flatters himself that so far he has got the better of me. That is because I am drawing him on. I am maturing a plan which will make him a poor and a very miserable man at one and the same time. If that scheme succeeds, and I am satisfied with the way you three men have performed the parts I shall call on you to play in it, I shall pay to each of you the sum of 10,000 pounds. If it doesn't succeed, then you will each receive a thousand and your expenses. Do you follow me?'

It was evident from their faces that they hung upon his every word.

'But, remember, I demand from you your whole and entire labour. While you are serving me you are mine body and soul. I know you are trustworthy. I have had good proof that you are – pardon the expression – unscrupulous, and I flatter myself you are silent. What is more, I shall tell you nothing beyond what is necessary for the carrying out of my scheme, so that you could not betray me if you would. Now for my plans!'

He sat down again and took a paper from his pocket. Having perused it, he turned to Eastover.

'You will leave at once – that is to say, by the boat on Wednesday – for Sydney. You will book your passage tomorrow morning, first thing, and join her in Plymouth. You will meet me tomorrow evening at an address I will send you and receive your final instructions. Good-night.'

Seeing that he was expected to go, Eastover rose, shook hands, and left the room without a word. He was too astonished to hesitate or to say anything.

Nikola took another letter from his pocket and turned to Prendergast.

'You will go down to Dover tonight, cross to Paris tomorrow morning, and leave this letter personally at the address you will find written on it. On Thursday, at half-past two precisely, you will deliver me an answer in the porch at Charing Cross. You will find sufficient money in that envelope to pay all your expenses. Now go!'

'At half-past two you shall have your answer. Good-night.'

'Good-night.'

When Prendergast had left the room, Dr Nikola lit another cigar and turned his attentions to Mr Baxter.

'Six months ago, Mr Baxter, I found for you a situation as tutor to the young Marquis of Beckenham. You still hold it, I suppose?'

'I do.'

'Is the Duke, the lad's father, well disposed towards you?'

'In every way. I have done my best to ingratiate myself with him. That was one of your instructions, if you will remember.'

'Yes, yes! But I was not certain that you would succeed. If the old man is anything like what he was when I last met him, he must still be a difficult person to deal with. Does the boy like you?'

'I hope so.'

'Have you brought me his photograph as I directed?'

'I have. Here it is.'

Baxter took a photograph from his pocket and handed it across the table.

'Good. You have done very well, Mr Baxter. I am pleased with you. Tomorrow morning you will go back to Yorkshire – '

'I beg your pardon, Bournemouth. His Grace owns a house near Bournemouth, which he occupies during the summer mouths.'

'Very well – then tomorrow morning you will go back to Bournemouth and continue to ingratiate yourself with father and son. You will also begin to implant in the boy's mind a desire for travel. Don't let him become aware that his desire has its source in you – but do not fail to foster it all you can. I will communicate with you further in a day or two. Now go.'

Baxter in his turn left the room. The door closed. Dr Nikola picked up the photograph and studied it carefully.

'The likeness is unmistakable – or it ought to be. My friend, my very dear friend, Wetherell, my toils are closing on you. My arrangements are perfecting themselves admirably. Presently when all is complete I shall press the lever, the machinery will be set in motion, and you will find yourself being slowly but surely ground into powder. Then you will hand over what I want, and be sorry you thought fit to baulk Dr Nikola!'

He rang the bell and ordered his bill. This duty discharged, he placed the cat back in its prison, shut the lid, descended with the basket to the hall, and called a hansom. When he had closed the apron, the porter enquired to what address he should order the cabman to drive. Dr Nikola did not reply for a moment, then he said, as if he had been thinking something out: 'The *Green Sailor* public-house, East India Dock Road.'

CHAPTER ONE

I determine to take a holiday – Sydney,
and what befell me there

First and foremost, my name, age, description, and occupation, as they say in the *Police Gazette*. Richard Hatteras, at your service, commonly called Dick, of Thursday Island, North Queensland, pearler, copra merchant, *bêche-de-mer* and tortoise-shell dealer, and South Sea trader generally. Eight-and-twenty years of age, neither particularly good-looking nor, if some people are to be believed, particularly amiable, six feet two in my stockings, and forty-six inches round the chest; strong as a Hakodate wrestler, and perfectly willing at any moment to pay ten pounds sterling to the man who can put me on my back.

And big shame to me if I were not so strong, considering the free, open-air, devil-may-care life I've led. Why, I was doing man's work at an age when most boys are wondering when they're going to be taken out of knickerbockers. I'd been half round the world before I was fifteen, and had been wrecked twice and marooned once before my beard showed signs of sprouting. My father was an Englishman, not very much profit to himself, so he used to say, but of a kindly disposition, and the best husband to my mother, during their short married life, that any woman could possibly have desired. She, poor soul, died of fever in the Philippines the year I was born, and he went to the bottom in the schooner *Helen of Troy*, a degree west of the Line Islands, within six months of her decease; struck the tail end of a cyclone, it was thought, and went down, lock, stock, and barrel, leaving only one man to tell the tale. So I lost father and mother in the same twelve months, and that being so, when I put my cabbage-tree on my head it covered, as far as I knew, all my family in the world.

Any way you look at it, it's calculated to give you a turn, at fifteen years of age, to know that there's not a living soul on the face of God's globe that you can take by the hand and call relation. That old saying about 'blood being thicker than water' is a pretty true one, I reckon: friends may be kind – they were so to me – but after all they're not the same thing, nor can they be, as your own kith and kin.

However, I had to look my trouble in the face and stand up to it as a man should, and I suppose this kept me from brooding over my loss as much as I should otherwise have done. At any rate, ten days after the news reached me, I had shipped aboard the *Little Emily*, trading schooner, for Papeete, booked for five years among the islands, where I was to learn to water copra, to cook my balances, and to lay the foundation of the strange adventures that I am going to tell you about in this book.

After my time expired and I had served my Trading Company on half the mudbanks of the Pacific, I returned to Australia and went up inside the Great Barrier Reef to Somerset – the pearling station that had just come into existence on Cape York. They were good days there then, before all the new-fangled laws that now regulate the pearling trade had come into force; days when a man could do almost as he liked among the islands in those seas. I don't know how other folk liked it, but the life just suited me – so much so that when Somerset proved inconvenient and the settlement shifted across to Thursday, I went with it, and, what was more to the point, with money enough at my back to fit myself out with a brand new lugger and full crew, so that I could go pearling on my own account.

For many years I went at it head down, and this brings me up to four years ago, when I was a grown man, the owner of a house, two luggers, and as good a diving plant as any man could wish to possess. What was more, just before this I had put some money into a mining concern on the mainland, which had, contrary to most ventures of the sort, turned up trumps, giving me as my share the nice round sum of £5,000. With all this wealth at my back, and having been in harness for a greater number of years on end than I cared to count, I made up my mind to take a holiday and go home to England to see the place where my father was born, and had lived his early life (I found the name of it written in the flyleaf of an old Latin book he left me), and to have a look at a country I'd heard so much about, but never thought to have the good fortune to set my foot upon.

Accordingly I packed my traps, let my house, sold my luggers and gear, intending to buy new ones when I returned, said goodbye to my friends and shipmates, and set off to join an Orient liner in Sydney. You will see from this that I intended doing the thing in style! And why not? I'd got more money to my hand to play with than most of the swells who patronise the first saloon; I had earned it honestly, and was resolved to enjoy myself with it to the top of my bent, and hang the consequences.

I reached Sydney a week before the boat was advertised to sail, but I didn't fret much about that. There's plenty to see and do in such a big place, and when a man's been shut away from theatres and amusements for years at a stretch, he can put in his time pretty well looking about him. All the same, not knowing a soul in the place, I must confess there were moments when I did think regretfully of the tight little island hidden away up north under the wing of New Guinea, of the luggers dancing to the breeze in the harbour, and the warm welcome that always awaited me among my friends in the saloons. Take my word for it, there's something in even being a leader on a small island. Anyway, it's better than being a deadbeat in a big city like Sydney, where nobody knows you, and your next-door neighbour wouldn't miss you if he never saw or heard of you again.

I used to think of these things as I marched about the streets looking in at shop windows, or took excursions up and down the Harbour. There's no place like Sydney Harbour in the wide, wide world for beauty, and before I'd been there a week I was familiar with every part of it. Still, it would have been *more* enjoyable, as I hinted just now, if I had had a friend to tour about with me; and by the same token I'm doing one man an injustice.

There was one fellow, I remember, who did offer to show me round: I fell across him in a saloon in George Street. He was tall and handsome, and as spic and span as a new pin till you came to look under the surface. When he entered the bar he winked at the girl who was serving me, and as soon as I'd finished my drink asked me to take another with him. Seeing what his little game was, and wanting to teach him a lesson, I lured him on by consenting. I drank with him, and then he drank with me.

'Been long in Sydney?' he enquired casually, looking at me, and, at the same time, stroking his fair moustache.

'Just come in,' was my reply.

'Don't you find it dull work going about alone?' he enquired. 'I shall never forget my first week of it.'

'You're about right,' I answered. 'It is dull! I don't know a soul, bar my banker and lawyer, in the town.'

'Dear me!' (more curling of the moustache). 'If I can be of any service to you while you're here, I hope you'll command me. For the sake of "Auld Lang Syne", don't you know. I believe we're both Englishmen, eh?'

'It's very good of you,' I replied modestly, affecting to be over-come by his condescension. 'I'm just off to lunch. I am staying at the *Quebec*. Is it far enough for a hansom?' As he was about to answer, a lawyer, with whom I had done a little business the day before, walked into the room. I turned to my patronising friend and said, 'Will you excuse me for one moment? I want to speak to this gentleman on business.'

He was still all graciousness.

'I'll call a hansom and wait for you in it.'

When he had left the saloon I spoke to the new arrival. He had noticed the man I had been talking to, and was kind enough to warn me against him.

'That man,' he said, 'bears a very bad reputation. He makes it his trade to meet new arrivals from England – weak-brained young pigeons with money. He shows them round Sydney, and plucks them so clean that, when they leave his hands, in nine cases out of ten, they haven't a feather left to fly with. You ought not, with your experience of rough customers, to be taken in by him.'

'Nor am I,' I replied. 'I am going to teach him a lesson. Would you like to see it? Then come with me.'

Arm in arm we walked into the street, watched by Mr Hawk from his seat in the cab. When we got there we stood for a moment chat-ting, and then strolled together down the pavement. Next moment I heard the cab coming along after us, and my friend hailing me in his silkiest tones; but though I looked him full in the face I pretended not to know him. Seeing this he drove past us – pulled up a little further down and sprang out to wait for me.

'I was almost afraid I had missed you,' he began, as we came up with him. 'Perhaps as it is such a fine day you would rather walk than ride?'

'I beg your pardon,' I answered; 'I'm really afraid you have the advantage of me.'

'But you have asked me to lunch with you at the *Quebec*. You told me to call a hansom.'

'Pardon me again! but you are really mistaken. I said I was going to lunch at the *Quebec*, and asked you if it was far enough to be worth while taking a hansom. That is your hansom, not mine. If you don't require it any longer, I should advise you to pay the man and let him go.'

'You are a swindler, sir. I refuse to pay the cabman. It is your hansom.'

I took a step closer to my fine gentleman, and, looking him full in the face, said as quietly as possible, for I didn't want all the street to hear: 'Mr *Dorunda* Dodson, let this be a lesson to you. Perhaps you'll think twice next time before you try your little games on me!'

He stepped back as if he had been shot, hesitated a moment, and then jumped into his cab and drove off in the opposite direction. When he had gone I looked at my astonished companion.

'Well, now,' he ejaculated at last, 'how on earth did you manage that?'

'Very easily,' I replied. 'I happened to remember having met that gentleman up in our part of the world when he was in a very awkward position – very awkward for him. By his action just now I should say that he has not forgotten the circumstance any more than I have.'

'I should rather think not. Good-day.'

We shook hands and parted, he going on down the street, while I branched off to my hotel.

That was the first of the only two adventures of any importance I met with during my stay in New South Wales. And there's not much in that, I fancy I can hear you saying. Well, that may be so, I don't deny it, but it was nevertheless through that that I became mixed up with the folk who figure in this book, and indeed it was to that very circumstance, and that alone, I owe my connection with the queer story I have set myself to tell. And this is how it came about.

Three days before the steamer sailed, and about four o'clock in the afternoon, I chanced to be walking down Castlereagh Street, wondering what on earth I should do with myself until dinner-time, when I saw approaching me the very man whose discomfiture I have just described. Being probably occupied planning the plucking of some unfortunate new chum, he did not see me. And as I had no desire to meet him again, after what had passed between us, I crossed the road and meandered off in a different direction, eventually finding myself located on a seat in the Domain, lighting a cigarette and looking down over a broad expanse of harbour.

One thought led to another, and so I sat on and on long after dusk had fallen, never stirring until a circumstance occurred on a neighbouring path that attracted my attention. A young and well-dressed lady was pursuing her way in my direction, evidently intending to leave the park by the entrance I had used to come into it. But unfortunately for her, at the junction of two paths to my right, three of Sydney's typical larrikins were engaged in earnest conversation. They had observed the girl coming towards them, and were evidently preparing some plan for accosting her. When she was only about fifty yards away, two of them walked to a distance, leaving the third and biggest ruffian to waylay her. He did so, but without success; she passed him and continued her walk at increased speed.

The man thereupon quickened his pace, and, secure in the knowledge that he was unobserved, again accosted her. Again she tried to escape him, but this time he would not leave her. What was worse, his two friends were now blocking the path in front. She looked to right and left, and was evidently uncertain what to do. Then, seeing escape was hopeless, she stopped, took out her purse, and gave it to the man who had first spoken to her. Thinking this was going too far, I jumped up and went quickly across the turf towards them. My footsteps made no sound on the soft grass, and as they were too much occupied in examining what she had given them, they did not notice my approach.

'You scoundrels!' I said, when I had come up with them. 'What do you mean by stopping this lady? Let her go instantly; and you, my friend, just hand over that purse.'

The man addressed looked at me as if he were taking my measure, and were wondering what sort of chance he'd have against me in a fight. But I suppose my height must have rather scared him, for he changed his tone and began to whine.

'I haven't got the lady's purse, s'help me, I ain't! I was only a asking of 'er the time; I'll take me davy I was!'

'Hand over that purse!' I said sternly, approaching a step nearer to him.

One of the others here intervened: 'Let's stowch 'im, Dog! There ain't a copper in sight!'

With that they began to close upon me. But, as the saying goes, 'I'd been there before.' I'd not been knocking about the rough side of the world for fifteen years without learning how to take care of myself. When they had had about enough of it, which was most likely more than they had bargained for, I took the purse and went down the path to where the innocent cause of it all was standing. She was looking very white and scared, but she plucked up sufficient courage to thank me prettily.

I can see her now, standing there looking into my face with big tears in her pretty blue eyes. She was a girl of about twenty-one or two years of age, I should think – tall, but slenderly built, with a sweet oval face, bright brown hair, and the most beautiful eyes I have ever seen in my life. She was dressed in some dark green material, wore a fawn jacket, and, because the afternoon was cold, had a boa of marten fur round her neck. I can remember also that her hat was of some flimsy make, with lace and glittering spear points in it, and that the whole structure was surmounted by two bows, one of black ribbon, the other of salmon pink.

'Oh, how can I thank you?' she began, when I had come up with her. 'But for your appearance I don't know what those men might not have done to me.'

'I am very glad that I was there to help you,' I replied, looking into her face with more admiration for its warm young beauty than perhaps I ought to have shown. 'Here is your purse. I hope you will find its contents safe. At the same time will you let me give you a little piece of advice. From what I have seen this afternoon this is evidently not the sort of place for a young lady to be walking in alone and after dark. I don't think I would risk it again if I were you.'

She looked at me for a moment and then said: 'You are quite right. I have only myself to thank for my misfortune. I met a friend and walked across the green with her; I was on my way back to my carriage – which is waiting for me outside – when I met those men. However, I think I can promise you that it will not happen again, as I am leaving Sydney in a day or two.'

Somehow, when I heard that, I began to feel glad I was booked to leave the place too. But of course I didn't tell her so.

'May I see you safely to your carriage?' I said at last. 'Those fellows may still be hanging about on the chance of overtaking you.'

Her courage must have come back to her, for she looked up into my face with a smile.

'I don't think they will be rude to me again after the lesson you have given them. But if you will walk with me I shall be very grateful.'

Side by side we proceeded down the path, through the gates and out into the street. A neat brougham was drawn up alongside the herb, and towards this she made her way. I opened the door and held it for her to get in. But before she did so she turned to me and stretched out her little hand.

'Will you tell me your name, that I may know to whom I am indebted?'

'My name is Hatteras. Richard Hatteras, of Thursday Island, Torres Straits. I am staying at the *Quebec*.'

'Thank you, Mr Hatteras, again and again. I shall always be grateful to you for your gallantry!'

This was attaching too much importance to such a simple action, and I was about to tell her so, when she spoke again: 'I think I ought to let you know who I am. My name is Wetherell, and my father is the Colonial Secretary. I'm sure he will be quite as grateful to you as I am. Goodbye.'

She seemed to forget that we had already shaken hands, for she extended her own a second time. I took it and tried to say something polite, but she stepped into her carriage and shut the door before I could think of anything, and next moment she was being whirled away up the street.

Now old fogies and disappointed spinsters can say what they please about love at first sight. I'm not a romantic sort of person – far from it – the sort of life I had hitherto led was not of a nature calculated to foster a belief in that sort of thing. But if I wasn't over head and ears in love when I resumed my walk that evening, well, I've never known what the passion is.

A daintier, prettier, sweeter little angel surely never walked the earth than the girl I had just been permitted the opportunity of rescuing; and from that moment forward I found my thoughts constantly reverting to her. I seemed to retain the soft pressure of her fingers in mine for hours afterwards, and as a proof of the perturbed state of my feelings I may add that I congratulated myself warmly on having worn that day my new and fashionable Sydney suit, instead of the garments in which I had travelled down from Torres Straits, and which I had hitherto considered quite good enough for even high days and holidays. That she herself would remember me for more than an hour never struck me as being likely.

Next morning I donned my best suit again, gave myself an extra brush up, and sauntered down town to see if I could run across her in the streets. What reason I had for thinking I should is more than I can tell you, but at any rate I was not destined to be disappointed. Crossing George Street a carriage passed me, and in it sat the girl whose fair image had exercised such an effect upon my mind. That she saw and recognised me was evidenced by the gracious bow and smile with which she favoured me. Then she passed out of sight, and it was a wonder that that minute didn't see the end of my career, for

I stood like one in a dream looking in the direction in which she had gone, and it was not until two hansoms and a brewer's wagon had nearly run me down that I realised it would be safer for me to pursue my meditations on the side walk.

I got back to my hotel by lunch-time, and during the progress of that meal a brilliant idea struck me. Supposing I plucked up courage and called? Why not? It would be only a polite action to enquire if she were any the worse for her fright. The thought was no sooner born in my brain than I was eager to be off. But it was too early for such a formal business, so I had to cool my heels in the hall for an hour. Then, hailing a hansom and enquiring the direction of their residence, I drove off to Potts Point. The house was the last in the street – an imposing mansion standing in well-laid-out grounds. The butler answered my ring, and in response to my enquiry dashed my hopes to the ground by informing me that Miss Wetherell was out.

'She's very busy, you see, at present, sir. She and the master leave for England on Friday in the *Orizaba*.'

'What!' I cried, almost forgetting myself in my astonishment. 'You don't mean to say that Miss Wetherell goes to England in the *Orizaba*?'

'I do, sir. And I do hear she's goin' 'ome to be presented at Court, sir!'

'Ah! Thank you. Will you give her my card, and say that I hope she is none the worse for her fright last evening?'

He took the card, and a substantial tip with it, and I went back to my cab in the seventh heaven of delight. I was to be shipmates with this lovely creature! For six weeks or more I should be able to see her every day! It seemed almost too good to be true. Instinctively I began to make all sorts of plans and preparations. Who knew but what – but stay, we must bring ourselves up here with a round turn, or we shall be anticipating what's to come.

To make a long story short – for it must be remembered that what I am telling you is only the prelude to all the extraordinary things that will have to be told later on – the day of sailing came. I went down to the boat on the morning of her departure, and got my baggage safely stowed away in my cabin before the rush set in. My cabin mate was to join the ship in Adelaide, so for the first few days of the voyage I should be alone.

About three o'clock we hove our anchor and steamed slowly down the Bay. It was a perfect afternoon, and the harbour, with its multitudinous craft of all nationalities and sizes, the blue water backed by stately hills, presented a scene the beauty of which would have appealed to the mind of the most prosaic. I had been below when the Wetherells arrived on board, so the young lady had not yet become aware of my presence. Whether she would betray any astonishment when she did find out was beyond my power to tell; at any rate, I know that I was by a long way the happiest man aboard the boat that day. However, I was not to be kept long in suspense. Before we had reached the Heads it was all settled, and satisfactorily so. I was standing on the promenade deck, just abaft the main saloon entrance, watching the panorama spread out before me, when I heard a voice I recognised only too well say behind me: 'And so goodbye to you, dear old Sydney. Great things will have happened when I set eyes on you again.'

Little did she know how prophetic were her words. As she spoke I turned and confronted her. For a moment she was overwhelmed with surprise, then, stretching out her hand, she said: 'Really, Mr Hatteras, this is most wonderful. You are the last person I expected to meet on board the Orizaba.'

'And perhaps,' I replied, 'I might with justice say the same of you. It looks as if we are destined to be fellow-travellers.'

She turned to a tall, white-bearded man beside her.

'Papa, I must introduce you to Mr Hatteras. You will remember I told you how kind Mr Hatteras was when those larrikins were rude to me in the Domain.'

'I am sincerely obliged to you, Mr Hatteras,' he said, holding out his hand and shaking mine heartily. 'My daughter did tell me, and I called yesterday at your hotel to thank you personally, but you were unfortunately not at home. Are you visiting Europe?'

'Yes; I'm going home for a short visit to see the place where my father was born.'

'Are you then, like myself, an Australian native? I mean, of course, as you know, colonial born?' asked Miss Wetherell with a little laugh. The idea of her calling herself an Australian native in any other sense! The very notion seemed preposterous.

'I was born at sea, a degree and a half south of Mauritius,' I answered; 'so I don't exactly know what you would call me. I hope you have comfortable cabins?'

'Very. We have made two or three voyages in this boat before, and we always take the same places. And now, papa, we must really go and see where poor Miss Thompson is. We are beginning to feel the swell, and she'll be wanting to go below. Goodbye for the present, Mr Hatteras.'

I raised my cap and watched her walk away down the deck, balancing herself as if she had been accustomed to a heaving plank all her life. Then I turned to watch the fast receding shore, and to my own thoughts, which were none of the saddest, I can assure you. For it must be confessed here, and why should I deny it? that I was in love from the soles of my deck shoes to the cap upon my head. But as to the chance that I, a humble pearler, would stand with one of Sydney's wealthiest and most beautiful daughters – why, that's another matter, and one that, for the present, I was anxious to keep behind me.

Within the week we had left Adelaide behind us, and four days later Albany was also a thing of the past. By the time we had cleared the Lewin we had all settled down to our life aboard ship, the bad sailors were beginning to appear on deck again, and the medium voyagers to make various excuses for their absences from meals. One thing was evident, that Miss Wetherell was the belle of the ship. Everybody paid her attention, from the skipper down to the humblest deck hand. And this being so, I prudently kept out of the way, for I had no desire to be thought to presume on our previous acquaintance. Whether she noticed this I cannot tell, but at any rate her manner to me when we *did* speak was more cordial than I had any right or reason to expect it would be. Seeing this, there were not wanting people on board who scoffed and sneered at the idea of the Colonial Secretary's daughter noticing so humble a person as myself, and when it became known what my exact social position was, I promise you these malicious whisperings did not cease.

One evening, two or three days after we had left Colombo behind us, I was standing at the rails on the promenade deck a little abaft the smoking-room entrance, when Miss Wetherell came up and took her place beside me. She looked very dainty and sweet in her evening dress, and I felt, if I had known her better, I should have liked to tell her so.

'Mr Hatteras,' said she, when we had discussed the weather and the sunset, 'I have been thinking lately that you desire to avoid me.'

'Heaven forbid! Miss Wetherell,' I hastened to reply. 'What on earth can have put such a notion into your head?'

'All the same, I believe it to be true. Now, why do you do it?'

'I have not admitted that I do it. But, perhaps, if I *do* seem to deny myself the pleasure of being with you as much as some other people

I could mention, it is only because I fail to see what possible enjoyment you can derive from my society.'

'That is a very pretty speech,' she answered, smiling, 'but it does not tell me what I want to know.'

'And what is it that you want to know, my dear young lady?'

'I want to know why you are so much changed towards me. At first we got on splendidly – you used to tell me of your life in Torres Straits, of your trading ventures in the Southern Seas, and even of your hopes for the future. Now, however, all that is changed. It is "Good-morning, Miss Wetherell", "Good-evening, Miss Wetherell", and that is all. I must own I don't like such treatment.'

'I must crave your pardon – but – '

'No, we won't have any "buts". If you want to be forgiven, you must come and talk to me as you used to do. You will like the rest of the people I'm sure when you get to know them. They are very kind to me.'

'And you think I shall like them for that reason?'

'No, no. How silly you are! But I do so want you to be friendly.'

After that there was nothing for it but for me to push myself into a circle where I had the best reasons for knowing that I was not wanted. However, it had its good side: I saw more of Miss Wetherell; so much more indeed that I began to notice that her father did not quite approve of it. But, whatever he may have thought, he said nothing to me on the subject.

A fortnight or so later we were at Aden, leaving that barren rock about four o'clock, and entering the Red Sea the same evening. The Suez Canal passed through, and Port Said behind us, we were in the Mediterranean, and for the first time in my life I stood in Europe.

At Naples the Wetherells were to say goodbye to the boat, and continue the rest of their journey home across the Continent. As the hour of separation approached, I must confess I began to dread it more and more. And somehow, I fancy, she was not quite as happy as she used to be. You will probably ask what grounds I had for believing that a girl like Miss Wetherell would take any interest in a man like myself; and it is a question I can no more answer than I can fly. And yet, when I came to think it all out, I was not without my hopes.

We were to reach port the following morning. The night was very still, the water almost unruffled. Somehow it came about that Miss Wetherell and I found ourselves together in the same sheltered spot where she had spoken to me on the occasion referred to before. The stars in the east were paling preparatory to the rising of the moon. I glanced at my companion as she leant against the rails scanning the quiet sea, and noticed the sweet wistfulness of her expression. Then, suddenly, a great desire came over me to tell her of my love. Surely, even if she could not return it, there would be no harm in letting her know how I felt towards her. For this reason I drew a little closer to her.

'And so, Miss Wetherell,' I said, 'tomorrow we are to bid each other goodbye; never, perhaps, to meet again.'

'Oh, no, Mr Hatteras,' she answered, 'we won't say that. Surely we shall see something of each other somewhere. The world is very tiny after all.'

'To those who desire to avoid each other, perhaps, but for those who wish to *find* it is still too large.'

'Well, then, we must hope for the best. Who knows but that we may run across each other in London. I think it is very probable.'

'And will that meeting be altogether distasteful to you?' I asked, quite expecting that she would answer with her usual frankness. But to my surprise she did not speak, only turned half away from me. Had I offended her?

'Miss Wetherell, pray forgive my rudeness,' I said hastily. 'I ought to have known I had no right to ask you such a question.'

'And why shouldn't you?' she replied, this time turning her sweet face towards me. 'No, Mr Hatteras, I will tell you frankly, I should very much like to see you again.'

With that all the blood in my body seemed to rush to my head. Could I be dreaming? Or had she really said she would like to see me again? I would try my luck now whatever came of it.

'You cannot think how pleasant our intercourse has been to me,' I said. 'And now I have to go back to my lonely, miserable existence again.'

'But you should not say that; you have your work in life!'

'Yes, but what is that to me when I have no one to work for? Can you conceive anything more awful than my loneliness? Remember as far as I know I am absolutely without kith and kin. There is not a single soul to care for me in the whole world – not one to whom my death would be a matter of the least concern.'

'Oh, don't – don't say that!'

Her voice faltered so that I turned from the sea and contemplated her.

'It is true, Miss Wetherell, bitterly true.'

'It is not true. It cannot be true!'

'If only I could think it would be some little matter of concern to you I should go back to my work with a happier heart.'

Again she turned her face from me. My arm lay beside hers upon the bulwarks, and I could feel that she was trembling. Brutal though it may seem to say so, this gave me fresh courage. I said slowly, bending my face a little towards her: 'Would it affect you, Phyllis?'

One little hand fell from the bulwarks to her side, and as I spoke I took possession of it. She did not appear to have heard my question, so I repeated it. Then her head went down upon the bulwarks, but not before I had caught the whispered 'yes' that escaped her lips.

Before she could guess what was going to happen, I had taken her in my arms and smothered her face with kisses.

Nor did she offer any resistance. I knew the whole truth now. She was mine, she loved me – me – me – me! The whole world seemed to re-echo the news, the very sea to ring with it, and just as I learned from her own dear lips the story of her love, the great moon rose as if to listen. Can you imagine my happiness, my delight? She was mine, this lovely girl, my very own! bound to me by all the bonds of love. Oh, happy hour! Oh, sweet delight!

I pressed her to my heart again and again. She looked into my face and then away from me, her sweet eyes suffused with tears, then suddenly her expression changed. I turned to see what ailed her, and to my discomfiture discovered her father stalking along the silent deck towards us.

Whispering to her to leave us she sped away, and I was left alone with her angry parent. That he was angry I judged from his face; nor was I wrong in my conjecture.

'Mr Hatteras,' he said severely, 'pray what does this mean? How is it that I find you in this undignified position with my daughter?'

'Mr Wetherell,' I answered, 'I can see that an explanation is due to you. Just before you came up I was courageous enough to tell your daughter that I loved her. She has been generous enough to inform me that she returns my affection. And now the best course for me to pursue is to ask your permission to make her my wife.'

'You presume, sir, upon the service you rendered my daughter in Sydney. I did not think you would follow it up in this fashion.'

'Your daughter is free to love whom she pleases, I take it,' I said, my temper, fanned by the tone he adopted, getting a little the better of my judgment. 'She has been good enough to promise to marry me – if I can obtain your permission. Have you any objection to raise?'

'Only one, and that one is insuperable! Understand me, I forbid it once and for all! In every particular – without hope of change – I forbid it!'

'As you must see it is a matter which affects the happiness of two lives, I feel sure you will be good enough to tell me your reasons?'

'I must decline any discussion on the matter at all. You have my answer, I forbid it!'

'This is to be final, then? I am to understand that you are not to be brought to change your mind by any actions of mine?'

'No, sir, I am not! What I have said is irrevocable. The idea is not to be thought of for a moment. And while I am on this subject let me tell you that your conduct towards my daughter on board this ship has been very distasteful to me. I have the honour to wish you a very good-evening.'

'Stay, Mr Wetherell,' I said, as he turned to go. 'You have been kind enough to favour me with your views. Now I will give you mine. Your daughter loves me. I am an honest and an industrious man, and I love her with my whole heart and soul. I tell you now, and though you decline to treat me with proper fairness, I give you warning that I intend to marry her if she will still have me – with your consent or without it!'

'You are insolent, sir.'

'I assure you I have no desire to be. I endeavour to remember that you are her father, though I must own you lack her sense of what is fair and right.'

'I will not discuss the question any further with you. You know my absolute decision. Good-night!'

'Good-night!'

With anger and happiness struggling in my breast for the mastery, I paced that deck for hours. My heart swelled with joy at the knowledge that my darling loved me, but it sank like lead when I considered the difficulties which threatened us if her father persisted in his present determination. At last, just as eight bells was striking (twelve o'clock), I went below to my cabin. My fellow-passenger was fast asleep – a fact which I was grateful for when I discovered propped against my bottle-rack a tiny envelope with my name inscribed upon it. Tearing it open I read the following.

My own Dearest,

My father has just informed me of his interview with you. I cannot understand it or ascribe a reason for it. But whatever happens, remember that I will be your wife, and the wife of no other. May God bless and keep you always.

Your own,

Phyllis

P.S. – Before we leave the ship you must let me know your address in London.

With such a letter under my pillow, can it be doubted that my dreams were good? How little I guessed the accumulation of troubles to which this little unpleasantness with Mr Wetherell was destined to be the prelude!

CHAPTER TWO

London

Now that I come to think the matter out, I don't know that I could give you any definite idea of what my first impressions of London were. One thing at least is certain, I had never had experience of anything approaching such a city before, and, between ourselves, I can't say that I ever want to again. The constant rush and roar of traffic, the crowds of people jostling each other on the pavements, the happiness and the misery, the riches and the poverty, all mixed up together in one jumble, like good and bad fruit in a basket, fairly took my breath away; and when I went down, that first afternoon, and saw the Park in all its summer glory, my amazement may be better imagined than described.

I could have watched the carriages, horsemen, and promenaders for hours on end without any sense of weariness. And when a bystander, seeing that I was a stranger, took compassion upon my ignorance and condescended to point out to me the various celebrities present, my pleasure was complete. There certainly is no place like London for show and glitter, I'll grant you that; but all the same I'd no more think of taking up my permanent abode in it than I'd try to cross the Atlantic in a Chinese sampan.

Having before I left Sydney been recommended to a quiet hotel in a neighbourhood near the Strand, convenient both for sightseeing and business, I had my luggage conveyed thither, and prepared to make myself comfortable for a time. Every day I waited eagerly for a letter from my sweetheart, the more impatiently because its non-arrival convinced me that they had not yet arrived in London. As it turned out, they had delayed their departure from Naples for two days, and had spent another three in Florence, two in Rome, and a day and a half in Paris.

One morning, however, my faithful watch over the letter rack, which was already becoming a standing joke in the hotel, was rewarded. An envelope bearing an English stamp and postmark, and addressed in a handwriting as familiar to me as my own, stared me in the face. To take it out and break the seal was the work of a moment. It was only a matter of a few lines, but it brought me news that raised me to the seventh heaven of delight.

Mr and Miss Wetherell had arrived in London the previous afternoon, they were staying at the *Hôtel Metropole*, would leave town for the country at the end of the week, but in the meantime, if I wished to see her, my sweetheart would be in the entrance hall of the British Museum the following morning at eleven o'clock.

How I conducted myself in the interval between my receipt of the letter and the time of the appointment, I have not the least remembrance; I know, however, that half-past ten, on the following morning, found me pacing up and down the street before that venerable pile, scanning with eager eyes every conveyance that approached me from the right or left. The minutes dragged by with intolerable slowness, but at length the time arrived.

A kindly church clock in the neighbourhood struck the hour, and others all round it immediately took up the tale. Before the last stroke had died away a hansom turned towards the gates from Bury Street, and in it, looking the picture of health and dainty beauty, sat the girl who, I had good reason to know, was more than all the world to me. To attract her attention and signal to the driver to pull up was the work of a second, and a minute later I had helped her to alight, and we were strolling together across the square towards the building.

'Ah, Dick,' she said, with a roguish smile, in answer to a question of mine, 'you don't know what trouble I had to get away this morning. Papa had a dozen places he wished me to go to with him. But when I told him that I had some very important business of my own to attend to before I could go calling, he was kind enough to let me off.'

'I'll be bound he thought you meant business with a dressmaker,' I laughingly replied, determined to show her that I was not unversed in the ways of women.

'I'm afraid he did,' she answered, blushing, 'and for that very reason alone I feel horribly guilty. But my heart told me I must see you at once, whatever happened.'

Could any man desire a prettier speech than that? If so, I was not that man. We were inside the building by this time, ascending the great staircase. A number of pretty, well-dressed girls were to be seen moving about the rooms and corridors, but not one who could in any way compare with the fair Australian by my side. As we entered the room at the top of the stairs, I thought it a good opportunity to ask the question I had been longing to put to her.

'Phyllis, my sweetheart,' I said, with almost a tremor in my voice, 'it is a fortnight now since I spoke to you. You have had plenty of time to consider our position. Have you regretted giving me your love?'

We came to a standstill, and leant over a case together, but what it contained I'm sure I haven't the very vaguest idea.

She looked up into my face with a sweet smile.

'Not for one single instant, Dick! Having once given you my love, is it likely I should want it back again?'

'I don't know. Somehow I can't discover sufficient reason for your giving it to me at all.'

'Well, be sure I'm not going to tell you. You might grow conceited. Isn't it sufficient that I do love you, and that I am not going to give you up, whatever happens?'

'More than sufficient,' I answered solemnly. 'But, Phyllis, don't you think I can induce your father to relent? Surely as a good parent he must be anxious to promote your happiness at any cost to himself?'

'I can't understand it at all. He has been so devoted to me all my life that his conduct now is quite inexplicable. Never once has he denied me anything I really set my heart upon, and he always promised me that I should be allowed to marry whomsoever I pleased, provided he was a good and honourable man, and one of whom he could in any way approve. And you are all that, Dick, or I shouldn't have loved you, I know.'

'I don't think I'm any worse than the ordinary run of men, dearest, if I am no better. At any rate I love you with a true and honourable love. But don't you think he will come round in time?'

'I'm almost afraid not. He referred to it only yesterday, and seemed quite angry that I should have dared to entertain any thought of you after what he said to me on board ship. It was the first time in my life he ever spoke to me in such a tone, and I felt it keenly. No, Dick, there is something behind it all that I cannot understand. Some mystery that I would give anything to fathom. Papa has not been himself ever since we started for England. Indeed, his very reason for coming at all is an enigma to me. And now that he is here, he seems in continual dread of meeting somebody – but who that somebody is, and why my father, who has the name and reputation of being such a courageous, determined, honourable man, should be afraid, is a thing I cannot understand.'

'It's all very mysterious and unfortunate. But surely something can be done? Don't you think if I were to see him again, and put the matter more plainly before him, something might be arranged?'

'It would be worse than useless at present, I fear. No, you must just leave it to me, and I'll do my best to talk him round. Ever since my mother died I have been as his right hand, and it will be strange if he does not listen to me and see reason in the end.'

Seeing who it was that would plead with him I did not doubt it.

By this time we had wandered through many rooms, and now found ourselves in the Egyptian Department, surrounded by embalmed dead folk and queer objects of all sorts and descriptions. There was something almost startling about our love-making in such a place, among these men and women, whose wooings had been conducted in a country so widely different to ours, and in an age that was dead and gone over two thousand years ere we were born. I spoke of this to Phyllis. She laughed and gave a little shiver.

'I wonder,' she said, looking down on the swathed-up figure of a princess of the royal house of Egypt, lying stretched out in the case beside which we sat, 'if this great lady, who lies so still and silent now, had any trouble with her love affair?'

'Perhaps she had more than one beau to her string, and not being allowed to have one took the other,' I answered; 'though from what we can see of her now she doesn't look as if she were ever capable of exercising much fascination, does she?'

As I spoke I looked from the case to the girl and compared the swaddled-up figure with the healthy, living, lovely creature by my side. But I hadn't much time for comparison. My sweetheart had taken her watch from her pocket and was glancing at the dial.

'A quarter to twelve!' she cried in alarm. 'Oh, Dick, I must be going. I promised to meet papa at twelve, and whatever happens I must not keep him waiting.'

She rose and was about to pull on her gloves. But before she had time to do so I had taken a little case from my pocket and opened it. When she saw what it contained she could not help a little womanly cry of delight.

'Oh, Dick! you naughty, extravagant boy!'

'Why, dearest? Why naughty or extravagant to give the woman I love a little token of my affection?' As I spoke I slipped the ring over her pretty finger and raised the hand to my lips.

'Will you try,' I said, 'whenever you look at that ring, to remember that the man who gave it to you loves you with his whole heart and soul, and will count no trouble too great, or no exertion too hard, to make you happy?'

'I will remember,' she said solemnly, and when I looked I saw that tears stood in her eyes. She brushed them hastily away, and after an interlude which it hardly becomes me to mention here, we went down the stairs again and out into the street, almost in silence.

Having called a cab, I placed her in it and nervously asked the question that had been sometime upon my mind: 'When shall I see you again?'

'I cannot tell,' she answered. 'Perhaps next week. But I'll let you know. In the meantime don't despair; all will come right yet! Goodbye.'

'Goodbye and God bless you!'

I lifted my hat, she waved her hand, and next moment the hansom had disappeared round the corner.

Having seen the last of her I wandered slowly down the pavement towards Oxford Street, then turning to my left hand, made my way citywards. My mind was full of my interview with the sweet girl who had just left me, and I wandered on and on, wrapped in my own thoughts, until I found myself in a quarter of London into which I had never hitherto penetrated. The streets were narrow, and, as if to be in keeping with the general air of gloom, the shops were small and their wares of a peculiarly sordid nature; hand-carts, barrows, and stalls lined the grimy pavements, and the noise was deafening.

A church clock somewhere in the neighbourhood struck 'One', and as I was beginning to feel hungry, and knew myself to be a long way from my hotel, I cast about me for a lunching-place. But it was some time before I encountered the class of restaurant I wanted. When I did it was situated at the corner of two streets, carried a foreign name over the door, and, though considerably the worse for wear, presented a cleaner appearance than any other I had as yet experienced.

Pushing the door open I entered. An unmistakable Frenchman, whose appearance, however, betokened long residence in England, stood behind a narrow counter polishing an absinthe glass. He bowed politely and asked my business.

'Can I have lunch?' I asked.

'Oui, monsieur! Cer-tain-lee. If monsieur will walk upstairs I will take his order.'

Waving his hand in the direction of a staircase in the corner of the shop he again bowed elaborately, while I, following the direction he indicated, proceeded to the room above. It was long and lofty, commanded an excellent view of both thoroughfares, and was furnished with a few inferior pictures, a much worn oilcloth, half a dozen small marble-top tables, and four times as many chairs.

When I entered three men were in occupation. Two were playing chess at a side table, while the third, who had evidently no connection with them, was watching the game from a distance, at the same time pretending to be absorbed in his paper. Seating myself at a table near the door, I examined the bill of fare, selected my lunch, and in order to amuse myself while it was preparing, fell to scrutinising my companions.

Of the chess-players, one was a big, burly fellow, with enormous arms, protruding rheumy eyes, a florid complexion, and a voluminous red beard. His opponent was of a much smaller build, with pale features, a tiny moustache, and watery blue eyes. He wore a pince-nez, and from the length of his hair and a dab of crimson lake upon his shirt cuff, I argued him an artist.

Leaving the chess-players, my eyes lighted on the stranger on the other side. He was more interesting in every way. Indeed, I was surprised to see a man of his stamp in the house at all. He was tall and slim, but exquisitely formed, and plainly the possessor of enormous strength. His head, if only from a phrenological point of view, was a magnificent one, crowned with a wealth of jet black hair. His eyes were dark as night, and glittered like those of a snake. His complexion was of a decidedly olive hue, though, as he sat in the shadow of the corner, it was difficult to tell this at first sight.

But what most fascinated me about this curious individual was the interest he was taking in the game the other men were playing. He kept his eyes fixed upon the board, looked anxiously from one to the other as a move trembled in the balance, smiled sardonically when his desires were realised, and sighed almost aloud when a mistake was made.

Every moment I expected his anxiety or disappointment to find vent in words, but he always managed to control himself in time. When he became excited I noticed that his whole body quivered under its influence, and once when the smaller of the players made an injudicious move a look flew into his face that was full of such malignant intensity that I'll own I was influenced by it. What effect it would have had upon the innocent cause of it all, had he seen it, I should have been sorry to conjecture.

Just as my lunch made its appearance the game reached a conclusion, and the taller of the two players, having made a remark in German, rose to leave. It was evident that the smaller man had won, and in an excess of pride, to which I gathered his nature was not altogether a stranger, he looked round the room as if in defiance.

Doing so, his eyes met those of the man in the corner. I glanced from one to the other, but my gaze rested longest on the face of the smaller man. So fascinated did he seem to be by the other's stare that his eyes became set and stony. It was just as if he were being mesmerised. The person he looked at rose, approached him, sat down at the table and began to arrange the men on the board without a word. Then he looked up again.

'May I have the pleasure of giving you a game?' he asked in excellent English, bowing slightly as he spoke, and moving a pawn with his long white fingers.

The little man found voice enough to murmur an appropriate reply, and they began their game, while I turned to my lunch. But, in spite of myself, I found my eyes continually reverting to what was happening at the other table. And, indeed, it was a curious sight I saw there.

The tall man had thrown himself into the business of the game, heart and soul. He half sat, half crouched over the board, reminding me more of a hawk hovering over a poultry yard than anything else I can liken him to.

His eyes were riveted first on the men before him and then on his opponent – his long fingers twitched and twined over each move, and seemed as if they would never release their hold. Not once did he speak, but his attitude was more expressive than any words.

The effect on the little man, his companion, was overwhelming. He was quite unable to do anything, but sat huddled up in his chair as if terrified by his demoniacal companion. The result even a child might have foreseen. The tall man won, and the little man, only too glad to have come out of the ordeal with a whole skin, seized his hat and, with a half-uttered apology, darted from the room.

For a moment or two his extraordinary opponent sat playing with the chessmen. Then he looked across at me and without hesitation said, accompanying his remark with a curious smile, for which I could not at all account: 'I think you will agree with me that the limitations of the fool are the birth gifts of the wise!'

Not knowing what reply to make to this singular assertion, I wisely held my tongue. This brought about a change in his demeanour; he rose from his seat, and came across to where I sat. Seating himself in a chair directly opposite me, he folded his hands in his lap, after the manner of a demure old spinster, and, having looked at me earnestly, said with an almost indescribable sweetness of tone: 'I think you will allow, Mr Hatteras, that half the world is born for the other half to prey upon!'

For a moment I was too much astonished to speak; how on earth had he become aware of my name? I stumbled out some sort of reply, which evidently did not impress him very much, for he began again: 'Our friend who has just left us will most certainly be one of those preyed upon. I pity him because he will not have the smallest grain of pleasure in his life. You, Mr Hatteras, on the other hand, will, unwittingly, be in the other camp. Circumstances will arrange that for you. Some have, of course, no desire to prey; but necessity forces it on them. Yourself, for instance. Some only prey when they are quite sure there will be no manner of risk. Our German friend who played the previous game is an example. Others, again, never lose an opportunity. Candidly speaking, to which class should you imagine I belong?'

He smiled as he put the question, and, his thin lips parting, I could just catch the glitter of the short teeth with which his mouth was furnished. For the third time since I had made his acquaintance I did not know which way to answer. However, I made a shot and said something.

'I really know nothing about you,' I answered. 'But from your kindness in giving our artist friend a game, and now in allowing me the benefit of your conversation, I should say you only prey upon your fellow-men when dire extremity drives you to it.'

'And you would be wrong. I am of the last class I mentioned. There is only one sport of any interest to me in life, and that is the opportunity of making capital out of my fellow humans. You see, I am candid with you, Mr Hatteras!'

'Pray excuse me. But you know my name! As I have never, to my knowledge, set eyes on you before, would you mind telling me how you became acquainted with it?'

'With every pleasure. But before I do so I think it only fair to tell you that you will not believe my explanation. And yet it *should* convince you. At any rate we'll try. In your right-hand top waistcoat pocket you have three cards.' Here he leant his head on his hands and shut his eyes. 'One is crinkled and torn, but it has written on it, in pencil, the name of Edward Braithwaite, Macquarrie Street, Sydney. I presume the name is Braithwaite, but the *t* and *e* are almost illegible. The second is rather a high sounding one – the Hon. Sylvester Wetherell, Potts Point, Sydney, New South Wales, and the third is, I take it, your own, Richard Hatteras. Am I right?'

I put my fingers in my pocket, and drew out what it contained – a half-sovereign, a shilling, a small piece of pencil, and three cards. The first, a well-worn piece of pasteboard, bore, surely enough, the name of Edward Braithwaite, and was that of the solicitor with whom I transacted my business in Sydney; the second was given me by my sweetheart's father the day before we left Australia; and the third was certainly my own.

Was this witchcraft or only some clever conjuring trick? I asked myself the question, but could give it no satisfactory answer. At any rate you may be sure it did not lessen my respect for my singular companion.

'Ah! I am right then!' he cried exultingly. 'Isn't it strange how the love of being right remains with us, when we think we have safely combated every other self-conceit. Well, Mr Hatteras, I am very pleased to have made your acquaintance. Somehow I think we are destined to meet again – where I cannot say. At any rate, let us hope that that meeting will be as pleasant and successful as this has been.'

But I hardly heard what he said. I was still puzzling my brains over his extraordinary conjuring trick – for trick I am convinced it was. He had risen and was slowly drawing on his gloves when I spoke.

'I have been thinking over those cards,' I said, 'and I am considerably puzzled. How on earth did you know they were there?'

'If I told you, you would have no more faith in my powers. So with your permission I will assume the virtue of modesty. Call it a conjuring trick, if you like. Many curious things are hidden under that comprehensive term. But that is neither here nor there. Before I go would you like to see one more?'

'Very much, indeed, if it's as good as the last!' I replied.

In the window stood a large glass dish, half full of water and having a dark brown fly paper floating on the surface. He brought it across to the table at which I sat, and having drained the water into a jug nearby, left the paper sticking to the bottom.

This done, he took a tiny leather case from his pocket and a small bottle out of that again. From this bottle he poured a few drops of some highly pungent liquid on to the paper, with the result that it grew black as ink and threw off a tiny vapour, which licked the edges of the bowl and curled upwards in a faint spiral column.

'There, Mr Hatteras, this is a – well, a trick – I learned from an old woman in Benares. It is a better one than the last and will repay your interest. If you will look on that paper for a moment, and try to concentrate your attention, you will see something that will, I think, astonish you.'

Hardly believing that I should see anything at all I looked. But for some seconds without success. My scepticism, however, soon left me. At first I saw only the coarse grain of the paper and the thin vapour rising from it. Then the knowledge that I was gazing into a dish vanished, I forgot my companion and the previous conjuring trick. I saw only a picture opening out before me – that of a handsomely furnished room, in which was a girl sitting in an easy chair crying as if her heart were breaking. The room I had never seen before, but the girl I should have known among a thousand. *She was Phyllis, my sweetheart!*

I looked and looked, and as I gazed at her I heard her call my name. 'Oh, Dick! Dick! come to me!' Instantly I sprang to my feet, meaning to cross the room to her. Next moment I became aware of a loud crash. The scene vanished, my senses came back to me, and to my astonishment I found myself standing alongside the overturned restaurant table. The glass dish lay on the floor shattered into a thousand fragments. My friend, the conjuror, had disappeared.

Having righted the table again, I went downstairs and explained my misfortune. When I had paid my bill I took my departure, more troubled in mind than I cared to confess. That it was only what he had called it, a conjuring trick, I felt I ought to be certain, but still it was clever and uncanny enough to render me very uncomfortable.

In vain I tried to drive the remembrance of the scene I had witnessed from my brain, but it would not be dispelled. At length, to satisfy myself, I resolved that if the memory of it remained with me so vividly in the morning I would take the bull by the horns and call at the *Metropôle* to make enquiries.

I returned to my hotel in time for dinner, but still I could not rid myself of the feeling that some calamity was approaching. Having sent my meal away almost untouched, I called a hansom and drove to the nearest theatre, but the picture of Phyllis crying and calling for me in vain kept me company throughout the performance, and brought me home more miserable at the end than I had started.

All night long I dreamed of it, seeing the same picture again and again, and hearing the same despairing cry, 'Oh, Dick! Dick! come to me!'

In the morning there was only one thing to be done. Accordingly, after breakfast I set off to make sure that nothing was the matter. On the way I tried to reason with myself. I asked how it was that I, Dick Hatteras, a man who thought he knew the world so well, should have been so impressed with a bit of wizardry as to be willing to risk making a fool of myself before the two last people in the world I wanted to think me one. Once I almost determined to turn back, but while the intention held me the picture rose again before my mind's eye, and on I went more resolved to solve the mystery than before.

Arriving at the hotel, I paid my cabman and entered the hall. A gorgeously caparisoned porter stood on the steps, and of him I enquired where I could find Miss Wetherell. Imagine my surprise when he replied: '*They've left, sir. Started yesterday afternoon, quite suddenly, for Paris, on their way back to Australia!*'

For the moment I could hardly believe my ears. Gone? Why had they gone? What could have induced them to leave England so suddenly? I questioned the hall porter on the subject, but he could tell me nothing save that they had departed for Paris the previous day, intending to proceed across the Continent in order to catch the first Australian boat at Naples.

Feeling that I should only look ridiculous if I stayed questioning the man any longer, I pressed a tip into his hand and went slowly back to my own hotel to try and think it all out. But though I devoted some hours to it, I could arrive at no satisfactory conclusion. The one vital point remained and was not to be disputed – they were gone. But the mail that evening brought me enlightenment in the shape of a letter, written in London and posted in Dover. It ran as follows.

Monday afternoon

MY OWN DEAREST – Something terrible has happened to papa! I cannot tell you what, because I do not know myself. He went out this morning in the best of health and spirits, and returned half an hour ago trembling like a leaf and white as a sheet. He had only strength enough left to reach a chair in my sitting-room before he fainted dead away. When he came to himself again he said, 'Tell your maid to pack at once. There is not a moment to lose. We start for Paris this evening to catch the next boat leaving Naples for Australia.' I said, 'But, papa!' 'Not a word,' he answered. 'I have seen somebody this morning whose presence renders it impossible for us to remain an instant longer in England. Go and pack at once, unless you wish my death to lie at your door.' After that I could, of course, say nothing. I have packed, and now, in half an hour, we leave England again. If I could only see you to say goodbye; but that, too, is impossible. I cannot tell what it all means, but that it is very serious business that takes us away so suddenly I feel convinced. My father seems frightened to remain in London a minute longer than he can help. He even stands at the window as I write, earnestly scrutinising everybody who enters the hotel. And now, my own –

But what follows, the reiterations of her affection, her vows to be true to me, etc., etc., could have no possible interest for anyone save lovers. And even those sympathetic ones I have, unfortunately, not the leisure now to gratify.

I sat like one stunned. All enjoyment seemed suddenly to have gone out of life for me. I could only sit twirling the paper in my hand and picturing the train flying remorselessly across France, bearing away from me the girl I loved better than all the world. I went down to the Park, but the scene there had no longer any interest in my eyes. I went later on to a theatre, but I found no enjoyment in the piece performed. London had suddenly become distasteful to me. I felt I must get out of it; but where could I go? Every place was alike in my present humour. Then one of the original motives of my journey rose before me, and I determined to act on the suggestion.

Next morning I accordingly set off for Hampshire to try, if possible, to find my father's old home. What sort of a place it would turn out to be I had not the very remotest idea. But I'd got the address by heart, and, with the help of a Bradshaw, for that place I steered.

Leaving the train at Lyndhurst Road – for the village I was in search of was situated in the heart of the New Forest – I hired a ramshackle conveyance from the nearest innkeeper and started off for it. The man who drove me had lived in the neighbourhood, so he found early occasion to inform me, all his seventy odd years, and it struck him as a humorous circumstance that he had never in his life been even as far as Southampton, a matter of only a few miles by road and ten minutes by rail.

And that self-same sticking at home is one of the things about England and yokel Englishmen that for the life of me I cannot understand. It seems to me – of course, I don't put it forward that I'm right – that a man might just as well be dead as only know God's world for twenty miles around him. It argues a poverty of interest in the rest of creation – a sort of mud-turtle existence, that's neither encouraging nor particularly ornamental. And yet if everybody went a-travelling where would the prosperity of England be? That's a point against my argument, I must confess. Well, perhaps we had travelled a matter of two miles when it struck me to ask my charioteer about the place to which we were proceeding. It was within the bounds of possibility, I thought, that he might once have known my father. I determined to try him. So waiting till we had passed a load of hay coming along the lane, I put the question to him.

To my surprise, he had no sooner heard the name than he became as excited as it was possible for him to be.

'Hatteras!' he cried. 'Be ye a Hatteras? Well, well, now, dearie me, who'd ha' thought it!'

'Do you know the name so well, then?'

'Ay! ay! I know the name well enough; who doesn't in these parts? There was the old squire and Lady Margaret when first I remember. Then Squire Jasper and his son, the captain, as was killed in the mutiny in foreign parts – and Master James – '

'James – that was my father's name. James Dymoke Hatteras.'

'You Master James' son – you don't say! Well! well! Now to think of that too! Him that ran away from home after words with the Squire and went to foreign parts. Who'd have thought it! Lawksee me! Sir William will be right down glad to see ye, I'll be bound.'

'Sir William, and who's Sir William?'

'He's the only one left now, sir. Lives up at the House. Ah, dear! Ah, dear! There's been a power o' trouble in the family these years past.'

By this time the aspect of the country was changing. We had left the lane behind us, ascended a short hill, and were now descending it again through what looked to my eyes more like a stately private avenue than a public road. Beautiful elms reared themselves on either hand and intermingled their branches overhead; while before us, through a gap in the foliage, we could just distinguish the winding river, with the thatched roofs of the village of which we had come in search, lining its banks, and the old grey tower of the church keeping watch and ward over all.

There was to my mind something indescribably peaceful and even sad about that view, a mute sympathy with the Past that I could hardly account for, seeing that I was Colonial born and bred. For the first time since my arrival in England the real beauty of the place came home upon me. I felt as if I could have looked for ever on that quiet and peaceful spot.

When we reached the bottom of the hill, and had turned the corner, a broad, well-made stone bridge confr·nted us. On the other side of this was an old-fashioned country inn, with its signboard dangling from the house front, and opposite it again a dilapidated cottage lolling beside two iron gates. The gates were eight feet or more in height, made of finely wrought iron, and supported by big stone posts, on the top of which two stone animals, griffins, I believe they are called, holding shields in their claws, looked down on passers-by in ferocious grandeur. From behind the gates an avenue wound and disappeared into the wood.

Without consulting me, my old charioteer drove into the inn yard, and, having thrown the reins to an ostler, descended from the vehicle. I followed his example, and then enquired the name of the place inside the gates. My guide, philosopher, and friend looked at me rather queerly for a second or two, and then recollecting that I was a stranger to the place, said: 'That be the Hall I was telling 'ee about. That's where Sir William lives!'

'Then that's where my father was born?'

He nodded his head, and as he did so I noticed that the ostler stopped his work of unharnessing the horse, and looked at me in rather a surprised fashion.

'Well, that being so,' I said, taking my stick from the trap, and preparing to stroll off, 'I'm just going to investigate a bit. You bring yourself to an anchor in yonder, my friend, and don't stir till I come for you again.'

He took himself into the inn without more ado, and I crossed the road towards the gates. They were locked, but the little entrance by the tumbledown cottage stood open, and passing through this I started up the drive. It was a perfect afternoon, the sunshine straggled in through the leafy canopy overhead and danced upon my path. To the right were the thick fastnesses of the preserves; while on my left, across the meadows I could discern the sparkle of water on a weir. I must have proceeded for nearly a mile through the wood before I caught sight of the house. Then, what a strange experience was mine.

Leaving the shelter of the trees, I opened on to as beautiful a park as the mind of man could imagine. A herd of deer were grazing quietly just before me, a woodman was eating his dinner in the shadow of an oak; but it was not upon deer or woodman that I looked, but at the house that stared at me across the undulating sea of grass.

It was a noble building, of grey stone, in shape almost square, with many curious buttresses and angles. The drive ran up to it with a grand sweep, and upon the green that fronted it some big trees reared their stately heads. In my time I'd heard a lot of talk about the stately homes of England, but this was the first time I had ever set eyes on one. And to think that this was my father's birthplace, the house where my ancestors had lived for centuries! I could only stand and stare at it in sheer amazement.

You see, my father had always been a very silent man, and though he used sometimes to tell us yarns about scrapes he'd got into as a boy, and how his father was a very stern man, and had sent him to a public school, because his tutor found him unmanageable, we never thought that he'd been anything very much in the old days – at any rate, not one of such a family as owned this house.

To tell the truth, I felt a bit doubtful as to what I'd better do. Somehow I was rather nervous about going up to the house and introducing myself as a member of the family without any credentials to back my assertion up; and yet, on the other hand, I did not want to go away and have it always rankling in my mind that I'd seen the old place and been afraid to go inside. My mind once made up, however, off I went, crossed the park, and made towards the front door. On nearer approach, I discovered that everything showed the same neglect I had noticed at the lodge. The drive was overgrown with weeds; no carriage seemed to have passed along it for ages. Shutters enclosed many of the windows, and where they did not, not one but several of the panes were broken. Entering the great stone porch, in which it would have been possible to seat a score of people, I pulled the antique doorbell, and waited, while the peal re-echoed down the corridors, for the curtain to go up on the next scene in my domestic drama.

Presently I heard footsteps approaching. A key turned in the lock, and the great door swung open. An old man, whose years could hardly have totalled less than seventy, stood before me, dressed in a suit of solemn black; almost green with age. He enquired my business in a wheezy whisper. In reply I asked if Sir William Hatteras were at home. Informing me that he would find out, he left me to cool my heels where I stood, and to ruminate on the queerness of my position. In five minutes or so he returned, and signed to me to follow him.

The hall was in keeping with the outside of the building, lofty and imposing. The floor was of oak, almost black with age, the walls were beautifully wainscoted and carved, and here and there tall armoured figures looked down upon me in disdainful silence. But the crowning glory of all was the magnificent staircase that ran up from the centre.

It was wide enough and strong enough to have taken a coach and four, the pillars that supported it were exquisitely carved, as were the banisters and rails. Half-way up was a sort of landing, from which again the stairs branched off to right and left.

Above this landing-place, and throwing a stream of coloured light down into the hall, was a magnificent stained-glass window, and on a lozenge in the centre of it the arms that had so much puzzled me on the gateway. A nobler hall no one could wish to possess, but brooding over it was the same air of poverty and neglect I had noticed all about the place. By the time I had taken in these things, my guide had reached a door at the further end. Pushing it open he bade me enter, and I did so, to find a tall, elderly man of stern aspect awaiting my coming.

He, like his servant, was dressed entirely in black, with the exception of a white tie, which gave his figure a semi-clerical appearance. His face was long and somewhat pinched, his chin and upper lip were shaven, and his snow-white, close-cropped whiskers ran in two straight lines from his jaw up to level with his piercing, hawk-like eyes. He would probably have been about seventy-five years of age, but he did not carry it well. In a low, monotonous voice he bade me welcome, and pointed to a chair, himself remaining standing.

'My servant tells me you say your name is Hatteras?' he began.

'That is so,' I replied. 'My father was James Dymoke Hatteras.'

He looked at me very sternly for almost a minute, not for a second betraying the slightest sign of surprise. Then putting his hands together, finger tip to finger tip, as I discovered later was his invariable habit while thinking, he said solemnly: 'James was my younger brother. He misconducted himself gravely in England and was sent abroad. After a brief career of spendthrift extravagance in Australia, we never heard of him again. You may be his son, but then, on the other hand, of course, you may not. I have no means of judging.'

'I give you my word,' I answered, a little nettled by his speech and the insinuation contained in it; 'but if you want further proof, I've got a Latin book in my portmanteau with my father's name upon the flyleaf, and an inscription in his own writing setting forth that it was given by him to me.'

'A Catullus?'

'Exactly! a Catullus.'

'Then I'll have to trouble you to return it to me at your earliest convenience. The book is my property: I paid eighteenpence for it about eleven o'clock a.m. on the 3rd of July, 1833, in the shop of John Burns, Fleet Street, London. My brother took it from me a week later, and I have not been able to afford myself another copy since.'

'You admit then that the book is evidence of my father's identity?'

'I admit nothing. What do you want with me? What do you come here for? You must see for yourself that I am too poor to be of any service to you, and I have long since lost any public interest I may once have possessed.'

'I want neither one nor the other. I am home from Australia on a trip, and I have a sufficient competence to render me independent of anyone.'

'Ah! That puts a different complexion on the matter. You say you hail from Australia? And what may you have been doing there?'

'Gold-mining – pearling – trading!'

He came a step closer, and as he did so I noticed that his face had assumed a look of indescribable cunning that was evidently intended to be of an ingratiating nature. He spoke in little jerks, pressing his fingers together between each sentence.

'Gold-mining! Ah! And pearling! Well, well! And I suppose you have been fortunate in your ventures?'

'Very!' I replied, having by this time determined on my line of action. 'I daresay my cheque for ten thousand pounds would not be dishonoured by the Bank of England.'

'Ten thousand pounds! Ten thousand pounds! Dear me, dear me!' He shuffled up and down the dingy room, all the time looking at me out of the corners of his eyes, as if to make sure that I was telling him the truth.

'Come, come, uncle,' I said, resolving to bring him to his bearings without further waste of time. 'This is not a very genial welcome to the son of a long-lost brother!'

'Well, well, you mustn't expect too much, my boy! You see for yourself the position I'm in. The old place is shut up, going to rack and ruin. Poverty is staring me in the face; I am cheated by everybody. Robbed right and left, not knowing which way to turn. But I'll not be put upon. They may call me what they please, but they can't get blood out of a stone. Can they? Answer me that, now!'

This speech showed me everything as plain as a pikestaff. I mean, of course, the reason of the deserted and neglected house, and his extraordinary reception of myself. I rose to my feet.

'Well, uncle – for my uncle you certainly are, whatever you may say to the contrary – I must be going. I'm sorry to find you like this, and from what you tell me I couldn't think of worrying you with my society! I want to see the old church and have a talk with the parson, and then I shall go off never to trouble you again.'

He immediately became almost fulsome in his effort to detain me. 'No, no! You mustn't go like that. It's not hospitable. Besides, you mustn't talk with parson. He's a bad lot is parson – a hard man with a cruel tongue. Says terrible things about me does parson. But I'll be even with him yet. Don't speak to him, laddie, for the honour of the family. Now ye'll stay and take lunch with me? – pot luck, of course – I'm too poor to give ye much of a meal; and in the meantime I'll show ye the house and estate.'

This was just what I wanted, though I did not look forward to the prospect of lunch in his company.

With trembling hands he took down an old-fashioned hat from a peg and turned towards the door. When we had passed through it he carefully locked it and dropped the key into his breeches' pocket. Then he led the way upstairs by the beautiful oak staircase I had so much admired on entering the house.

When we reached the first landing, which was of noble proportions and must have contained upon its walls nearly a hundred family portraits all coated with the dust of years, he approached a door and threw it open. A feeble light straggled in through the closed shutters, and revealed an almost empty room. In the centre stood a large canopied bed, of antique design. The walls were wainscoted, and the massive chimney-piece was carved with heraldic designs. I enquired what room this might be.

'This is where all our family were born,' he answered. ''Twas here your father first saw the light of day.'

I looked at it with a new interest. It seemed hard to believe that this was the birthplace of my own father, the man whom I remembered so well in a place and life so widely different. My companion noticed the look upon my face, and, I suppose, felt constrained to say something.

'Ah! James!' he said sorrowfully, 'ye were always a giddy, roving lad. I remember ye well.' (He passed his hand across his eyes, to brush away a tear, I thought, but his next speech disabused me of any such notion.) 'I remember that but a day or two before ye went ye blooded my nose in the orchard, and the very morning ye decamped ye borrowed half a crown of me, and never paid it back.'

A sudden something prompted me to put my hand in my pocket. I took out half a crown, and handed it to him without a word. He took it, looked at it longingly, put it in his pocket, took it out again, ruminated a moment, and then reluctantly handed it back to me.

'Nay, nay! my laddie, keep your money, keep your money. Ye can send me the Catullus.' Then to himself, unconscious that he was speaking his thoughts aloud: 'It was a good edition, and I have no doubt would bring five shillings any day.'

From one room we passed into another, and yet another. They were all alike – shut up, dust-ridden, and forsaken. And yet with it all what a noble place it was – one which any man might be proud to call his own. And to think that it was all going to rack and ruin because of the miserly nature of its owner. In the course of our ramble I discovered that he kept but two servants, the old man who had admitted me to his presence, and his wife, who, as that peculiar phrase has it, cooked and did for him. I discovered later that he had not paid either of them wages for some years past, and that they only stayed on with him because they were too poor and proud to seek shelter elsewhere.

When we had inspected the house we left it by a side door, and crossed a courtyard to the stables. There the desolation was, perhaps, even more marked than in the house. The great clock on the tower above the main building had stopped at a quarter to ten on some long-forgotten day, and a spider now ran his web from hand to hand.

At our feet, between the stones, grass grew luxuriantly, thick moss covered the coping of the well, the doors were almost off their hinges, and rats scuttled through the empty loose boxes at our approach. So large was the place, that thirty horses might have found a lodging comfortably, and as far as I could gather, there was room for half as many vehicles in the coach-houses that stood on either side. The intense quiet was only broken by the cawing of the rooks in the giant elms overhead, the squeaking of the rats, and the low grumbling of my uncle's voice as he pointed out the ruin that was creeping over everything.

Before we had finished our inspection it was lunch time, and we returned to the house. The meal was served in the same room in which I had made my relative's acquaintance an hour before. It consisted, I discovered, of two meagre mutton chops and some home-made bread and cheese, plain and substantial fare enough in its way, but hardly the sort one would expect from the owner of such a house. For a beverage, water was placed before us, but I could see that my host was deliberating as to whether he should stretch his generosity a point or two further.

Presently he rose, and with a muttered apology left the room, to return five minutes later carrying a small bottle carefully in his hand. This, with much deliberation and no small amount of sighing, he opened. It proved to be claret, and he poured out a glassful for me. As I was not prepared for so much liberality, I thought something must be behind it, and in this I was not mistaken.

'Nephew,' said he after a while, 'was it ten thousand pounds you mentioned as the amount of your fortune?'

I nodded. He looked at me slyly and cleared his throat to gain time for reflection. Then seeing that I had emptied my glass, he refilled it with another scarce concealed sigh, and sat back in his chair.

'And I understand you to say you are quite alone in the world, my boy?'

'Quite! Until I met you this morning I was unaware that I had a single relative on earth. Have I any more connections?'

'Not a soul – only Gwendoline.'

'Gwendoline!' I cried, 'and who may Gwendoline be?'

'My daughter – your cousin. My only child! Would you like to see her?'

'I had no idea you had a daughter. Of course I should like to see her!'

He left the table and rang the bell. The ancient man-servant answered the summons.

'Tell your wife to bring Miss Gwendoline to us.'

'Miss Gwendoline here, sir? You do not mean it surely, sir?'

'Numbskull! numbskull! numbskull!' cried the old fellow in an ecstasy of fury that seemed to spring up as suddenly as a squall does between the islands, 'bring her without another word or I'll be the death of you.'

Without further remonstrance the old man left the room, and I demanded an explanation.

'Good servant, but an impudent rascal, sir!' he said. 'Of course you must see my daughter, my beautiful daughter, Gwendoline. He's afraid you'll frighten her, I suppose! Ha! ha! Frighten my bashful, pretty one. Ha! ha!'

Anything so supremely devilish as the dried-up mirth of this old fellow it would be difficult to imagine. His very laugh seemed as if it had to crack in his throat before it could pass his lips. What would his daughter be like, living in such a house, with such companions? While I was wondering, I heard footsteps in the corridor, and then an old woman entered and curtsied respectfully. My host rose and went over to the fireplace, where he stood with his hands behind his back and the same devilish grin upon his face.

'Well, where is my daughter?'

'Sir, do you really mean it?'

'Of course, I mean it. Where is she?'

In answer the old lady went to the door and called to someone in the hall.

'Come in, dearie. It's all right. Come in, do'ee now, that's a little dear.'

But the girl made no sign of entering, and at last the old woman had to go out and draw her in. And then – but I hardly know how to write it. How shall I give you a proper description of the – *thing* that entered.

She – if *she* it could be called – was about three feet high, dressed in a shapeless print costume. Her hair stood and hung in a tangled mass upon her head, her eyes were too large for her face, and to complete the horrible effect, a great patch of beard grew on one cheek, and descended almost to a level with her chin. Her features were all awry, and now and again she uttered little moans that were more like those of a wild beast than of a human being. In spite of the old woman's endeavours to make her do so, she would not venture from her side, but stood slobbering and moaning in the half dark of the doorway.

It was a ghastly sight, one that nearly turned me sick with loathing. But the worst part of it all was the inhuman merriment of her father.

'There, there!' he cried; 'had ever man such a lovely daughter? Isn't she a beauty? Isn't she fit to be a prince's bride? Isn't she fit to be the heiress of all this place? Won't the young dukes be asking her hand in marriage? Oh, you beauty! You – but there, take her away – take her away, I say, before I do her mischief.'

The words had no sooner left his mouth than the old woman seized her charge and bundled her out of the room, moaning as before. I can tell you there was at least one person in that apartment who was heartily glad to be rid of her.

When the door had closed upon them my host came back to his seat, and with another sigh refilled my glass. I wondered what was coming next. It was not long, however, before I found out.

'Now you know everything,' he said. 'You have seen my home, you have seen my poverty, and you have seen my daughter. What do you think of it all?'

'I don't know what to think.'

'Well, then, I'll tell you. That child wants doctors; that child wants proper attendance. She can get neither here. I am too poor to help her in any way. You're rich by your own telling. I have today taken you into the bosom of my family, recognised you without doubting your assertions. Will you help me? Will you give me one thousand pounds towards settling that child in life? With that amount it could be managed.'

'Will I what?' I cried in utter amazement – dumbfounded by his impudence.

'Will you settle one thousand pounds upon her, to keep her out of her grave?'

'Not one penny!' I cried; 'and, what's more, you miserable, miserly old wretch, I'll give you a bit of my mind.'

And thereupon I did! Such a talking to as I suppose the old fellow had never had in his life before, and one he'd not be likely to forget in a hurry. He sat all the time, white with fury, his eyes blazing, and his fingers quivering with impotent rage. When I had done he ordered me out of his house. I took him at his word, seized my hat, and strode across the hall through the front door, and out into the open air.

But I was not to leave the home of my ancestors without a parting shot. As I closed the front door behind me I heard a window go up, and on looking round there was the old fellow shaking his fist at me from the second floor.

'Leave my house – leave my park!' he cried in a shrill falsetto, 'or I'll send for the constable to turn you off. Bah! You came to steal. You're no nephew of mine; I disown you! You're a common cheat – a swindler – an impostor! Go!'

I took him at his word, and went. Leaving the park, I walked straight across to the rectory, and enquired if I might see the clergyman. To him I told my tale, and, among other things, asked if anything could be done for the child – my cousin. He only shook his head.

'I fear it is hopeless, Mr Hatteras,' the clergyman said. 'The old gentleman is a terrible character, and as he owns half the village, and every acre of the land hereabouts, we all live in fear and trembling of him. We have no shadow of a claim upon the child, and unless we can prove that he actually ill-treats it, I'm sorry to say I think there is nothing to be done.'

So ended my first meeting with my father's family.

From the rectory I returned to my inn. What should I do now? London was worse than a desert to me now that my sweetheart was gone from it, and every other place seemed as bad. Then an advertisement on the wall of the bar parlour caught my eye.

FOR SALE OR HIRE

THE YACHT *ENCHANTRESS*

Ten tons

Apply, SCREW & MATCHEM

Bournemouth

It was just the very thing. I was pining for a breath of sea air again. It was perfect weather for a cruise. I would go to Bournemouth, inspect the yacht at once, and, if she suited me, take her for a month or so. My mind once made up, I hunted up my Jehu, and set off for the train, never dreaming that by so doing I was taking the second step in that important chain of events that was to affect all the future of my life.

CHAPTER FOUR

I save an important life

I travelled to Bournemouth by a fast train, and immediately on arrival made my way to the office of Messrs. Screw & Matchem with a view to instituting enquiries regarding the yacht they had advertised for hire. It was with the senior partner I transacted my business, and a shrewd but pleasant gentleman I found him.

Upon my making known my business to him, he brought me a photograph of the craft in question, and certainly a nice handy boat she looked. She had been built, he went on to inform me, for a young nobleman, who had made two very considerable excursions in her before he had been compelled to fly the country, and was only three years old. I learned also that she was lying in Poole harbour, but he was good enough to say that if I wished to see her she should be brought round to Bournemouth the following morning, when I could inspect her at my leisure. As this arrangement was one that exactly suited me, I closed with it there and then, and thanking Mr Matchem for his courtesy, betook myself to my hotel. Having dined, I spent the evening upon the pier – the first of its kind I had ever seen – listened to the band, and diverted myself with thoughts of her to whom I had plighted my troth, and whose unexpected departure from England had been such a sudden and bitter disappointment to me.

Next morning, faithful to promise, the *Enchantress* sailed into the bay and came to an anchor within a biscuit throw of the pier. Chartering a dinghy, I pulled myself off to her, and stepped aboard. An old man and a boy were engaged washing down, and to them I introduced myself and business. Then for half an hour I devoted myself to overhauling her thoroughly. She was a nice enough little craft, well set up, and from her run looked as if she might possess a fair turn of speed; the gear was in excellent order, and this was accounted for when the old man told me she had been repaired and thoroughly overhauled that selfsame year.

Having satisfied myself on a few other minor points, I pulled ashore and again went up through the gardens to the agents' office. Mr Matchem was delighted to hear that I liked the yacht well enough to think of hiring her at their own price (a rather excessive one, I must admit), and, I don't doubt, would have supplied me with a villa in Bournemouth, and a yachting box in the Isle of Wight, also on their own terms, had I felt inclined to furnish them with the necessary order. But fortunately I was able to withstand their temptations, and having given them my cheque for the requisite amount, went off to make arrangements, and to engage a crew.

Before nightfall I had secured the services of a handy lad in place of the old man who had brought the boat round from Poole, and was in a position to put to sea. Accordingly next morning I weighed anchor for a trip round the Isle of Wight. Before we had brought the Needles abeam I had convinced myself that the boat was an excellent sailer, and when the first day's cruise was over I had found no reason to repent having hired her.

And I would ask you here, is there any other amusement to compare with yachting? Can anything else hope to vie with it? Suppose a man to be a lover of human craftmanship – then what could be more to his taste than a well-built yacht? Is a man a lover of speed? Then what more could he wish for than the rush over the curling seas, with the graceful fabric quivering under him like an eager horse, the snowy line of foam driving away from either bow, and the fresh breeze singing merrily through the shrouds, bellying out the stretch of canvas overhead till it seems as if the spars must certainly give way beneath the strain they are called upon to endure!

Is a man a lover of the beautiful in nature? Then from what better place can he observe earth, sky, and sea than from a yacht's deck? Thence he views the stretch of country ashore, the dancing waves around him, the blue sky flaked with fleecy clouds above his head, while the warm sunshine penetrates him through and through till it finds his very heart and stays there, making a better, and certainly a healthier, man of him.

Does the world ever look so fair as at daybreak, when Dame Nature is still half asleep, and the water lies like a sheet of shimmering glass, and the great sun comes up like a ball of gold, with a solemnity that makes one feel almost afraid? Or at night when, anchored in some tiny harbour, the lights are twinkling ashore, and the sound of music comes wafted across the water, with a faintness that only adds to its beauty, to harmonise with the tinkling of the waves alongside. Review these things in your mind and then tell me what recreation can compare with yachting.

Not having anything to hurry me, and only a small boy and my own thoughts to keep my company, I took my time; remained two days in the Solent, sailed round the island, put in a day at Ventnor, and so back to Bournemouth. Then, after a day ashore, I picked up a nice breeze and ran down to Torquay to spend another week sailing slowly back along the coast, touching at various ports, and returning eventually to the place I had first hailed from.

In relating these trifling incidents it is not my wish to bore my readers, but to work up gradually to that strange meeting to which they were the prelude. Now that I can look back in cold blood upon the circumstances that brought it about, and reflect how narrowly I escaped missing the one event which was destined to change my whole life, I can hardly realise that I attached such small importance to it at the time. Somehow I have always been a firm believer in Fate, and indeed it would be strange, all things considered, if I were not. For when a man has passed through so many extraordinary adventures as I have, and not only come out of them unharmed, but happier and a great deal more fortunate than he has really any right to be, he may claim the privilege, I think, of saying he knows something about his subject.

And, mind you, I date it all back to that visit to the old home, and to my uncle's strange reception of me, for had I not gone down into the country I should never have quarrelled with him, and if I had not quarrelled with him I should not have gone back to the inn in such a dudgeon, and in that case I should probably have left the place without a visit to the bar, never have seen the advertisement, visited Bournemouth, hired the yacht or – but there I must stop. You must work out the rest for yourself when you have heard my story.

The morning after my third return to Bournemouth I was up by daybreak, had had my breakfast, and was ready to set off on a cruise across the bay, before the sun was a hand's breath above the horizon. It was as perfect a morning as any man could wish to see. A faint breeze just blurred the surface of the water, tiny waves danced in the sunshine, and my barkie nodded to them as if she were anxious to be off. The town ashore lay very quiet and peaceful, and so still was the air that the cries of a few white gulls could be heard quite distinctly, though they were half a mile or more away. Having hove anchor, we tacked slowly across the bay, passed the pier-head, and steered for

Old Harry Rock and Swanage Bay. My crew was for'ard, and I had possession of the tiller.

As we went about between Canford Cliffs and Alum Chine, something moving in the water ahead of me attracted my attention. We were too far off to make out exactly what it might be, and it was not until five minutes later, when we were close abreast of it, that I discovered it to be a bather. The foolish fellow had ventured further out than was prudent, had struck a strong current, and was now being washed swiftly out to sea. But for the splashing he made to show his whereabouts, I should in all probability not have seen him, and in that case his fate would have been sealed. As it was, when we came up with him he was quite exhausted.

Heaving my craft to, I leapt into the dinghy, and pulled towards him, but before I could reach the spot he had sunk. At first I thought he was gone for good and all, but in a few seconds he rose again. Then, grabbing him by the hair, I passed an arm under each of his, and dragged him unconscious into the boat. In less than three minutes we were alongside the yacht again, and with my crew's assistance I got him aboard. Fortunately a day or two before I had had the forethought to purchase some brandy for use in case of need, and my Thursday Island experiences having taught me exactly what was best to be done under such circumstances, it was not long before I had brought him back to consciousness.

In appearance he was a handsome young fellow, well set up, and possibly nineteen or twenty years of age. When I had given him a stiff nobbler of brandy to stop the chattering of his teeth, I asked him how he came to be so far from shore.

'I am considered a very good swimmer,' he replied, 'and often come out as far as this, but today I think I must have got into a strong outward current, and certainly but for your providential assistance I should never have reached home alive.'

'You have had a very narrow escape,' I answered, 'but thank goodness you're none the worse for it. Now, what's the best thing to be done? Turn back, I suppose, and set you ashore.'

'But what a lot of trouble I'm putting you to.'

'Nonsense! I've nothing to do, and I count myself very fortunate in having been able to render you this small assistance. The breeze is freshening, and it won't take us any time to get back. Where do you live?'

'To the left there! That house standing back upon the cliff. Really I don't know how to express my gratitude.'

'Just keep that till I ask you for it; and now, as we've got a twenty minutes' sail before us, the best thing for you to do would be to slip into a spare suit of my things. They'll keep you warm, and you can return them to my hotel when you get ashore.'

I sang out to the boy to come aft and take the tiller, while I escorted my guest below into the little box of a cabin, and gave him a rig out. Considering I am six feet two, and he was only five feet eight, the things were a trifle large for him; but when he was dressed I couldn't help thinking what a handsome, well-built, aristocratic-looking young fellow he was. The work of fitting him out accomplished, we returned to the deck. The breeze was freshening, and the little hooker was ploughing her way through it, nose down, as if she knew that under the circumstances her best was expected of her.

'Are you a stranger in Bournemouth?' my companion asked as I took the tiller again.

'Almost,' I answered. 'I've only been in England three weeks. I'm home from Australia.'

'Australia! Really! Oh, I should so much like to go out there.'

His voice was very soft and low, more like a girl's than a boy's, and I noticed that he had none of the mannerisms of a man – at least, not of one who has seen much of the world.

'Yes, Australia's as good a place as any other for the man who goes out there to work,' I said, 'But somehow you don't look to me like a chap that is used to what is called roughing it. Pardon my bluntness.'

'Well, you see, I've never had much chance. My father is considered by many a very peculiar man. He has strange ideas about me, and so you see I've never been allowed to mix with other people. But I'm stronger than you'd think, and I shall be twenty in October next.'

I wasn't very far out in his age, then.

'And now, if you don't mind telling me, what is your name?'

'I suppose there can be no harm in letting you know it. I was told if ever I met anyone and they asked me, not to tell them. But since you saved my life it would be ungrateful not to let you know. I am the Marquis of Beckenham.'

'Is that so? Then your father is the Duke of Glenbarth?'

'Yes. Do you know him?'

'Never set eyes on him in my life, but I heard him spoken of the other day.'

I did not add that it was Mr Matchem who, during my conversation with him, had referred to his Grace, nor did I think it well to say that he had designated him the 'Mad Duke.' And so the boy I had saved from drowning was the young Marquis of Beckenham. Well, I was moving in good society with a vengeance. This boy was the first nobleman I had ever clapped eyes on, though I knew the Count de Panuroff well enough in Thursday Island. But then foreign Counts, and shady ones at that, ought not to reckon, perhaps.

'But you don't mean to tell me,' I said at length, 'that you've got no friends? Don't you ever see anyone at all?'

'No, I am not allowed to. My father thinks it better not. And as he does not wish it, of course I have nothing left but to obey. I must own, however, I should like to see the world – to go a long voyage to Australia, for instance.'

'But how do you put in your time? You must have a very dull life of it.'

'Oh, no! You see, I have never known anything else, and then I have always the future to look forward to. As it is now, I bathe every morning, I have my yacht, I ride about the park, I have my studies, and I have a tutor who tells me wonderful stories of the world.'

'Oh, your tutor has been about, has he?'

'Dear, yes! He was a missionary in the South Sea Islands, and has seen some very stirring adventures.'

'A missionary in the South Seas, eh? Perhaps I know him.'

'Were you ever in those seas?'

'Why, I've spent almost all my life there.'

'Were you a missionary?'

'You bet not. The missionaries and my friends don't cotton to one another.'

'But they are such good men!'

'That may be. Still, as I say, we don't somehow cotton. D'you know, I'd like to set my eyes upon your tutor.'

'Well, you will. I think I see him on the beach now. I expect he has been wondering what has become of me. I've never been out so long before.'

'Well, you're close home now, and as safe as eggs in a basket.'

Another minute brought us into as shallow water as I cared to go. Accordingly, heaving to, I brought the dinghy alongside, and we got into her. Then casting off, I pulled my lord ashore. A small, clean-shaven, parsonish-looking man, with the regulation white choker, stood by the water waiting for us. As I beached the boat he came forward and said: 'My lord, we have been very anxious about you. We feared you had met with an accident.'

'I have been very nearly drowned, Mr Baxter. Had it not been for this gentleman's prompt assistance I should never have reached home again.'

'You should really be more careful, my lord. I have warned you before. Your father has been nearly beside himself with anxiety about you!'

'Eh?' said I to myself. 'Somehow this does not sound quite right. Anyhow, Mr Baxter, I've seen your figure-head somewhere before – but you were not a missionary then, I'll take my affidavit.'

Turning to me, my young lord held out his hand.

'You have never told me your name,' he said almost reproachfully.

'Dick Hatteras,' I answered, 'and very much at your service.'

'Mr Hatteras, I shall never forget what you have done for me. That I am most grateful to you I hope you will believe. I know that I owe you my life.'

Here the tutor's voice chipped in again, as I thought, rather impatiently.

'Come, come, my lord. This delay will not do. Your father will be growing still more nervous about you. We must be getting home!'

Then they went off up the cliff path together, and I returned to my boat.

'Mr Baxter,' I said to myself again as I pulled off to the yacht, 'I want to know where I've seen your face before. I've taken a sudden dislike to you. I don't trust you; and if your employer's the man they say he is, well, he won't either.'

Then, having brought the dinghy alongside, I made the painter fast, clambered aboard, and we stood out of the bay once more.

CHAPTER FIVE
Mystery

The following morning I was sitting in my room at the hotel idly scanning the *Standard*, and wondering in what way I should employ myself until the time arrived for me to board the yacht, when I heard a carriage roll up to the door.

On looking out I discovered a gorgeous landau, drawn by a pair of fine thoroughbreds, and resplendent with much gilded and crested harness, standing before the steps. A footman had already opened the door, and I was at the window just in time to see a tall, soldierly man alight from it. To my astonishment, two minutes later a waiter entered my room and announced 'His Grace the Duke of Glenbarth'. It was the owner of the carriage and the father of my young friend, if by such a title I might designate the Marquis of Beckenham.

'Mr Hatteras, I presume?' said he, advancing towards me and using that dignified tone that only an English gentleman can assume with anything approaching success.

'Yes, that is my name. I am honoured by your visit. Won't you sit down?'

'Thank you.'

He paused for a moment, and then continued: 'Mr Hatteras, I have to offer you an apology. I should have called upon you yesterday to express the gratitude I feel to you for having saved the life of my son, but I was unavoidably prevented.'

'I beg you will not mention it,' I said. 'His lordship thanked me sufficiently himself. And after all, when you look at it, it was not very much to do. I would, however, venture one little suggestion. Is it wise to let him swim so far unaccompanied by a boat? The same thing might happen to him on another occasion, and no one be near enough to render him any assistance.'

'He will not attempt so much again. He has learned a lesson from this experience. And now, Mr Hatteras, I trust you will forgive what I am about to say. My son has told me that you have just arrived in

England from Australia. Is there any way I can be of service to you? If there is, and you will acquaint me with it, you will be conferring a great favour upon me.'

'I thank your Grace,' I replied – I hope with some little touch of dignity – 'it is very kind of you, but I could not think of such a thing. But, stay, there is one service perhaps you *could* do me.'

'I am delighted to hear it, sir. And pray what may it be?'

'Your son's tutor, Mr Baxter! His face is strangely familiar to me. I have seen him somewhere before, but I cannot recall where. Could you tell me anything of his history?'

'Very little, I fear, save that he seems a worthy and painstaking man, an excellent scholar, and very capable in his management of young men. I received excellent references with him, but of his past history I know very little. I believe, however, that he was a missionary in the South Seas for some time, and that he was afterwards for many years in India. I'm sorry I cannot tell you more about him since you are interested in him.'

'I've met him somewhere, I'm certain. His face haunts me. But to return to your son – I hope he is none the worse for his adventure?'

'Not at all, thank you. Owing to the system I have adopted in his education, the lad is seldom ailing.'

'Pardon my introducing the subject. But do you think it is quite wise to keep a youth so ignorant of the world? I am perhaps rather presumptuous, but I cannot help feeling that such a fine young fellow would be all the better for a few companions.'

'You hit me on rather a tender spot, Mr Hatteras. But, as you have been frank with me, I will be frank with you. I am one of those strange beings who govern their lives by theories. I was brought up by my father, I must tell you, in a fashion totally different from that I am employing with my son. I feel now that I was allowed a dangerous amount of licence. And what was the result? I mixed with everyone, was pampered and flattered far beyond what was good for me, derived a false notion of my own importance, and when I came to man's estate was, to all intents and purposes, quite unprepared and unfitted to undertake the duties and responsibilities of my position.

'Fortunately I had the wit to see where the fault lay, and there and then I resolved that if ever I were blessed with a son, I would conduct his education on far different lines. My boy has not met a dozen strangers in his life. His education has been my tenderest care. His position, his duties towards his fellow-men, the responsibilities of his rank, have always been kept rigorously before him. He has been brought up to understand that to be a Duke is not to be a titled nonentity or a pampered *roué*, but to be one whom Providence has blessed with an opportunity of benefiting and watching over the welfare of those less fortunate than himself in the world's good gifts.

'He has no exaggerated idea of his own importance; a humbler lad, I feel justified in saying, you would nowhere find. He has been educated thoroughly, and he has all the best traditions of his race kept continually before his eyes. But you must not imagine, Mr Hatteras, that because he has not mixed with the world he is ignorant of its temptations. He may not have come into personal contact with them, but he has been warned against their insidious influences, and I shall trust to his personal pride and good instincts to help him to withstand them when he has to encounter them himself. Now, what do you think of my plan for making a nobleman?'

'A very good one, with such a youth as your son, I should think, your Grace; but I would like to make one more suggestion, if you would allow me?'

'And that is?'

'That you should let him travel before he settles down. Choose some fit person to accompany him. Let him have introductions to good people abroad, and let him use them; then he will derive different impressions from different countries, view men and women from different standpoints, and enter gradually into the great world and station which he is some day to adorn.'

'I had thought of that myself, and his tutor has lately spoken to me a good deal upon the subject. I must own it is an idea that commends itself strongly to me. I will think it over. And now, sir, I must wish you good-day. You will not let me thank you, as I should have wished, for the service you have rendered my house, but, believe me, I am none the less grateful. By the way, your name is not a common one. May I ask if you have any relatives in this county?'

'Only one at present, I fancy – my father's brother, Sir William Hatteras, of Murdlestone, in the New Forest.'

'Ah! I never met him. I knew his brother James very well in my younger days. But he got into sad trouble, poor fellow, and was obliged to fly the country.'

'You are speaking of my father. And you knew him?'

'Knew him? Indeed I did. And a better fellow never stepped; but, like most of us in those days, too wild – much too wild! And so you are James's son? Well, well! This is indeed a strange coincidence.

But dear me, I am forgetting; I must beg your pardon for speaking so candidly of your father.'

'No offence, I'm sure.'

'And pray tell me where my old friend is now?'

'Dead, your Grace! He was drowned at sea.'

The worthy old gentleman seemed really distressed at this news. He shook his head, and I heard him murmur: 'Poor Jim! Poor Jim!' Then, turning to me again, he took my hand.

'This makes our bond a doubly strong one. You must let me see more of you! How long do you propose remaining in England?'

'Not very much longer, I fear. I am already beginning to hunger for the South again.'

'Well, you must not go before you have paid us a visit. Remember we shall always be pleased to see you. You know our house, I think, on the cliff. Good-day, sir, good-day.'

So saying, the old gentleman accompanied me downstairs to his carriage, and, shaking me warmly by the hand, departed.

Again I had cause to ponder on the strangeness of the fate that had led me to Hampshire – first to the village where my father was born, and then to Bournemouth, where by saving this young man's life I had made a firm friend of a man who again had known my father. By such small coincidences are the currents of our lives diverted.

That same afternoon, while tacking slowly down the bay, I met the Marquis. He was pulling himself in a small skiff, and when he saw me he made haste to come alongside and hitch on. At first I wondered whether it would not be against his father's wishes that he should enter into conversation with such a worldly person as myself. But he evidently saw what was passing in my mind, and banished all doubts by saying: 'I have been on the lookout for you, Mr Hatteras. My father has given me permission to cultivate your acquaintance, if you will allow me.'

'I shall be very pleased,' I answered. 'Won't you come aboard and have a chat? I'm not going out of the bay this afternoon.'

He clambered over the side and seated himself in the well, clear of the boom, as nice-looking and pleasant a young fellow as any man could wish to set eyes on. 'Well,' I thought to myself, 'if all peers were like this boy there'd be less talk of abolishing the House of Lords.'

'You can't imagine how I've been thinking over all you told me the other day,' he began when we were fairly on our way. 'I want you to tell me more about Australia and the life you lead out there, if you will.'

'I'll tell you all I can with pleasure,' I answered. 'But you ought to go and see the places and things for yourself. That's better than any telling. I wish I could take you up and carry you off with me now; away down to where you can make out the green islands peeping out of the water to port and starboard, like bits of the Garden of Eden gone astray and floated out to sea. I'd like you to smell the breezes that come off from them towards evening, to hear the "trades" whistling overhead, and the thunder of the surf upon the reef. Or at another time to get inside that selfsame reef and look down through the still, transparent water, at the rainbow-coloured fish dashing among the coral boulders, in and out of the most beautiful fairy grottoes the brain of man can conceive.'

'Oh, it must be lovely! And to think that I may live my life and never see these wonders. Please go on; what else can you tell me?'

'What more do you want to hear? There is the pick of every sort of life for you out there. Would you know what real excitement is? Then I shall take you to a new gold rush. To begin with you must imagine yourself setting off for the field, with your trusty mate marching step by step beside you, pick and shovel on your shoulders, and both resolved to make your fortunes in the twinkling of an eye. When you get there, there's the digger crowd, composed of every nationality. There's the warden and his staff, the police officers, the shanty keepers, the blacks, and dogs.

'There's the tented valley stretching away to right and left of you, with the constant roar of sluice boxes and cradles, the creak of windlasses, and the perpetual noise of human voices. There's the excitement of pegging out your claim and sinking your first shaft, wondering all the time whether it will turn up trumps or nothing. There's the honest, manly labour from dawn to dusk. And then, when daylight fails, and the lamps begin to sparkle over the field, songs drift up the hillside from the drinking shanties in the valley, and you and your mate weigh up your day's returns, and, having done so, turn into your blankets to dream of the monster nugget you intend to find upon the morrow. Isn't that real life for you?'

He did not answer, but there was a sparkle in his eyes which told me I was understood.

'Then if you want other sorts of enterprise, there is Thursday Island, where I hail from, with its extraordinary people. Let us suppose ourselves wandering down the Front at nightfall, past the Kanaka billiard saloons and the Chinese stores, into, say, the *Hotel of All Nations*. Who is that handsome, dark, mysterious fellow, smoking a cigarette and idly flirting with the pretty bar girl? You don't know him, but I do! There's indeed a history for you. You didn't notice, perhaps, that rakish schooner that came to anchor in the bay early in the forenoon. What lines she had! Well, that was his craft. Tomorrow she'll be gone, it is whispered, to try for pearl in prohibited Dutch waters. Can't you imagine her slinking round the islands, watching for the patrolling gunboat, and ready, directly she has passed, to slip into the bay, skim it of its shell, and put to sea again. Sometimes they're chased – and then?'

'What then?'

'Well, a clean pair of heels or trouble with the authorities, and possibly a year in a Dutch prison before you're brought to trial! Or would you do a pearling trip in less exciting but more honest fashion? Would you ship aboard a lugger with five good companions, and go a-cruising down the New Guinea coast, working hard all day long, and lying out on deck at night, smoking and listening to the lip-lap of the water against the counter, or spinning yarns of all the world?'

'What else?'

'Why, what more do you want? Do you hanker after a cruise aboard a stinking *bêche-de-mer* boat inside the Barrier Reef, or a run with the sandalwood cutters or tortoiseshell gatherers to New Guinea; or do you want to go ashore again and try an overlanding trip half across the continent, riding behind your cattle all day long, and standing your watch at night under dripping boughs, your teeth chattering in your head, waiting for the bulls to break, while every moment you expect to hear the Bunyip calling in that lonely water-hole beyond the fringe of Mulga scrub?'

'You make me almost mad with longing.'

'And yet, somehow, it doesn't seem so fine when you're at it. It's when you come to look back upon it all from a distance of twelve thousand miles that you feel its real charm. Then it calls to you to return in every rustle of the leaves ashore, in the blue of the sky above, in the ripple of the waves upon the beach. And it eats into your heart, so that you begin to think you will never be happy till you're back in the old tumultuous devil-may-care existence again.'

'What a life you've led! And how much more to be envied it seems than the dull monotony of our existence here in sleepy old England.'

'Don't you believe it. If you wanted to change I could tell you of dozens of men, living exactly the sort of life I've described, who would only too willingly oblige you. No, no! Believe me, you've got chances of doing things we would never dream of. Do them, then, and let the other go. But all the same, I think you ought to see more of the world I've told you of before you settle down. In fact, I hinted as much to your father only yesterday.'

'He said that you had spoken of it to him. Oh, how I wish he would let me go!'

'Somehow, d'you know, I think he will.'

I put the cutter over on another tack, and we went crashing back through the blue water towards the pier. The strains of the band came faintly off to us. I had enjoyed my sail, for I had taken a great fancy to this bright young fellow sitting by my side. I felt I should like to have finished the education his father had so gallantly begun. There was something irresistibly attractive about him, so modest, so unassuming, and yet so straightforward and gentlemanly.

Dropping him opposite the bathing machines, I went on to my own anchorage on the other side of the pier. Then I pulled myself ashore and went up to the town. I had forgotten to write an important letter that morning, and as it was essential that the business should be attended to at once, to repair my carelessness, I crossed the public gardens and went through the gardens to the post office to send a telegram.

I must tell you here that since my meeting with Mr Baxter, the young Marquis's tutor, I had been thinking a great deal about him, and the more I thought the more certain I became that we had met before. To tell the truth, a great distrust of the man was upon me. It was one of those peculiar antipathies that no one can explain. I did not like his face, and I felt sure that he did not boast any too much love for me.

As my thoughts were still occupied with him, my astonishment may be imagined, on arriving at the building, at meeting him face to face upon the steps. He seemed much put out at seeing me, and hummed and hawed over his 'Good-afternoon', for all the world as if I had caught him in the middle of some guilty action.

Returning his salutation, I entered the building and looked about me for a desk at which to write my wire. There was only one vacant, and I noticed that the pencil suspended on the string was still swinging to and fro as it had been dropped. Now Baxter had only just left the building, so there could be no possible doubt that it was he who had last used the stand. I pulled the form towards me and prepared to write. But as I did so I noticed that the previous writer had pressed so hard upon his pencil that he had left the exact impression of his message plainly visible upon the pad. It ran as follows.

LETTER RECEIVED. YOU OMITTED REVEREND. THE TRAIN IS
LAID, BUT A NEW ELEMENT OF DANGER HAS ARISEN.

It was addressed to 'Nikola, *Green Sailor Hotel*, East India Dock
Road, London', and was signed 'Nineveh'.

The message was so curious that I looked at it again, and the
longer I looked the more certain I became that Baxter was the
sender. Partly because its wording interested me, and partly for
another reason which will become apparent later on, I inked the
message over, tore it from the pad, and placed it carefully in
my pocket-book. One thing at least was certain, and that was, if
Baxter were the sender, there was something underhand going
on. If he were not, well, then there could be no possible harm
in my keeping the form as a little souvenir of a rather curious
experience.

I wrote my own message, and having paid for it left the office. But
I was not destined to have the society of my own thoughts for long.
Hardly had I reached the Invalids' Walk before I felt my arm touched.
To my supreme astonishment I found myself again confronted by
Mr Baxter. He was now perfectly calm and greeted me with extra-
ordinary civility.

'Mr Hatteras, I believe,' he said. 'I think I had the pleasure of
meeting you on the sands a few days ago. What a beautiful day it is,
isn't it? Are you proceeding this way? Yes? Then perhaps I may be
permitted the honour of walking a short distance with you.'

'With pleasure,' I replied. 'I am going up the cliff to my hotel, and
I shall be glad of your company. I think we met in the telegraph
office just now.'

'In the post office, I think. I had occasion to go in there to register
a letter.'

His speech struck me as remarkable. My observation was so trivial
that it hardly needed an answer, and yet not only did he vouchsafe
me one, but he corrected my statement and volunteered a further
one on his own account. What reason could he have for wanting to
make me understand that he had gone in there to post a letter? What
would it have mattered to me if he *had* been there, as I suggested, to
send a telegram?

'Mr Baxter,' I thought to myself, 'I've got a sort of conviction that
you're not the man you pretend to be, and what's more I'd like to bet
a shilling to a halfpenny that, if the truth were only known, you're
our mysterious friend Nineveh.'

We walked for some distance in silence. Presently my companion began to talk again – this time, however, in a new strain and perhaps with a little more caution.

'You have been a great traveller, I understand, Mr Hatteras.'

'A fairly great one, Mr Baxter. You also, I am told, have seen something of the world.'

'A little – very little.'

'The South Seas, I believe. D'you know Papeete?'

'I have been there.'

'D'you know New Guinea at all?'

'No. I was never near it. I am better acquainted with the Far East – China, Japan, etc.'

Suddenly something, I shall never be able to tell what, prompted me to say: 'And the Andamans?'

The effect on my companion was as sudden as it was extraordinary. For a moment he staggered on the path like a drunken man; his face grew ashen pale, and he had to give utterance to a hoarse choking sound before be could get out a word. Then he said: 'No – no – you are quite mistaken, I assure you. I never knew the Andamans.'

Now, on the Andamans, as all the world knows, are located the Indian penal establishments, and noting his behaviour, I became more and more convinced in my own mind that there was some mystery about Mr Baxter that had yet to be explained. I had still a trump card to play.

'I'm afraid you are not very well, Mr Baxter,' I said at length 'Perhaps the heat is too much for you, or we are walking too fast? This is my hotel. Won't you come inside and take a glass of wine or something to revive you?'

He nodded his head eagerly. Large drops of perspiration stood on his forehead, and I saw that he was quite unstrung.

'I am not well – not at all well.'

As soon as we reached the smoking-room I rang for two brandies and sodas. When they arrived he drank his off almost at a gulp, and in a few seconds was pretty well himself again.

'Thank you for your kindness, Mr Hatteras,' he said. 'I think we must have walked up the hill a little too fast for my strength. Now, I must be going back to the town. I find I have forgotten something.' Almost by instinct I guessed his errand. He was going to dispatch another telegram. Resolved to try the effect of one part-ing shot, I said: 'Perhaps you do not happen to be going near the telegraph office again? If you are, should I be taxing your kindness too much if I asked you to leave a message there for me? I find I have forgotten one.'

He bowed and simply said: 'With much pleasure.'

He pronounced it 'pleesure', and as he said it he licked his lips in his usual self-satisfied fashion. I wondered how he would conduct himself when he saw the message I was going to write.

Taking a form from a table near where I sat, I wrote the following.

JOHN NICHOLSON
Langham Hotel, London
The train is laid, but a new danger has arisen.
HATTERAS

Blotting it carefully, I gave it into his hands, at the same time asking him to read it, lest my writing should not be decipherable and any question might be asked concerning it. As he read I watched his face intently. Never shall I forget the expression that swept over it. I had scored a complete victory. The shaft went home. But only for an instant. With wonderful alacrity he recovered himself and, shaking me feebly by the hand, bade me goodbye, promising to see that my message was properly delivered.

When he had gone I laid myself back in my chair for a good think. The situation was a peculiar one in every way. If he were up to some devilry I had probably warned him. If not, why had he betrayed himself so openly?

Half an hour later an answer to my first telegram arrived, and, such is the working of Fate, it necessitated my immediate return to London. I had been thinking of going for some days past, but had put it off. Now it was decided for me.

As I did not know whether I should return to Bournemouth again, I determined to call upon the Marquis to bid him goodbye. Accordingly, donning my hat, I set off for the house.

Now if Burke may be believed, the Duke of Glenbarth possesses houses in half the counties of the kingdom; but I am told his seaside residence takes precedence of them all in his affections. Standing well out on the cliffs, it commands a lovely view of the bay – looks toward the Purbeck Hills on the right, and the Isle of Wight and Hengistbury Head on the left. The house itself, as far as I could see, left nothing to be desired, and the grounds had been beautified in the highest form of landscape gardening.

I found my friend and his father in a summer-house upon the lawn. Both appeared unaffectedly glad to see me, and equally sorry to hear that I had come to bid them goodbye. Mr Baxter was not visible, and it was with no little surprise I learned that he, too, was contemplating a trip to the metropolis.

'I hope, if ever you visit Bournemouth again, you will come and see us,' said the Duke as I rose to leave.

'Thank you,' said I, 'and I hope if ever your son visits Australia you will permit me to be of some service to him.'

'You are very kind. I will bear your offer in mind.'

Shaking hands with them both, I bade them goodbye, and went out through the gate.

But I was not to escape without an interview with my clerical friend after all. As I left the grounds and turned into the public road I saw a man emerge from a little wicket gate some fifty yards or so further down the hedge. From the way he made his appearance, it was obvious he had been waiting for me to leave the house.

It was, certainly enough, my old friend Baxter. As I came up with him he said, with the same sanctimonious grin that usually encircled his mouth playing round it now: 'A nice evening for a stroll, Mr Hatteras.'

'A very nice evening, as you say, Mr Baxter.'

'May I intrude myself upon your privacy for five minutes?'

'With pleasure. What is your business?'

'Of small concern to you, sir, but of immense importance to me. Mr Hatteras, I have it in my mind that you do not like me.'

'I hope I have not given you cause to think so. Pray what can have put such a notion into your head?'

I half hoped that he would make some allusion to the telegram he had dispatched for me that morning, but he was far too cunning for that. He looked me over and over out of his small ferrety eyes before he replied: 'I cannot tell you why I think so, Mr Hatteras, but instinct generally makes us aware when we are not quite all we might be to other people. Forgive me for speaking in this way to you, but you must surely see how much it means to me to be on good terms with friends of my employer's family.'

'You are surely not afraid lest I should prejudice the Duke against you?'

'Not afraid, Mr Hatteras! I have too much faith in your sense of justice to believe that you would willingly deprive me of my means of livelihood – for of course that is what it would mean in plain English.'

'Then you need have no fear. I have just said goodbye to them. I am going away tomorrow, and it is very improbable that I shall ever see either of them again.'

'You are leaving for Australia?'

'Very shortly, I think.'

'I am much obliged to you for the generous way you have treated me. I shall never forget your kindness.'

'Pray don't mention it. Is that all you have to say to me? Then good-evening!'

'Good-evening, Mr Hatteras.' He turned back by another gate into the garden, and I continued my way along the cliff, reflecting on the curious interview I had just passed through. If the truth must be known, I was quite at a loss to understand what he meant by it! Why had he asked that question about Australia? Was it only chance that had led him to put it, or was it done designedly, and for some reason connected with that mysterious 'Train' mentioned in his telegram?

I was to find out later, and only too thoroughly!

CHAPTER SIX

I meet Dr Nikola again

It is strange with what ease, rapidity, and apparent unconsciousness the average man jumps from crisis to crisis in that strange medley he is accustomed so flippantly to call His Life. It was so in my case. For two days after my return from Bournemouth I was completely immersed in the toils of Hatton Garden, had no thought above the sale of pearls and the fluctuations in the price of shell; yet, notwithstanding all this, the afternoon of the third day found me kicking my heels on the pavement of Trafalgar Square, my mind quite made up, my passage booked, and my ticket for Australia stowed away in my waistcoat pocket.

As I stood there the grim, stone faces of the lions above me were somehow seen obscurely, Nelson's monument was equally unregarded, for my thoughts were far away with my mind's eye, following an ocean mail-steamer as she threaded her tortuous way between the Heads and along the placid waters of Sydney Harbour.

So wrapped up was I in the folds of this agreeable reverie, that when I felt a heavy hand upon my shoulder and heard a masculine voice say joyfully in my ear, 'Dick Hatteras, or I'm a Dutchman', I started as if I had been shot.

Brief as was the time given me for reflection, it was long enough for that voice to conjure up a complete scene in my mind. The last time I had heard it was on the bridge of the steamer *Yarraman*, lying in the land-locked harbour of Cairns, on the Eastern Queensland coast; a canoeful of darkies were jabbering alongside, and a cargo of bananas was being shipped aboard.

I turned and held out my hand.

'Jim Percival!' I cried, with as much pleasure as astonishment. 'How on earth does it come about that you are here?'

'Arrived three days ago,' the good-looking young fellow replied. 'We're lying in the River just off the West India Docks. The old man kept us at it like galley slaves till I began to think we should never get the cargo out. Been up to the office this morning, coming back saw you standing here looking as if you were thinking of something ten thousand miles away. I tell you I nearly jumped out of my skin with astonishment, thought there couldn't be two men with the same face and build, so smacked you on the back, discovered I was right, and here we are. Now spin your yarn. But stay, let's first find a more convenient place than this.'

We strolled down the Strand together, and at last had the good fortune to discover a 'house of call' that met with even his critical approval. Here I narrated as much of my doings since we had last met, as I thought would satisfy his curiosity. My meeting with that mysterious individual at the French restaurant and my suspicions of Baxter particularly amused him.

'What a rum beggar you are, to be sure!' was his disconcerting criticism when I had finished. 'What earthly reason have you for thinking that this chap, Baxter, has any designs upon your young swell, Beckenham, or whatever his name may be?'

'What makes you stand by to shorten sail when you see a suspicious look about the sky? Instinct, isn't it?'

'That's a poor way out of the argument, to my thinking.'

'Well, at any rate, time will show how far I'm right or wrong; though I don't suppose I shall hear any more of the affair, as I return to Australia in the *Saratoga* on Friday next.'

'And what are you going to do now?'

'I haven't the remotest idea. My business is completed, and I'm just kicking my heels in idleness till Friday comes and it is time for me to set off for Plymouth.'

'Then I have it. You'll just come along down to the docks with me; I'm due back at the old hooker at five sharp. You'll dine with us – pot luck, of course. Your old friend Riley is still chief officer; I'm second; young Cleary, whom you remember as apprentice, is now third; and, if I'm not very much mistaken, we'll find old Donald Maclean aboard too, tinkering away at his beloved engines. I don't believe that fellow could take a holiday away from his thrust blocks and piston rods if he were paid to. We'll have a palaver about old times, and I'll put you ashore myself when you want to go. There, what do you say?'

'I'm your man,' said I, jumping at his offer with an alacrity which must have been flattering to him.

The truth was, I was delighted to have secured some sort of companionship, for London, despite its multitudinous places of amusement, and its five millions of inhabitants, is but a dismal caravanserai to be left alone in. Moreover, the *Yarraman*'s officers and I were old friends, and, if the truth must be told, my heart yearned for the sight of a ship and a talk about days gone by.

Accordingly, we made our way down to the Embankment, took the underground train at Charing Cross for Fenchurch Street, proceeding thence by the 'London and Blackwall' to the West India Docks.

The *Yarraman*, travel-stained, and bearing on her weather-beaten plates evidences of the continuous tramp-like life she had led, lay well out in the stream. Having chartered a waterman, we were put on board, and I had the satisfaction of renewing my acquaintance with the chief officer, Riley, at the yawning mouth of the for'ard hatch. The whilom apprentice, Cleary, now raised to the dignity of third officer, grinned a welcome to me from among the disordered raffle of the fo'c'stle head, while that excellent artificer, Maclean, oil-can and spanner in hand, greeted me affectionately in Gaelic from the entrance to the engine-room. The skipper was ashore, so I seated myself on the steps leading to the hurricane deck, and felt at home immediately.

Upon the circumstances attending that reunion there is no necessity for me to dwell. Suffice it that we dined in the deserted saloon, and adjourned later to my friend Percival's cabin in the alleyway just for'ard of the engine-room, where several bottles of Scotch whisky, a strange collection of glassware, and an assortment of excellent cigars, were produced. Percival and Cleary, being the juniors, ensconced themselves on the top bunk; Maclean (who had been induced to abandon his machinery in honour of our meeting) was given the washhandstand. Riley took the cushioned locker in the corner, while I, as their guest, was permitted the luxury of a canvas-backed deck-chair, the initials on the back of which were not those of its present owner. At first the conversation was circumscribed, and embraced Plimsoll, the attractions of London, and the decline in the price of freight; but, as the contents of the second bottle waned, speech became more unfettered, and the talk drifted into channels and latitudes widely different. Circumstances connected with bygone days were recalled; the faces of friends long hidden in the mists of time were brought again to mind; anecdotes illustrative of various types of maritime character succeeded each other in brisk succession, till Maclean, without warning, finding his voice, burst into incongruous melody. One song suggested another; a banjo was produced, and tuned to the noise of clinking glasses; and every moment the atmosphere grew thicker.

How long this concert would have lasted I cannot say, but I remember, after the third repetition of the chorus of the sea-chanty that might have been heard a mile away, glancing at my watch and discovering to my astonishment that it was past ten o'clock. Then rising to my feet I resisted all temptations to stay the night, and reminded my friend Percival of his promise to put me ashore again. He was true to his word, and five minutes later we were shoving off from the ship's side amid the valedictions of my hosts. I have a recollection to this day of the face of the chief engineer gazing sadly down upon me from the bulwarks, while his quavering voice asserted the fact, in dolorous tones, that:

> Aft hae I rov'd by bonny Doon,
> To see the rose and woodbine twine;
> And ilka bird sang o' its luve,
> And fondly sae did I o' mine.

With this amorous farewell still ringing in my ears I landed at Limehouse Pier, and bidding my friend goodbye betook myself by the circuitous route of Emmett and Ropemaker Streets and Church Row to that aristocratic thoroughfare known as the East India Dock Road.

The night was dark and a thick rain was falling, presenting the mean-looking houses, muddy road, and foot-stained pavements in an aspect that was even more depressing than was usual to them. Despite the inclemency of the weather and the lateness of the hour, however, the street was crowded; blackguard men and foul-mouthed women, such a class as I had never in all my experience of rough folk encountered before, jostled each other on the pavements with scant ceremony; costermongers cried their wares, small boys dashed in and out of the crowd at top speed, and flaring gin palaces took in and threw out continuous streams of victims.

For some minutes I stood watching this melancholy picture, contrasting it with others in my mind. Then turning to my left hand I pursued my way in the direction I imagined the Stepney railway station to lie. It was not pleasant walking, but I was interested in the life about me – the people, the shops, the costermongers' barrows, and I might even say the public-houses.

I had not made my way more than a hundred yards along the street when an incident occurred that was destined to bring with it a train of highly important circumstances. As I crossed the entrance to a small side street, the door of an ill-looking tavern was suddenly thrust open and the body of a man was propelled from it, with a considerable amount of violence, directly into my arms. Having no desire to act as his support I pushed him from me, and as I did so glanced at the door through which he had come. Upon the glass was a picture, presumably nautical, and under it this legend, 'The Green Sailor'. In a flash Bournemouth post office rose before my mind's eye, the startled face of Baxter on the doorstep, the swinging pencil on the telegraph stand, and the imprint of the mysterious message addressed to 'Nikola, *Green Sailor Hotel*, East India Dock Road'. So complete was my astonishment that at first I could do nothing but stand stupidly staring at it, then my curiosity asserted itself and, seeking the private entrance, I stepped inside. A short passage conducted me to a small and evil-smelling room abutting on the bar. On the popular side of the counter the place was crowded; in the chamber where I found myself I was the sole customer. A small table stood in the centre, and round this two or three chairs were ranged, while several pugnacious prints lent an air of decoration to the walls.

On the other side, to the left of that through which I had entered, a curtained doorway hinted at a similar room beyond. A small but heavily-built man, whom I rightly judged to be the landlord, was busily engaged with an assistant, dispensing liquor at the counter, but when I rapped upon the table he forsook his customers, and came to learn my wishes. I called for a glass of whisky, and seated myself at the table preparatory to commencing my enquiries as to the existence of Baxter's mysterious friend. But at the moment that I was putting my first question the door behind the half-drawn curtain, which must have been insecurely fastened, opened about an inch, and a voice greeted my ears that brought me up all standing with surprise. *It was the voice of Baxter himself.*

'I assure you,' he was saying, 'it was desperate work from beginning to end, and I was never so relieved in my life as when I discovered that he had really come to say goodbye.'

At this juncture one of them must have realised that the door was open, for I heard someone rise from his chair and come towards it. Acting under the influence of a curiosity which was as baneful to himself as it was fortunate for me, before closing it he opened the door wider and looked into the room where I sat. It was Baxter, and if I live to be an hundred I shall not forget the expression on his face as his eyes fell upon me.

'Mr Hatteras!' he gasped, clutching at the wall for support.

Resolved to take him at a disadvantage, I rushed towards him and shook him warmly by the hand, at the same time noticing that he had discarded his clerical costume. It was too late now for him to pretend that he did not know me, and as I had taken the precaution to place my foot against it, it was equally impossible for him to shut the door. Seeing this he felt compelled to surrender, and I will do him the justice to admit that he did it with as good a grace as possible.

'Mr Baxter,' I said, 'this is the last place I should have expected to meet you in. May I come in and sit down?'

Without giving him time to reply I entered the room, resolved to see who his companion might be. Of course, in my own mind I had quite settled that it was the person to whom he had telegraphed from Bournemouth – in other words Nikola. But who was Nikola? And had I ever seen him before?

My curiosity was destined to be satisfied, and in a most unexpected fashion. For there, sitting at the table, a half-smoked cigarette between his fingers, and his face turned towards me, was the man whom I had seen playing chess in the restaurant, the man who had told me my name by the cards in my pocket, and the man who had warned me in such a mysterious fashion about my sweetheart's departure. He was Baxter's correspondent! He was Nikola!

Whatever my surprise may have been, he was not in the least disconcerted, but rose calmly from his seat and proffered me his hand, saying as he did so: 'Good-evening, Mr Hatteras. I am delighted to see you, and still more pleased to learn that you and my worthy old friend, Baxter, have met before. Won't you sit down?'

I seated myself on a chair at the further end of the table; Baxter meanwhile looked from one to the other of us as if uncertain whether to go or stay. Presently, however, he seemed to make up his mind, and advancing towards Nikola, said, with an earnestness that I could see was assumed for the purpose of putting me off the scent: 'And so I cannot induce you, Dr Nikola, to fit out an expedition for the work I have named?'

'If I had five thousand pounds to throw away,' replied Nikola, 'I might think of it, Mr Baxter, but as I haven't you must understand that it is impossible.' Then seeing that the other was anxious to be going, he continued, 'Must you be off? Then good-night.'

Baxter shook hands with us both with laboured cordiality, and having done so slunk from the room. When the door closed upon him Nikola turned to me.

'There must be some fascination about a missionary's life after all,' he said. 'My old tutor, Baxter, as you are aware, has a comfortable position with the young Marquis of Beckenham, which, if he conducts himself properly, may lead to something really worth having in the future, and yet here he is anxious to surrender it in order to go back to his missionary work in New Guinea, to his hard life, insufficient food, and almost certain death.'

'He was in New Guinea then?'

'Five years – so he tells me.'

'Are you certain of that?'

'Absolutely!'

'Then all I can say is that, in spite of his cloth, Mr Baxter does not always tell the truth.'

'I am sorry you should think that. Pray what reason have you for saying so?'

'Simply because in a conversation I had with him at Bournemouth he deliberately informed me that he had never been near New Guinea in his life.'

'You must have misunderstood him. However that has nothing to do with us. Let us turn to a pleasanter subject.'

He rang the bell, and the landlord having answered it, ordered more refreshment. When it arrived he lit another cigarette, and leaning back in his chair glanced at me through half-closed eyes.

Then occurred one of the most curious and weird circumstances connected with this meeting. Hardly had he laid himself back in his chair before I heard a faint scratching against the table leg, and next moment an enormous cat, black as the Pit of Tophet, sprang with a bound upon the table and stood there steadfastly regarding me, its eyes flashing and its back arched. I have seen cats without number, Chinese, Persian, Manx, the Australian wild cat, and the English tabby, but never in the whole course of my existence such another as that owned by Dr Nikola. When it had regarded me with its evil eyes for nearly a minute, it stepped daintily across to its master, and rubbed itself backwards and forwards against his arm, then to my astonishment it clambered up on to his shoulder and again gave me the benefit of its fixed attention. Dr Nikola must have observed the amazement depicted in my face, for he smiled in a curious fashion, and coaxing the beast down into his lap fell to stroking its fur with his long, white fingers. It was as uncanny a performance as ever I had the privilege of witnessing.

'And so, Mr Hatteras,' he said slowly, 'you are thinking of leaving us?'

'I am,' I replied, with a little start of natural astonishment. 'But how did you know it?'

'After the conjuring tricks – we agreed to call them conjuring tricks, I think – I showed you a week or two ago, I wonder that you should ask such a question. You have the ticket in your pocket even now.'

All the time he had been speaking his extraordinary eyes had never left my face; they seemed to be reading my very soul, and his cat ably seconded his efforts.

'By the way, I should like to ask you a few questions about those self-same conjuring tricks,' I said. 'Do you know you gave me a most peculiar warning?'

'I am very glad to hear it; I hope you profited by it.'

'It cost me a good deal of uneasiness, if that's any consolation to you. I want to know how you did it!'

'My fame as a wizard would soon evaporate if I revealed my methods,' he answered, still looking steadfastly at me. 'However, I will give you another exhibition of my powers, if you like. In fact, another warning. Have you confidence enough in me to accept it?'

'I'll wait and see what it is first,' I replied cautiously, trying to remove my eyes from his.

'Well, my warning to you is this – you intend to sail in the *Saratoga* for Australia on Friday next, don't you? Well, then, don't go; as you love your life, don't go!'

'Good gracious! and why on earth not?' I cried.

He stared fixedly at me for more than half a minute before he answered. There was no escaping those dreadful eyes, and the regular sweep of those long white fingers on the cat's black fur seemed to send a cold shiver right down my spine. Bit by bit I began to feel a curious sensation of dizziness creeping over me.

'Because you will *not* go. You cannot go. I forbid you to go.'

I roused myself with an effort, and sprang to my feet, crying as I did so: 'And what right have *you* to forbid me to do anything? I'll go on Friday, come what may. And I'd like to see the man who will prevent me.'

Though he must have realised that his attempt to hypnotise me (for attempt it certainly was) had proved a failure, he was not in the least disconcerted.

'My dear fellow,' he murmured gently, knocking off the ash of his cigarette against the table edge as he did so, 'no one is seeking to prevent you. I gave you, at your own request – you will do me the justice to admit that – a little piece of advice. If you do not care to follow it, that is your concern, not mine; but pray do not blame me. Must you really go now? Then good-night, and goodbye, for I don't suppose I shall see you this side of the Line again.'

I took his proffered hand, and wished him good-night. Having done so, I left the house, heartily glad to have said goodbye to the only man in my life whom I have really feared.

When in the train, on my way back to town, I came to review the meeting in the *Green Sailor*, I found myself face to face with a series of problems very difficult to work out. How had Nikola first learned my name? How had he heard of the Wetherells? Was he the mysterious person his meeting with whom had driven Wetherell out of England? Why had Baxter telegraphed to him that 'the train was laid?' Was I the new danger that had arisen? How had Baxter come to be at the *Green Sailor* in non-clerical costume? Why had he been so disturbed at my entry? Why had Nikola invented such a lame excuse to account for his presence there? Why had he warned me not to sail in the *Saratoga*? And, above all, why had he resorted to hypnotism to secure his ends?

I asked myself these questions, but one by one I failed to answer them to my satisfaction. Whatever other conclusion I might have come to, however, one thing at least was certain: that was, that my original supposition was a correct one. There was a tremendous mystery somewhere. Whether or not I was to lose my interest in it after Friday remained to be seen.

Arriving at Fenchurch Street, I again took the Underground, and, bringing up at the Temple, walked to my hotel off the Strand. It was nearly twelve o'clock by the time I entered the hall; but late as it was I found time to examine the letter rack. It contained two envelopes bearing my name, and taking them out I carried them with me to my room. One, to my delight, bore the postmark of Port Said, and was addressed in my sweetheart's handwriting. You may guess how eagerly I tore it open, and with what avidity I devoured its contents. From it I gathered that they had arrived at the entrance of the Suez Canal safely; that her father had recovered his spirits more and more with every mile that separated him from Europe. He was now almost himself again, she said, but still refused with characteristic determination to entertain the smallest notion of myself as a son-in-law. But Phyllis herself did not despair of being able to talk him round. Then came a paragraph which struck me as being so peculiar as to warrant my reproducing it here.

The passengers, what we have seen of them, appear to be, with one exception, a nice enough set of people. That exception, however, is intolerable; his name is Prendergast, and his personal appearance is as objectionable as his behaviour is extraordinary; his hair is snow-white and his face is deeply pitted with small-pox. This is, of course, not his fault, but it seems somehow to aggravate the distaste I have for him. Unfortunately we were thrown into his company in Naples, and since then the creature has so far presumed upon that introduction, that he scarcely leaves me alone for a moment. Papa does not seem to mind him so much, but I continually thank goodness that, as he leaves the boat in Port Said, the rest of the voyage will be performed without him.

The remainder of the letter had no concern for anyone but myself, so I do not give it. Having read it I folded it up and put it in my pocket, feeling that if I had been on board the boat I should in all probability have allowed Mr Prendergast to understand that his attentions were distasteful and not in the least required. If I could only have foreseen that within a fortnight I was to be enjoying the doubtful pleasure of that very gentleman's society, under circumstances as important as life and death, I don't doubt I should have thought still more strongly on the subject.

The handwriting of the second envelope was bold, full of character but quite unknown to me. I opened it with a little feeling of curiosity and glanced at the signature, 'Beckenham'. It ran as follows.

West Cliff, Bournemouth
Tuesday Evening

MY DEAR MR HATTERAS

I have great and wonderful news to tell you! This week has proved an extraordinarily eventful one for me, for what do you think? My father has suddenly decided that I shall travel. All the details have been settled in a great hurry. You will understand this when I tell you that Mr Baxter and I sail for Sydney in the steamship *Saratoga* next week. My father telegraphed to Mr Baxter, who is in London, to book our passages and to choose our cabins this morning. I can only say that my greatest wish is that you were coming with us. Is it so impossible? Cannot you make your arrangements fit in? We shall travel overland to Naples and join the boat there. This is Mr Baxter's proposition, and you may be sure, considering what I shall see *en route*, I have no objection to urge against it. Our tour will be an extensive one. We visit Australia and New Zealand, go thence to Honolulu, thence to San Francisco, returning, across the United States, via Canada, to Liverpool.

You may imagine how excited I am at the prospect, and as I feel that I owe a great measure of my good fortune to you, I want to be the first to acquaint you of it.

Yours ever sincerely,
BECKENHAM

I read the letter through a second time, and then sat down on my bed to think it out. One thing was self-evident. I knew now how Nikola had become aware that I was going to sail in the mail boat on Friday; Baxter had seen my name in the passenger list, and had informed him.

I undressed and went to bed, but not to sleep. I had a problem to work out, and a more than usually difficult one it was. Here was the young Marquis of Beckenham, I told myself, only son of his father, heir to a great name and enormous estates, induced to travel by my representations. There was a conspiracy afoot in which, I could not help feeling certain, the young man was in some way involved. And yet I had no right to be certain about it after all, for my suspicions at best were only conjectures. Now the question was whether I ought to warn the Duke or not? If I did I might be frightening him without cause, and might stop his son's journey; and if I did not, and things went wrong – well, in that case, I should be the innocent means of bringing a great and lasting sorrow upon his house. Hour after hour I turned this question over and over in my mind, uncertain how to act. The clocks chimed their monotonous round, the noises died down and rose again in the streets, and daylight found me only just come to a decision. I would not tell him; but at the same time I would make doubly sure that I sailed aboard that ship myself, and that throughout the voyage I was by the young man's side to guard him from ill.

Breakfast time came, and I rose from my bed wearied with thought. Even a bath failed to restore my spirits. I went downstairs and crossing the hall again, examined the rack. Another letter awaited me. I passed into the dining-room and, seating myself at my table, ordered breakfast. Having done so, I turned to my correspondence. Fate seemed to pursue me. On this occasion the letter was from the lad's father, the Duke of Glenbarth himself, and ran as follows.

Sandridge Castle, Bournemouth
Wednesday

DEAR MR HATTERAS

My son tells me he has acquainted you with the news of his
departure for Australia next week. I don't doubt this will cause
you some little surprise; but it has been brought about by a
curious combination of circumstances. Two days ago I received
a letter from my old friend, the Earl of Amberley, who, as you
know, has for the past few years been Governor of the colony
of New South Wales, telling me that his term of Office will
expire in four months. Though he has not seen my boy since the
latter was two years old, I am anxious that he should be at the
head of affairs when he visits the colony. Hence this haste. I
should have liked nothing better than to have accompanied him
myself, but business of the utmost importance detains me in
England. I am, however, sending Mr Baxter with him, with
powerful credentials, and if it should be in your power to do
anything to assist them you will be adding materially to the debt
of gratitude I already owe you.

Believe me, my dear Mr Hatteras, to be,

Very truly yours,

GLENBARTH

My breakfast finished, I answered both these letters, informed my
friends of my contemplated departure by the same steamer, and
promised that I would do all that lay in my power to ensure both the
young traveller's pleasure and his safety.

For the rest of the morning I was occupied inditing a letter to my
sweetheart, informing her of my return to the Colonies, and telling
her all my adventures since her departure.

The afternoon was spent in saying goodbye to the few business
friends I had made in London, and in the evening I went for the last
time to a theatre.

Five minutes to eleven o'clock next morning found me at Water-
loo sitting in a first-class compartment of the West of England
express, bound for Plymouth and Australia. Though the platform
was crowded to excess, I had the carriage so far to myself, and was
about to congratulate myself on my good fortune, when a porter
appeared on the scene, and deposited a bag in the opposite corner. A
moment later, and just as the train was in motion, a man jumped in
the carriage, tipped the servant, and then placed a basket upon the

rack. The train was half-way out of the station before he turned round, and my suspicions were confirmed. *It was Dr Nikola!*

Though he must have known who his companion was, he affected great surprise.

'Mr Hatteras,' he cried, 'I think this is the most extraordinary coincidence I have ever experienced in my life.'

'Why so?' I asked. 'You knew I was going to Plymouth today, and one moment's reflection must have told you, that as my boat sails at eight, I would be certain to take the morning express, which lands me there at five. Should I be indiscreet if I asked where you may be going?'

'Like yourself, I am also visiting Plymouth,' he answered, taking the basket, before mentioned, down from the rack, and drawing a French novel from his coat pocket. 'I expect an old Indian friend home by the mail boat that arrives tonight. I am going down to meet him.'

I felt relieved to hear that he was not thinking of sailing in the *Saratoga*, and after a few polite commonplaces, we both lapsed into silence. I was too suspicious, and he was too wary, to appear over friendly. Clapham, Wimbledon, Surbiton, came and went. Weybridge and Woking flashed by at lightning speed, and even Basingstoke was reached before we spoke again. That station behind us, Dr Nikola took the basket before mentioned on his knee, and opened it. When he had done so, the same enormous black cat, whose acquaintance I had made in the East India Dock Road, stepped proudly forth. In the daylight the brute looked even larger and certainly fiercer than before. I felt I should have liked nothing better than to have taken it by the tail and hurled it out of the window. Nikola, on the other hand, seemed to entertain for it the most extraordinary affection.

Now such was this marvellous man's power of fascination that by the time we reached Andover Junction his conversation had roused me quite out of myself, had made me forget my previous distrust of him, and enabled me to tell myself that this railway journey was one of the most enjoyable I had ever undertaken.

In Salisbury we took luncheon baskets on board, with two bottles of champagne, for which my companion, in spite of my vigorous protest, would insist upon paying.

As the train rolled along the charming valley, in which lie the miniature towns of Wilton, Dinton, and Tisbury, we pledged each other in right good fellowship, and by the time Exeter was reached were friendly enough to have journeyed round the world together.

Exeter behind us, I began to feel drowsy, and before the engine came to a standstill at Okehampton was fast asleep.

I remember no more of that ill-fated journey; nor, indeed have I any recollection of anything at all, until I woke up in Room No. 37 of the *Ship and Vulture Hotel* in Plymouth.

The sunshine was streaming in through the slats of the Venetian blinds, and a portly gentleman, with a rosy face, and grey hair, was standing by my bedside, holding my wrist in his hand, and calmly scrutinising me. A nurse in hospital dress stood beside him.

'I think he'll do now,' he said to her as he rubbed his plump hands together; 'but I'll look round in the course of the afternoon.'

'One moment,' I said feebly, for I found I was too weak to speak above a whisper. 'Would you mind telling me where I am, and what is the matter with me?'

'I should very much like to be able to do so,' was the doctor's reply. 'My opinion is, if you want me to be candid, that you have been drugged and well-nigh poisoned, by a remarkably clever chemist. But what the drug and the poison were, and who administered it to you, and the motive for doing so, is more than I can tell you. From what I can learn from the hotel proprietors you were brought here from the railway station in a cab last night by a gentleman who happened to find you in the carriage in which you travelled down from London. You were in such a curious condition that I was sent for and this nurse procured. Now you know all about – '

'What day did you say this is?'

'Saturday, to be sure.'

'Saturday!' I cried. 'You don't mean that! Then, by Jove, I've missed the *Saratoga* after all. Here, let me get up! And tell them downstairs to send for the Inspector of Police. I have got to get to the bottom of this.'

I sat up in bed, but was only too glad to lie down again, for my weakness was extraordinary. I looked at the doctor.

'How long before you can have me fit to travel?'

'Give yourself three days' rest and quiet,' he replied, 'and we'll see what we can do.'

'Three days? And two days and a half to cross the continent, that's five and a half – say six days. Good! I'll catch the boat in Naples, and then, Dr Nikola, if you're aboard, as I suspect, I should advise you to look out.'

CHAPTER SEVEN

Port Said, and what befell us there

Fortunately for me my arrangements fitted in exactly, so that at one thirty p.m., on the seventh day after my fatal meeting with Dr Nikola in the West of England express, I had crossed the continent, and stood looking out on the blue waters of Naples Bay. To my right was the hill of San Martino, behind me that of Capo di Monte, while in the distance, to the southward, rose the cloud-tipped summit of Vesuvius. The journey from London is generally considered, I believe, a long and wearisome one; it certainly proved so to me, for it must be remembered that my mind was impatient of every delay, while my bodily health was not as yet recovered from the severe strain that had been put upon it.

The first thing to be done on arrival at the terminus was to discover a quiet hotel; a place where I could rest and recoup during the heat of the day, and, what was perhaps more important, where I should run no risk of meeting with Dr Nikola or his satellites. I had originally intended calling at the office of the steamship company in order to explain the reason of my not joining the boat in Plymouth, planning afterwards to cast about me, among the various hotels, for the Marquis of Beckenham and Mr Baxter. But, on second thoughts, I saw the wisdom of abandoning both these courses. If you have followed the thread of my narrative, you will readily understand why.

Nor for the same reason did I feel inclined to board the steamer which I could see lying out in the harbour, until darkness had fallen. I ascertained, however, that she was due to sail at midnight, and that the mails were already being got aboard.

Almost exactly as eight o'clock was striking, I mounted the gangway, and strolled down the promenade deck to the first saloon entrance; then calling a steward to my assistance, I had my baggage conveyed to my cabin, where I set to work arranging my little knick-nacks, and making myself comfortable for the five weeks' voyage that lay before us. So far I had seen nothing of my friends, and, on making enquiries, I discovered that they had not yet come aboard. Indeed, they did not do so until the last boat had discharged its burden at the gangway. Then I met Lord Beckenham on the promenade deck, and unaffected was the young man's delight at seeing me.

'Mr Hatteras,' he cried, running forward to greet me with out-stretched hand, 'this was all that was wanting to make my happiness complete. I *am* glad to see you. I hope your cabin is near ours.'

'I'm on the port side just abaft the pantry,' I answered, shaking him by the hand. 'But tell me about yourself. I expect you had a pleasant journey across the continent.'

'Delightful!' was his reply. 'We stayed a day in Paris, and another in Rome, and since we have been here we have been rushing about seeing everything, like a regulation pair of British tourists.'

At this moment Mr Baxter, who had been looking after the luggage, I suppose, made his appearance, and greeted me with more cordiality than I had expected him to show. To my intense surprise, however, he allowed no sign of astonishment to escape him at my having joined the boat after all. But a few minutes later, as we were approaching the companion steps, he said: 'I understood from his lordship, Mr Hatteras, that you were to embark at Plymouth; was I mistaken, therefore, when I thought I saw you coming off with your luggage this evening?'

'No, you were not mistaken,' I answered, being able now to account for his lack of surprise. 'I came across the continent like yourselves, and only joined the vessel a couple of hours ago.'

Here the Marquis chimed in, and diverted the conversation into another channel.

'Where is everybody?' he asked, when Mr Baxter had left us and gone below. 'There are a lot of names on the passenger list, and yet I see nobody about!'

'They are all in bed,' I answered. 'It is getting late, you see, and, if I am not mistaken, we shall be under way in a few minutes.'

'Then, I think, if you'll excuse me for a few moments, I'll go below to my cabin. I expect Mr Baxter will be wondering where I am.'

When he had left me I turned to the bulwarks and stood looking across the water at the gleaming lights ashore. One by one the boats alongside pushed off, and from the sounds that came from for'ard, I gathered that the anchor was being got aboard. Five minutes later we had swung round to our course and were facing for the open sea. For the first mile or so my thoughts chased each other in rapid succession. You must remember that it was in Naples I had learnt that my darling loved me, and it was in Naples now that I was bidding goodbye to Europe and to all the strange events that had befallen me there. I leant upon the rail, looked at the fast-receding country in our wake, at old Vesuvius, fire-capped, away to port, at the Great Bear swinging in the heavens to the nortard, and then thought of the Southern Cross which, before many weeks were passed, would be lifting its head above our bows to welcome me back to the sunny land and to the girl I loved so well. Somehow I felt glad that the trip to England was over, and that I was really on my way home at last.

The steamer ploughed her almost silent course, and three-quarters of an hour later we were abreast of Capri. As I was looking at it, Lord Beckenham came down the deck and stood beside me. His first speech told me that he was still under the influence of his excitement; indeed, he spoke in rapturous terms of the enjoyment he expected to derive from his tour.

'But are you sure you will be a good sailor?' I asked.

'Oh, I have no fear of that,' he answered confidently. 'As you know, I have been out in my boat in some pretty rough weather and never felt in the least ill, so I don't think it is likely that I shall begin to be a bad sailor on a vessel the size of the *Saratoga*. By the way, when are we due to reach Port Said?'

'Next Thursday afternoon, I believe, if all goes well.'

'Will you let me go ashore with you if you go? I don't want to bother you, but after all you have told me about the place, I should like to see it in your company.'

'I'll take you with pleasure,' I answered, 'provided Mr Baxter gives his consent. I suppose we must regard him as skipper.'

'Oh, I don't think we need fear his refusing. He is very good-natured, you know, and lets me have my own way a good deal.'

'Where is he now?'

'Down below, asleep. He has had a lot of running about today and thought he would turn in before we got under way. I think I had better be going now. Good-night.'

'Good-night,' I answered, and he left me again.

When I was alone I returned to my thoughts of Phyllis and the future, and as soon as my pipe was finished, went below to my bunk. My berth mate I had discovered earlier in the evening was a portly English merchant of the old school, who was visiting his agents in Australia; and, from the violence of his snores, I should judge had not much trouble on his mind. Fortunately mine was the lower bunk, and, when I had undressed, I turned into it to sleep like a top until roused by the bathroom steward at half-past seven next morning. After a good bathe I went back to my cabin and set to work to dress. My companion by this time was awake, but evidently not much inclined for conversation. His usual jovial face, it struck me, was not as rosy as when I had made his acquaintance the night before, and from certain signs I judged that his good spirits were more than half assumed.

All this time a smart sea was running, and, I must own, the *Saratoga* was rolling abominably.

'A very good morning to you, my dear sir,' my cabin mate said, with an air of enjoyment his pallid face belied, as I entered the berth. 'Pray how do you feel today?'

'In first-class form,' I replied, 'and as hungry as a hunter.'

He laid himself back on his pillow with a remark that sounded very much like 'Oh dear,' and thereafter I was suffered to shave and complete my toilet in silence. Having done so I put on my cap and went on deck.

It was indeed a glorious morning; bright sunshine streamed upon the decks, the sea was a perfect blue, and so clear was the air that, miles distant though it was from us, the Italian coastline could be plainly discerned above the port bulwarks. By this time I had cross-examined the chief steward, and satisfied myself that Nikola was not aboard. His absence puzzled me considerably. Was it possible that I could have been mistaken in the whole affair, and that Baxter's motives were honest after all? But in that case why had Nikola drugged me? And why had he warned me against sailing in the *Saratoga*? The better to think it out I set myself for a vigorous tramp round the hurricane deck, and was still revolving the matter in my mind, when, on turning the corner by the smoking-room entrance, I found myself face to face with Baxter himself. As soon as he saw me, he came smiling towards me, holding out his hand.

'Good-morning, Mr Hatteras,' he said briskly; 'what a delightful morning it is, to be sure. You cannot tell how much I am enjoying it. The sea air seems to have made a new man of me already.'

'I am glad to hear it. And pray how is your charge?' I asked, more puzzled than ever by this display of affability.

'Not at all well, I am sorry to say.'

'Not well? You don't surely mean to say that he is seasick?'

'I'm sorry to say I do. He was perfectly well until he got out of his bunk half an hour ago. Then a sudden, but violent, fit of nausea seized him, and drove him back to bed again.'

'I am very sorry to hear it, I hope he will be better soon. He would have been one of the last men I should have expected to be bowled over. Are you coming for a turn round?'

'I shall feel honoured,' he answered, and thereupon we set off, step for step, for a constitutional round the deck. By the time we had finished it was nine o'clock, and the saloon gong had sounded for breakfast.

The meal over, I repaired to the Marquis's cabin, and having knocked, was bidden enter. I found my lord in bed, retching violently; his complexion was the colour of zinc, his hands were cold and clammy; and after every spasm his face streamed with perspiration.

'I am indeed sorry to see you like this,' I said, bending over him. 'How do you feel now?'

'Very bad indeed!' he answered, with a groan. 'I cannot understand it at all. Before I got out of bed this morning I felt as well as possible. Then Mr Baxter was kind enough to bring me a cup of coffee, and within five minutes of drinking it, I was obliged to go back to bed feeling hopelessly sick and miserable.'

'Well, you must try and get round as soon as you can, and come on deck; there's a splendid breeze blowing, and you'll find that will clear the sickness out of you before you know where you are.'

But his only reply was another awful fit of sickness, that made as if it would tear his chest asunder. While he was under the influence of it, his tutor entered, and set about ministering to him with a care and fatherly tenderness that even deceived me. I can see things more plainly now, on looking back at them, than I could then, but I must own that Baxter's behaviour towards the boy that morning was of a kind that would have hoodwinked the very Master of All Lies himself. I could easily understand now how this man had come to have such an influence over the kindly-natured Duke of Glenbarth, who, when all was said and done, could have had but small experience of men of Baxter's type.

Seeing that, instead of helping, I was only in the way, I expressed a hope that the patient would soon be himself again, and returned to the deck.

Luncheon came, and still Lord Beckenham was unable to leave his berth. In the evening he was no better. The following morning he was, if anything, stronger; but towards midday, just as he was thinking of getting up, his nausea returned upon him, and he was obliged to postpone the attempt. On Wednesday there was no improvement, and, indeed, it was not until Thursday afternoon, when the low-lying coast of Port Said was showing above the sea-line, that he felt in any way fit to leave his bunk. In all my experience of seasickness I had never known a more extraordinary case.

It was almost dark before we dropped our anchor off the town, and as soon as we were at a standstill I went below to my friend's cabin. He was sitting on the locker fully dressed.

'Port Said,' I announced. 'Now, how do you feel about going ashore? Personally, I don't think you had better try it.'

'Oh! but I want to go. I have been looking forward to it so much. I am much stronger than I was, believe me, and Mr Baxter doesn't think it could possibly hurt me.'

'If you don't tire yourself too much,' that gentleman put in.

'Very well, then,' I said. 'In that case I'm your man. There are plenty of boats alongside, so we'll have no difficulty about getting there. Won't you come, too, Mr Baxter?'

'I think not, thank you,' he answered. 'Port Said is not a place of which I am very fond, and as we shall not have much time here, I am anxious to utilise our stay in writing His Grace a letter detailing our progress so far.'

'In that case I think we had better be going,' I said, turning to his lordship.

We made our way on deck, and, after a little chaffering, secured a boat, in which we were pulled ashore. Having arrived there, we were immediately beset by the usual crowd of beggars and donkey boys, but withstanding their importunities, we turned into the Rue de Commerce and made our way inland. To my companion the crowded streets, the diversity of nationalities and costume, and the strange variety of shops and wares, were matters of absorbing interest. This will be the better understood when it is remembered that, poor though Port Said is in orientalism, it was nevertheless the first Eastern port he had encountered. We had both a few purchases to make, and this business satisfactorily accomplished, we hired a guide and started off to see the sights.

Passing out of the Rue de Commerce, our attention was attracted by a lame young beggar who, leaning on his crutches, blocked our way while he recited his dismal catalogue of woes. Our guide bade him be off, and indeed I was not sorry to be rid of him, but I could see, by glancing at his face, that my companion had taken his case more seriously. In fact we had not proceeded more than twenty yards before he asked me to wait a moment for him, and taking to his heels ran back to the spot where we had left him.

When he rejoined us I said: 'You don't mean to say that you gave that rascal money?'

'Only half a sovereign,' he answered. 'Perhaps you didn't hear the pitiful story he told us? His father is dead, and now, if it were not for his begging, his mother and five young sisters would all be starving.' I asked our guide if he knew the man, and whether his tale were true.

'No, monsieur,' he replied promptly, 'it is all one big lie. His father is in the jail, and, if she had her rights, his mother would be there too.' Not another word was said on the subject, but I could see that the boy's generous heart had been hurt. How little he guessed the effect that outburst of generosity was to have upon us later on.

At our guide's suggestion, we passed from the commercial, through the European quarter, to a large mosque situated in Arab Town. It was a long walk, but we were promised that we should see something there that would amply compensate us for any trouble we might be put to to reach it. This turned out to be the case, but hardly in the fashion he had predicted.

The mosque was certainly a fine building, and at the time of our visit was thronged with worshippers. They knelt in two long lines, reaching from end to end, their feet were bare, and their heads turned towards the east. By our guide's instructions we removed our boots at the entrance, but fortunately, seeing what was to transpire later, took the precaution of carrying them into the building with us. From the main hall we passed into a smaller one, where a number of Egyptian standards, relics of the war of '82, were unrolled for our inspection. While we were examining them, our guide, who had for a moment left us, returned with a scared face to inform us that there were a number of English tourists in the mosque who had refused to take their boots off, and were evidently bent on making trouble. As he spoke the ominous hum of angry voices drifted in to us, increasing in volume as we listened. Our guide pricked up his ears and looked anxiously at the door.

'There will be trouble directly,' he said solemnly, 'if those young men do not behave themselves. If messieurs will be guided by me, they will be going. I can show them a back way out.'

For a moment I felt inclined to follow his advice, but Beckenham's next speech decided me to stay.

'You will not go away and leave those stupid fellows to be killed?' he said, moving towards the door into the mosque proper. 'However foolish they may have been, they are still our countrymen, and whatever happens we ought to stand by them.'

'If you think so, of course we will,' I answered, 'but remember it may cost us our lives. You still want to stay? Very good, then, come along, but stick close to me.'

We left the small ante-room, in which we had been examining the flags, and passed back into the main hall. Here an extraordinary scene presented itself.

In the furthest corner, completely hemmed in by a crowd of furious Arabs, were three young Englishmen, whose faces plainly showed how well they understood the dangerous position into which their own impudence and folly had enticed them.

Elbowing our way through the crowd, we reached their side, and immediately called upon them to push their way towards the big doors; but before this manoeuvre could be executed, someone had given an order in Arabic, and we were all borne back against the wall.

'There is no help for it!' I cried to the biggest of the strangers. 'We must fight our way out. Choose your men and come along.'

So saying, I gave the man nearest me one under the jaw to remember me by, which laid him on his back, and then, having room to use my arms, sent down another to keep him company. All this time my companions were not idle, and to my surprise I saw the young Marquis laying about him with a science that I had to own afterwards did credit to his education. Our assailants evidently did not expect to meet with this resistance, for they gave way and began to back towards the door. One or two of them drew knives, but the space was too cramped for them to do much harm with them.

'One more rush,' I cried, 'and we'll turn them out.'

We made the rush, and next moment the doors were closed and barred on the last of them. This done, we paused to consider our position. True we had driven the enemy from the citadel, but then unless we could find a means of escape, we ourselves were equally prisoners in it. What was to be done?

Leaving three of our party to guard the doors, the remainder searched the adjoining rooms for a means of escape; but though we were unsuccessful in our attempt to find an exit, we did what was the next best thing to it, discovered our cowardly guide in a corner skulking in a curious sort of cupboard.

By the time we had proved to him that the enemy were really driven out, and that we had possession of the mosque, he recovered his wits a little, and managed, after hearing our promise to throw him to the mob outside unless he discovered a means of escape for us, to cudgel his brains and announce that he knew of one.

No sooner did we hear this, than we resolved to profit by it. The mob outside was growing every moment more impatient, and from the clang of steel-shod rifle butts on the stone steps we came to the conclusion that the services of a force of soldiery had been called in. The situation was critical, and twice imperious demands were made upon us to open the door. But, as may be supposed, this we did not feel inclined to do.

'Now, for your way out,' I said, taking our trembling guide, whose face seemed to blanch whiter and whiter with every knock upon the door, by the shoulders, and giving him a preliminary shake. 'Mind what you're about, and remember, if you lead us into any trap, I'll wring your miserable neck, as sure as you're alive. Go ahead.'

Collecting our boots and shoes, which, throughout the tumult, had been lying scattered about upon the floor, we passed into the ante-room, and put them on. Then creeping softly out by another door, we reached a small courtyard in the rear, surrounded on all sides by high walls. Our way, so our guide informed us, lay over one of these. But how we were to surmount them was a puzzle, for the lowest scaling place was at least twelve feet high. However, the business had to be done, and, what was more to the point, done quickly.

Calling the strongest of the tourists, who were by this time all quite sober, to my side, I bade him stoop down as if he were playing leap-frog; then, mounting his back myself, I stood upright, and stretched my arms above my head. To my delight my fingers reached to within a few inches of the top of the wall.

'Stand as steady as you can,' I whispered, 'for I'm going to jump.'

I did so, and clutched the edge. Now, if anybody thinks it is an easy thing to pull oneself to the top of the wall in that fashion, let him try it, and I fancy he'll discover his mistake. I only know I found it a harder business than I had anticipated, so much harder that when I reached the top I was so completely exhausted as to be unable to do anything for more than a minute. Then I whispered to another man to climb upon the first man's back, and stretch his hands up to mine. He did so, and I pulled him up beside me. The guide came next, then the other tourist, then Lord Beckenham. After which I took off and lowered my coat to the man who had stood for us all, and having done so, took a firm grip of the wall with my legs, and dragged him up as I had done the others.

It had been a longer business than I liked, and every moment, while we were about it, I expected to hear the cries of the mob inside the mosque, and to find them pouring into the yard to prevent our escape. The bolts on the door, however, must have possessed greater strength than we gave them credit for. At any rate, they did not give way.

When we were all safely on the wall, I asked the guide in which direction we should now proceed; he pointed to the adjoining roofs, and in Indian file, and with the stealthiness of cats, we accordingly crept across them.

The third house surmounted, we found ourselves overlooking a narrow alley, into which we first peered carefully, and, having discovered that no one was about, eventually dropped.

'Now,' said the guide, as soon as we were down, 'we must run along here, and turn to the left.'

We did so, to find ourselves in a broader street, which eventually brought us out into the thoroughfare through which we had passed to reach the mosque.

Having got our bearings now, we headed for the harbour, or at least for that part of the town with which I was best acquainted, as fast as our legs would carry us. But, startling as they had been, we had not yet done with adventures for the night.

Once in the security of the gaslit streets, we said goodbye to the men who had got us into all the trouble, and having come to terms with our guide, packed him off and proceeded upon our way alone.

Five minutes later the streaming lights of an open doorway brought us to a standstill, and one glance told us we were looking into the Casino. The noise of the roulette tables greeted our ears, and as we had still plenty of time, and my companion was not tired, I thought it a good opportunity to show him another phase of the seamy side of life.

But before I say anything about that I must chronicle a curious circumstance. As we were entering the building, something made me look round. To my intense astonishment I saw, or believed I saw, Dr Nikola standing in the street, regarding me. Bidding my companion remain where he was for a moment, I dashed out again and ran towards the place where I had seen the figure. But I was too late. If it were Dr Nikola, he had vanished as suddenly as he had come. I hunted here, there, and everywhere, in doorways, under verandahs, and down lanes, but it was no use, not a trace of him could I discover. So abandoning my search, I returned to the Casino. Beckenham was waiting for me, and together we entered the building.

The room was packed, and consequently all the tables were crowded, but as we did not intend playing, this was a matter of small concern to us. We were more interested in the players than the game. And, indeed, the expressions on the faces around us were extraordinary. On some hope still was in the ascendant, on others a haggard despair seemed to have laid its grisly hand; on every one was imprinted the lust of gain. The effect on the young man by my side was peculiar. He looked from face to face, as if he were observing the peculiarities of some strange animals. I watched him, and then I saw his expression suddenly change.

Following the direction of his eyes, I observed a young man putting down his stake upon the board. His face was hidden from me, but by taking a step to the right I could command it. It was none other than the young cripple who had represented his parents to be in such poverty-stricken circumstances; the same young man whom Beckenham had assisted so generously only two hours before. As we looked, he staked his last coin, and that being lost, turned to leave the building. To do this, it was necessary that he should pass close by where we stood. Then his eyes met those of his benefactor, and with a look of what might almost have been shame upon his face, he slunk down the steps and from the building.

'Come, let us get out of this place,' cried my companion impatiently, 'I believe I should go mad if I stayed here long.'

Thereupon we passed out into the street, and without further ado proceeded in the direction in which I imagined the *Saratoga* to lie. A youth of about eighteen chequered summers requested, in broken English, to be permitted the honour of piloting us, but feeling confident of being able to find my way I declined his services.

For fully a quarter of an hour we plodded on, until I began to wonder why the harbour did not heave in sight. It was a queer part of the town we found ourselves in; the houses were perceptibly meaner and the streets narrower. At last I felt bound to confess that I was out of my reckoning, and did not know where we were.

'What are we to do?' asked my lord, looking at his watch. 'It's twenty minutes to eleven, and I promised Mr Baxter I would not be later than the hour.'

'What an idiot I was not to take that guide!'

The words were hardly out of my mouth before that personage appeared round the corner and came towards us. I hailed his coming with too much delight to notice the expression of malignant satisfaction on his face, and gave him the name of the vessel we desired to find. He appeared to understand, and the next moment we were marching off under his guidance in an exactly contrary direction.

We must have walked for at least ten minutes without speaking a word. The streets were still small and ill-favoured, but, as this was probably a short cut to the harbour, such minor drawbacks were not worth considering.

From one small and dirty street we turned into another and broader one. By this time not a soul was to be seen, only a vagrant dog or two lying asleep in the road. In this portion of the town gas lamps were at a discount, consequently more than half the streets lay in deep shadow. Our guide walked ahead, we followed half-a-dozen paces or so behind him. I remember noticing a Greek cognomen upon a signboard, and recalling a similar name in Thursday Island, when something very much resembling a thin cord touched my nose and fell over my chin. Before I could put my hand up to it, it had begun to tighten round my throat. Just at the same moment I heard my companion utter a sharp cry, and after that I remember no more.

CHAPTER EIGHT

Our imprisonment and attempt at escape

For what length of time I lay unconscious after hearing Beckenham's cry, and feeling the cord tighten round my throat, as narrated in the preceding chapter, I have not the remotest idea; I only know that when my senses returned to me again I found myself in complete darkness. The cord was gone from my neck, it is true, but something was still encircling it in a highly unpleasant fashion. On putting my hand up to it, to my intense astonishment I discovered it to be a collar of iron, padlocked at the side, and communicating with a wall at the back by means of a stout chain fixed in a ring, which again was attached to a swivel.

This ominous discovery set me hunting about to find out where I was, and for a clue as to what these things might mean. That I was in a room was evident from the fact that, by putting my hands behind me, I could touch two walls forming a corner. But in what part of the town such a room might be was beyond my telling. One thing was evident, however, the walls were of brick, unplastered and quite innocent of paper.

As not a ray of light relieved the darkness I put my hand into my ticket pocket, where I was accustomed to carry matches, and finding that my captors had not deprived me of them, lit one and looked about me. It was a dismal scene that little gleam illumined. The room in which I was confined was a small one, being only about ten feet long by eight wide, while, if I had been able to stand upright, I might have raised my hand to within two or three inches of the ceiling. In the furthest left-hand corner was a door, while in the wall on the right, but hopelessly beyond my reach, was a low window almost completely boarded up. I had no opportunity of seeing more, for by the time I had realised these facts the match had burnt down to my fingers. I blew it out and hastened to light another.

Just as I did so a low moan reached my ear. It came from the further end of the room. Again I held the match aloft; this time to discover a huddled-up figure in the corner opposite the door. One glance at it told me that it was none other than my young friend the Marquis of Beckenham. He was evidently still unconscious, for though I called him twice by name, he did not answer, but continued in the same position, moaning softly as before. I had only time for a hurried glance at him before my last match burned down to my fingers, and had to be extinguished. With the departure of the light a return of faintness seized me, and I fell back into my corner, if not quite insensible, certainly unconscious of the immediate awkwardness of our position.

It was daylight when my power of thinking returned to me, and long shafts of sunshine were percolating into us through the chinks in the boards upon the window. To my dismay the room looked even smaller and dingier than when I had examined it by the light of my match some hours before. The young Marquis lay unconscious in his corner just as I had last seen him, but with the widening light I discovered that his curious posture was due more to extraneous circumstances than to his own weakness, for I could see that he was fastened to the wall by a similar collar to my own.

I took out my watch, which had not been taken from me as I might have expected, and examined the dial. It wanted five minutes of six o'clock. So putting it back into my pocket, I set myself for the second time to try and discover where we were. By reason of my position and the chain that bound me, this could only be done by listening, so I shut my eyes and put all my being into my ears. For some moments no sound rewarded my attention. Then a cock in a neighbouring yard on my right crowed lustily, a dog on my left barked, and a moment later I heard the faint sound of someone coming along the street. The pedestrian, whoever he might be, was approaching from the right hand, and, what was still more important, my trained ear informed me that he was lame of one leg, and walked with crutches. Closer and closer he came. But to my surprise he did not pass the window; indeed, I noticed that when he came level with it the sound was completely lost to me. This told me two things: one, that the window, which, as I have already said, was boarded up, did not look into the main thoroughfare; the other, that the street itself ran along on the far side of the very wall to which my chain was attached.

As I arrived at the knowledge of this fact, Beckenham opened his eyes; he sat up as well as his chain would permit, and gazed about him in a dazed fashion. Then his right hand went up to the iron collar enclosing his neck, and when he had realised what it meant he appeared even more mystified than before. He seemed to doze again for a minute or so, then his eyes opened, and as they did so they fell upon me, and his perplexity found relief in words.

'Mr Hatteras,' he said, in a voice like that of a man talking in his sleep, 'where are we and what on earth does this chain mean?'

'You ask me something that I want to know myself,' I answered. 'I cannot tell you where we are, except that we are in Port Said. But if you want to know what I think it means, well, I think it means treachery. How do you feel now?'

'Very sick indeed, and my head aches horribly. But I can't understand it at all. What do you mean by saying that it is treachery?'

This was the one question of all others I had been dreading, for I could not help feeling that when all was said and done I was bitterly to blame. However, unpleasant or not, the explanation had to be got through, and without delay.

'Lord Beckenham,' I began, sitting upright and clasping my hands round my knees, 'this is a pretty bad business for me. I haven't the reputation of being a coward, but I'll own I feel pretty rocky and mean when I see you sitting there on the floor with that iron collar round your neck and that chain holding you to the wall, and know that it's, in a measure, all my stupid, blundering folly that has brought it about.'

'Oh, don't say that, Mr Hatteras!' was the young man's generous reply. 'For whatever or whoever may be to blame for it, I'm sure you're not.'

'That's because you don't know everything, my lord. Wait till you have heard what I have to tell you before you give me such complete absolution.'

'I'm not going to blame you whatever you may tell me; but please go on!'

There and then I set to work and told him all that had happened to me since my arrival in London; informed him of my meeting with Nikola, of Wetherell's hasty departure for Australia, of my distrust for Baxter, described the telegram incident and Baxter's curious behaviour afterwards, narrated my subsequent meeting with the two men in the *Green Sailor Hotel*, described my journey to Plymouth, and finished with the catastrophe that had happened to me there.

'Now you see,' I said in conclusion, 'why I regard myself as being so much to blame.'

'Excuse me,' he answered, 'but I cannot say that I see it in the same light at all.'

'I'm afraid I must be more explicit then. In the first place you must understand that, without a shadow of a doubt, Baxter was chosen for your tutor by Nikola, whose agent he undoubtedly is, for a specific purpose. Now what do you think that purpose was? You don't know? To induce your father to let you travel, to be sure. You ask why they should want you to travel? We'll come to that directly. Their plan is succeeding admirably, when I come upon the scene and, like the great blundering idiot I am, must needs set to work unconsciously to assist them in their nefarious designs. Your father eventually consents, and it is arranged that you shall set off for Australia at once. Then it is discovered that I am going to leave in the same boat. This does not suit Nikola's plans at all, so he determines to prevent my sailing with you. By a happy chance he is unsuccessful, and I follow and join the boat in Naples. Good gracious! I see something else now.'

'What is that?'

'Simply this. I could not help thinking at the time that your bout of seasickness between Naples and this infernal place was extraordinary. Well, if I'm not very much mistaken, *you were physicked, and it was Baxter's doing*.'

'But why?'

'Ah! That's yet to be discovered. But you may bet your bottom dollar it was some part of their devilish conspiracy. I'm as certain of that as that we are here now. Now here's another point. Do you remember my running out of the Casino last night? Well, that was because I saw Nikola standing in the roadway watching us.'

'Are you certain? How could he have got here? And what could his reasons be for watching us?'

'Why, can't you see? To find out how his plot is succeeding, to be sure.'

'And that brings us back to our original question – what is that plot?'

'That's rather more difficult to answer! But if you ask my candid opinion I should say nothing more nor less than to make you prisoner and blackmail your father for a ransom.'

For some few minutes neither of us spoke. The outlook seemed too hopeless for words, and the Marquis was still too weak to keep up an animated conversation for any length of time. He sat leaning his head on his hand. But presently he looked up again.

'My poor father!' he said. 'What a state he will be in!'

'And what worries me more,' I answered, 'is how he will regret ever having listened to my advice. What a dolt I was not to have told him of my suspicions.'

'You must not blame yourself for that. I am sure my father would hold you as innocent as I do. Now let us consider our position. In the first place, where are we, do you think? In the second, is there any possible chance of escape?'

'To the first my answer is, "don't know"; to the second, "can't say". I have discovered one thing, however, and that is that the street does not lie outside that window, but runs along on the other side of this wall behind me. The window, I suspect, looks out on to some sort of a courtyard. But unfortunately that information is not much use to us, as we can neither of us move away from where we are placed.'

'Is there no other way?'

'Not one, as far as I can tell. Can you see anything on your side?'

'Nothing at all, unless we could get at the door. But what's that sticking out of the wall near your feet?'

To get a better view of it I stooped as much as I was able.

'It looks like a pipe.'

The end of a pipe it certainly was, and sticking out into the room, but where it led to, and why it had been cut off in this peculiar fashion, were two questions I could no more answer than I could fly.

'Does it run out into the street, do you think?' was Beckenham's immediate query. 'If so, you might manage to call through it to some passer-by, and ask him to obtain assistance for us!'

'A splendid notion if I could get my mouth anywhere within a foot of it, but as this chain will not permit me to do that, it might as well be a hundred miles off. It's as much as I can do to touch it with my fingers.'

'Do you think if you had a stick you could push a piece of paper through? We might write a message on it.'

'Possibly, but there's another drawback to that. I haven't the necessary piece of stick.'

'Here is a stiff piece of straw; try that.'

He harpooned a piece of straw, about eight inches long, across the room towards me, and, when I had received it, I thrust it carefully into the pipe. A disappointment, however, was in store for us.

'It's no use,' I reported sorrowfully, as I threw the straw away. 'It's an elbow half-way down, and that would prevent any message from being pushed through.'

'Then we must try to discover some other plan. Don't lose heart!'

'Hush! I hear somebody coming.'

True enough a heavy footfall was approaching down the passage. It stopped at the door of the room in which we were confined, and a key was inserted in the lock. Next moment the door swung open and a tall man entered the room. A ray of sunlight, penetrating between the boards that covered the window, fell upon him, and showed us that his hair was white and that his face was deeply pitted with smallpox marks. Now, where had I met or heard of a man with those two peculiarities before? Ah! I remembered!

He stood for a moment in the doorway looking about him, and then strolled into the centre of the room.

'Good morning, gentlemen,' he said, with an airy condescension that stung like an insult; 'I trust you have no fault to find with the lodging our poor hospitality is able to afford you.'

'Mr Prendergast,' I answered, determined to try him with the name of the man mentioned by my sweetheart in her letter. 'What does this mean? Why have we been made prisoners like this? I demand to be released at once. You will have to answer to our consul for this detention.'

For a brief space he appeared to be dumbfounded by my knowledge of his name. But he soon recovered himself and leaned his back against the wall, looking us both carefully over before he answered.

'I shall be only too pleased,' he said sneeringly, 'but if you'll allow me to say so, I don't think we need trouble about explanations yet awhile.'

'Pray, what do you mean by that?'

'Exactly what I say; as you are likely to be our guests for some considerable time to come, there will be no need for explanation.'

'You mean to keep us prisoners, then, do you? Very well, Mr Prendergast, be assured of this, when I do get loose I'll make you feel the weight of my arm.'

'I think it's very probable there will be a fight if ever we do meet,' he answered, coolly taking a cigarette from his pocket and lighting it. 'And it's my impression you'd be a man worth fighting, Mr Hatteras.'

'If you think my father will let me remain here very long you're much mistaken,' said Beckenham. 'And as for the ransom you expect him to pay, I don't somehow fancy you'll get a halfpenny.'

At the mention of the word 'ransom' I noticed that a new and queer expression came into our captor's face. He did not reply, however, except to utter his usual irritating laugh. Having done so he went to the door and called something in Arabic. In answer a gigantic negro made his appearance, bearing in his hands a tray on which were set two basins of food and two large mugs of water. These were placed before us, and Prendergast bade us, if we were hungry, fall to.

'You must not imagine that we wish to starve you,' he said. 'Food will be served to you twice a day. And if you want it, you can even be supplied with spirits and tobacco. Now, before I go, one word of advice: Don't indulge in any idea of escape. Communication with the outside world is absolutely impossible, and you will find that those collars and chains will stand a good strain before they will give way. If you behave yourselves you will be well looked after; but if you attempt any larks you will be confined in different rooms, and there will be a radical change in our behaviour towards you.'

So saying he left the room, taking the precaution to lock the door carefully behind him.

When we were once more alone, a long silence fell upon us. It would be idle for me to say that the generous behaviour of the young Marquis with regard to my share in this wretched business had set my mind at rest. But if it had not done that it had at least served to intensify another resolution. Come what might, I told myself, I would find a way of escape, and he should be returned to his father safe and sound, if it cost me my life to do it. But how *were* we to escape? We could not move from our places on account of the chains that secured us to the walls, and, though I put all my whole strength into it, I found I could not dislodge the staple a hundredth part of an inch from its holding-place.

The morning wore slowly on, midday came and went, the afternoon dragged its dismal length, and still there was no change in our position. Towards sundown the same gigantic negro entered the room again, bringing us our evening meal. When he left we were locked up for the night, with only the contemplation of our woes, and the companionship of the multitudes of mice that scampered about the floor, to enliven us.

The events of the next seven days are hardly worth chronicling, unless it is to state that every morning at daylight the same cock crew and the same dog barked, while at six o'clock the same cripple invariably made his way down the street behind me. At eight o'clock, almost to the minute, breakfast was served to us, and, just as punctually, the evening meal made its appearance as the sun was declining behind the opposite housetop. Not again did we see any sign of Mr Prendergast, and though times out of number I tugged at my chain I was never a whit nearer loosening it than I had been on the first occasion. One after another plans of escape were proposed, discussed, and invariably rejected as impracticable. So another week passed and another, until we had been imprisoned in that loathsome place not less than twenty days. By the end of that time, as may be supposed, we were as desperate as men could well be. I must, however, admit here that anything like the patience and pluck of my companion under such trying circumstances I had never in my life met with before. Not once did he reproach me in the least degree for my share in the wretched business, but took everything just as it came, without unnecessary comment and certainly without complaint.

One fact had repeatedly struck me as significant, and that was the circumstance that every morning between six and half-past, as already narrated, the same cripple went down the street; and in connection with this, within the last few days of the time, a curious coincidence had revealed itself to me. From the tapping of his crutches on the stones I discovered that while one was shod with iron, the other was not. Now where and when had I noticed that peculiarity in a cripple before? That I had observed it somewhere I felt certain. For nearly half the day I turned this over and over in my mind, and then, in the middle of our evening meal, enlightenment came to me.

I remembered the man whose piteous tale had so much affected Beckenham on the day of our arrival, and the sound his crutches made upon the pavement as he left us. If my surmise proved correct, and we could only manage to communicate with him, here was a golden opportunity. But how were we to do this? We discussed it, and discussed it, times out of number, but in vain. That he must be stopped on his way down the street need not to be argued at all. In what way, however, could this be done? The window was out of the question, the door was not to be thought of; in that case the only communicating place would be the small pipe by my side. But as I have already pointed out, by reason of the elbow it would be clearly impossible to force a message through it. All day we devoted our-selves to attempts to solve what seemed a hopeless difficulty. Then like a flash another brilliant inspiration burst upon me.

'By Jove, I have it!' I said, taking care to whisper lest anyone might be listening at the door. 'We must manage by hook or crook to catch a mouse *and let him carry our appeal for help to the outside world.*'

'A magnificent idea! If we can catch one I do believe you've saved us!'

But to catch a mouse was easier said than done. Though the room was alive with them they were so nimble and so cunning, that, try how we would, we could not lay hold of one. But at length my efforts were rewarded, and after a little struggle I held my precious captive in my hand. By this time another idea had come to me. If we wanted to bring Nikola and his gang to justice, and to discover their reason for hatching this plot against us, it would not do to ask the public at large for help – and I must own, in spite of our long imprisonment, I was weak enough to feel a curiosity as to their motive. No! It must be to the beggar who passed the house every morning that we must appeal.

'This letter concerns you more than me,' I said to my fellow prisoner. 'Have you a lead pencil in your pocket?'

He had, and immediately threw it across to me. Then, taking a small piece of paper from my pocket, I set myself to compose the following in French and English, assisted by my companion: 'If this should meet the eye of the individual to whom a young Englishman gave half a sovereign in charity three weeks ago, he is implored to assist one who assisted him, and who has been imprisoned ever since that day in the room with the blank wall facing the street and the boarded-up window on the right hand side. To do this he must obtain a small file and discover a way to convey it into the room by means of the small pipe leading through the blank wall into the street; perhaps if this could be dislodged it might be pushed in through the aperture thus made. On receipt of the file an English five-pound note will be conveyed to him in the same way as this letter, and another if secrecy is observed and those imprisoned in the house escape.'

This important epistle had hardly been concocted before the door was unlocked and our dusky servitor entered with the evening meal. He had long since abandoned his first habit of bringing us our food in separate receptacles, but conveyed it to us now in the saucepan in which it was cooked, dividing it thence into our basins. These latter, it may be interesting to state, had not been washed since our arrival.

All the time that our jailer was in the room I held my trembling prisoner in my hand, clinging to him as to the one thing which connected us with liberty. But the door had no sooner closed upon him than I had tilted out my food upon the floor and converted my basin into a trap.

It may be guessed how long that night seemed to us, and with what trembling eagerness we awaited the first signs of breaking day. Directly it was light I took off and unravelled one of my socks. The thread thus obtained I doubled, and having done this, secured one end of it to the note, which I had rolled into a small compass, attaching the other to my captive mouse's hind leg. Then we set ourselves to wait for six o'clock. The hour came; and minute after minute went by before we heard in the distance the tapping of the crutches on the stones. Little by little the sound grew louder, and then fainter, and when I judged he was nearly at my back I stooped and thrust our curious messenger into the pipe. Then we sat down to await the result.

As the mouse, only too glad to escape, ran into the aperture, the thread, on which our very lives depended, swiftly followed, dragging its message after it. Minutes went by; half an hour; an hour; and then the remainder of the day; and still nothing came to tell us that our appeal had been successful.

That night I caught another mouse, wrote the letter again, and at six o'clock next morning once more dispatched it on its journey. Another day went by without reply. That night we caught another, and at six o'clock next morning sent it off; a third, and even a fourth, followed, but still without success. By this time the mice were almost impossible to catch, but our wits were sharpened by despair, and we managed to hit upon a method that eventually secured for us a plentiful supply. For the sixth time the letter was written and dispatched at the moment the footsteps were coming down the street. Once more the tiny animal crawled into the pipe, and once more the message disappeared upon its journey.

Another day was spent in anxious waiting, but this time we were not destined to be disappointed. About eight o'clock that night, just as we were giving up hope, I detected a faint noise near my feet; it was for all the world as if someone were forcing a stick through a hole in a brick wall. I informed Beckenham of the fact in a whisper, and then put my head down to listen. Yes, there was the sound again. Oh, if only I had a match! But it was no use wishing for what was impossible, so I put my hand down to the pipe. It was moving! It turned in my hand, moved to and fro for a brief space and then disappeared from my grasp entirely; next moment it had left the room. A few seconds later something cold was thrust into my hand, *and from its rough edge I knew it to be a file*. I drew it out as if it were made of gold and thrust it into my pocket. A piece of string was attached to it, and the reason of this I was at first at some loss to account for. But a moment's reflection told me that it was to assist in the fulfilment of our share of the bargain. So, taking a five-pound note from the secret pocket in which I carried my paper money, I tied the string to it, and it was instantly withdrawn.

A minute could not have elapsed before I was at work upon the staple of my collar, and in less than half an hour it was filed through and the iron was off my neck.

If I tried for a year I could not make you understand what a relief it was to me to stand upright. I stretched myself again and again, and then crossed the room on tiptoe in the dark to where the Marquis lay.

'You are free!' he whispered, clutching and shaking my hand. 'Oh, thank God!'

'Hush! Put down your head and let me get to work upon your collar before you say anything more.'

As I was able this time to get at my work standing up, it was not very long before Beckenham was as free as I was. He rose to his feet with a great sigh of relief, and we shook hands warmly in the dark.

'Now,' I said, leading him towards the door, 'we will make our escape, and I pity the man who attempts to stop us.'

CHAPTER NINE

Dr Nicola permits us a free passage

The old saying, 'Don't count your chickens before they're hatched,' is as good a warning as any I know. Certainly it proved so in our case. For if we had not been so completely occupied filing through the staples of our collars we should not have omitted to take into consideration the fact that, even when we should have removed the chains that bound us, we would still be prisoners in the room. I'm very much afraid, however, even had we remembered this point, we should only have considered it of minor importance and one to be easily overcome. As it was, the unwelcome fact remained that the door was locked, and, what was worse, that the lock itself had, for security's sake, been placed on the outside, so that there was no chance of our being able to pick it, even had our accomplishments lain in that direction. 'Try the window,' whispered Beckenham, in answer to the heavy sigh which followed my last discovery.

Accordingly we crossed the room, and I put my hands upon one of the boards and pulled. But I might as well have tried to tow a troopship with a piece of cotton, for all the satisfactory result I got; the planks were trebly screwed to the window frame, and each in turn defied me. When I was tired Beckenham put his strength to it, but even our united efforts were of no avail, and, panting and exhausted, we were at length obliged to give it up as hopeless.

'This is a pretty fix we've got ourselves into,' I said as soon as I had recovered sufficient breath to speak. 'We can't remain here, and yet how on earth are we to escape?'

'I can't say, unless we manage to burst that door open and fight our way out. I wonder if that could be done.'

'First, let's look at the door.'

We crossed the room again, and I examined the door carefully with my fingers. It was not a very strong one; but I was sufficient of a carpenter to know that it would withstand a good deal of pressure before it would give way.

'I've a good mind to try it,' I said; 'but in that case, remember, it will probably mean a hand-to-hand fight on the other side, and, unarmed and weak as we are, we shall be pretty sure to get the worst of it.'

'Never mind that,' my intrepid companion replied, with a confidence in his voice that I was very far from feeling. 'In for a penny, in for a pound; even if we're killed it couldn't be worse than being buried alive in here.'

'That's so, and if fighting's your idea, I'm your man,' I answered. 'Let me first take my bearings, and then I'll see what I can do against it. You get out of the way, but be sure to stand by to rush the passage directly the door goes.'

Again I felt the door and wall in order that I might be sure where it lay, and having done so crossed the room. My heart was beating like a Nasmyth hammer, and it was nearly a minute before I could pull myself together sufficiently for my rush. Then summoning every muscle in my body to my assistance, I dashed across and at it with all the strength my frame was capable of. Considering the darkness of the room, my steering was not so bad, for my shoulder caught the door just above its centre; there was a great crash – a noise of breaking timbers – and amid a shower of splinters and general *débris* I fell headlong through into the passage. By the time it would have taken me to count five, Beckenham was beside me helping me to rise.

'Now stand by for big trouble!' I said, rubbing my shoulder, and every moment expecting to see a door open and a crowd of Prendergast's ruffians come rushing out. 'We shall have them on us in a minute.'

But to our intense astonishment it was all dead silence. Not a sound of any single kind, save our excited breathing, greeted our ears. We might have broken into an empty house for all we knew the difference.

For nearly five minutes we stood, side by side, waiting for the battle which did not come.

'What on earth does it mean?' I asked my companion. 'That crash of mine was loud enough to wake the dead. Can they have deserted the place, think you, and left us to starve?'

'I can't make it out any more than you can,' he answered. 'But don't you think we'd better take advantage of their not coming to find a way out?'

'Of course. One of us had better creep down the passage and discover how the land lies. As I'm the stronger, I'll go. You wait here.'

I crept along the passage, treading cautiously as a cat, for I knew that both our lives depended on it. Though it could not have been more than sixty feet, it seemed of interminable length, and was as black as night. Not a glimmer of light, however faint, met my eyes.

On and on I stole, expecting every moment to be pounced upon and seized; but no such fate awaited me. If, however, our jailers did not appear, another danger was in store for me.

In the middle of my walk my feet suddenly went from under me, and I found myself falling I knew not where. In reality it was only a drop of about three feet down a short flight of steps. Such a noise as my fall made, however, was surely never heard, but still no sound came. Then Beckenham fumbled his way cautiously down the steps to my side, and whispered an enquiry as to what had happened. I told him in as few words as possible, and then struggled to my feet again.

Just as I did so my eyes detected a faint glimmer of light low down on the floor ahead of us. From its position it evidently emanated from the doorway of a room.

'Oh! if only we had a match,' I whispered.

'It's no good wishing,' said Beckenham. 'What do you advise?'

'It's difficult to say,' I answered; 'but I should think we'd better listen at that door and try to discover if there is anyone inside. If there is, and he is alone, we must steal in upon him, let him see that we are desperate, and, willy-nilly, force him to show us a way out. It's ten chances to one, if we go on prowling about here, we shall stumble upon the whole nest of them – then we'll be caught like rats in a trap. What do you think?'

'I agree with you. Go on.'

Without further ado we crept towards the light, which, as I expected, came from under a door, and listened. Someone was plainly moving about inside; but though we waited for what seemed a quarter of an hour, but must in reality have been less than a minute and a half, we could hear no voices.

'Whoever he is, he's alone – that's certain,' whispered my companion. 'Open the door softly, and we'll creep in upon him.'

In answer, and little by little, a cold shiver running down my back lest it should creak and so give warning to the person within, I turned the handle, pushed open the door, and we looked inside. Then – but, my gracious! if I live to be a thousand I shall never forget even the smallest particular connected with the sight that met my eyes.

The room itself was a long and low one: its measurements possibly sixty feet by fifteen. The roof – for there was no ceiling – was of wood, crossed by heavy rafters, and much begrimed with dirt and smoke. The floor was of some highly polished wood closely resembling oak and was completely bare. But the shape and construction of the room itself were as nothing compared with the strangeness of its furniture and occupants. Words would fail me if I tried to give you a true and accurate description of it. I only know that, strong man as I was, and used to the horrors of life and death, what I saw before me then made my blood run cold and my flesh creep as it had never done before.

To begin with, round the walls were arranged, at regular intervals, more than a dozen enormous bottles, each of which contained what looked, to me, only too much like human specimens pickled in some light-coloured fluid resembling spirits of wine. Between these gigantic but more than horrible receptacles were numberless smaller ones holding other and even more dreadful remains; while on pedestals and stands, bolt upright and reclining, were skeletons of men, monkeys, and quite a hundred sorts of animals. The intervening spaces were filled with skulls, bones, and the apparatus for every kind of murder known to the fertile brain of man. There were European rifles, revolvers, bayonets, and swords; Italian stilettos, Turkish scimitars, Greek knives, Central African spears and poisoned arrows, Zulu knobkerries, Afghan yataghans, Malay krises, Sumatra blowpipes, Chinese dirks, New Guinea head-catching implements, Australian spears and boomerangs, Polynesian stone hatchets, and numerous other weapons the names of which I cannot now remember. Mixed up with them were implements for every sort of wizardry known to the superstitious; from old-fashioned English love charms to African Obi sticks, from spiritualistic planchettes to the most horrible of Fijian death potions.

In the centre of the wall, opposite to where we stood, was a large fireplace of the fashion usually met with in old English manor-houses, and on either side of it a figure that nearly turned me sick with horror. That on the right hand was apparently a native of Northern India, if one might judge by his dress and complexion. He sat on the floor in a constrained attitude, accounted for by the fact that his head, which was at least three times too big for his body, was so heavy as to require an iron tripod with a ring or collar in the top of it to keep it from overbalancing him and bringing him to the floor. To add to the horror of this awful head, it was quite bald; the skin was drawn tensely over the bones, and upon this great veins stood out as large as macaroni stems.

On the other side of the hearth was a creature half-ape and half-man – the like of which I remember once to have seen in a museum of monstrosities in Sydney, where, if my memory serves me, he was described upon the catalogue as a Burmese monkey-boy. He was chained to the wall in somewhat the same fashion as we had been, and was chattering and scratching for all the world like a monkey in a Zoo.

But, horrible as these things were, the greatest surprise of all was yet to come. For, standing at the heavy oaken table in the centre of the room, was a man I should have known anywhere if I had been permitted half a glance at him. *It was Dr Nikola.*

When we entered he was busily occupied with a scalpel, dissecting an animal strangely resembling a monkey. On the table, and watching the work upon which his master was engaged, sat his constant companion, the same fiendish black cat I have mentioned elsewhere. While at the end nearest us, standing on tiptoe, the better to see what was going on, was an albino dwarf, scarcely more than two feet eight inches high.

Now, though it has necessarily taken me some time to describe the scene which greeted our eyes, it must not be supposed that anything like the same length of time had really elapsed since our entry. Three seconds at the very most would have sufficed to cover the whole period.

So stealthily, however, had our approach been made, and so carefully had I opened the door, that we were well into the room before our appearance was discovered, and also before I had realised into whose presence we had stumbled. Then my foot touched a board that creaked, and Dr Nikola looked up from the work upon which he was engaged.

His pale, thin face did not show the slightest sign of surprise as he said, in his usual placid tone: 'So you have managed to escape from your room, gentlemen. Well, and pray what do you want with me?'

For a moment I was so much overcome with surprise that my tongue refused to perform its office. Then I said, advancing towards him as I spoke, closely followed by the Marquis: 'So, Dr Nikola, we have met at last!'

'At last, Mr Hatteras, as you say,' this singular being replied, still without showing a sign of either interest or embarrassment. 'All things considered, I suppose you would deem me ironical if I ventured to say that I am pleased to see you about again. However, don't let me keep you standing; won't you sit down? My lord, let me offer you a chair.'

All this time we were edging up alongside the table, and I was making ready for a rush at him. But he was not to be taken off his guard. His extraordinary eyes had been watching me intently, taking in my every movement; and a curious effect their steady gaze had upon me.

'Dr Nikola,' I said, pulling myself together, 'the game is up. You beat me last time; but now you must own I come out on top. Don't utter a word or call for assistance – if you do you're a dead man. Now drop that knife you hold in your hand, and show us the way out!'

The Marquis was on his right, I was on his left, and we were close upon him as I spoke. Still he showed no sign of fear, though he must have known the danger of his position. But his eyes glowed in his head like living coals.

You will ask why we did not rush at him? Well, if I am obliged to own it, I must – the truth was, such was the power that emanated from this extraordinary man, that though we both knew the crucial moment of our enterprise had arrived, while his eyes were fixed upon us, neither of us could stir an inch. When he spoke his voice seemed to cut like a knife.

'So you think my game is up, Mr Hatteras, do you? I'm afraid once more I must differ from you. Look behind you.'

I did so, and that glance showed me how cleverly we'd been trapped. Leaning against the door, watching us with cruel, yet smiling eyes, was our old enemy Prendergast, revolver in hand. Just behind me were two powerful Soudanese, while near the Marquis was a man looking like a Greek – and a very stalwart Greek at that. Observing our discomfiture, Nikola seated himself in a big chair near the fireplace and folded his hands in the curious fashion I have before described; as he did so his black cat sprang to his shoulder and sat there watching us all. Dr Nikola was the first to speak.

'Mr Hatteras,' he said, with devilish clearness and deliberation, 'you should really know me better by this time than to think you could outwit me so easily. Is my reputation after all so small? And, while I think of it, pray let me have the pleasure of returning to you your five pound note and your letters. Your mice were perfect messengers, were they not?' As he spoke he handed me the self-same Bank of England note I had dispatched through the pipe that very evening in payment for the file; then he shook from a box he had taken from the chimney-piece all the communications I had written imploring assistance from the outside world. To properly estimate my chagrin and astonishment would be very difficult. I could only sit and stare, first at the money and then at the letters, in blankest amazement. So we had not been rescued by the cripple after all. Was it possible that while we had been so busy arranging our escape we had in reality been all the time under the closest surveillance? If that were so, then this knowledge of our doings would account for the silence with which my attack upon the door had been received. Now we were in an even worse position than before. I looked at Beckenham, but his head was down and his right hand was picking idly at the table edge. He was evidently waiting for what was coming next. In sheer despair I turned to Nikola.

'Since you have outwitted us again, Dr Nikola, do not play with us – tell us straight out what our fate is to be.'

'If it means going back to that room again,' said Beckenham, in a voice I hardly recognised, 'I would far rather die and be done with it.'

'Do not fear, my lord, you shall not die,' Nikola said, turning to him with a bow. 'Believe me, you will live to enjoy many happier hours than those you have been compelled to spend under my roof!'

'What do you mean?'

The doctor did not answer for nearly a moment; then he took what looked to me suspiciously like a cablegram form from his pocket and carefully examined it. Having done so, he said quietly: 'Gentlemen, you ask what I mean? Well, I mean this – if you wish to leave this house this very minute, you are free to do so on one condition!'

'And that condition is?'

'That you allow yourselves to be blindfolded in this room and conducted by my servants to the harbour side. I must furthermore ask your words of honour that you will not seek to remove your bandages until you are given permission to do so. Do you agree to this?'

Needless to say we both signified our assent.

This free permission to leave the house was a second surprise, and one for which we were totally unprepared.

'Then let it be so. Believe me, my lord Marquis, and you, Mr Hatteras, it is with the utmost pleasure I restore your liberty to you again!'

He made a sign to Prendergast, who instantly stepped forward. But I had something to say before we were removed.

'One word first, Dr Nikola. You have – '

'Mr Hatteras, if you will be guided by me, you will keep a silent tongue in your head. Let well alone. Take warning by the proverb, and beware how you disturb a sleeping dog. Why I have acted as I have done towards you, you may some day learn; in the meantime rest assured it was from no idle motive. Now take me at my word, and go while you have the chance. I may change my mind in a moment, and then – '

He stopped and did not say any more. At a sign, Prendergast clapped a thick bandage over my eyes, while another man did the same for Beckenham; a man on either side of me took my arms, and next moment we had passed out of the room, and before I could have counted fifty were in the cool air of the open street.

How long we were walking, after leaving the house, I could not say, but at last our escort called a halt. Prendergast was evidently in command, for he said: 'Gentlemen, before we leave you, you will renew your words of honour not to remove your bandages for five full minutes?'

We complied with his request, and instantly our arms were released; a moment later we heard our captors leaving us. The minutes went slowly by. Presently Beckenham said: 'How long do you think we've been standing here?'

'Nearly the stipulated time, I should fancy,' I answered. 'However, we'd better give them a little longer, to avoid any chance of mistake.'

Again a silence fell on us. Then I tore off my bandage, to find Beckenham doing the same.

'They're gone, and we're free again,' he cried. 'Hurrah!'

We shook hands warmly on our escape, and having done so looked about us. A ship's bell out in the stream chimed half an hour after midnight, and a precious dark night it was. A number of vessels were to be seen, and from the noise that came from them it was evident they were busy coaling.

'What's to be done now?' asked Beckenham.

'Find an hotel, I think,' I answered; 'get a good night's rest, and first thing in the morning hunt up our consul and the steamship authorities.'

'Come along, then. Let's look for a place. I noticed one that should suit us close to where we came ashore that day.'

Five minutes' walking brought us to the house we sought. The proprietor was not very fastidious, and whatever he may have thought of our appearances he took us in without demur. A bath and a good meal followed, and then after a thorough overhauling of all the details connected with our imprisonment we turned into bed, resolved to thrash it out upon the morrow.

Next morning, true to our arrangement, as soon as breakfast was over, I set off for the steamship company's office, leaving the Marquis behind me at the hotel for reasons which had begun to commend themselves to me, and which will be quite apparent to you.

I found the *Saratoga*'s agent hard at work in his private office. He was a tall, thin man, slightly bald, wearing a pair of heavy gold pincenez, and very slow and deliberate in his speech.

'I beg your pardon,' he began, when I had taken possession of his proffered chair, 'but did I understand my clerk to say that your name was Hatteras?'

'That is my name,' I answered. 'I was a passenger in your boat the *Saratoga* for Australia three weeks ago, but had the misfortune to be left behind when she sailed.'

'Ah! I remember the circumstances thoroughly,' he said. 'The young Marquis of Beckenham went ashore with you, I think, and came within an ace of being also left behind.'

'Within an ace!' I cried; 'but he was left behind.'

'No, no! there you are mistaken,' was the astounding reply; 'he would have been left behind had not his tutor and I gone ashore at the last moment to look for him and found him wandering about on the outskirts of Arab Town. I don't remember ever to have seen a man more angry than the tutor was, and no wonder, for they only just got out to the boat again as the gangway was being hauled aboard.'

'Then you mean to tell me that the Marquis went on to Australia after all!' I cried. 'And pray how did this interesting young gentleman explain the fact of his losing sight of me?'

'He lost you in a crowd, he said,' the agent continued. 'It was a most extraordinary business altogether.'

It certainly was, and even more extraordinary than he imagined. I could hardly believe my ears. The world seemed to be turned upside down. I was so bewildered that I stumbled out a few lame enquiries about the next boat sailing for Australia, and what would be done with my baggage on its arrival at the other end, and then made my way as best I could out of the office.

Hastening back to the hotel, I told my story from beginning to end to my astonished companion, who sat on his bed listening open-mouthed. When I had finished he said feebly: 'But what does it all mean? Tell me that! What does it mean?'

'It means,' I answered, 'that our notion about Nikola's abducting us in order to blackmail your father was altogether wrong, and, if you ask me, I should say not half picturesque enough. No, no! this mystery is a bigger one by a hundred times than even we expected, and there are more men in it than those we have yet seen. It remains with you to say whether you will assist in the attempt to unravel it or not.'

'What do you mean by saying it remains with me? Do I understand that you intend following it up?'

'Of course I do. Nikola and Baxter between them have completely done me – now I'm going to do my best to do them. By Jove!'

'What is it now?'

'I see it all as plain as a pikestaff. I understand exactly now why Baxter came for you, why he telegraphed that the train was laid, why I was drugged in Plymouth, why you were seasick between Naples and this place, and why we were both kidnapped so mysteriously!'

'Then explain, for mercy's sake!'

'I will. See here. In the first place, remember your father's peculiar education of yourself. If you consider that, you will see that you are the only young nobleman of high rank whose face is not well known to his brother peers. That being so, Nikola wants to procure you for some purpose of his own in Australia. Your father advertises for a tutor; he sends one of his agents – Baxter – to secure the position. Baxter, at Nikola's instruction, puts into your head a desire for travel. You pester your father for the necessary permission. Just as this is granted I come upon the scene. Baxter suspects me. He telegraphs to Nikola "The train is laid", which means that he has begun to sow the seeds of a desire for travel, when a third party steps in – in other words, I am the new danger that has arisen. He arranges your sailing, and all promises to go well. Then Dr Nikola finds out I intend going in the same boat. He tries to prevent me; and I – by Jove! I see another thing. Why did Baxter suggest that you should cross the continent and join the boat at Naples? Why, simply because if you started from Plymouth you would soon have got over your sickness, if you had ever been ill at all, and in that case the passengers would have become thoroughly familiar with your face by the time you reached Port Said. That would never have done, so he takes you to Naples, drugs you next morning – for you must remember you were ill after the coffee he gave you – and by that means keeps you ill and confined to your cabin throughout the entire passage to Port Said. Then he persuades you to go ashore with me. You do so, with what result you know. Presently he begins to bewail your non-return, invites the agent to help in the search. They set off, and eventually find you near the Arab quarter. You must remember that neither the agent, the captain, nor the passengers have seen you, save at night, so the substitute, who is certain to have been well chosen and schooled for the part he is to play, is not detected. Then the boat goes on her way, while we are left behind languishing in durance vile.'

'Do you really think those are the facts of the case?'

'Upon my word, I do!'

'Then what do you advise me to do? Remember, Baxter has letters to the different Governors from my father.'

'I know what I should do myself!'

'Go to the consul and get him to warn the authorities in Australia, I suppose?'

'No. That would do little or no good – remember, they've three weeks' start of us.'

'Then what shall we do? I'm in your hands entirely, and whatever you advise I promise you I'll do.'

'If I were you I should doff my title, take another name, and set sail with me for Australia. Once there, we'll put up in some quiet place and set ourselves to unmask these rascals and to defeat their little game, whatever it may be. Are you prepared for so much excitement as that?'

'Of course I am. Come what may, I'll go with you, and there's my hand on it.'

'Then we'll catch the next boat – not a mail-steamer – that sails for an Australian port, and once ashore there we'll set the ball a-rolling with a vengeance.'

'That scoundrel Baxter! I'm not vindictive as a rule, but I feel I should like to punish him.'

'Well, if they've not flown by the time we reach Australia, you'll probably be able to gratify your wish. It's Nikola, however, I want.'

Beckenham shuddered as I mentioned the Doctor's name. So to change the subject I said: 'I'm thinking of taking a little walk. Would you care to accompany me?'

'Where are you going?' he asked.

'I'm going to try and find the house where we were shut up,' I answered. 'I want to be able to locate it for future reference, if necessary.'

'Is it safe to go near it, do you think?'

'In broad daylight, yes! But, just to make sure, we'll buy a couple of revolvers on the way. And, what's more, if it becomes necessary we'll use them.'

'Come along, then.'

With that we left our hotel and set off in the direction of the Casino, stopping, however, on the way to make the purchases above referred to.

On arrival at the place we sought, we halted and looked about us. I pointed to a street on our right.

'That was the way we came from the mosque,' I said. Then, pointing to a narrow alley way almost opposite where we stood, I continued, 'And that was where I saw Nikola standing watching us. Now when we came out of this building we turned to our left hand, and, if I mistake not, went off in that direction. I think, if you've no objection, we'll go that way now.'

We accordingly set off at a good pace, and after a while arrived at the spot where the guide had caught us up. It looked a miserably dirty neighbourhood in the bright sunlight. Beckenham gazed about him thoughtfully, and finally said: 'Now we turn to our right, I think.'

'Quite so. Come along!'

We passed down one thoroughfare and up another, and at last reached the spot where I had commented on the sign-boards, and where we had been garrotted. Surely the house must be near at hand now? But though we hunted high and low, up one street and down another, not a single trace of any building, answering the description of the one we wanted, could we discover. At last, after nearly an hour's search, we were obliged to give it up, and return to our hotel, unsuccessful.

As we finished lunch a large steamer made her appearance in the harbour, and brought up opposite the town. When we questioned our landlord, who was an authority on the subject, he informed us that she was the S.S. *Pescadore*, of Hull, bound to Melbourne.

Hearing this we immediately chartered a boat, pulled off to her, and interviewed the captain. As good luck would have it, he had room for a couple of passengers. We therefore paid the passage money, went ashore again and provided ourselves with a few necessaries, rejoined her, and shortly before nightfall steamed into the Canal. Port Said was a thing of the past. Our eventful journey was resumed – what was the end of it all to be?

PART TWO

CHAPTER ONE

We reach Australia, and the result

The *Pescadore*, if she was slow, was certainly sure, and so the thirty-sixth day after our departure from Port Said, as recorded in the previous chapter, she landed us safe and sound at Williamstown, which, as all the Australian world knows, is one of the principal railway termini, and within an hour's journey of Melbourne. Throughout the voyage nothing occurred worth chronicling, if I except the curious behaviour of Lord Beckenham, who, for the first week or so, seemed sunk in a deep lethargy, from which neither chaff nor sympathy could rouse him. From morning till night he mooned aimlessly about the decks, had visibly to pull himself together to answer such questions as might be addressed to him, and never by any chance sustained a conversation beyond a few odd sentences. To such a pitch did this depression at last bring him that, the day after we left Aden, I felt it my duty to take him to task and to try to bully or coax him out of it. We were standing at the time under the bridge and a little forrard of the chart-room.

'Come,' I said, 'I want to know what's the matter with you. You've been giving us all the miserables lately, and from the look of your face at the present moment I'm inclined to believe it's going to continue. Out with it! Are you homesick, or has the monotony of this voyage been too much for you?'

He looked into my face rather anxiously, I thought, and then said: 'Mr Hatteras, I'm afraid you'll think me an awful idiot when I *do* tell you, but the truth is I've got Dr Nikola's face on my brain, and do what I will I cannot rid myself of it. Those great, searching eyes, as we saw them in that terrible room, have got on my nerves, and I can think of nothing else. They haunt me night and day!'

'Oh, that's all fancy!' I cried. 'Why on earth should you be frightened of him? Nikola, in spite of his demoniacal cleverness, is only a man, and even then you may consider that we've seen the last of him.

So cheer up, take as much exercise as you possibly can, and believe me, you'll soon forget all about him.'

But it was no use arguing with him. Nikola had had an effect upon the youth that was little short of marvellous, and it was not until we had well turned the Leuwin, and were safely in Australian waters, that he in any way recovered his former spirits.

And here, lest you should give me credit for a bravery I did not possess, I must own that I was more than a little afraid of another meeting with Nikola, myself. I had had four opportunities afforded me of judging of his cleverness – once in the restaurant off Oxford Street, once in the *Green Sailor* public-house in the East India Dock Road, once in the West of England express, and lastly, in the house in Port Said. I had not the slightest desire, therefore, to come to close quarters with him again.

Arriving in Melbourne we caught the afternoon express for Sydney, reaching that city the following morning a little after breakfast. By the time we arrived at our destination we had held many consultations over our future, and the result was a decision to look for a quiet hotel on the outskirts of the city, and then to attempt to discover what the mystery, in which we had been so deeply involved, might mean. The merits of all the various suburbs were severally discussed, though I knew but little about them, and the Marquis less. Paramatta, Penrith, Woolahra, Balmain, and even many of the bays and harbours, received attention, until we decided on the last named as the most likely place to answer our purpose.

This settled, we crossed Darling harbour, and, after a little hunting about, discovered a small but comfortable hotel situated in a side street, called the *General Officer*. Here we booked rooms, deposited our meagre baggage, and having installed ourselves, sat down and discussed the situation.

'So this is Sydney,' said Beckenham, stretching himself out comfortably upon the sofa by the window as he spoke. 'And now that we've got here, what's to be done first?'

'Have lunch,' I answered promptly.

'And then?' he continued.

'Hunt up a public library and take a glimpse of the *Morning Herald*'s back numbers. They will tell us a good deal, though not all we want to know. Then we'll make a few enquiries. Tomorrow morning I shall ask you to excuse me for a couple of hours. But in the afternoon we ought to have acquired sufficient information to enable us to make a definite start on what we've got to do.'

'Then let's have lunch at once and be off. I'm all eagerness to get to work.'

We accordingly ordered lunch, and, when it was finished, set off in search of a public library. Having found it – and it was not a very difficult matter – we sought the reading room and made for a stand of *Sydney Morning Herald*s in the corner. Somehow I felt as certain of finding what I wanted there as any man could possibly be, and as it happened I was not disappointed. On the second page, beneath a heading in bold type, was a long report of a horse show, held the previous afternoon, at which it appeared a large vice-regal and fashionable party were present. The list included His Excellency the Governor and the Countess of Amberley, the Ladies Maud and Ermyntrude, their daughters, the Marquis of Beckenham, Captain Barrenden, an aide-de-camp, and Mr Baxter. In a voice that I hardly recognised as my own, so shaken was it with excitement, I called Beckenham to my side and pointed out to him his name. He stared, looked away, then stared again, hardly able to believe his eyes.

'What does it mean?' he whispered, just as he had done in Port Said. 'What does it mean?'

I led him out of the building before I answered, and then clapped him on the shoulder.

'It means, my boy,' I said, 'that there's been a hitch in their arrangements, and that we're not too late to circumvent them after all.'

'But where do you think they are staying – these two scoundrels?'

'At Government House, to be sure. Didn't you see that the report said, "The Earl and Countess of Amberley and a distinguished party from Government House, including the Marquis of Beckenham", etc.?'

'Then let us go to Government House at once and unmask them. That is our bounden duty to society.'

'Then all I can say is, if it is our duty to society, society will have to wait. No, no! We must find out first what their little game is. That once decided, the unmasking will fall in as a natural consequence. Don't you understand?'

'I am afraid I don't quite. However, I expect you're right.'

By this time we were back again at the ferry. It was not time for the boat to start, so while we waited we amused ourselves staring at the placards pasted about on the wharf hoardings. Then a large theatrical poster caught my eye and drew me towards it. It announced a grand vice-regal 'command' night at one of the principal theatres for that very evening, and further set forth the fact that the most

noble the Marquis of Beckenham would be amongst the distinguished company present.

'Here we are,' I called to my companion, who was at a little
distance. 'We'll certainly go to this. The Marquis of Beckenham
shall honour it with his patronage and presence after all.'

Noting the name and address of the theatre, we went back to our
hotel for dinner, and as soon as it was eaten returned to the city to
seek the theatre.

When we entered it the building was crowded, and the arrival of
the Government House party was momentarily expected. Presently
there was a hush, then the orchestra and audience rose while 'God
save the Queen' was played, and the Governor and a brilliant party
entered the vice-regal box. You may be sure of all that vast con-
course of people there were none who stared harder than Beckenham and myself. And it was certainly enough to make any man
stare, for there, sitting on her ladyship's right hand, faultlessly
dressed, was the exact image of the young man by my side. The
likeness was so extraordinary that for a moment I could hardly
believe that Beckenham had not left me to go up and take his seat
there. And if I was struck by the resemblance, you may be sure that
he was a dozen times more so. Indeed, his bewilderment was most
comical, and must have struck those people round us, who were
watching, as something altogether extraordinary. I looked again,
and could just discern behind the front row the smug, self-satisfied
face of the tutor Baxter. Then the play commenced, and we were
compelled to turn and give it our attention.

Here I must stop to chronicle one circumstance that throughout
the day had struck me as peculiar. When our vessel arrived at
Williamstown it so happened that we had travelled up in the train to
Melbourne with a tall, handsome, well-dressed man of about thirty
years of age. Whether he, like ourselves, was a new arrival in the
Colony, and only passing through Melbourne, I cannot say; at any
rate he went on to Sydney in the mail train with us. Then we lost
sight of him, only to find him standing near the public library when
we had emerged from it that afternoon, and now here he was sitting
in the stalls of the theatre not half a dozen chairs from us. Whether
this continual companionship was designed or only accidental, I
could not of course say, but I must own that I did not like the look of
it. Could it be possible, I asked myself, that Nikola, learning our
departure for Australia in the *Pescadore*, had cabled from Port Said to
this man to watch us?

The performance over, we left the theatre and set off for the ferry, only reaching it just as the boat was casting off. As it was I had to jump for it, and on reaching the deck should have fallen in a heap but for a helping hand that was stretched out to me. I looked up to tender my thanks, when to my surprise I discovered that my benefactor was none other than the man to whom I have just been referring. His surprise was even greater than mine, and muttering something about 'a close shave', he turned and walked quickly aft. My mind was now made up, and I accordingly reported my discovery to Beckenham, pointing out the man and warning him to watch for him when he was abroad without me. This he promised to do.

Next morning I donned my best attire (my luggage having safely arrived), and shortly before eleven o'clock bade Beckenham goodbye and betook myself to Potts Point to call upon the Wetherells.

It would be impossible for me to say with what varied emotions I trod that well-remembered street, crossed the garden, and approached the ponderous front door, which somehow had always seemed to me so typical of Mr Wetherell himself. The same butler who had opened the door to me on the previous occasion opened it now, and when I asked if Miss Wetherell were at home, he gravely answered, 'Yes, sir,' and invited me to enter. Though I had called there before, it must be remembered that this was the first time I had been inside the house, and I must confess the display of wealth in the hall amazed me.

I was shown into the drawing-room – a large double chamber beautifully furnished and possessing an elegantly painted ceiling – while the butler went in search of his mistress. A few moments later I heard a light footstep outside, a hand was placed upon the handle of the door, and before I could have counted ten, Phyllis – my Phyllis! was in the room and in my arms! Over the next five minutes, gentle reader, we will draw a curtain with your kind permission. If you have ever met your sweetheart after an absence of several months, you will readily understand why!

When we had become rational again I led her to a sofa, and, seating myself beside her, asked if her father had in any way relented towards me. At this she looked very unhappy, and for a moment I thought was going to burst into tears.

'Why! what is the matter, Phyllis, my darling?' I cried in sincere alarm, 'What is troubling you?'

'Oh, I am so unhappy,' she replied. 'Dick, there is a gentleman in Sydney now to whom papa has taken an enormous fancy, and he is exerting all his influence over me to induce me to marry him.'

'The deuce he is, and pray who may – ' but I got no further in my enquiries, for at that moment I caught the sound of a footstep in the hall, and next moment Mr Wetherell opened the door. He remained for a brief period looking from one to the other of us without speaking, then he advanced, saying, 'Mr Hatteras, please be so good as to tell me when this persecution will cease? Am I not even to be free of you in my own house. Flesh and blood won't stand it, I tell you, sir – won't stand it! You pursued my daughter to England in a most ungentlemanly fashion, and now you have followed her out here again.'

'Just as I shall continue to follow her all my life, Mr Wetherell,' I replied warmly, 'wherever you may take her. I told you on board the *Orizaba*, months ago, that I loved her; well, I love her ten thousand times more now. She loves me – won't you hear her tell you so? Why then should you endeavour to keep us apart?'

'Because an alliance with you, sir, is distasteful to me in every possible way. I have other views for my daughter, you must learn.' Here Phyllis could keep silence no longer, and broke in with: 'If you mean by that that you will force me into this hateful marriage with a man I despise, papa, you are mistaken. I will marry no one but Mr Hatteras, and so I warn you.'

'Silence, Miss! How dare you adopt that tone with me! You will do as I wish in this and all other matters, and so we'll have no more talk about it. Now, Mr Hatteras, you have heard what I have to say, and I warn you that, if you persist in this conduct, I'll see if something can't be found in the law to put a stop to it. Meanwhile, if you show yourself in my grounds again, I'll have my servants throw you out into the street! Good-day.'

Unjust as his conduct was to me, there was nothing for it but to submit, so picking up my hat I bade poor little frightened Phyllis farewell and went towards the door. But before taking my departure I was determined to have one final shot at her irascible parent, so I said, 'Mr Wetherell, I have warned you before, and I do so again: your daughter loves me, and, come what may, I will make her my wife. She is her own mistress, and you cannot force her into marrying anyone against her will. Neither can you prevent her marrying me if she wishes it. You will be sorry some day that you have behaved like this to me.'

But the only answer he vouchsafed was a stormy one.

'Leave my house this instant. Not another word, sir, or I'll call my servants to my assistance!'

The stately old butler opened the front door for me, and assuming as dignified an air as was possible, I went down the drive and passed out into the street.

When I reached home again Beckenham was out, for which I was not sorry, as I wanted to have a good quiet think by myself. So, lighting a cigar, I pulled a chair into the verandah and fell to work. But I could make nothing of the situation, save that, by my interview this morning, my position with the father was, if possible, rendered even more hopeless than before. Who was this more fortunate suitor? Would it be any use my going to him and – but no, that was clearly impossible. Could I induce Phyllis to run away with me? That was possible, of course, but I rather doubted if she would care to take such an extreme step until every other means had proved unsuccessful. Then what was to be done? I began to wish that Beckenham would return in order that we might consult together.

Half an hour later our lunch was ready, but still no sign came of the youth. Where could he have got to? I waited an hour and then fell to work. Three o'clock arrived and still no sign – four, five, and even six. By this time I was in a fever of anxiety. I remembered the existence of the man who had followed us from Melbourne, and Beckenham's trusting good nature. Then and there I resolved, if he did not return before half-past seven, to set off for the nearest police station and have a search made for him. Slowly the large hand of the clock went round, and when, at the time stated, he had not appeared, I donned my hat and, enquiring the way, set off for the home of the law.

On arriving there and stating my business I was immediately conducted to the inspector in charge, who questioned me very closely as to Beckenham's appearance, age, profession, etc. Having done this, he said: 'But what reason have you, sir, for supposing that the young man has been done away with? He has only been absent from his abode, according to your statement, about eight or nine hours.'

'Simply because,' I answered, 'I have the best of reasons for knowing that ever since his arrival in Australia he has been shadowed. This morning he said he would only go for a short stroll before lunch, and I am positively certain, knowing my anxiety about him, he would not have remained away so long of his own accord without communicating with me.'

'Is there any motive you can assign for this shadowing?'

'My friend is heir to an enormous property in England. Perhaps that may assist you in discovering one?'

'Very possibly. But still I am inclined to think you are a little hasty in coming to so terrible a conclusion, Mr — ?'

'Hatteras is my name, and I am staying at the *General Officer* hotel in Palgrave Street.'

'Well, Mr Hatteras, if I were you I would go back to your hotel. You will probably find your friend there eating his dinner and thinking about instituting a search for you. If, however, he has not turned up, and does not do so by tomorrow morning, call here again and report the matter, and I will give you every assistance in my power.'

Thanking him for his courtesy I left the station and walked quickly back to the hotel, hoping to find Beckenham safely returned and at his dinner. But when the landlady met me in the verandah, and asked if I had any news of my friend, I realised that a disappointment was in store for me. By this time the excitement and worry were getting too much for me. What with Nikola, the spy, Beckenham, Phyllis, the unknown lover, and old Mr Wetherell, I had more than enough to keep my brain occupied. I sat down on a chair on the verandah with a sigh and reviewed the whole case. Nine o'clock struck by the time my reverie was finished. Just as I did so a newspaper boy came down the street lustily crying his wares. To divert my mind from its unpleasant thoughts, I called him up and bought an *Evening Mercury*. Having done so I passed into my sitting-room to read it. The first, second, and third pages held nothing of much interest to me, but on the fourth was an item which was astonishing enough to almost make my hair stand on end. It ran as follows.

IMPORTANT ENGAGEMENT IN HIGH LIFE

We have it on the very best authority that an engagement will shortly be announced between a certain illustrious young nobleman, now a visitor in our city, and the beautiful daughter of one of Sydney's most prominent politicians, who has lately returned from a visit to England. The *Evening Mercury* tenders the young couple their sincerest congratulations.

Could this be the solution of the whole mystery? Could it be that the engagement of Baxter, the telegram, the idea of travel, the drugging, the imprisonment in Port Said, the substitution of the false marquis were all means to this end? Was it possible that this man, who was masquerading as a man of title, was to marry Phyllis (for there could be no possible doubt as to the persons to whom that paragraph referred)? The very thought of such a thing was not to be endured.

There must be no delay now, I told myself, in revealing all I knew. The villains must be unmasked this very night. Wetherell should know all as soon as I could tell him.

As I came to this conclusion I crushed my paper into my pocket and set off, without a moment's delay, for Potts Point. The night was dark, and now a thick drizzle was falling.

Though it really did not take me very long, it seemed an eternity before I reached the house and rang the bell. The butler opened the door, and was evidently surprised to see me.

'Is Mr Wetherell at home?' I asked. For a moment he looked doubtful as to what he should say, then compromising matters, answered that he would see.

'I know what that means,' I said in reply. 'Mr Wetherell is in, but you don't think he'll see me. But he must! I have news for him of the very utmost importance. Will you tell him that?'

He left me and went along the hall and upstairs. Presently he returned, shaking his head.

'I'm very sorry, sir, but Mr Wetherell's answer is, if you have anything to tell him you must put it in writing; he cannot see you.'

'But he must! In this case I can accept no refusal. Tell him, will you, that the matter upon which I wish to speak to him has nothing whatsoever to do with the request I made to him this morning. I pledge him my word on that.'

Again the butler departed, and once more I was left to cool my heels in the portico. When he returned it was with a smile upon his face.

'Mr Wetherell will be glad if you will step this way, sir.' I followed him along the hall and up the massive stone staircase. Arriving at the top he opened a door on the left-hand side and announced 'Mr Hatteras.'

I found Mr Wetherell seated in a low chair opposite the fire, and from the fact that his right foot was resting on a sort of small trestle, I argued that he was suffering from an attack of his old enemy the gout.

'Be good enough to take a chair, Mr Hatteras,' he said, when the door had been closed. 'I must own I am quite at a loss to understand what you can have to tell me of so much importance as to bring you to my house at this time of night.'

'I think I shall be able to satisfy you on that score, Mr Wetherell,' I replied, taking the *Evening Mercury* from my pocket and smoothing it out. 'In the first place will you be good enough to tell me if there is any truth in the inference contained in that paragraph?'

I handed the paper to him and pointed to the lines in question. Having put on his glasses he examined it carefully.

'I am sorry they should have made it public so soon, I must admit,' he said. 'But I don't deny that there is a considerable amount of truth in what that paragraph reports.'

'You mean by that that you intend to try and marry Phyllis – Miss Wetherell – to the Marquis of Beckenham?'

'The young man has paid her a very considerable amount of attention ever since he arrived in the colony, and only last week he did me the honour of confiding his views to me. You see, I am candid with you.'

'I thank you for it. I, too, will be candid with you. Mr Wetherell, you may set your mind at rest at once, this marriage will never take place!'

'And pray be so good as to tell me your reason for such a statement!'

If you want it bluntly, because the young man now staying at Government House is no more the Marquis of Beckenham than I am. He is a fraud, an impostor, a cheat of the first water, put up to play his part by one of the cleverest scoundrels unhung.'

'Mr Hatteras, this is really going too far. I can quite understand your being jealous of his lordship, but I cannot understand your having the audacity to bring such a foolish charge against him. I, for one, must decline to listen to it. If he had been the fraud you make him out, how would his tutor have got those letters from his Grace the Duke of Glenbarth? Do you imagine his Excellency the Governor, who has known the family all his life, would not have discovered him ere this? No, no, sir! It won't do! If you think so, who has schooled him so cleverly? Who has pulled the strings so wonderfully?'

'Why, Nikola to be sure!'

Had I clapped a revolver to the old gentleman's head, or had the walls opened and Nikola himself stepped into the room, a greater effect of terror and consternation could not have been produced in the old gentleman's face than did those five simple words. He fell back in his chair gasping for breath, his complexion became ashen in its pallor, and for a moment his whole nervous system seemed unstrung. I sprang to his assistance, thinking he was going to have a fit, but he waved me off, and when he had recovered himself sufficiently to speak, said hoarsely: 'What do you know of Dr Nikola? Tell me for God's sake! – what do you know of him? Quick, quick!'

Thereupon I set to work and told him my story, from the day of my arrival in Sydney from Thursday Island up to the moment of my reaching his house, described my meeting and acquaintance with the real Beckenham, and all the events consequent upon it. He listened, with an awful terror growing in his face, and when I had finished my narrative with the disappearance of my friend he nearly choked. 'Mr Hatteras,' he gasped, 'will you swear this is the truth you are telling me?'

'I solemnly swear it,' I answered. 'And will do so in public when and where you please.'

'Then before I do anything else I will beg your pardon for my conduct to you. You have taken a noble revenge. I cannot thank you sufficiently. But there is not a moment to lose. My daughter is at a ball at Government House at the present moment. I should have accompanied her, but my gout would not permit me. Will you oblige me by ringing that bell?'

I rang the bell as requested, and then asked what he intended doing.

'Going off to his Excellency at once, gout or no gout, and telling him what you have told me. If it is as you have said, we must catch these scoundrels and rescue your friend without an instant's delay!'

Here the butler appeared at the door.

'Tell Jenkins to put the grey mare in my brougham and bring her round at once.'

Half an hour later we were at Government House waiting in his Excellency's study for an interview. The music of the orchestra in the ballroom came faintly in to us, and when Lord Amberley entered the room he seemed surprised, as well he might be, to see us. But as soon as he had heard what we had to tell him his expression changed. 'Mr Wetherell, this is a very terrible charge you bring against my guest. Do you think it can possibly be true?'

'I sadly fear so,' said Mr Wetherell. 'But perhaps Mr Hatteras will tell you the story exactly as he told it to me.'

I did so, and, when I had finished, the Governor went to the door and called a servant.

'Find Lord Beckenham, Johnson, at once, and ask him to be so good as to come to me here. Stay – on second thoughts I'll go and look for him myself.'

He went off, leaving us alone again to listen to the ticking of the clock upon the mantelpiece, and to wonder what was going to happen next. Five minutes went by and then ten, but still he did not return. When he did do so it was with a still more serious countenance.

'You are evidently right, gentlemen. Neither the spurious marquis, nor his tutor, Mr Baxter, can be found anywhere. I have discovered, too, that all their valuables and light luggage have been smuggled out of the house tonight without the knowledge of my servants. This is a very terrible business. But I have given instructions, and the police will be communicated with at once. Now we must do our best to find the real Beckenham.'

'Lord Amberley,' said Wetherell, in a choking voice, 'do you think one of your servants could tell my daughter to come to me at once; I am not feeling very well.'

The Governor hesitated a moment, and then said: 'I am sorry to say, Mr Wetherell, your daughter left the House an hour ago. A message was brought to her that you had been suddenly taken ill and needed her. She went off at once.'

Wetherell anxiety was piteous to see.

'My God!' he cried in despair. 'If that is so, I am ruined. This is Nikola's revenge.'

Then he uttered a curious little sigh, moved a step forward, and fell in a dead faint upon the floor.

CHAPTER TWO
On the trail

As soon as Wetherell was able to speak again he said as feebly as an old man of ninety, 'Take me home, Mr Hatteras, take me home, and let us think out together there what is best to be done to rescue my poor child.' The Governor rose to his feet and gave him his arm.

'I think you're right, Mr Wetherell,' he said. 'It is of course just possible that you will find your daughter at her home when you arrive. God grant she may be! But in case she is not I will communicate all I know to the Police Commissioner on his arrival, and send him and his officers on to you. We must lose no time if we wish to catch these scoundrels.' Then turning to me, he continued: 'Mr Hatteras, it is owing to your promptness that we are able to take such early steps. I shall depend upon your further assistance in this matter.'

'You may do so with perfect confidence, my lord,' I answered. 'If you knew all you would understand that I am more anxious perhaps than anyone to discover the whereabouts of the young lady and my unfortunate friend.'

If his Excellency thought anything he did not give utterance to it, and Mr Wetherell's carriage being at the door we went out to it without another word. As we stepped into it Mr Wetherell cried to the coachman: 'Home, and as fast as you can go.'

Next moment we were being whirled down the drive at a pace which at any other time I should have thought dangerous. Throughout the journey we sat almost silent, wrapped in our anxieties and forebodings; hoping almost against hope that when we arrived at Potts Point we should find Phyllis awaiting us there. At last we turned into the grounds, and on reaching the house I sprang out and rang the bell, then I went down to help my companion to alight. The butler opened the door and descended the steps to take the rugs. Wetherell stopped him almost angrily, crying: 'Where is your mistress? Has she come home?'

The expression of surprise on the man's face told me, before he had time to utter a word, that our hopes were not to be realised.

'Miss Phyllis, sir?' the man said. 'Why, she's at the ball at Government 'Ouse.'

Wetherell turned from him with a deep sigh, and taking my arm went heavily up the steps into the hall.

'Come to my study, Mr Hatteras,' he said, 'and let me confer with you. For God's sake don't desert me in my hour of need!'

'You need have no fear of that,' I answered. 'If it is bad for you, think what it is for me.' And then we went upstairs together.

Reaching his study, Mr Wetherell led the way in and sat down. On a side table I noticed a decanter of whisky and some glasses. Without asking permission I went across to them and poured out a stiff nobbler for him.

'Drink this,' I said; 'it will pull you together a little; remember you will want all your strength for the work that lies before us.'

Like a child he did as he was ordered, and then sank back into his chair. I went across to the hearthrug and stood before him.

'Now,' I said, 'we must think this out from the very beginning, and to do that properly we must consider every detail. Have you any objection to answering my questions?'

'Ask any questions you like,' he replied, 'and I will answer them.'

'In the first place, then, how soon after his arrival in the colony did your daughter get to know this sham Beckenham?'

'Three days,' he answered.

'At a dance, dinner party, picnic, or what?'

'At none of these things. The young man, it appears, had seen my daughter in the street, and having been struck with her beauty asked one of the aides-de-camp at Government House, with whom we are on intimate terms, to bring him to call. At the time, I remember, I thought it a particularly friendly action on his part.'

'I don't doubt it,' I answered. 'Well that, I think, should tell us one thing.'

'And what is that?'

'That his instructions were to get to know your daughter without delay'

'But what could his reason have been, do you think?'

'Ah, that I cannot tell you just yet. Now you must pardon what I am going to say: do you think he was serious in his intentions regarding Phyllis – I mean your daughter?'

'Perfectly, as far as I could tell. His desire, he said, was, if she would have him, to be allowed to marry her on his twenty-first birthday, which would be next week, and in proof of permission he showed me a cablegram from his father.'

'A forgery, I don't doubt. Well, then, the only construction I can put upon it is that the arrival of the real Beckenham in Sydney must have frightened him, thus compelling the gang to resort to other means of obtaining possession of her at once. Now our next business must be to find out how that dastardly act was accomplished. May I ring the bell and have up the coachman who drove your daughter to the ball?'

'By all means. Please act in every way in this matter as if this house were your own.'

I rang the bell, and when the butler appeared to answer it Mr Wetherell instructed him to find the man I wanted and send him up. The servant left the room again, and for five minutes we awaited his re-appearance in silence. When he did come back he said, 'Thompson has not come home yet, sir.'

'Not come home yet! Why, it's nearly eleven o'clock! Send him in directly he arrives. Hark! What bell is that?'

'Front door, sir.'

'Go down and answer it then, and if it should be the Commissioner of Police show him up here at once.'

As it turned out it was not the Commissioner of Police, but an Inspector.

'Good evening,' said Mr Wetherell. 'You have come from Government House, I presume?'

'Exactly so, sir,' replied the Inspector. 'His Excellency gave us some particulars and then sent us on to you.'

'You know the nature of the case?'

'His Excellency informed us himself.'

'And what steps have you taken?'

'Well, sir, to begin with, we have given orders for a thorough search throughout the city and suburbs for the tutor and the sham nobleman, at the same time more men are out looking for the real Lord Beckenham. We are also trying to find your coachman, who was supposed to have driven Miss Wetherell away from Government House, and also the carriage, which is certain to be found before very long.'

He had hardly finished speaking before there was another loud ring at the bell, and presently the butler entered the room once more. Crossing to Mr Wetherell, he said: 'Two policemen are at the front door, and they have brought Thompson home, sir.'

'Ah! we are likely to have a little light thrown upon the matter now. Let them bring him up here instantly.'

'He's not in a very nice state, sir.'

'Never mind that. Let them bring him up here, instantly!' Again the butler departed, and a few moments later heavy footsteps ascended the stairs and approached the study door. Then two stalwart policemen entered the room supporting between them a miserable figure in coachman's livery. His hat and coat were gone and his breeches were stained with mud, while a large bruise totally obscured his left eye. His master surveyed him with unmitigated disgust.

'Stand him over there opposite me,' said Mr Wetherell, pointing to the side of the room furthest from the door.

The policemen did as they were ordered, while the man looked more dead than alive.

'Now, Thompson,' said Wetherell, looking sternly at him, 'what have you got to say for yourself?'

But the man only groaned. Seeing that in his present state he could say nothing, I went across to the table and mixed him a glass of grog. When I gave it to him he drank it eagerly. It seemed to sharpen his wits, for he answered instantly: 'It wasn't my fault, sir. If I'd only ha' known what their game was I'd have been killed afore I'd have let them do anything to hurt the young lady. But they was too cunnin' for me, sir.'

'Be more explicit, sir!' said Wetherell sternly. 'Don't stand there whining, but tell your story straightforwardly and at once.'

The poor wretch pulled himself together and did his best. 'It was in this way, sir,' he began. 'Last week I was introduced by a friend of mine to as nice a spoken man as ever I saw. He was from England, he said, and having a little money thought he'd like to try his 'and at a bit o' racing in Australia, like. He was on the lookout for a smart man, he said, who'd be able to put him up to a wrinkle or two, and maybe train for him later on. He went on to say that he'd 'eard a lot about me, and thought I was just the man for his money. Well, we got more and more friendly till the other night, Monday, when he said as how he'd settled on a farm a bit out in the country, and was going to sign the agreement, as he called it, for to rent it next day. He was goin' to start a stud farm and trainin' establishment combined, and would I take the billet of manager at three 'undred a year? Anyway, as he said, "Don't be in a 'urry to decide; take your time and think it over. Meet me at the *Canary Bird 'Otel* on Thursday night (that's tonight, sir) and give me your decision." Well, sir, I drove Miss Wetherell to Government

'Ouse, sir, according to orders, and then, comin' 'ome, went round by the *Canary Bird* to give 'im my answer, thinkin' no 'arm could ever come of it. When I drove up he was standin' at the door smoking his cigar, an' bein' an affable sort of fellow, invited me inside to take a drink. "I don't like to leave the box," I said. "Oh, never mind your horse," says he. " 'Ere's a man as will stand by it for five minutes." He gave a respectable lookin' chap, alongside the lamp-post, a sixpence, and he 'eld the 'orse, so in I went. When we got inside I was for goin' to the bar, but 'e says, "No. This is an important business matter, and we don't want to be over'eard." With that he leads the way into a private room at the end of the passage and shuts the door. "What's yours?" says he. "A nobbler o' rum," says I. Then he orders a nobbler of rum for me and a nobbler of whisky for 'imself. And when it was brought we sat talkie' of the place he'd thought o' takin' an' the 'orses he was goin' to buy, an' then' e says, " 'Ullo! Somebody listenin' at the door. I 'eard a step. Jump up and look." I got up and ran to the door, but there was nobody there, so I sat down again and we went on talking. Then he says, takin' up his glass: " 'Ere's to your 'ealth, Mr Thompson, and success to the farm." We both drank it an' went on talkin' till I felt that sleepy I didn't know what to do. Then I dropped off, an' after that I don't remember nothin' of what 'appened till I woke up in the Domain, without my hat and coat, and found a policeman shakin' me by the shoulder.'

'The whole thing is as plain as daylight,' cried Wetherell bitterly. 'It is a thoroughly organised conspiracy, having me for its victim. Oh, my girlie! My poor little girlie! What has my obstinacy brought you to!'

Seeing the old man in this state very nearly broke me down, but I mastered myself with an effort and addressed a question to the unfortunate coachman: 'Pull yourself together, Thompson, and try and tell me as correctly as you can what this friend of yours was like.'

I fully expected to hear him give an exact description of the man who had followed us from Melbourne, but I was mistaken.

'I don't know, sir,' said Thompson, 'as I could rightly tell you, my mind being still a bit dizzy-like. He was tall, but not by any manner of means big made; he had very small 'ands an' feet, a sort o' what they call death's-'ead complexion; 'is 'air was black as soot, an' so was 'is eyes, an' they sparkled like two diamonds in 'is' ead.'

'Do you remember noticing if he had a curious gold ring on his little finger, like a snake?'

'He had, sir, with two eyes made of some black stone. That's just as true as you're born.'

'Then it was Nikola,' I cried in an outburst of astonishment, 'and he followed us to Australia after all!'

Wetherell gave a deep sigh that was more like a groan than anything else; then he became suddenly a new man.

'Mr Inspector,' he cried to the police officer, 'that man, or traces of him, must be found before daylight. I know him, and he is as slippery as an eel; if you lose a minute he'll be through your fingers.'

'One moment first,' I cried. 'Tell me this, Thompson: when you drove up to the *Canary Bird* hotel where did you say this man was standing?'

'In the verandah, sir.'

'Had he his hat on?'

'Yes, sir.'

'And then you went towards the bar, but it was crowded, so he took you to a private room?'

'Yes, sir.'

'And once there he began giving you the details of this farm he proposed starting. Did he work out any figures on paper?'

'Yes, sir.'

'On what?'

'On a letter or envelope; I'm not certain which.'

'Which of course he took from his pocket?'

'Yes, sir.'

'Very good,' I said. Then turning to the police officer, 'Now, Mr Inspector, shall we be off to the *Canary Bird*?'

'If you wish it, sir. In the meantime I'll send instructions back by these men to the different stations. Before breakfast time we must have the man who held the horse in our hands.'

'You don't know him, I suppose?' I asked Thompson.

'No, sir; but I've seen him before,' he answered.

'He's a Sydney fellow then?'

'Oh yes, sir.'

'Then there should be no difficulty in catching him. Now let us be going.'

Mr Wetherell rose to accompany us, but hard though it was to stop him I eventually succeeded in dissuading him from such a course.

'But you will let me know directly you discover anything, won't you, Mr Hatteras?' he cried as we were about to leave the room. 'Think what my anxiety will be.'

I gave my promise and then, accompanied by the Inspector, left the house. Hailing a passing cab we jumped into it and told the driver to proceed as fast as he could to the hotel in question. Just as we started a clock in the neighbourhood struck twelve. Phyllis had been in Nikola's hands three hours.

Pulling up opposite the *Canary Bird* (the place where the coachman had been drugged), we jumped out and bade the cabman wait. The hotel was in complete darkness, and it was not until we had pealed the bell twice that we succeeded in producing any sign of life. Then the landlord, half dressed, carrying a candle in his hand, came downstairs and called out to know who was there and what we wanted. My companion immediately said 'Police', and in answer to that magic word the door was unbarred.

'Good-evening, Mr Bartrell,' said the Inspector politely. 'May we come in for a moment on business?'

'Certainly, Mr Inspector,' said the landlord, who evidently knew my companion. 'But isn't this rather a late hour for a call. I hope there is nothing the matter?'

'Nothing much,' returned the Inspector; 'only we want to make a few enquiries about a man who was here tonight, and for whom we are looking.'

'If that is so I'm afraid I must call my barman. I was not in the bar this evening. If you'll excuse me I'll go and bring him down. In the meantime make yourselves comfortable.'

He left us to kick our heels in the hall while he went upstairs again. In about ten minutes, and just as my all-consuming impatience was well-nigh getting the better of me, he returned, bringing with him the sleepy barman.

'These gentlemen want some information about a man who was here tonight,' the landlord said by way of introduction. 'Perhaps you can give it?'

'What was he like, sir?' asked the barman of the Inspector.

The latter, however, turned to me.

'Tall, slim, with a sallow complexion,' I said, 'black hair and very dark restless eyes. He came in here with the Hon. Sylvester Wetherell's coachman.'

The man seemed to recollect him at once.

'I remember him,' he said. 'They sat in No. 5 down the passage there, and the man you mention ordered a nobbler of rum for his friend and a whisky for himself.'

'That's the fellow we want,' said the Inspector. 'Now tell me this, have you ever seen him in here before?'

'Never once,' said the barman, 'and that's a solemn fact, because if I had I couldn't have forgotten it. His figurehead wouldn't let you do that. No, sir, tonight was the first night he's ever been in the *Canary Bird*.'

'Did anyone else visit them while they were in the room together?'

'Not as I know of. But stay, I'm not so certain. Yes; I remember seeing a tall, good-looking chap come down the passage and go in there. But it was some time, half an hour maybe, after I took in the drinks.'

'Did you see him come out again?'

'No. But I know the coachman got very drunk, and had to be carried out to the carriage.'

'How do you know that?'

'Because I saw the other two doing it.'

The Inspector turned to me.

'Not very satisfactory, is it?'

'No,' I answered. 'But do you mind letting us look into No. 5 – the room they occupied?'

'Not at all,' said the landlord. 'Will you come with me?'

So saying he led the way down the passage to a little room on the right-hand side, the door of which he threw open with a theatrical flourish. It was in pitch darkness, but a few seconds later the gas was lit and we could see all that it contained. A small table stood in the centre of the room and round the walls were ranged two or three wooden chairs. A small window was at the further end and a fireplace opposite the door. On the table was a half-smoked cigar and a torn copy of the *Evening Mercury*. But that was not what I wanted, so I went down on my hands and knees and looked about upon the floor.

Presently I descried a small ball of paper near the grate. Picking it up I seated myself at the table and turned to the barman, who was watching my movements attentively.

'Was this room used by any other people after the party we are looking for left?'

'No, sir. There was nobody in either of these two bottom rooms.'

'You are quite certain of that?'

'Perfectly certain.'

I took up the ball of paper, unrolled it and spread it out upon the table. To my disgust it was only the back half of an envelope, and though it had a few figures dotted about upon it, was of no possible use to us.

'Nothing there?' asked the Inspector.

'Nothing at all,' I answered bitterly, 'save a few incomprehensible figures.'

'Well, in that case, we'd better be getting up to the station and see if they've discovered anything yet.'

'Come along, then,' I answered. 'We must be quick though, for we've lost a lot of precious time, and every minute counts.'

I took up the *Evening Mercury* and followed him out to the cab, after having sincerely thanked the hotel proprietor and the barman for their courtesy. The Inspector gave the driver his orders and we set off. As we went we discussed our next movements, and while we were doing so I idly glanced at the paper I held in my hand. There was a lamp in the cab, and the light showed me on the bottom right-hand corner a round blue india-rubber stamp mark, 'W. E. Maxwell, stationer and newsagent, 23, Ipswell Street, Woolahra.'

'Stop the cab!' I almost shouted. 'Tell the man to drive us back to the *Canary Bird* as fast as he can go.'

The order was given, the cab faced round, and in less than a minute we were on our way back.

'What's up now?' asked the astonished Inspector.

'Only that I believe I've got a clue,' I cried.

I did not explain any further, and in five minutes we had brought the landlord downstairs again.

'I'm sorry to trouble you in this fashion,' I cried, 'but life and death depend on it. I want you to let me see No. 5 again.'

He conducted us to the room, and once more the gas was lit. The small strip of envelope lay upon the table just as I had thrown it down. I seated myself and again looked closely at it. Then I sprang to my feet.

'I thought so!' I cried excitedly, pointing to the paper; 'I told you I had a clue. Now, Mr Inspector, who wrote those figures?'

'The man you call Nikola, I suppose.'

'That's right. Now who would have bought this newspaper? You must remember that Thompson only left his box to come in here.'

'Nikola, I suppose.'

'Very good. Then according to your own showing Nikola owned this piece of envelope and this *Evening Mercury*. If that is certain, look here!'

He came round and looked over my shoulder. I pointed to what was evidently part of the gummed edge of the top of the envelope. On it were these three important words, ' – swell Street, Woolahra.'

'Well,' he said, 'what about it?'

'Why, look here!' I said, as I opened the *Evening Mercury* and pointed to the stamp-mark at the bottom. 'The man who bought this newspaper at Mr Maxwell's shop also bought this envelope there. The letters "swell" before "street" constitute the last half of Ipswell, the name of the street. If that man be Nikola, as we suspect, the person who served him is certain to remember him, and it is just within the bounds of possibility he may know his address.'

'That's so,' said the Inspector, who was struck with the force of my argument. 'I know Mr Maxwell's shop, and our best plan will be to go on there as fast as we can.'

Again thanking the landlord for his civility, we returned to our cab and once more set off, this time for Mr Maxwell's shop in Ipswell Street. By the time we reached it, it was nearly three o'clock, and gradually growing light.

As the cab drew up alongside the curb the Inspector jumped out and rang the bell at the side door. It was opened after a while by a shock-headed youth, about eighteen years of age, who stared at us in sleepy astonishment.

'Does Mr Maxwell live at the shop?' asked the Inspector.

'No, sir.'

'Where then?'

'Ponson Street – third house on the left-hand side.'

'Thank you.'

Once more we jumped into the cab and rattled off. It seemed to me, so anxious and terrified was I for my darling's safety, that we were fated never to get the information we wanted; the whole thing was like some nightmare, in which, try how I would to move, every step was clogged.

A few minutes' drive brought us to Ponson Street, and we drew up at the third house on the left-hand side. It was a pretty little villa, with a nice front garden and a creeper-covered verandah. We rang the bell and waited. Presently we heard someone coming down the passage, and a moment later the door was unlocked.

'Who is there?' cried a voice from within.

'Police,' said my companion as before.

The door was immediately opened, and a very small sandy-complexioned man, dressed in a flaring suit of striped pyjamas, stood before us.

'Is anything wrong, gentlemen?' he asked nervously.

'Nothing to affect you, Mr Maxwell,' my companion replied. 'We only want a little important information, if you can give it us. We are anxious to discover a man's whereabouts before daylight, and we have been led to believe that you are the only person who can give us the necessary clue.'

'Good gracious! I never heard of such a thing. But I shall be happy to serve you if I can,' the little man answered, leading the way into his dining-room and opening the shutters with an air of importance his appearance rather belied. 'What is it?'

'Well, it's this,' I replied, producing the piece of envelope and the *Evening Mercury*. 'You see these letters on the top of this paper, don't you?' He nodded, his attention at once secured by seeing his own name. 'Well, that envelope was evidently purchased in your shop. So was this newspaper.'

'How can you tell that?'

'In the case of the envelope, by these letters; in that of the paper, by your rubber stamp on the bottom.'

'Ah! Well, now, and in what way can I help you?'

'We want to know the address of the man who bought them.'

'That will surely be difficult. Can you give me any idea of what he was like?'

'Tall, slightly foreign in appearance, distinctly handsome, sallow complexion, very dark eyes, black hair, small hands and feet.'

As my description progressed the little man's face brightened. Then he cried with evident triumph: 'I know the man; he came into the shop yesterday afternoon.'

'And his address is?'

His face fell again. His information was not quite as helpful as he had expected it would be.

'There I can't help you, I'm sorry to say. He bought a packet of paper and envelopes and the *Evening Mercury* and then left the shop. I was so struck by his appearance that I went to the door and watched him cross the road.'

'And in which direction did he go?'

'Over to Podgers' chemist shop across the way. That was the last I saw of him.'

'I'm obliged to you, Mr Maxwell,' I said, shaking him by the hand. 'But I'm sorry you can't tell us something more definite about him.' Then turning to the Inspector: 'I suppose we had better go off and find Podgers. But if we have to spend much more time in rushing about like this we shall be certain to lose them altogether.'

'Let us be off to Podgers, then, as fast as we can go.'

Bidding Mr Maxwell goodbye, we set off again, and in ten minutes had arrived at the shop and had Mr Podgers downstairs. We explained our errand as briefly as possible, and gave a minute description of the man we wanted.

'I remember him perfectly,' said the sedate Podgers. 'He came into my shop last night and purchased a bottle of chloroform.'

'You made him sign the poison book, of course?'

'Naturally I did, Mr Inspector. Would you like to see his signature?'

'Very much,' we both answered at once, and the book was accordingly produced.

Podgers ran his finger down the list.

'Brown, Williams, Davis – ah! here it is. "Chloroform: J. Venneage, 22, Calliope Street, Woolahra." '

'Venneage!' I cried. 'Why, that's not his name!'

'Very likely not,' replied Podgers; 'but it's the name he gave me.'

'Never mind, we'll try 22, Calliope Street on the chance,' said the Inspector. 'Come along, Mr Hatteras.'

Again we drove off, this time at increased pace. In less than fifteen minutes we had turned into the street we wanted, and pulled up about a hundred yards from the junction. It was a small thoroughfare, with a long line of second-class villa residences on either side. A policeman was sauntering along on the opposite side of the way, and the Inspector called him over. He saluted respectfully, and waited to be addressed.

'What do you know of number 22?' asked the Inspector briefly. The constable considered for a few moments, and then said: 'Well, to tell you the truth, sir, I didn't know until yesterday that it was occupied.'

'Have you seen anybody about there?'

'I saw three men go in just as I came on the beat tonight.'

'What were they like?'

'Well, I don't know that I looked much at them. They were all pretty big, and they seemed to be laughing and enjoying themselves.'

'Did they! Well, we must go in there and have a look at them. You had better come with us.'

We walked on down the street till we arrived at No. 22. Then opening the gate we went up the steps to the hall door. It was quite light enough by this time to enable us to see everything distinctly. The Inspector gave the bell a good pull and the peal re-echoed inside the house. But not a sound of any living being came from within in answer. Again the bell was pulled, and once more we waited patiently, but with the same result.

'Either there's nobody at home or they refuse to hear,' said the Inspector. 'Constable, you remain where you are and collar the first man you see. Mr Hatteras, we will go round to the back and try to effect an entrance from there.'

We left the front door, and finding a path reached the yard. The house was only a small one, with a little verandah at the rear on to which the back door opened. On either side of the door were two fair-sized windows, and by some good fortune it chanced that the catch of one of these was broken.

Lifting the sash up the Inspector jumped into the room, and its soon as he was through I followed him. Then we looked about us. The room, however, was destitute of furniture or occupants.

'I don't hear anybody about,' my companion said, opening the door that led into the hall. Just at that moment I heard a sound, and touching his arm signed to him to listen. We both did so, and sure enough there came again the faint muttering of a human voice. In the half-dark of the hall it sounded most uncanny.

'Somebody in one of the front rooms,' said the Inspector. 'I'll slip along and open the front door, bring in the man from outside, and then we'll burst into the room and take our chance of capturing them.'

He did as he proposed, and when the constable had joined us we moved towards the room on the left.

Again the mutterings came from the inside, and the Inspector turned the handle of the door. It was locked, however.

'Let me burst it in,' I whispered.

He nodded, and I accordingly put my shoulder against it, and bringing my strength to bear sent it flying in.

Then we rushed into the room, to find it, at first glance, empty. Just at that moment, however, the muttering began again, and we looked towards the darkest corner; somebody was there, lying on the ground. I rushed across and knelt down to look. *It was Beckenham; his mouth gagged and his hands and feet bound. The noise we had heard was that made by him trying to call us to his assistance.*

In less time than it takes to tell I had cut his bonds and helped him to sit up. Then I explained to the Inspector who he was.

'Thank God you're found!' I cried. 'But what does it all mean? How long have you been like this? And where is Nikola?'

'I don't know how long I've been here,' he answered, 'and I don't know where Nikola is.'

'But you must know something about him!' I cried. 'For Heaven's sake tell me all you can! I'm in awful trouble, and your story may give me the means of saving a life that is dearer to me than my own.'

'Get me something to drink first, then,' he replied; 'I'm nearly dying of thirst; after that I'll tell you all I can.'

Fortunately I had had the foresight to put a flask of whisky into my pocket, and I now took it out and gave him a stiff nobbler. It revived him somewhat, and he prepared to begin his tale. But the Inspector interrupted: 'Before you commence, my lord, I must send word to the Commissioner that you have been found.'

He wrote a message on a piece of paper and dispatched the constable with it. Having done so he turned to Beckenham and said: 'Now, my lord, pray let us hear your story.'

Beckenham forthwith commenced.

CHAPTER THREE
Lord Beckenham's story

'When you left me, Mr Hatteras, to visit Miss Wetherell at Potts Point, I remained in the house for half an hour or so reading. Then, thinking no harm could possibly come of it, I started out for a little excursion on my own account. It was about half-past eleven then. Leaving the hotel I made for the ferry and crossed Darling Harbour to Millers Point; then, setting myself for a good ramble, off I went through the city, up one street and down another, to eventually bring up in the botanical gardens. The view was so exquisite that I sat myself down on a seat and resigned myself to rapturous contemplation of it. How long I remained there I could not possibly say. I only know that while I was watching the movements of a man-o'-war in the cove below me I became aware, by intuition – for I did not look at him – that I was the object of close scrutiny by a man standing some little distance from me. Presently I found him drawing closer to me, until he came boldly up and seated himself beside me. He was a queer-looking little chap, in some ways not unlike my old tutor Baxter, with a shrewd, clean-shaven face, grey hair, bushy eyebrows, and a long and rather hooked nose. He was well dressed, and when he spoke did so with some show of education. When we had been sitting side by side for some minutes he turned to me and said: "It is a beautiful picture we have spread before us, is it not?"

' "It is, indeed," I answered. "And what a diversity of shipping?"

' "You may well say that," he continued. "It would be an interesting study, would it not, to make a list of all the craft that pass in and out of this harbour in a day – to put down the places where they were built and whence they hail, the characters of their owners and commanders, and their errands about the world. What a book it would make, would it not? Look at that man-o'-war in Farm Cove; think of the money she cost, think of where that money came from – the rich people who paid without thinking, the poor who dreaded the coming of the tax collector like a visit from the Evil One; imagine the busy dockyard in which she was built – can't you seem to hear the clang of the riveters and the buzzing of the steam saws? Then take that Norwegian boat passing the fort there; think of her birthplace in far Norway, think of the places she has since seen, imagine her masts growing in the forests on the mountainside of lonely fjords, where the silence is so intense that a stone rolling down and dropping into the water echoes like thunder. Then again, look at that emigrant vessel steaming slowly up the harbour; think of the folk aboard her, every one with his hopes and fears, confident of a successful future in this *terra incognita*, or despondent of that and everything else. Away to the left there you see a little island schooner making her way down towards the blue Pacific; imagine her in a few weeks among the islands – tropical heavens dropped down into sunlit waters – buying such produce as perhaps you have never heard of. Yes, it is a wonderful picture – a very wonderful picture?"

' "You seem to have studied it very carefully," I said, after a moment's silence.

' "Perhaps I have," he answered. "I am deeply interested in the life of the sea – few more so. Are you a stranger in New South Wales?"

' "Quite a stranger," I replied. "I only arrived in Australia a few days since."

' "Indeed! Then you have to make the acquaintance of many entrancing beauties yet. Forgive my impertinence, but if you are on a tour, let me recommend you to see the islands before you return to your home."

' "The South Sea Islands, I presume you mean?" I said.

' "Yes; the bewitching islands of the Southern Seas! The most entrancingly beautiful spots on God's beautiful earth! See them before you go. They will amply repay any trouble it may cost you to reach them."

' "I should like to see them very much," I answered, feeling my enthusiasm rising at his words.

' "Perhaps you are interested in them already," he continued.

' "Very much indeed," I replied.

' "Then, in that case, I may not be considered presumptuous if I offer to assist you. I am an old South Sea merchant myself, and I have amassed a large collection of beautiful objects from the islands. If you would allow me the pleasure I should be delighted to show them to you."

' "I should like to see them very much indeed," I answered, thinking it extremely civil of him to make the offer.

' "If you have time we might perhaps go and overhaul them now. My house is but a short distance from the Domain, and my carriage is waiting at the gates."

' "I shall be delighted," I said, thinking there could be no possible harm in my accepting his courteous invitation.

' "But before we go, may I be allowed to introduce myself," the old gentleman said, taking a card-case from his pocket and withdrawing a card. This he handed to me, and on it I read – "Mr Mathew Draper." "I am afraid I have no card to offer you in return," I said; "but I am the Marquis of Beckenham."

' "Indeed! Then I am doubly honoured," the old gentleman said with a low bow. "Now shall we wend our way up towards my carriage?"

'We did so, chatting as we went. At the gates a neat brougham was waiting for us, and in it we took our places.

' "Home," cried my host, and forthwith we set off down the street. Up one thoroughfare and down another we passed, until I lost all count of our direction. Throughout the drive my companion talked away in his best style; commented on the architecture of the houses, had many queer stories to tell of the passers-by, and in many other ways kept my attention engaged till the carriage came to a standstill before a small but pretty villa in a quiet street.

'Mr Draper immediately alighted, and when I had done so, dismissed his coachman, who drove away as we passed through the little garden and approached the dwelling. The front door was opened by a dignified man-servant, and we entered. The hall, which was a spacious one for so small a dwelling, was filled with curios and weapons, but I had small time for observing them, as my host led me towards a room at the back. As we entered it he said, "I make you welcome to my house, my lord. I hope, now that you have taken the trouble to come, I shall be able to show you something that will repay your visit." Thereupon, bidding me seat myself for a few moments, he excused himself and left the room. When he returned he began to do the honours of the apartment. First we examined a rack of Australian spears, nulla-nullas, and boomerangs, then another containing New Zealand hatchets and clubs. After this we crossed to a sort of alcove where reposed in cases a great number of curios collected from the further islands of the Pacific. I was about to take up one of these when the door on the other side of the room opened and someone entered. At first I did not look round, but hearing the newcomer approaching me I turned, to find myself, to my horrified surprise, face to face *with no less a person than Dr Nikola*. He was dressed entirely in black, his coat was buttoned and displayed all the symmetry of his peculiar figure, while his hair seemed blacker and his complexion even paler than before. He had evidently been prepared for my visit, for he held out his hand and greeted me without a sign of astonishment upon his face.

'"This is indeed a pleasure, my lord," he said, still with his hand outstretched, looking hard at me with his peculiar cat-like eyes. "I did not expect to see you again so soon. And you are evidently a little surprised at meeting me."

'"I am more than surprised," I answered bitterly, seeing how easily I had been entrapped. "I am horribly mortified and angry. Mr Draper, you had an easy victim."

'Mr Draper said nothing, but Dr Nikola dropped into a chair and spoke for him.

'"You must not blame my old friend Draper," he said suavely. "We have been wondering for the last twenty-four hours how we might best get hold of you, and the means we have employed so successfully seemed the only possible way. Have no fear, my lord, you shall not be hurt. In less than twenty-four hours you will enjoy the society of your energetic friend Mr Hatteras again."

'"What is your reason for abducting me like this?" I asked. "You are foolish to do so, for Mr Hatteras will leave no stone unturned to find me."

'"I do not doubt that at all," said Dr Nikola quietly; "but I think Mr Hatteras will find he will have all his work cut out for him this time."

'"If you imagine that your plans are not known in Sydney you are mistaken," I cried. "The farce you are playing at Government House is detected, and Mr Hatteras, directly he finds I am lost, will go to Lord Amberley and reveal everything."

'"I have not the slightest objection," returned Dr Nikola quietly. "By the time Mr Hatteras can take those steps – indeed, by the time he discovers your absence at all, we shall be beyond the reach of his vengeance."

'I could not follow his meaning, of course, but while he had been speaking I had been looking stealthily round me for a means of escape. The only way out of the room was, of course, by the door, but both Nikola and his ally were between me and that. Then a big stone hatchet hanging on the wall near me caught my eye. Hardly had I seen it before an idea flashed through my brain. Supposing I seized it and fought my way out. The door of the room stood open, and I noticed with delight that the key was in the lock on the outside. One rush, armed with the big hatchet, would take me into the passage; then before my foes could recover their wits I might be able to turn the key, and, having locked them in, make my escape from the house before I could be stopped.

'Without another thought I made up my mind, sprang to the wall, wrenched down the hatchet, and prepared for my rush. But by the time I had done it both Nikola and Draper were on their feet.

' "Out of my way!" I cried, raising my awful weapon aloft. "Stop me at your peril!"

'With my hatchet in the air I looked at Nikola. He was standing rigidly erect, with one arm outstretched, the hand pointing at me. His eyes glared like living coals, and when he spoke his voice came from between his teeth like a serpent's hiss.

' "Put down that axe!" he said.

'With that the old horrible fear of him which had seized me on board ship came over me again. His eyes fascinated me so that I could not look away from them. I put down the hatchet without another thought. Still he gazed at me in the same hideous fashion.

' "Sit down in that chair," he said quietly. "You cannot disobey me." And indeed I could not. My heart was throbbing painfully, and an awful dizziness was creeping over me. Still I could not get away from those terrible eyes. They seemed to be growing larger and fiercer every moment. Oh! I can feel the horror of them even now. As I gazed his white right hand was moving to and fro before me with regular sweeps, and with each one I felt my own will growing weaker and weaker. That I was being mesmerised, I had no doubt, but if I had been going to be murdered I could not have moved a finger to save myself.

'Then there came a sudden but imperative knock at the door, and both Nikola and Draper rose. Next moment the man whom we had noticed in the train as we came up from Melbourne, and against whom you, Mr Hatteras, had warned me in Sydney, entered the room. He crossed and stood respectfully before Nikola.

' "Well, Mr Eastover, what news?" asked the latter. "Have you done what I told you?"

' "Everything," the man answered, taking an envelope from his pocket. "Here is the letter you wanted."

'Nikola took it from his subordinate's hand, broke the seal, and having withdrawn the contents, read it carefully. All this time, seeing resistance was quite useless, I did not move. I felt too sick and giddy for anything. When he had finished his correspondence Nikola said something in an undertone to Draper, who immediately left the room. During the time he was absent none of us spoke. Presently he returned, bringing with him a wine glass filled with water, which he presented to Nikola.

' "Thank you," said that gentleman, feeling in his waistcoat pocket. Presently he found what he wanted and produced what looked like a small silver scent-bottle. Unscrewing the top, he poured from it into the wine glass a few drops of some dark-coloured liquid. Having done this he smelt it carefully and then handed it to me.

' "I must ask you to drink this, my lord,"'he said. "You need have no fear of the result: it is perfectly harmless."

'Did ever man hear such a cool proposition? Very naturally I declined to do as he wished.

' "You must drink it!" he reiterated. "Pray do so at once. I have no time to waste bandying words with you."

' "I will not drink it!" I cried, rising to my feet, and prepared to make a fight for it if need should be.

'Once more those eyes grew terrible, and once more that hand began to make the passes before my face. Again I felt the dizziness stealing over me. His will was growing every moment too strong for me. I could not resist him. So when he once more said, "Drink!" I took the glass and did as I was ordered. After that I remember seeing Nikola, Draper, and the man they called Eastover engaged in earnest conversation on the other side of the room. I remember Nikola cross- ing to where I sat and gazing steadfastly into my face, and after that I recollect no more until I came to my senses in this room, to find myself bound and gagged. For what seemed like hours I lay in agony, then I heard footsteps in the verandah, and next moment the sound of voices. I tried to call for help, but could utter no words. I thought you would go away without discovering me, but fortunately for me you did not do so. Now, Mr Hatteras, I have told you everything; you know my story from the time you left me up to the present moment.'

For some time after the Marquis had concluded his strange story both the Inspector and I sat in deep thought. That Beckenham had been kidnapped in order that he should be out of the way while the villainous plot for abducting Phyllis was being enacted there could be no doubt. But why had he been chosen, and what clues were we to gather from what he had told us? I turned to the Inspector and said: 'What do you think will be the best course for us to pursue now?'

'I have been wondering myself. I think, as there is nothing to be learned from this house, the better plan would be for you two gentleman to go back to Mr Wetherell, while I return to the detective office and see if anything has been discovered by the men there. As soon as I have found out I will join you at Potts Point. What do you think?'

I agreed that it would be the best course; so, taking the Marquis by the arms (for he was still too weak to walk alone), we left the house and were about to step into the street when I stopped, and asking them to wait for me ran back into the room again. In the corner, just as it had been thrown down, lay the rope with which Beckenham had been bound and the pad which had been fitted over his mouth. I picked both up and carried them into the verandah.

'Come here, Mr Inspector,' I cried. 'I thought I should learn something from this. Take a look at this rope and this pad, and tell me what you make of them.'

He took each up in turn and looked them over and over. But he only shook his head.

'I don't see anything to guide us,' he said as he laid them down again.

'Don't you?' I cried. 'Why, they tell me more than I have learnt from anything else I've seen. Look at the two ends of this.' (Here I took up the rope and showed it to him.) 'They're seized!'

I looked triumphantly at him, but he only stared at me in surprise, and said, 'What do you mean by "seized"?'

'Why, I mean that the ends are bound up in this way – look for yourself. Now not one landsman in a hundred *seizes* a rope's end. This line was taken from some ship in the harbour, and – By Jove! here's another discovery!'

'What now?' he cried, being by this time almost as excited as I was myself.

'Why, look here,' I said, holding the middle of the rope up to the light, so that we could get a better view of it. 'Not very many hours ago this rope was running through a block, and that block was rather an uncommon one.'

'How do you know that it was an uncommon one?'

'Because it has been newly painted, and what's funnier still, painted green, of all other colours. Look at this streak of paint along the line; see how it's smudged. Now let's review the case as we walk along.'

So saying, with the Marquis between us, we set off down the street, hoping to be able to pick up an early cab.

'First and foremost,' I said, 'remember old Draper's talk of the South Seas – remember the collection of curios he possessed. Probably he owns a schooner, and it's more than probable that this line and this bit of canvas came from it.'

'I see what you're driving at,' said the Inspector. 'It's worth considering. Directly I get to the office I will set men to work to try and find this mysterious gentleman. You would know him again, my lord?'

'I should know him anywhere,' was Beckenham's immediate reply.

'And have you any idea at all where this house, to which he conducted you, is located?'

'None at all. I only know that it was about half-way down a street of which all the houses, save the one at the corner – which was a grocer's shop – were one-storeyed villas.'

'Nothing a little more definite, I suppose?'

'Stay! I remember that there was an empty house with broken windows almost opposite, and that on either side of the steps leading up to the front door were two stone eagles with outstretched wings. The head of one of the eagles – the left, I think – was missing.'

The Inspector noted these things in his pocket-book, and just as he had finished we picked up a cab and called it to the sidewalk. When we had got in and given the driver Mr Wetherell's address, I said to the Inspector: 'What are you going to do first?'

'Put some men on to find Mr Draper, and some more to find an island schooner with her blocks newly painted green.'

'You won't be long in letting us know what you discover, will you?' I said. 'Remember how anxious we are.'

'You may count on my coming to you at once with any news I may procure,' he answered.

A few moments later we drew up at Mr Wetherell's door. Bidding the Inspector goodbye we went up the steps and rang the bell. By the time the cab was out in the street again we were in the house making our way, behind the butler, to Mr Wetherell's study.

The old gentleman had not gone to bed, but sat just as I had left him so many hours before. As soon as we were announced he rose to receive us.

'Thank God, Mr Hatteras, you have come back!' he said. 'I have been in a perfect fever waiting for you. What have you to report?'

'Not very much, I'm afraid,' I answered. 'But first let me have the pleasure of introducing the real Marquis of Beckenham to you, whom we have had the good fortune to find and rescue.'

Mr Wetherell bowed gravely and held out his hand.

'My lord,' he said, 'I am thankful that you have been discovered. I look upon it as one step towards the recovery of my poor girl. I hope now that both you and Mr Hatteras will take up your abode with me during the remainder of your stay in the colony. You have had a scurvy welcome to New South Wales. We must see if we can't make up to you for it. But you look thoroughly worn out; I expect you would like to go to bed.'

He rang the bell, and when his butler appeared, gave him some instructions about preparing rooms for us.

Ten minutes later the man returned and stated that our rooms were ready, whereupon Mr Wetherell himself conducted Beckenham to the apartment assigned to him. When he returned to me, he asked if I would not like to retire too, but I would not hear of it. I could not have slept a wink, so great was my anxiety. Seeing this, he seated himself and listened attentively while I gave him an outline of Beckenham's story. I had hardly finished before I heard a carriage roll up to the door. There was a ring at the bell, and presently the butler, who, like ourselves, had not dreamt of going to bed, though his master had repeatedly urged him to do so, entered and announced the Inspector.

Wetherell hobbled across to receive him with an anxious face.

'Have you any better tidings for me?' he asked

'Not very much, I'm afraid, sir,' the Inspector said, shaking his head. 'The best I have to tell you is that your carriage and horse have been found in the yard of an empty house off Pitt Street.'

'Have you been able to discover any clue as to who put them there?'

'Not one! The horse was found out of the shafts tied to the wall. There was not a soul about the place.'

Wetherell sat down again and covered his face with his hands. At that instant the telephone bell in the corner of the room rang sharply. I jumped up and went across to it. Placing the receivers to my ears, I heard a small voice say, 'Is that Mr Wetherell's house, Potts Point?'

'Yes,' I answered.

'Who is speaking?'

'Mr Hatteras. Mr Wetherell, however, is in the room. Who are you?'

'Detective officer. Will you tell Mr Wetherell that Mr Draper's house has been discovered?'

I communicated the message to Mr Wetherell, and then the Inspector joined me at the instrument and spoke.

'Where is the house?' he enquired.

'83, Charlemagne Street – north side.'

'Very good. Inspector Murdkin speaking. Let plain clothes men be stationed at either end of the street, and tell them to be on the lookout for Draper, and to wait for me. I'll start for the house at once.'

'Very good, sir.'

He rang off and then turned to me.

'Are you too tired to come with me, Mr Hatteras?' he enquired.

'Of course not,' I answered. 'Let us go at once.'

'God bless you!' said Wetherell. 'I hope you may catch the fellow.'

Bidding him goodbye, we went downstairs again, and jumped into the cab, which was directed to the street in question.

Though it was a good distance from our starting-point, in less than half an hour we had pulled up at the corner. As the cab stopped, a tall man, dressed in blue serge, who had been standing near the lamp-post, came forward and touched his hat.

'Good-morning, Williams,' said the Inspector. 'Any sign of our man?'

'Not one, sir. He hasn't come down the street since I've been here.'

'Very good. Now come along and we'll pay the house a visit.'

So saying he told the cabman to follow us slowly, and we proceeded down the street. About half-way along he stopped and pointed to a house on the opposite side.

'That is the house his lordship mentioned, with the broken windows, and this is where Mr Draper dwells, if I am not much mistaken – see the eagles are on either side of the steps, just as described.'

It was exactly as Beckenham had told us, even to the extent of the headless eagle on the left of the walk. It was a pretty little place, and evidently still occupied, as a maid was busily engaged cleaning the steps.

Pushing open the gate, the Inspector entered the little garden and accosted the girl.

'Good-morning,' he said politely. 'Pray, is your master at home?'

'Yes, sir; he's at breakfast just now.'

'Well, would you mind telling him that two gentlemen would like to see him?'

'Yes, sir.'

The girl rose to her feet, and, wiping her hands on her apron, led the way into the house. We followed close behind her. Then, asking us to wait a moment where we were, she knocked at a door on the right and opening it, disappeared within.

'Now,' said the Inspector, 'our man will probably appear, and we shall have him nicely.'

The Inspector had scarcely spoken before the door opened again, and a man came out. To our surprise, however, he was very tall and stout, with a round, jovial face, and a decided air of being satisfied with himself and the world in general.

'To what do I owe the honour of this visit?' he said, looking at the Inspector.

'I am an Inspector of Police, as you see,' answered my companion, 'and we are looking for a man named Draper, who yesterday was in possession of this house.'

'I am afraid you have made some little mistake,' returned the other. 'I am the occupier of this house, and have been for some months past. No Mr Draper has anything at all to do with it.'

The Inspector's face was a study for perfect bewilderment. Nor could mine have been much behind it. The Marquis had given such a minute description of the dwelling opposite and the two stone birds on the steps, that there could be no room for doubt that this was the house. And yet it was physically impossible that this man could be Draper; and, if it were the place where Beckenham had been drugged, why were the weapons, etc., he had described not in the hall?

'I cannot understand it at all,' said the Inspector, turning to me. 'This is the house, and yet where are the things with which it ought to be furnished?'

'You have a description of the furniture, then?' said the owner. 'That is good, for it will enable me to prove to you even more clearly that you are mistaken. Pray come and see my sitting-rooms for yourselves.'

He led the way into the apartment from which he had been summoned, and we followed him. It was small and nicely furnished, but not a South Sea curio or native weapon was to be seen in it. Then we followed him to the corresponding room at the back of the house. This was upholstered in the latest fashion; but again there was no sign of what Beckenham had led us to expect we should find. We were completely nonplussed.

'I am afraid we have troubled you without cause,' said the Inspector, as we passed out into the hall again.

'Don't mention it,' the owner answered; 'I find my compensation in the knowledge that I am not involved in any police unpleasantness.'

'By the way,' said the Inspector suddenly, 'have you any idea who your neighbours may be?'

'Oh, dear, yes!' the man replied. 'On my right I have a frigidly respectable widow of Low Church tendencies. On my left, the

Chief Teller of the Bank of New Holland. Both very worthy members of society, and not at all the sort of people to be criminally inclined.'

'In that case we can only apologise for our intrusion and wish you good-morning.'

'Pray don't apologise. I should have been glad to have assisted you. Good-morning.'

We went down the steps again and out into the street. As we passed through the gate, the Inspector stopped and examined a mark on the right hand post. Then he stooped and picked up what looked like a pebble. Having done so we resumed our walk.

'What on earth can be the meaning of it all?' I asked. 'Can his lordship have made a mistake?'

'No, I think not. We have been cleverly duped, that's all.'

'What makes you think so?'

'I didn't think so until we passed through the gate on our way out. Now I'm certain of it. Come across the street.'

I followed him across the road to a small plain-looking house, with a neatly-curtained bow window and a brass plate on the front door. From the latter I discovered that the proprietress of the place was a dressmaker, but I was completely at a loss to understand why we were visiting her.

As soon as the door was opened the Inspector asked if Miss Tiffins were at home, and, on being told that she was, enquired if we might see her. The maid went away to find out, and presently returned and begged us to follow her. We did so down a small passage towards the door of the room which contained the bow window.

Miss Tiffins was a lady of uncertain age, with a prim, precise manner, and corkscrew curls. She seemed at a loss to understand our errand, but bade us be seated, and then asked in what way she could be of service to us.

'In the first place, madam,' said the Inspector, 'let me tell you that I am an officer of police. A serious crime has been perpetrated, and I have reason to believe that it may be in your power to give us a clue to the persons who committed it.'

'You frighten me, sir,' replied the lady. 'I cannot at all see in what way I can help you. I lead a life of the greatest quietness. How, therefore, can I know anything of such people?'

'I do not wish to imply that you do know anything of them. I only want you to carry your memory back as far as yesterday, and to answer me the few simple questions I may ask you.'

'I will answer them to the best of my ability.'

'Well, in the first place, may I ask if you remember seeing a brougham drive up to that house opposite about midday yesterday?'

'No, I cannot say that I do,' the old lady replied after a moment's consideration.

'Do you remember seeing a number of men leave the house during the afternoon?'

'No. If they came out I did not notice them.'

'Now, think for one moment, if you please, and tell me what vehicles, if any, you remember seeing stop there.'

'Let me try to remember. There was Judge's baker's cart, about three, the milk about five, and a furniture van about half-past six.'

'That's just what I want to know. And have you any recollection whose furniture van it was?'

'Yes. I remember reading the name as it turned round. Goddard & James, George Street. I wondered if the tenant was going to move.'

The Inspector rose, and I followed his example.

'I am exceedingly obliged to you, Miss Tiffins. You have helped me materially.'

'I am glad of that,' she answered; 'but I trust I shall not be wanted to give evidence in court. I really could not do it.'

'You need have no fear on that score,' the Inspector answered. 'Good-day.'

'Good-day.'

When we had left the house the Inspector turned to me and said: 'It was a great piece of luck finding a dressmaker opposite. Commend me to ladies of that profession for knowing what goes on in the street. Now we will visit Messrs Goddard & James and see who hired the things. Meantime, Williams' (here he called the plain-clothes constable to him), 'you had better remain here and watch that house. If the man we saw comes out, follow him, and let me know where he goes.'

'Very good, sir,' the constable replied, and we left him to his vigil.

Then, hailing a passing cab, we jumped into it and directed the driver to convey us to George Street. By this time it was getting on for midday, and we were both worn out. But I was in such a nervous state that I could not remain inactive. Phyllis had been in Nikola's hands nearly fourteen hours, and so far we had not obtained one single definite piece of information as to her whereabouts.

Arriving at the shop of Messrs Goddard & James, we went inside and asked to see the chief partner. An assistant immediately conveyed us to an office at the rear of the building, where we found an elderly gentleman writing at a desk. He looked up as we entered, and then, seeing the Inspector's uniform, rose and asked our business.

'The day before yesterday,' began my companion, 'you supplied a gentleman with a number of South Sea weapons and curios on hire did you not?'

'I remember doing so – yes,' was the old gentleman's answer. 'What about it?'

'Only I should be glad if you would favour me with a description of the person who called upon you about them – or a glimpse of his letter, if he wrote.'

'He called and saw me personally.'

'Ah! that is good. Now would you be so kind as to describe him?'

'Well, in the first place, he was very tall and rather handsome; he had, if I remember rightly, a long brown moustache, and was decidedly well dressed.'

'That doesn't tell us very much, does it? Was he alone?'

'No. He had with him, when he came into the office, an individual whose face singularly enough remains fixed in my memory – indeed I cannot get it out of my head.'

Instantly I became all excitement.

'What was this second person like?' I asked.

'Well, I can hardly tell you – that is to say, I can hardly give you a good enough description of him to make you see him as I saw him. He was tall and yet very slim, had black hair, a sallow complexion, and the blackest eyes I ever saw in a man. He was clean-shaven and exquisitely dressed, and when he spoke, his teeth glittered like so many pearls. I never saw another man like him in my life.'

'Nikola for a thousand!' I cried, bringing my hand down with a thump upon the table.

'It looks as if we're on the track at last,' said the Inspector. Then turning to Mr Goddard again: 'And may I ask now what excuse thee made to you for wanting these things?'

'They did not offer any; they simply paid a certain sum down for the hire of them, gave me their address, and then left.'

'And the address was?'

'83, Charlemagne Street. Our van took the things there and fetched them away last night.'

'Thank you. And now one or two other questions. What name did the hirer give?'

'Eastover.'

'And when they left your shop how did they go away?'

'A cab was waiting at the door for them, and I walked out to it with them.'

'There were only two of them, you think?'

'No. There was a third person waiting for them in the cab, and it was that very circumstance which made me anxious to have my things brought back as soon as possible. If I had been able to, I should have even declined to let them go.'

'Why so?'

'Well, to tell you that would involve a story. But perhaps I had better tell you. It was in this way. About three years ago, through a distant relative, I got to know a man named Draper.'

'Draper!' I cried. 'You don't mean – but there, I beg your pardon. Pray go on.'

'As I say, I got to know this man Draper, who was a South Sea trader. We met once or twice, and then grew more intimate. So friendly did we at last become, that I even went so far as to put some money into a scheme he proposed to me. It was a total failure. Draper proved a perfect fraud and a most unbusinesslike person, and all I got out of the transaction was the cases of curios and weapons which this man Eastover hired from me. It was because – when I went out with my customers to their cab – I saw this man Draper waiting for them that I became uneasy about my things. However, all's well that ends well, and as they returned my goods and paid the hire I must not grumble.'

'And now tell me what you know of Draper's present life,' the Inspector said.

'Ah! I'm afraid of that I can tell you but little. He has been twice declared bankrupt, and the last time there was some fuss made over his schooner, the *Merry Duchess*.'

'He possesses a schooner, then?'

'Oh, yes! A nice boat, She's in harbour now, I fancy.'

'Thank you very much, Mr Goddard. I am obliged to you for your assistance in this matter.'

'Don't mention it. I hope that what I have told you may prove of service to you.'

'I'm sure it will. Good-day.'

'Good-day, gentlemen.'

He accompanied us to the door, and then bade us farewell.

'Now what are we to do?' I asked.

'Well, first, I am going back to the office to put a man on to find this schooner, and then I'm going to take an hour or two's rest. By that time we shall know enough to be able to lay our hands on Dr Nikola and his victim, I hope.'

'God grant we may!'

'Where are you going now?'

'Back to Potts Point,' I answered.

We thereupon bade each other farewell and set off in different directions.

When I reached Mr Wetherell's house I learned from the butler that his master had fallen asleep in the library. Not wishing to disturb him, I enquired the whereabouts of my own bedroom, and on being conducted to it, laid myself down fully dressed upon the bed. So utterly worn out was I, that my head had no sooner touched the pillow than I was fast asleep. How long I lay there I do not know, but when I woke it was to find Mr Wetherell standing beside me, holding a letter in his hand. He was white as a sheet, and trembling in every limb.

'Read this, Mr Hatteras,' he cried. 'For Heaven's sake tell me what we are to do!'

I sat up on the side of the bed and read the letter he handed to me. It was written in what was evidently a disguised hand, on common notepaper, and ran:

To Mr Wetherell
Potts Point, Sydney

Dear Sir

This is to inform you that your daughter is in very safe keeping. If you wish to find her you had better be quick about it. What's more, you had better give up consulting the police, and such like, in the hope of getting hold of her. The only way you can get her will be to act as follows: at eight o'clock tonight charter a boat and pull down the harbour as far as Shark Point. When you get there, light your pipe three times, and someone in a boat nearby will do the same. Be sure to bring with you the sum of *one hundred thousand pounds in gold, and – this is most important – bring with you the little stick you got from China Pete, or do not come at all*. Above all, do not bring more than one man. If you do not put in an appearance you will not hear of your daughter again.

Yours obediently,
The Man who Knows

CHAPTER FOUR

Following up a clue

For some moments after I had perused the curious epistle Mr
Wetherell had brought to my room I remained wrapped in
thought.

'What do you make of it?' my companion asked.

'I don't know what to say,' I answered, looking at it again. 'One
thing, however, is quite certain, and that is that, despite its curious
wording, it is intended you should take it seriously.'

'You think so?'

'I do indeed. But I think when the Inspector arrives it would be just
as well to show it to him. What do you say?'

'I agree with you. Let us defer consideration of it until we see him.'

When, an hour later, the Inspector put in an appearance, the letter
was accordingly placed before him, and his opinion asked concerning it. He read it through without comment, carefully examined the
writing and signature, and finally held it up to the light. Having done
this he turned to me and said: 'Have you that envelope we found at
the *Canary Bird*, Mr Hatteras?'

I took it out of my pocket and handed it to him. He then placed it
on the table side by side with the letter, and through a magnifying-
glass scrutinised both carefully. Having done so, he asked for the
envelope in which it had arrived. Mr Wetherell had thrown it into
the waste-paper basket, but a moment's search brought it to light.
Again he scrutinised both the first envelope and the letter, and then
compared them with the second cover.

'Yes, I thought so,' he said. 'This letter was written either by
Nikola, or at his desire. The paper is the same as that he purchased at
the stationer's shop we visited.'

'And what had we better do now?' queried Wetherell, who had
been eagerly waiting for him to give his opinion.

'We must think,' said the Inspector. 'In the first place, I suppose
you don't feel inclined to pay the large sum mentioned here?'

'Not if I can help it, of course,' answered Wetherell. 'But if the worst comes to the worst, and I cannot rescue my poor girl any other way, I would sacrifice even more than that.'

'Well, we'll see if we can find her without compelling you to pay anything at all,' the Inspector cried. 'I've got an idea in my head.'

'And what is that?' I cried; for I, too, had been thinking out a plan.

'Well, first and foremost,' he answered, 'I want you, Mr Wetherell, to tell me all you can about your servants. Let us begin with the butler. How long has he been with you?'

'Nearly twenty years.'

'A good servant, I presume, and a trustworthy man?'

'To the last degree. I have implicit confidence in him.'

'Then we may dismiss him from our minds. I think I saw a footman in the hall. How long has he been with you?'

'Just about three months.'

'And what sort of a fellow is he?'

'I really could not tell you very much about him. He seems intelligent, quick and willing, and up to his work.'

'Is your cook a man or a woman?'

'A woman. She has been with me since before my wife's death – that is to say, nearly ten years. You need have no suspicion of her.'

'Housemaids?'

'Two. Both have been with me some time, and seem steady respectable girls. There is also a kitchen-maid; but she has been with me nearly as long as my cook, and I would stake my reputation on her integrity.'

'Well, in that case, the only person who seems at all suspicious is the footman. May we have him up?'

'With pleasure. I'll ring for him.'

Mr Wetherell rang the bell, and a moment later it was answered by the man himself.

'Come in, James, and shut the door behind you,' his master said. The man did as he was ordered, but not without looking, as I thought, a little uncomfortable. The Inspector I could see had noticed this too, for he had been watching him intently ever since he had appeared in the room.

'James,' said Mr Wetherell, 'the Inspector of Police wishes to ask you a few questions. Answer him to the best of your ability.'

'To begin with,' said the Inspector, 'I want you to look at this envelope. Have you seen it before?'

He handed him the envelope of the anonymous letter addressed to Mr Wetherell. The man took it and turned it over in his hands.

'Yes, sir,' he said, 'I have seen it before; I took it in at the front door.'

'From whom?'

'From a little old woman, sir,' the man answered.

'A little old woman!' cried the Inspector, evidently surprised. 'What sort of woman?'

'Well, sir, I don't know that I can give you much of a description of her. She was very small, had a sort of nut-cracker face, a little black poke bonnet, and walked with a stick.'

'Should you know her again if you saw her?'

'Oh yes, sir.'

Did she say anything when she gave you the letter?'

'Only, "For Mr Wetherell, young man." That was all, sir.'

'And you didn't ask if there was an answer? That was rather a singular omission on your part, was it not?'

'She didn't give me time, sir. She just put it into my hand and went down the steps again.'

'That will do. Now, Mr Wetherell, I think we'd better see about getting that money from the bank. You need not wait, my man.'

The footman thereupon left the room, while both Mr Wetherell and I stared at the Inspector in complete astonishment. He laughed.

'You are wondering why I said that,' he remarked at last.

'I must confess it struck me as curious,' answered Wetherell.

'Well, let me tell you I did it with a purpose. Did you notice that young man's face when he entered the room and when I gave him the letter? There can be no doubt about it, he is in the secret.'

'You mean that he is in Nikola's employ? Then why don't you arrest him?'

'Because I want to be quite certain first. I said that about the money because, if he is Nikola's agent, he will carry the information to him, and by so doing keep your daughter in Sydney for at least a day longer. Do you see?'

'I do, and I admire your diplomacy. Now what is your plan?'

'May I first tell mine?' I said.

'Do,' said the Inspector, 'for mine is not quite matured yet.'

'Well,' I said, 'my idea is this. I propose that Mr Wetherell shall obtain from his bank a number of gold bags, fill them with lead discs to represent coin, and let it leak out before this man that he has got the money in the house. Then tonight Mr Wetherell will set off for the waterside. I will row him down the harbour disguised as a boat-man. We will pick up the boat, as arranged in that letter. In the meantime you must start from the other side in a police boat, pull up to meet us, and arrest the man. Then we will force him to disclose Miss Wetherell's whereabouts, and act upon his information. What do you say?'

'It certainly sounds feasible,' said the Inspector, and Mr Wetherell nodded his head approvingly. At that moment the Marquis entered the room, looking much better than when we had found him on the preceding night, and the conversation branched off into a different channel.

My plot seemed to commend itself so much to Mr Wetherell's judgement, that he ordered his carriage and drove off there and then to his bank, while I went down to the harbour, arranged about a boat and having done so, proceeded up to the town, where I purchased a false beard, an old dungaree suit, such as a man loafing about the harbour might wear, and a slouch hat of villainous appearance. By the time I got back to the house Mr Wetherell had returned. With great delight he conducted me to his study, and, opening his safe, showed me a number of canvas bags, on each of which was printed £1,000.

'But surely there are not £100,000 there?'

'No,' said the old gentleman with a chuckle. 'There is the counter-feit of £50,000 there; for the rest I propose to show them these.'

So saying, he dived his hand into a drawer and produced a sheaf of crisp banknotes.

'There – these are notes for the balance of the amount.'

'But you surely are not going to pay? I thought we were going to try to catch the rascals without letting any money change hands.'

'So we are; do not be afraid. If you will only glance at these notes you will see that they are dummies, every one of them. They are for me to exhibit to the man in the boat; in the dark they'll pass muster, never fear.'

'Very good indeed,' I said with a laugh. 'By the time they can be properly examined we shall have the police at hand ready to capture him.'

'I believe we shall,' the old gentleman cried, rubbing his hands together in his delight – 'I believe we shall. And a nice example we'll make of the rascals. Nikola thinks he can beat me, I'll show him how mistaken he is!'

And for some time the old gentleman continued in this strain, confidently believing that he would have his daughter with him again by the time morning came. Nor was I far behind him in confidence. Since Nikola had not spirited her out of the country my plot seemed the one of all others to enable us to regain possession of her, and not only that, but we hoped it would give us an opportunity of punishing those who had so schemed against her. Suddenly an idea was born in my brain, and instantly I acted on it.

'Mr Wetherell,' I said, 'supposing, when your daughter is safe with you again, I presume so far as once more to offer myself for your son-in-law, what will you say?'

'What will I say?' he cried. 'Why, I will tell you that you shall have her, my boy, with ten thousand blessings on your head. I know you now; and since I've treated you so badly, and you've taken such a noble revenge, why, I'll make it up to you, or my name's not Wetherell. But we won't talk any more about that till we have got possession of her; we have other and more important things to think of. What time ought we to start tonight?'

'The letter fixes the meeting for ten o'clock; we had better be in the boat by half-past nine. In the meantime I should advise you to take a little rest. By the way, do you think your footman realises that you have the money?'

'He ought to, for he carried it up to this room for me; and, what's more, he has applied for a holiday this afternoon.'

'That's to carry the information. Very good; everything is working excellently. Now I'm off to rest for a little while.'

'I'll follow your example. In the meantime I'll give orders for an early dinner.'

We dined at seven o'clock sharp, and at half-past eight I went off to my room to don my disguise; then, bidding the Marquis good-bye – much to the young gentleman's disgust, for he was most anxious to accompany us – I slipped quietly out of my window, crossed the garden – I hoped unobserved – and then went down to the harbour side, where the boat I had chartered was waiting for me. A quarter of an hour later Wetherell's carriage drove up, and on seeing it I went across and opened the door. My disguise was so perfect that for a moment the old gentleman seemed undecided whether to trust me or not. But my voice, when I spoke, reassured him, and then we set to work carrying the bags of spurious money down to the boat. As soon as this was accomplished we stepped in. I seated myself amidships and got out the oars, Mr Wetherell taking the yoke-lines in the stern. Then we shoved off, and made our way out into the harbour.

It was a dull, cloudy night, with hardly a sign of a star in the whole length and breadth of heaven, while every few minutes a cold, cheerless wind swept across the water. So chilly indeed was it that before we had gone very far I began to wish I had added an overcoat to my other disguises. We hardly spoke, but pulled slowly down towards the island mentioned in the letter. The strain on our nerves was intense and I must confess to feeling decidedly nervous as I wondered what would happen if the police boat did not pull up to meet us, as we had that morning arranged.

A quarter to ten chimed from some church ashore as we approached within a hundred yards of our destination. Then I rested on my oars and waited. All round us were the lights of bigger craft, but no rowing-boat could I see. About five minutes before the hour I whispered to Wetherell to make ready, and in answer the old gentleman took a matchbox from his pocket. Exactly as the town clocks struck the hour he lit a vesta; it flared a little and then went out. As it did so a boat shot out of the darkness to port. He struck a second, and then a third. As the last one burned up and then died away, the man rowing the boat I have just referred to struck a light, then another, then another, in rapid succession. Having finished his display, he took up his oars and propelled his boat towards us. When he was within talking distance he said in a gruff voice: 'Is Mr Wetherell aboard?'

To this my companion immediately answered, not however without a tremble in his voice, 'Yes, here I am!'

'Money all right?'

'Can you see if I hold it up?' asked Mr Wetherell. As he spoke a long black boat came into view on the other side of our questioner, and pulled slowly towards him. It was the police boat.

'No, I don't want to see,' said the voice again. 'But this is the message I was to give you. Pull in towards Circular Quay and find the *Maid of the Mist* barque. Go aboard her, and take your money down into the cuddy. There you'll get your answer.'

'Nothing more?' cried Mr Wetherell.

'That's all I was told,' answered the man, and then said, 'Goodnight.'

At the same moment the police boat pulled up alongside him and made fast. I saw a dark figure enter his boat, and next moment the glare of a lantern fell upon the man's face. I picked up my oars and pulled over to them, getting there just in time to hear the Inspector ask the man his name.

'James Burbidge,' was the reply. 'I don't know as how you've got anything against me. I'm a licensed waterman, I am.'

'Very likely,' said the Inspector; 'but I want a little explanation from you. How do you come to be mixed up in this business?'

'What – about this 'ere message, d'you mean?'

'Yes, about this message. Where is it from? Who gave it to you?'

'Well, if you'll let me go, I'll tell you all about it,' growled the man. 'I was up at the *Hen and Chickens* this evenin', just afore dark, takin' a nobbler along with a friend. Presently in comes a cove in a cloak. He beckons me outside and says, "Do you want to earn a sufring?" – a sufring is twenty bob. So I says, "My word, I do!" Then he says, "Well, you go out on the harbour tonight, and be down agin Shark point at ten." I said I would, and so I was. "You'll see a boat there with an old gent in it," says he. "He'll strike three matches, and you do the same. Then ask him if he's Mr Wetherell. If he says 'Yes', ask him if the money's all right. And if he says 'Yes' to that, tell him to pull in towards Circular Quay and find the *Maid of the Mist* barque. He's to take his money down to the cuddy, and he'll get his answer there." That's the truth, so 'elp me bob! I don't know what you wants to go arrestin' of an honest man for.'

The Inspector turned to the water police. 'Does any man here know James Burbidge?'

Two or three voices immediately answered in the affirmative, and this seemed to decide the officer, for he turned to the waterman again and said, 'As some of my men seem to know you, I'll let you off. But for your own sake go home and keep a silent tongue in your head.' He thereupon clambered back into his own boat and bade the man depart. In less time than it takes to tell he was out of sight. We then drew up alongside the police boat.

'What had we better do, Mr Inspector?' asked Mr Wetherell.

'Find the *Maid of the Mist* at once. She's an untenanted ship, being for sale. You will go aboard, sir, with your companion, and down to the cuddy. Don't take your money, however. We'll draw up alongside as soon as you're below, and when one of their gang, whom you'll dispatch for it, comes up to get the coin, we'll collar him, and then come to your assistance. Do you understand?'

'Perfectly. But how are we to know the vessel?'

'Well, the better plan would be for you to follow us. We'll pull to within a hundred yards of her. I learn from one of my men here that she's painted white, so you'll have no difficulty in recognising her.'

'Very well, then, go on, and we'll follow you.'

The police boat accordingly set off, and we followed about fifty yards behind her. A thick drizzle was now falling, and it was by no means an easy matter to keep her in sight. For some time we pulled on. Presently we began to get closer to her. In a quarter of an hour we were alongside.

'There's your craft,' said the Inspector, pointing as he spoke to a big vessel showing dimly through the scud to starboard of us. 'Pull over to her.'

I followed his instructions, and, arriving at the vessel's side, hitched on, made the painter fast, and then, having clambered aboard, assisted Mr Wetherell to do the same. As soon as we had both gained the deck we stood and looked about us, at the same time listening for any sound which might proclaim the presence of the men we had come to meet; but save the sighing of the wind in the shrouds overhead, the dismal creaking of blocks, and the drip of moisture upon the deck, no sign was to be heard. There was nothing for it, therefore, but to make our way below as best we could. Fortunately I had had the forethought to bring with me a small piece of candle, which came in very handily at the present juncture, seeing that the cuddy, when we reached the companion ladder, was wrapt in total darkness. Very carefully I stepped inside, lit the candle, and then, with Mr Wetherell at my heels, made my way down the steps.

Arriving at the bottom we found ourselves in a fair-sized saloon of the old-fashioned type. Three cabins stood on either side, while from the bottom of the companion ladder, by which we had descended, to a long cushioned locker right aft under the wheel, ran a table covered with American cloth. But there was no man of any kind to be seen. I opened cabin after cabin, and searched each with a like result. We were evidently quite alone in the ship.

'What do you make of it all?' I asked of Mr Wetherell.

'It looks extremely suspicious,' he answered. 'Perhaps we're too early for them. But see, Mr Hatteras, there's something on the table at the further end.'

So there was – something that looked very much like a letter. Together we went round to the end of the table, and there, surely enough, found a letter pinned to the American cloth, and addressed to my companion in a bold but rather quaint handwriting.

'It's for you, Mr Wetherell,' I said, removing the pins and presenting it to him. Thereupon we sat down beside the table, and he broke the seal with trembling fingers. It was not a very long epistle, and ran as follows.

My dear Mr Wetherell

Bags of imitation money and spurious banknotes will not avail you, nor is it politic to arrange that the water police should meet you on the harbour for the purpose of arresting me. You have lost your opportunity, and your daughter accordingly leaves Australia tonight. I will, however, give you one more chance – take care that you make the most of it. The sum I now ask is £150,000, *with the stick given you by China Pete*, and must be paid without enquiry of any sort. If you are agreeable to this, advertise as follows, 'I will pay – W., and give stick!' in the agony column *Sydney Morning Herald*, on the 18th, 19th, and 20th of this present month. Further arrangements will then be made with you.

The Man who Knows

'Oh, my God, I've ruined all!' cried Mr Wetherell as he put the letter down on the table; 'and, who knows? I may have killed my poor child!'

Seeing his misery, I did my best to comfort him; but it was no use. He seemed utterly broken down by the failure of our scheme, and, if the truth must be told, my own heart was quite as heavy. One thing was very certain, there was a traitor in our camp. Someone had overheard our plans and carried them elsewhere. Could it be the footman? If so, he should have it made hot for him when I got sufficient proof against him; I could promise him that most certainly. While I was thinking over this, I heard a footstep on the companion stairs, and a moment later the Inspector made his appearance. His astonishment at finding us alone, reading a letter by the light of one solitary candle, was unmistakable, for he said, as he came towards us and sat down, 'Why, how's this? Where are the men?'

'There are none. We've been nicely sold,' I answered, handing him the letter. He perused it without further remark, and when he had done so, sat drumming with his fingers upon the table in thought.

'We shall have to look in your own house for the person who has given us away, Mr Wetherell!' he said at last. 'The folk who are running this affair are as cute as men are made nowadays; it's a pleasure to measure swords with them.'

'What do you think our next move had better be?'

'Get home as fast as we can. I'll return with you, and we'll talk it over there. It's no use our remaining here.'

We accordingly went on deck, and descended to our wherry again. This time the Inspector accompanied us, while the police boat set off down the harbour on other business. When we had seen it pull out into the darkness, we threw the imitation money overboard, pushed off for the shore, landed where we had first embarked, and then walked up to Mr Wetherell's house. It was considerably after two o'clock by the time we reached it, but the butler was still sitting up for us. His disappointment seemed as keen as ours when he discovered that we had returned without his young mistress. He followed us up to the study with spirits and glasses, and then at his master's instruction went off to bed.

'Now, gentlemen,' began Mr Wetherell, when the door had closed upon him, 'let us discuss the matter thoroughly. But before we begin, may I offer you cigars.'

The Inspector took one, but I declined, stating that I preferred a pipe. But my pipe was in my bedroom, which was on the other side of the passage; so asking them to wait for me, I went to fetch it. I left the room, shutting the door behind me. But it so happened that the pipe-case had been moved, and it was some minutes before I could find it. Having done so, however, I blew out my candle, and was about to leave the room, which was exactly opposite the study, when I heard the green baize door at the end of the passage open, and a light footstep come along the corridor. Instantly I stood perfectly still, and waited to see who it might be. Closer and closer the step came, till I saw in the half dark the pretty figure of one of the parlour maids. On tiptoe she crept up to the study door, and then stooping down, listened at the keyhole. Instantly I was on the alert, every nerve strained to watch her. For nearly five minutes she stood there, and then with a glance round, tiptoed quietly along the passage again, closing the baize door after her.

When she was safely out of hearing I crossed to the study. Both the Inspector and Mr Wetherell saw that something had happened, and were going to question me. But I held up my hand.

'Don't ask any questions, but tell me as quickly, and as nearly as you can, what you have been talking about during the last five minutes,' I said.

'Why?'

'Don't stop to ask questions. Believe in the importance of my haste. What was it?'

'I have only been giving Mr Wetherell a notion of the steps I propose to take,' said the Inspector.

'Thank you. Now I'm off. Don't sit up for me, Mr Wetherell; I'm going to follow up a clue that may put us on the right scent at last. I don't think you had better come, Mr Inspector, but I'll meet you here again at six o'clock.'

'You can't explain, I suppose?' said the latter, looking a little huffed.

'I'm afraid not,' I answered; 'but I'll tell you this much – I saw one of the female servants listening at this door just now. She'll be off, if I mistake not, with the news she has picked up, and I want to watch her. Good-night.'

'Good-night, and good luck to you.'

Without another word I slipped off my boots, and carrying them in my hand, left the room, and went downstairs to the morning-room. This apartment looked out over the garden, and possessed a window shaded by a big tree. Opening it, I jumped out and carefully closed it after me. Then, pausing for a moment to resume my boots, I crept quietly down the path, jumped a low wall, and so passed into the back street. About fifty yards from the tradesmen's entrance, but on the opposite side of the road, there was a big Moreton Bay fig-tree. Under this I took my stand, and turned a watchful eye upon the house. Fortunately it was a dark night, so that it would have been extremely difficult for anyone across the way to have detected my presence.

For some minutes I waited, and was beginning to wonder if I could have been deceived, when I heard the soft click of a latch, and next moment a small dark figure passed out into the street, and closed the gate after it. Then, pausing a moment as if to make up her mind, for the mysterious person was a woman, she set off quickly in the direction of the city. I followed about a hundred yards behind her.

With the exception of one policeman, who stared very hard at me, we did not meet a soul. Once or twice I nearly lost her, and when we reached the city itself I began to see that it would be well for me to decrease the difference that separated us, if I did not wish to bid goodbye to her altogether. I accordingly hastened my steps, and in this fashion we passed up one street and down another, until we reached what I cannot help thinking must have been the lowest quarter of Sydney. On either hand were Chinese names and sign-boards, marine stores, slop shops, with pawnbrokers and public-houses galore; while in this locality few of the inhabitants seemed to have any idea of what bed meant. Groups of sullen-looking men and women were clustered at the corners, and on one occasion the person I was pursuing was stopped by them. But she evidently knew how to take care of herself, for she was soon marching on her way again.

At the end of one long and filthily dirty street she paused and looked about her. I had crossed the road just before this, and was scarcely ten yards behind her. Pulling my hat well down to shade my face, and sticking my hands in my pockets, I staggered and reeled along, doing my best to imitate the gait of a drunken man. Seeing only me about, she went up to the window of a corner house and tapped with her knuckles thrice upon the glass. Before one could have counted twenty the door of the dwelling was opened, and she passed in. Now I was in a nasty fix – either I must be content to abandon my errand, or I must get inside the building, and trust to luck to procure the information I wanted. Fortunately, in my present disguise the girl would be hardly likely to recognise her master's guest. So giving them time to get into a room, I also went up to the door and turned the handle. To my delight it was unlocked. I opened it, and entered the house.

The passage was in total darkness; but I could make out where the door of the room I wanted to find was located by a thin streak of light low down upon the floor. As softly as I possibly could, I crept up to it, and bent down to look through the keyhole. The view was necessarily limited, but I could just make out the girl I had followed sitting upon a bed; while leaning against the wall, a dirty clay pipe in her mouth, was the vilest old woman I have ever in my life set eyes on. She was very small, with a pinched-up nut-cracker face, dressed in an old bit of tawdry finery, more than three sizes too large for her. Her hair fell upon her shoulders in a tangled mass, and from under it her eyes gleamed out like those of a wicked little Scotch terrier ready to bite. As I bent down to listen I heard her say: 'Well, my pretty dear, and what information have you got for the gentleman, that brings you down at this time of night?'

'Only that the *coppers* are going to start at daylight looking for the *Merry Duchess*. I heard the Inspector say so himself.'

'At daylight, are they?' croaked the old hag. 'Well, I wish 'em joy of their search, I do – them – them! Any more news, my dear?'

'The master and that long-legged slab of a Hatteras went out tonight down the harbour. The old man brought home a lot of money bags, but what was in 'em was only dummies.'

'I know that, too, my dear. Nicely they was sold. Ha! ha!' She chuckled like an old fiend, and then began to cut up another pipe of tobacco in the palm of her hand like a man. She smoked negro head, and the reek of it came out through the keyhole to me. But the younger woman was evidently impatient, for she rose and said: 'When do they sail with the girl, Sally?'

'They're gone, my dear. They went at ten tonight.'

At this piece of news my heart began to throb painfully, so much indeed that I could hardly listen for its beating.

'They weren't long about it,' said the younger girl critically.

'That Nikola's not long about anything,' remarked the old woman.

'I hope Pipa Lannu will agree with her health – the stuck-up minx – I do!' the younger remarked spitefully. 'Now where's the money he said I was to have. Give it to me and let me be off. I shall get the sack if this is found out.'

'It was five pound I was to give yer, wasn't it?' the elder woman said, pushing her hand deep down into her pocket.

'Ten,' said the younger sharply. 'No larks, Sally. I know too much for you!'

'Oh, you know a lot, honey, don't you? Of course you'd be expected to know more than old Aunt Sally, who's never seen anything at all, wouldn't you? Go along with you!'

'Hand me over the money I say, and let me be off!'

'Of course you do know a lot more, don't you? There's a pound!' While they were wrangling over the payment I crept down the passage again to the front door. Once I had reached it, I opened it softly and went out, closing it carefully behind me. Then I took to my heels and ran down the street in the direction I had come. Enquiring my way here and there from policemen, I eventually reached home, scaled the wall, and went across the garden to the morning-room window. This I opened, and by its help made my way into the house and upstairs. As I had expected that he would have gone to bed, my astonishment was considerable at meeting Mr Wetherell on the landing.

'Well, what have you discovered?' he asked anxiously as I came up to him.

'Information of the greatest importance,' I answered; 'but one other thing first. Call up your housekeeper, and tell her you have reason to believe that one of the maids is not in the house. Warn her not to mention you in the matter, but to discharge the girl before breakfast. By the time you've done that I'll have changed my things and be ready to tell you everything.'

'I'll go and rouse her at once; I'm all impatience to know what you have discovered.'

He left me and passed through the green baize door to the servants' wing; while I went to my bedroom and changed my things. This done, I passed into the study, where I found a meal awaiting me. To this I did ample justice, for my long walk and the excitement of the evening had given me an unusual appetite.

Just as I was cutting myself a third slice of beef Mr Wetherell returned, and informed me that the housekeeper was on the alert, and would receive the girl on her reappearance.

'Now tell me of your doings,' said old gentleman.

I thereupon narrated all that had occurred since I left the study in search of my pipe – how I had seen the girl listening at the door, how I had followed her into the town; gave him a description of old Sally, the maid's interview with her, and my subsequent return home. He listened eagerly, and, when I had finished, said: 'Do you believe then that my poor girl has been carried off by Nikola to this island called Pipa Lannu?'

'I do; there seems to be no doubt at all about it.'

'Well then, what are we to do to rescue her? Shall I ask the Government to send a gunboat down?'

'If you think it best; but, for my own part, I must own I should act independently of them. You don't want to make a big sensation, I presume; and remember, to arrest Nikola would be to open the whole affair.'

'Then what do you propose?'

'I propose,' I answered, 'that we charter a small schooner, fit her out, select half a dozen trustworthy and silent men, and then take our departure for Pipa Lannu. I am well acquainted with the island, and, what's more, I hold a master's certificate. We would sail in after dark, arm all our party thoroughly, and go ashore. I expect they will be keeping your daughter a prisoner in a hut. If that is so, we will surround it and rescue her without any trouble or fuss, and, what is better still, without any public scandal. What do you think?'

'I quite agree with what you say. I think it's an excellent idea; and, while you've been speaking, I too have been thinking of something. There's my old friend McMurtough, who has a nice steam yacht. I'm sure he'd be willing to let us have the use of her for a few weeks.'

'Where does he live? – Far from here?'

'His office would be best; we'll go over and see him directly after breakfast if you like.'

'By all means. Now I think I'll go and take a little nap; I feel quite worn out. When the Inspector arrives you will be able to explain all that has happened; but I think I should ask him to keep a quiet tongue in his head about the island. If it leaks out at all, it may warn them, and they'll be off elsewhere – to a place perhaps where we may not be able to find them.'

'I'll remember,' said Mr Wetherell, and thereupon I retired to my room, and, having partially undressed, threw myself upon my bed. In less than two minutes I was fast asleep, never waking until the first gong sounded for breakfast; then, after a good bath, which refreshed me wonderfully, I dressed in my usual habiliments, and went downstairs. Mr Wetherell and the Marquis were in the dining-room, and when I entered both he and the Marquis, who held a copy of the *Sydney Morning Herald* in his hand, seemed prodigiously excited.

'I say, Mr Hatteras,' said the latter (after I had said 'Good-morning'), 'here's an advertisement which is evidently intended for you!'

'What is it about?' I asked. 'Who wants to advertise for me?'

'Read for yourself,' said the Marquis, giving me the paper.

I took it, and glanced down the column to which he referred me until I came to the following:

Richard Hatteras. – If this should meet the eye of Mr Richard Hatteras of Thursday Island, Torres Straits, lately returned from England, and believed to be now in Sydney; he is earnestly requested to call at the office of Messrs Dawson & Gladman, Solicitors, Castlereagh Street, where he will hear of something to his advantage.

There could be no doubt at all that I was the person referred to; but what could be the reason of it all? What was there that I could possibly hear to my advantage, save news of Phyllis, and it would be most unlikely that I would learn anything about the movements of the gang who had abducted her from a firm of first-class solicitors such as I understood Messrs Dawson & Gladman to be. However, it was no use wondering about it, so I dismissed the matter from my mind for the present, and took my place at the table. In the middle of the meal the butler left the room, in response to a ring at the front door. When he returned, it was to inform me that a man was in the hall, who wished to have a few moments' conversation with me. Asking Mr Wetherell to excuse me, I left the room.

In the hall I found a seedy-looking individual of about middle age. He bowed, and on learning that my name was Hatteras, asked if he might be permitted five minutes alone with me. In response, I led him to the morning-room, and having closed the door, pointed to a seat.

'What is your business?' I enquired, when he had sat down.

'It is rather a curious affair to approach, Mr Hatteras,' the man began. 'But to commence, may I be permitted to suggest that you are uneasy in your mind about a person who has disappeared?'

'You may certainly suggest that, if you like,' I answered cautiously.

'If it were in a man's power to furnish a clue regarding that person's whereabouts, it might be useful to you, I suppose,' he continued, craftily watching me out of the corners of his eyes.

'Very useful,' I replied. 'Are you in a position to do so?'

'I might possibly be able to afford you some slight assistance,' he went on. 'That is, of course, provided it were made worth my while.'

'What do you call "worth your while"?'

'Well, shall we say five hundred pounds? That's not a large sum for really trustworthy information. I ought to ask a thousand, considering the danger I'm running in mixing myself up with the affair. Only I'm a father myself, and that's why I do it.'

'I see. Well, let me tell you, I consider five hundred too much.'

'Well then I'm afraid we can't trade. I'm sorry.'

'So am I. But I'm not going to buy a pig in a poke.'

'Shall we say four hundred, then?'

'No. Nor three – two, or one. If your information is worth anything, I don't mind giving you fifty pounds for it. But I won't give a halfpenny more.'

As I spoke, I rose as if to terminate the interview. Instantly my visitor adopted a different tone.

'My fault is my generosity,' he said. 'It's the ruin of me. Well, you shall have it for fifty. Give me the money, and I'll tell you.'

'By no means,' I answered. 'I must hear the information first. Trust to my honour. If what you tell me is worth anything, I'll give you fifty pounds for it. Now what is it?'

'Well, sir, to begin with, you must understand that I was standing at the corner of Pitt Street an evening or two back, when two men passed me talking earnestly together. One of 'em was a tall strapping fellow, the other a little chap. I never saw two eviller looking rascals in my life. Just as they came alongside me, one says to the other, "Don't be afraid; I'll have the girl at the station all right at eight o'clock sharp." The other said something that I could not catch, and then I lost sight of them. But what I had heard stuck in my head, and so I accordingly went off to the station, arriving there a little before the hour. I hadn't been there long before the smallest of the two chaps I'd seen in the street came on to the platform, and began looking about him. By the face of him he didn't seem at all pleased at not finding the other man waiting for him. A train drew up at the platform, and presently, just before it started, I saw the other and a young lady wearing a heavy veil come quickly along. The first man saw them, and gave a little cry of delight. "I thought you'd be too late," says he. "No fear of that," says the other, and jumps into a first-class carriage, telling the girl to get in after him, which she does, crying the while, as I could see. Then the chap on the platform says to the other who was leaning out of the window, "Write to me from Bourke, and tell me how she gets on." "You bet," says his friend. "And don't you forget to keep your eye on Hatteras." "Don't you be afraid," answered the man on the platform. Then the guard whistled, and the train went out of the station. Directly I was able to I got away, and first thing this morning came on here. Now you have my information, and I'll trouble you for that fifty pound.'

'Not so fast, my friend. Your story seems very good, but I want to ask a few questions first. Had the bigger man – the man who went up to Bourke, a deep cut over his left eye?'

'Now I come to think of it, he had. I'd forgotten to tell you that.'

'So it was he, then? But are you certain it was Miss Wetherell? Remember she wore a veil. Could you see if her hair was flaxen in colour?'

'Very light it was; but I couldn't see rightly which colour it was.'

'You're sure it was a light colour?'

'Quite sure. I could swear to it in a court of law if you wanted me to.'

'That's all right then, because it shows me your story is a fabrication. Come, get out of this house or I'll throw you out. You scoundrel, for two pins I'd give you such a thrashing as you'd remember all your life!'

'None o' that, governor. Don't you try it on. Hand us over that fifty quid.'

With that the scoundrel whipped out a revolver and pointed it at me. But before he could threaten again I had got hold of his wrist with one hand, snatched the pistol with the other, and sent him sprawling on his back upon the carpet.

'Now, you brute,' I cried, 'what am I going to do with you, do you think? Get up and clear out of the house before I take my boot to you.'

He got up and began to brush his clothes.

'I want my fifty pound,' he cried.

'You'll get more than you want if you come here again,' I said. 'Out you go!'

With that I got him by the collar and dragged him out of the room across the hall, much to the butler's astonishment, through the front door, and then kicked him down the steps. He fell in a heap on the gravel.

'All right, my fine bloke,' he said as he lay there; 'you wait till I get you outside. I'll fix you up, and don't you make no mistake.'

I went back to the dining-room without paying any attention to his threats. Both Mr Wetherell and Beckenham had been witnesses of what had occurred, and now they questioned me concerning his visit. I gave them an outline of the story the man had told me and convinced them of its absurdity. Then Mr Wetherell rose to his feet.

'Now shall we go and see McMurtough?'

'Certainly,' I said; 'I'll be ready as soon as you are.'

'You will come with us I hope, Lord Beckenham?' Wetherell said.

'With every pleasure,' answered his lordship, and thereupon we went off to get ready.

Three-quarters of an hour later we were sitting in Mr McMurtough's ante-room, waiting for an interview. At the end of ten minutes a commissionaire came in to inform us that Mr McMurtough was disengaged, and forthwith conducted us to his room. We found him a small, grey-haired, pleasant-looking gentleman, full of life and fun. He received Mr Wetherell as an old friend, and then waited to be introduced to us.

'Let me make you acquainted with my friends, McMurtough,' said Wetherell – 'the Marquis of Beckenham and Mr Hatteras.'

He bowed and then shook hands with us, after which we sat down and Wetherell proceeded to business. The upshot of it all was that he fell in with our plans as soon as we had uttered them, and expressed himself delighted to lend his yacht in such a good cause.

'I only wish I could come with you,' he said; 'but unfortunately that is quite impossible. However, you are more than welcome to my boat. I will give you a letter, or send one to the captain, so that she may be prepared for sea today. Will you see about provisioning her, or shall I?'

'We will attend to that,' said Wetherell. 'All the expenses must of course be mine.'

'As you please about that, my old friend,' returned McMurtough.

'Where is she lying?' asked Wetherell.

The owner gave us the direction, and then having sincerely thanked him, we set off in search of her. She was a nice craft of about a hundred and fifty tons burden, and looked as if she ought to be a good sea boat. Chartering a wherry, we were pulled off to her. The captain was below when we arrived, but a hail brought him on deck. Mr Wetherell then explained our errand, and gave him his owner's letter. He read it through, and having done so, said: 'I am at your service, gentlemen. From what Mr McMurtough says here I gather that there is no time to lose, so with your permission I'll get to work at once.'

'Order all the coal you want, and tell the steward to do the same for anything he may require in his department. The bills must be sent in to me.'

'Very good, Mr Wetherell. And what time will you be ready?'

'As soon as you are. Can you get away by three o'clock this afternoon, think you?'

'Well, it will be a bit of a scramble, but I think we can manage it. Anyhow, I'll do my best, you may be sure of that, sir.'

'I'm sure you will. There is grave need for it. Now we'll go back and arrange a few matters ashore. My man shall bring our baggage down later on.'

'Very good, sir. I'll have your berths prepared.' With that we descended to the boat again, and were pulled ashore. Arriving there, Mr Wetherell asked what we should do first.

'Hadn't we better go up to the town and purchase a few rifles and some ammunition?' I said. 'We can have them sent down direct to the boat, and so save time.'

'A very good suggestion. Let us go at once.'

We accordingly set off for George Street – to a shop I remembered having seen. There we purchased half a dozen Winchester repeaters, with a good supply of ammunition. They were to be sent down to the yacht without fail that morning. This done, we stood on the pavement debating what we should do next. Finally it was decided that Mr Wetherell and Beckenham should go home to pack, while I made one or two other small purchases, and then join them. Accordingly, bidding them goodbye, I went on down the street, completed my business, and was about to hail a cab and follow them, when a thought struck me: Why should I not visit Messrs Dawson & Gladman, and find out why they were advertising for me? This I determined to do, and accordingly set off for Castlereagh Street. Without much hunting about I discovered their office, and went inside.

In a small room leading off the main passage, three clerks were seated. To them I addressed myself, asking if I might see the partners.

'Mr Dawson is the only one in town, sir,' said the boy to whom I spoke. 'If you'll give me your name, I'll take it in to him.'

'My name is Hatteras,' I said. 'Mr Richard Hatteras.'

'Indeed, sir,' answered the lad. 'If you'll wait, Mr Dawson will see you in a minute, I'm sure.'

On hearing my name the other clerks began whispering together, at the same time throwing furtive glances in my direction. In less than two minutes the clerk returned, and begged me to follow him, which I did. At the end of a long passage we passed through a curtained doorway, and I stood in the presence of the chief partner, Mr Dawson. He was a short, podgy man, with white whiskers and a bald head, and painfully precise.

'I have great pleasure in making your acquaintance, Mr Hatteras,' he said, as I came to an anchor in a chair. 'You have noticed our advertisement, I presume?'

'I saw it this morning,' I answered. 'And it is on that account I am here.'

'One moment before we proceed any further. Forgive what I am about to say – but you will see yourself that it is a point I am compelled not to neglect. Can you convince me as to your identity?'

'Very easily,' I replied, diving my hand into my breast-pocket and taking out some papers. 'First and foremost, here is my bank-book. Here is my card-case. And here are two or three letters addressed to me by London and Sydney firms. The Hon. Sylvester Wetherell, Colonial Secretary, will be glad, I'm sure, to vouch for me. Is that sufficient to convince you?'

'More than sufficient,' he answered, smiling. 'Now let me tell you for what purpose we desired you to call upon us.' Here he opened a drawer and took out a letter.

'First and foremost, you must understand that we are the Sydney agents of Messrs Atwin, Dobbs & Forsyth, of Furnival's Inn, London. From them, by the last English mail, we received this letter. I gather that you are the son of James Dymoke Hatteras, who was drowned at sea in the year 1880 – is that so?'

'I am.'

'Your father was the third son of Sir Edward Hatteras of Murdlestone, in the county of Hampshire?'

'He was.'

'And the brother of Sir William, who had one daughter Gwendoline Mary?'

'That is so.'

'Well, Mr Hatteras, it is my sad duty to inform you that within a week of your departure from England your cousin, the young lady just referred to, was drowned by accident in a pond near her home and that her father, who had been ailing for some few days, died of heart disease on hearing the sad tidings. In that case, so my correspondents inform me, there being no nearer issue, you succeed to the title and estates – which I also learn are of considerable value, including the house and park, ten farms, and a large amount of house property, a rent roll of fifteen thousand a year, and accumulated capital of nearly a hundred thousand pounds.'

'Good gracious! Is this really true?'

'Quite true. You can examine the letter for yourself.'

I took it up from the table and read it through, hardly able to believe my eyes.

'You are indeed a man to be envied, Mr Hatteras,' said the lawyer. 'The title is an old one, and I believe the property is considered one of the best in that part of England.'

'It is! But I can hardly believe that it is really mine.'

'There is no doubt about that, however. You are a baronet as certainly as I am a lawyer. I presume you would like us to take whatever action is necessary in the matter?'

'By all means. This afternoon I am leaving Sydney, for a week or two, for the Islands. I will sign any papers when I come back.'

'I will bear that in mind. And your address in Sydney is – '

'Care of the Honourable Sylvester Wetherell, Potts Point.'

'Thank you. And, by the way, my correspondents have desired me on their behalf to pay in to your account at the Oceania the sum of five thousand pounds. This I will do today.'

'I am obliged to you. Now I think I must be going. To tell the truth, I hardly know whether I am standing on my head or my heels.'

'Oh, you will soon get over that.'

'Good-morning.'

'Good-morning, Sir Richard.'

With that, I bade him farewell, and went out of the office, feeling quite dazed by my good fortune. I thought of the poor idiot whose end had been so tragic, and of the old man as I had last seen him, shaking his fist at me from the window of the house. And to think that that lovely home was mine, and that I was a baronet, the principal representative of a race as old as any in the countryside! It seemed too wonderful to be true!

Hearty were the congratulations showered upon me at Potts Point, you may be sure, when I told my tale, and my health was drunk at lunch with much goodwill. But our minds were too much taken up with the arrangements for our departure that afternoon to allow us to think very much of anything else. By two o'clock we were ready to leave the house, by half-past we were on board the yacht, at three-fifteen the anchor was up, and a few moments later we were ploughing our way down the harbour.

Our search for Phyllis had reached another stage.

CHAPTER FIVE

The islands, and what we found there

To those who have had no experience of the South Pacific the
constantly recurring beauties of our voyage would have seemed like a
foretaste of Heaven itself. From Sydney, until the Loyalty Group lay
behind us, we had one long spell of exquisite weather. By night under
the winking stars, and by day in the warm sunlight, our trim little
craft ploughed her way across smooth seas, and our only occupation
was to promenade or loaf about the decks and to speculate as to the
result of the expedition upon which we had embarked.

Having sighted the Isle of Pines we turned our bows almost due
north and headed for the New Hebrides. Every hour our impatience
was growing greater. In less than two days, all being well, we should
be at our destination, and twenty-four hours after that, if our fortune
proved in the ascendant, we ought to be on our way back with Phyllis
in our possession once more. And what this would mean to me I can
only leave you to guess.

One morning, just as the faint outline of the coast of Aneityum
was peering up over the horizon ahead, Wetherell and I chanced to
be sitting in the bows. The sea was as smooth as glass, and the
tinkling of the water round the little vessel's nose as she turned it
off in snowy lines from either bow, was the only sound to be heard.
As usual the conversation, after wandering into other topics, came
back to the subject nearest our hearts. This led us to make a few
remarks about Nikola and his character. There was one thing I had
always noticed when the man came under discussion, and that was
the dread Wetherell had of him. My curiosity had been long excited
as to its meaning, and having an opportunity now, I could not help
asking him for an explanation.

'You want to know how it is that I am so frightened of Nikola?' he
asked, knocking the ash off his cigar on the upturned fluke of the
anchor alongside him. 'Well, to give you my reason will necessitate
my telling you a story. I don't mind doing that at all, but what I am

afraid of is that you may be inclined to doubt its probability. I must confess it is certainly more like the plot of a Wilkie Collins novel than a bit of sober reality. However, if you want to hear it you shall.'

'I should like to above all things,' I replied, making myself comfortable and taking another cigar from my pocket. 'I have been longing to ask you about it for some time past, but could not quite screw up my courage.'

'Well, in the first place,' Mr Wetherell said, 'you must understand that before I became a Minister of the Crown, or indeed a Member of Parliament at all, I was a barrister with a fairly remunerative practice. That was before my wife's death and when Phyllis was at school. Up to the time I am going to tell you about I had taken part in no very sensational case. But my opportunity for earning notoriety was, though I did not know it, near at hand. One day I was briefed to defend a man accused of the murder of a Chinaman aboard a Sydney vessel on a voyage from Shanghai. At first there seemed to be no doubt at all as to his guilt, but by a singular chance, with the details of which I will not bore you, I hit upon a scheme which got him off. I remember the man perfectly, and a queer fellow he was, half-witted, I thought, and at the time of the trial within an ace of dying of consumption. His gratitude was the more pathetic because he had not the wherewithal to pay me. However, he made it up to me in another way, and that's where my real story commences.

'One wet night, a couple of months or so after the trial, I was sitting in my drawing-room listening to my wife's music, when a servant entered to tell me that a woman wanted to see me. I went out into the passage to find waiting there a tall buxom lass of about five-and-twenty years of age. She was poorly dressed, but in a great state of excitement.

' "Are you Mr Wetherell?" she said; "the gentleman as defended China Pete in the trial the other day?"

' "I am," I answered. "What can I do for you? I hope China Pete is not in trouble again?"

' "He's in a worse trouble this time, sir," said the woman. "He's dyin', and he sent me to fetch you to 'im before he goes."

' "But what does he want me for?" I asked rather suspiciously.

' "I'm sure I dunno," was the girl's reply. "But he's been callin' for you all this blessed day: 'Send for Mr Wetherell! Send for Mr Wetherell!' So off I came, when I got back from work, to fetch you. If you're comin', sir, you'd best be quick, for he won't last till mornin'."

' "Very well, I'll come with you at once," I said, taking a mackintosh down from a peg as I spoke. Then, having told my wife not to sit up for me, I followed my strange messenger out of the house and down into the city.

'For nearly an hour we walked on and on, plunging deeper into the lower quarter of the town. All through the march my guide maintained a rigid silence, walking a few paces ahead, and only recognising the fact that I was following her by nodding in a certain direction whenever we arrived at cross thoroughfares or interlacing lanes.

'At last we arrived at the street she wanted. At the corner she came suddenly to a standstill, and putting her two first fingers into her mouth blew a shrill whistle, after the fashion of street boys. A moment later a shock-headed urchin about ten years old made his appearance from a dark alley and came towards us. The woman said something to him, which I did not catch, and then turning sharply to her left hand beckoned to me to follow her. This I did, but not without a feeling of wonderment as to what the upshot of it all would be.

'From the street itself we passed, by way of a villainous alley, into a large courtyard, where brooded a silence like that of death. Indeed, a more weird and desolate place I don't remember ever to have met with. Not a soul was to be seen, and though it was surrounded by houses, only two feeble lights showed themselves. Towards one of these my guide made her way, stopping on the threshold. Upon a panel she rapped with her fingers, and as she did so a window on the first floor opened, and the same boy we had met in the street looked out.

' "How many?" enquired the woman, who had brought me, in a loud whisper.

' "None now," replied the boy; "but there's been a power of Chinkies hereabouts all the evenin', an' 'arf an hour ago there was a gent in a cloak."

'Without waiting to hear any more the woman entered the house and I followed close on her heels. The adventure was clearly coming to a head now.

'When the door had been closed behind us the boy appeared at the top of a flight of stairs with a lighted candle. We accordingly ascended to him, and having done so made our way towards a door at the end of the abominably dirty landing. At intervals I could hear the sound of coughing coming from a room at the end. My companion, however, bade me stop, while she went herself into the room, shutting the door after her. I was left alone with the boy, who immediately took me under his protection, and for my undivided benefit performed a series of highly meritorious acrobatic performances upon the feeble banisters, to his own danger, but apparent satisfaction. Suddenly, just as he was about to commence what promised to be the most successful item in his *repertoire*, he paused, lay flat on his stomach upon the floor, and craned his head over the side, where once banisters had been, and gazed into the half dark well below. All was quiet as the grave. Then, without warning, an almond-eyed, pigtailed head appeared on the stairs and looked upwards. Before I could say anything to stop him, the youth had divested himself of his one slipper, taken it in his right hand, leaned over a bit further, and struck the ascending Celestial a severe blow on the mouth with the heel of it. There was the noise of a hasty descent and the banging of the street door a moment later, then all was still again, and the youngster turned to me.

' "That was Ah Chong," he said confidentially. 'He's the sixth Chinkie I've landed that way since dark.'

'This important piece of information he closed with a double-jointed oath of remarkable atrocity, and, having done so, would have recommenced the performance of acrobatic feats had I not stopped him by asking the reason of his action. He looked at me with a grin, and said: "I dunno, but all I cares is that China Pete in there gives me a sprat (sixpence) for every Chinkie what I keeps out of the 'ouse. He's a rum one is China Pete; an' can't he cough – my word!"

'I was about to put another question when the door opened and the girl who had brought me to the house beckoned me into the room. I entered and she left me alone with the occupant.

'Of all the filthy places I have ever seen – and I have had the ill-luck to discover a good many in my time – that one eclipsed them all. The room was at most ten feet long by seven wide, had a window at the far end, and the door, through which I had entered, opposite it. The bed-place was stretched between the door and the window, and was a horrible exhibition. On it, propped up by pillows and evidently in the last stage of collapse, was the man called China Pete, whom I had last seen walking out of the dock at the Supreme Court a couple of months before. When we were alone together he pointed to a box near the bed and signified that I should seat myself. I did so, at the same time taking occasion to express my sorrow at finding him in this lamentable condition. He made no reply to my civilities, but after a little pause found strength enough to whisper, "See if there's anybody at the door." I went across, opened the door and looked into the passage, but save the boy, who was now sitting on the top step of the stairs at the other end, there was not a soul in sight. I told him this and having again closed the door, sat down on the box and waited for him to speak.

' "You did me a good turn, Mr Wetherell, over that trial," the invalid said at last, "and I couldn't make it worth your while."

' "Oh, you mustn't let that worry you," I answered soothingly. "You would have paid me if you had been able."

' "Perhaps I should, perhaps I shouldn't, anyhow I didn't, and I want to make it up to you now. Feel under my pillow and bring out what you find there."

'I did as he directed me and brought to light a queer little wooden stick about three and a half inches long, made of some heavy timber and covered all over with Chinese inscriptions; at one end was a tiny bit of heavy gold cord much tarnished. I gave it to him and he looked at it fondly.

' "Do you know the value of this little stick?" he asked after a while.

' "I have no possible notion," I replied.

' "Make a guess," he said.

'To humour him I guessed five pounds. He laughed with scorn.

' "Five pounds! O ye gods! Why, as a bit of stick it's not worth five pence, but for what it really is there is not money enough in the world to purchase it. If I could get about again I would make myself the richest and most powerful man on earth with it. If you could only guess one particle of the dangers I've been through to get it you would die of astonishment. And the sarcasm of it all is that now I've got it I can't make use of it. On six different occasions the priests of the Llamaserai in Pekin have tried to murder me to get hold of it. I brought it down from the centre of China disguised as a wandering beggar. That business connected with the murder of the Chinaman on board the ship, against which you defended me, was on account of it. And now I lie here dying like a dog, with the key to over ten millions in my hand. Nikola has tried for five years to obtain it, without success however. He little dreams I've got it after all. If he did I'd be a dead man by this time."

' "Who is this Nikola then?" I asked.

' "Dr Nikola? Well, he's Nikola, and that's all I can tell you. If you're a wise man you'll want to know no more. Ask the Chinese mothers nursing their almond-eyed spawn in Pekin who he is; ask the Japanese, ask the Malays, the Hindoos, the Burmese, the coal porters in Port Said, the Buddhist priests of Ceylon; ask the King of

Corea, the men up in Thibet, the Spanish priests in Manilla, or the Sultan of Borneo, the ministers of Siam, or the French in Saigon – they'll all know Dr Nikola and his cat, and, take my word for it, they fear him."

'I looked at the little stick in my hand and wondered if the man had gone mad.

' "What do you wish me to do with this?" I asked.

' "Take it away with you," he answered, "and guard it like your life, and when you have occasion, use it. Remember you have in your hand what will raise a million men and the equivalent of over ten mil – "

'At this point a violent fit of coughing seized him and nearly tore him to pieces. I lifted him up a little in the bed, but before I could take my hands away a stream of blood had gushed from his lips. Like a flash of thought I ran to the door to call the girl, the boy on the stairs re-echoed my shout, and in less time than it takes to tell the woman was in the room. But we were too late – *China Pete was dead*.

'After giving her all the money I had about me to pay for the funeral, I bade her goodbye, and with the little stick in my pocket returned to my home. Once there I sat myself down in my study, took my legacy out of my pocket and carefully examined it. As to its peculiar power and value, as described to me by the dead man, I hardly knew what to think. My own private opinion was that China Pete was not sane at the time he told me. And yet, how was I to account for the affray with the Chinaman on the boat, and the evident desire the Celestials in Sydney had to obtain information concerning it? After half an hour's consideration of it I locked it up in a drawer of my safe and went upstairs to bed.

'Next day China Pete was buried, and by the end of the month I had well nigh forgotten that he had ever existed, and had hardly thought of his queer little gift, which still reposed in the upper drawer of my safe. But I was to hear more of it later on.

'One night, about a month after my coming into possession of the stick, my wife and I were entertaining a few friends at dinner. The ladies had retired to the drawing-room and I was sitting with the gentlemen at the table over our wine. Curiously enough we had just been discussing the main aspects of the politics of the East when a maid-servant entered to say that a gentleman had called, and would be glad to know if he might have an interview with me on important business. I replied to the effect that I was engaged, and told her to ask him if he would call again in the morning. The servant left the room only to return with the information that the man would be leaving Sydney shortly after daylight, but that if I would see him later on in the evening he would endeavour to return. I therefore told the girl to say I would see him about eleven o'clock, and then dismissed the matter from my mind.

'As the clock struck eleven I said good-night to the last of my guests upon the doorstep. The carriage had not gone fifty yards down the street before a hansom drew up before my door and a man dressed in a heavy cloak jumped out. Bidding the driver wait for him he ran up my steps.

' "Mr Wetherell, I believe?" he said. I nodded and wished him "good-evening", at the same time asking his business.

' "I will tell you with pleasure," he answered, "if you will permit me five minutes alone with you. It is most important, and as I leave Sydney early tomorrow morning you will see that there is not much time to spare."

'I led the way into the house and to my study, which was in the rear, overlooking the garden. Once there I bade him be seated, taking up my position at my desk.

'Then, in the light of the lamp, I became aware of the extra-ordinary personality of my visitor. He was of middle height, but beautifully made. His face was oval in shape, with a deadly white complexion. In contrast to this, however, his eyes and hair were dark as night. He looked at me very searchingly for a moment and then said: "My business will surprise you a little I expect, Mr Wetherell. First, if you will allow me I will tell you something about myself and then ask you a question. You must understand that I am pretty well known as an Eastern traveller; from Port Said to the Kuriles there is hardly a place with which I am not acquainted. I have a hobby. I am a collector of Eastern curios, but there is one thing I have never been able to obtain."

' "And that is?"

' "A Chinese executioner's symbol of office."

' "But how can I help you in that direction?" I asked, completely mystified.

' "By selling me one that has lately come into your possession," he said. "It is a little black stick, about three inches long and covered with Chinese characters. I happened to hear, quite by chance, that you had one in your possession, and I have taken a journey of some thousands of miles to endeavour to purchase it from you."

'I went across to the safe, unlocked it, and took out the little stick China Pete had given me. When I turned round I almost dropped it with surprise as I saw the look of eagerness that rose in my visitor's face. But he pulled himself together and said, as calmly as he had yet addressed me: "That is the very thing. If you will allow me to purchase it, it will complete my collection. What value do you place upon it?"

' "I have no sort of notion of its worth," I answered, putting it down on the table and looking at it. Then in a flash a thought came into my brain, and I was about to speak when he addressed me again.

' "Of course my reason for wishing to buy it is rather a hare-brained one, but if you care to let me have it I will give you fifty pounds for it with pleasure."

' "Not enough, Dr Nikola," I said with a smile.

'He jumped as if he had been shot, and then clasped his hands tight on the arm of his chair. My random bolt had gone straight to the heart of the bullseye. This man then was Dr Nikola, the extraordinary individual against whom China Pete had warned me. I was determined now that, come what might, he should not have the stick.

' "Do you not consider the offer I make you a good one then, Mr Wetherell?" he asked.

' "I'm sorry to say I don't think the stick is for sale," I answered. "It was left to me by a man in return for a queer sort of service I rendered him, and I think I should like to keep it as a souvenir."

' "I will raise my offer to a hundred pounds in that case," said Nikola.

' "I would rather not part with it," I said, and as I spoke, as if to clinch the matter, I took it up and returned it to the safe, taking care to lock the door upon it.

' "I will give you five hundred pounds for it," cried Nikola, now thoroughly excited. "Surely that will tempt you?"

' "I'm afraid an offer of ten times that amount would make no difference," I replied, feeling more convinced than ever that I would not part with it.

'He laid himself back in his chair, and for nearly a minute and a half stared me full in the face. You have seen Nikola's eyes, so I needn't tell you what a queer effect they are able to produce. I could not withdraw mine from them, and I felt that if I did not make an effort I should soon be mesmerised. So, pulling myself together, I sprang from my chair, and, by doing so, let him see that our interview was at an end. However, he was not going without a last attempt to drive a bargain. When he saw that I was not to be moved his temper gave way, and he bluntly told me that I would have to sell it to him.

'"There is no compulsion in the matter," I said warmly. "The curio is my own property, and I will do just as I please with it."

'He thereupon begged my pardon, asked me to attribute his impatience to the collector's eagerness, and after a few last words bade me "good-night", and left the house.

'When his cab had rolled away I went back to my study and sat thinking for a while. Then something prompted me to take the stick out from the safe. I did so, and sat at my table gazing at it, wondering what the mystery might be to which it was the key. That it was not what Dr Nikola had described it I felt certain.

'At the end of half an hour I put it in my pocket, intending to take it upstairs to show my wife, locked the safe again and went off to my dressing-room. When I had described the interview and shown the stick to my wife I placed it in the drawer of the looking-glass and went to bed.

'Next morning, about three o'clock, I was awakened by the sound of someone knocking violently at my door. I jumped out of bed and enquired who it might be. To my intense surprise the answer was "Police!" I therefore donned my dressing-gown, and went out to find a sergeant of police on the landing waiting for me.

'"What is the matter?" I cried.

'"A burglar!" was his answer. "We've got him downstairs; caught him in the act."

'I followed the officer down to the study. What a scene was there! The safe had been forced, and its contents lay scattered in every direction. One drawer of my writing-table was wide open, and in a corner, handcuffed, and guarded by a stalwart constable, stood a Chinaman.

'Well, to make a long story short, the man was tried, and after denying all knowledge of Nikola – who, by the way, could not be found – was convicted, and sentenced to five years' hard labour. For a month I heard no more about the curio. Then a letter arrived from an English solicitor in Shanghai demanding from me, on behalf of a Chinaman residing in that place, a little wooden stick covered with Chinese characters, which was said to have been stolen by an Englishman, known in Shanghai as China Pete. This was very clearly another attempt on Nikola's part to obtain possession of it, so I replied to the effect that I could not entertain the request.

'A month or so later – I cannot, however, be particular as to the exact date – I found myself again in communication with Nikola, this time from South America. But there was this difference this time: he used undisguised threats, not only against myself, in the event of my still refusing to give him what he wanted, but also against my wife and daughter. I took no notice, with the result that my residence was again broken into, but still without success. Now I no longer locked the talisman up in the safe, but hid it in a place where I knew no one could possibly find it. My mind, you will see, was perfectly made up; I was not going to be driven into surrendering it.

'One night, a month after my wife's death, returning to my house I was garrotted and searched within a hundred yards of my own front door, but my assailants could not find it on me. Then peculiar pressure from other quarters was brought to bear; my servants were bribed, and my life became almost a burden to me. What was more, I began to develop that extraordinary fear of Nikola which seems to seize upon everyone who has any dealings with him. When I went home to England some months back, I did it because my spirits had got into such a depressed state that I could not remain in Australia. But I took care to deposit the stick with my plate in the bank before I left. There it remained till I returned, when I put it back in its old hiding-place again.

'The day after I reached London I happened to be crossing Trafalgar Square. Believing that I had left him at least ten thousand miles away, you may imagine my horror when I saw Dr Nikola watching me from the other side of the road. Then and there I returned to my hotel, bade Phyllis pack with all possible dispatch, and that same afternoon we started to return to Australia. The rest you know. Now what do you think of it all?'

'It's an extraordinary story. Where is the stick at the present moment?'

'In my pocket. Would you like to see it?'

'Very much, if you would permit me to do so.' He unbuttoned his coat, and from a carefully contrived pocket under the arm drew out a little piece of wood of exactly the length and shape he had described. I took it from him and gazed at it carefully. It was covered all over with Chinese writing, and had a piece of gold silk attached to the handle. There was nothing very remarkable about it; but I must own I was strangely fascinated by it when I remembered the misery it had caused, the changes and chances it had brought about, the weird story told by China Pete, and the efforts that had been made by Nikola to obtain possession of it. I gave it back to its owner, and then stood looking out over the smooth sea, wondering where Phyllis was and what she was doing. Nikola, when I met him, would have a heavy account to settle with me, and if my darling reported any further cruelty on his part I would show no mercy. But why had Mr Wetherell brought the curio with him now?

I put the question to him.

'For one very good reason,' he answered. 'If it is the stick Nikola is after, as I have every right to suppose, he may demand it as a ransom for my girl, and I am quite willing to let him have it. The wretched thing has caused sufficient misery to make me only too glad to be rid of it.'

'I hope, however, we shall be able to get her without giving it up,' I said. 'Now let us go aft to lunch.'

The day following we were within a hundred miles of our destination, and by midday of the day following that again were near enough to render it advisable to hold a council over our intended movements. Accordingly, a little before lunch-time the Marquis, Wetherell, the skipper and myself, met under the after awning to consider our plan of war. The vessel herself was hove to, for we had no desire to put in an appearance at the island during daylight.

'The first matter to be taken into consideration, I think, Mr Wetherell,' said the skipper, 'is the point as to which side of the island we shall bring up on.'

'You will be able to settle that,' answered Wetherell, looking at me. 'You are acquainted with the place, and can best advise us.'

'I will do so to the best of my ability,' I said, sitting down on the deck and drawing an outline with a piece of chalk. 'The island is shaped like this. There is no reef. Here is the best anchorage, without doubt, but here is the point where we shall be most likely to approach without being observed. The trend of the land is all upward from the shore, and, as far as I remember, the most likely spot for a hut, if they are detaining Miss Wetherell there, as we suppose, will be on a little plateau looking south, and hard by the only fresh water on the island.'

'And what sort of anchorage shall we get there, do you think?' asked the skipper, who very properly wished to run no risk with his owner's boat.

'Mostly coral. None too good, perhaps, but as we shall have steam up, quite safe enough.'

'And how do you propose that we shall reach the hut when we land? Is there any undergrowth, or must we climb the hill under the enemy's fire?'

'I have been thinking that out,' I said, 'and I have come to the conclusion that the best plan would be for us to approach the island after dark, to heave to about three miles out and pull ashore in the boat. We will then ascend the hill by the eastern slope and descend upon them. They will probably not expect us from that quarter, and it will at least be easier than climbing the hill in the face of a heavy fire. What do you say?'

They all agreed that it seemed practicable.

'Very good then,' said the skipper, 'we'll have lunch and afterwards begin our preparations.' Then turning to me, 'I'll get you to come into my cabin, Mr Hatteras, by-and-by and take a look at the Admiralty chart, if you will. You will be able probably to tell me if you think it can be relied on.'

'I'll do so with pleasure,' I answered, and then we went below. Directly our meal was over I accompanied the skipper to look at the chart, and upon it we marked our anchorage. Then an adjournment was made aft, and our equipment of rifles and revolvers thoroughly overhauled. We had decided earlier that our landing party should consist of eight men – Wetherell, Beckenham, the mate of the yacht, myself, and four of the crew, each of whom would be supplied with a Winchester repeating rifle, a revolver, and a dozen cartridges. Not a shot was to be fired, however, unless absolutely necessary, and the greatest care was to be taken in order to approach the hut, if possible, without disturbing its inmates.

When the arms had been distributed and carefully examined, the sixteen foot surf-boat was uncovered and preparations made for hoisting her overboard. By the time this was done it was late in the afternoon, and almost soon enough for us to be thinking about overcoming the distance which separated us from our destination. Exactly at four o'clock the telegraph on the bridge signalled 'go ahead', and we were on our way once more. To tell the truth, I think we were all so nervous that we were only too thankful to be moving again.

About dusk I was standing aft, leaning against the taffrail, when Beckenham came up and stood beside me. It was wonderful what a difference these few months had made in him; he was now as brown as a berry, and as fine-looking a young fellow as any man could wish to see.

'We shall be picking up the island directly,' I said as he came to an anchor alongside me. 'Do you think you ought to go tonight? Remember you will run the risk of being shot!'

'I have thought of that,' he said. 'I believe it's my duty to do my best to help you and Mr Wetherell.'

'But what would your father say if he knew?'

'He would say that I only did what was right. I have just been writing to him, telling him everything. If anything should happen to me you will find the letter on the chest of drawers in your cabin. I know you will send it on to him. But if we both come out of it safely and rescue Miss Wetherell I'm going to ask a favour of you?'

'Granted before I know what it is!'

'It isn't a very big one. I want you to let me be your best man at your wedding?'

'So you shall. And a better I could not possibly desire.'

'I like to hear you say that. We've been through a good deal together since we left Europe, haven't we?'

'We have, and tonight will bring it to a climax, or I'm much mistaken.'

'Do you think Nikola will show fight?'

'Not a doubt about it I should think. If he finds himself cornered he'll probably fight like a demon.'

'It's Baxter I want to meet.'

'Nikola is my man. I've a big grudge against him, and I want to pay it.'

'How little we thought when we were cruising about Bournemouth Bay together that within such a short space of time we should be sailing the South Pacific on such an errand! It seems almost too strange to be possible.'

'So it does! All's well that ends well, however. Let's hope we're going to be successful tonight. Now I'm going on the bridge to see if I can pick the land up ahead.'

I left him and went forward to the captain's side. Dusk had quite fallen by this time, rendering it impossible to see very far ahead. A hand had been posted in the fore-rigging as a lookout, and every moment we expected to hear his warning cry; but nearly an hour passed, and still it did not come.

Then suddenly the shout rang out, 'Land ahead!' and we knew that our destination was in sight. Long before this all our lights had been obscured, and so, in the darkness – for a thick pall of cloud covered the sky – we crept up towards the coast. Within a couple of minutes of hearing the hail every man on board was on deck gazing ahead in the direction in which we were proceeding.

By tea-time we had brought the land considerably nearer, and by eight o'clock were within three miles of it. Not a sign, however, of any craft could we discover, and the greatest vigilance had to be exercised on our part to allow no sign to escape us to show our whereabouts to those ashore. Exactly at nine o'clock the shore party, fully armed, assembled on deck, and the surf-boat was swung overboard. Then in the darkness we crept down the gangway and took our places. The mate was in possession of the tiller, and when all was ready we set off for the shore.

CHAPTER SIX
Conclusion

Once we had left her side and turned our boat's nose towards the land, the yacht lay behind us, a black mass nearly absorbed in the general shadow. Not a light showed itself, and everything was as still as the grave; the only noise to be heard was the steady dip, dip of the oars in the smooth water and now and then the chirp of the rowlocks. For nearly half an hour we pulled on, pausing at intervals to listen, but nothing of an alarming nature met our ears. The island was every moment growing larger, the beach more plain to the eye, and the hill more clearly defined.

As soon as the boat grounded we sprang out and, leaving one hand to look after her, made our way ashore. It was a strange experience, that landing on a strange beach on such an errand and at such an hour, but we were all too much taken up with the work which lay before us to think of that. Having left the water's edge we came to a standstill beneath a group of palms and discussed the situation. As the command of the expedition had fallen upon me I decided upon the following course of action. To begin with, I would leave the party behind me and set out by myself to ascertain the whereabouts of the hut. Having discovered this I would return, and we would thereupon make our way inland and endeavour to capture it. I explained the idea in as few words as possible to my followers, and then, bidding them wait for me where they were, at the same time warning them against letting their presence be discovered, I set off up the hill in the direction I knew the plateau to lie. The undergrowth was very thick and the ground rocky; for this reason it was nearly twenty minutes before I reached the top of the hill. Then down the other side I crept, picking my way carefully, and taking infinite precautions that no noise should serve to warn our foes of my coming.

At last I reached the plateau and looked about me. A small perpendicular cliff, some sixty feet in height, was before me, so throwing myself down upon my stomach, I wriggled my way to its edge. When I got there I looked over and discovered three well-built huts on a little plateau at the cliff's base. At the same moment a roar of laughter greeted my ears from the building on the left. It was followed by the voice of a man singing to the accompaniment of a banjo. Under cover of his music I rose to my feet and crept back through the bushes, by the track along which I had come. I knew enough to distribute my forces now.

Having reached my friends again, I informed them of what I had seen, and we then arranged the mode of attack as follows: the mate of the yacht, with two of the hands, would pass round the hill to the left of the plateau, Wetherell and another couple of men would take the right side, while Beckenham and myself crept down from the back. Not a sound was to be made or a shot fired until I blew my whistle. Then, with one last word of caution, we started on our climb.

By this time the clouds had cleared off the sky and the stars shone brightly. Now and again a bird would give a drowsy 'caw' as we disturbed him, or a wild pig would jump up with a grunt and go trotting off into the undergrowth, but beyond these things all was very still. Once more I arrived at the small precipice behind the huts, and, having done so, sat down for a few moments to give the other parties time to take up their positions. Then, signing to Beckenham to accompany me, I followed the trend of the precipice along till I discovered a place where we might descend in safety. In less than a minute we were on the plateau below, creeping towards the centre hut. Still our approach was undetected. Bidding Beckenham in a whisper wait for me, I crept cautiously round to the front, keeping as much as possible in the shadow. As soon as I had found the door, I tiptoed towards it and prepared to force my way inside, but I had an adventure in store for me which I had not anticipated.

Seated in the doorway, almost hidden in the shadow, was the figure of a man. He must have been asleep, for he did not become aware of my presence until I was within a foot of him. Then he sprang to his feet and was about to give the alarm. Before he could do so, however, I was upon him. A desperate hand-to-hand struggle followed, in which I fought solely for his throat. This once obtained, I tightened my fingers upon it and squeezed until he fell back unconscious. It was like a horrible nightmare, that combat without noise in the dark entry of the hut, and I was more than thankful that it ended so satisfactorily for me. As soon as I had disentangled myself, I rose to my feet and proceeded across his body into the hut itself. A swing door led from the porch, and this I pushed open.

'Who is it, and what do you want?' said a voice which I should have recognised everywhere.

In answer I took Phyllis in my arms and, whispering my name, kissed her over and over again. She uttered a little cry of astonishment and delight. Then, bidding her step quietly, I passed out into the starlight, leading her after me. As we were about to make for the path by which I had descended, Beckenham stepped forward, and at the same instant the man with whom I had been wrestling came to his senses and gave a shout of alarm. In an instant there was a noise of scurrying feet and a great shouting of orders.

'Make for the boats!' I cried at the top of my voice, and, taking Phyllis by the hand, set off as quickly as I could go up the path, Beckenham assisting her on the other side.

If I live to be a hundred I shall never forget that rush up the hill. In and out of trees and bushes, scratching ourselves and tearing our clothes, we dashed; conscious only of the necessity for speed. Before we were halfway down the other side Phyllis's strength was quite exhausted, so I took her in my arms and carried her the remainder of the distance. At last we reached the boats and jumped on board. The rest of the party were already there, and the word being given we prepared to row out to the yacht. But before we could push off a painful surprise was in store for us. The Marquis, who had been counting the party, cried: '*Where is Mr Wetherell?*'

We looked round upon each other, and surely enough the old gentleman was missing. Discovering this, Phyllis nearly gave way and implored us to go back at once to find him. But having rescued her with so much difficulty I did not wish to run any risk of letting her fall into her enemies' hands again; so selecting four volunteers from the party, I bade the rest pull the boat out to the yacht and give Miss Wetherell into the captain's charge, while the balance accompanied me ashore again in search of her father. Having done this the boat was to return and wait for us.

Quickly we splashed our way back to the beach, and then, plunging into the undergrowth, began our search for the missing man. As we did not know where to search, it was like looking for a needle in a bundle of hay, but presently one of the hands remembered having seen him descending the hill, so we devoted our attentions to that side. For nearly two hours we toiled up and down, but without success. Not a sign of the old gentleman was to be seen. Could he have mistaken his way and be even now searching for us on another beach? To make sure of this we set off and thoroughly searched the two bays in the direction he would most likely have taken. But still without success. Perhaps he had been captured and carried back to the huts? In that case we had better proceed thither and try to rescue him. This, however, was a much more serious undertaking, and you may imagine it was with considerable care that we approached the plateau again.

When we reached it the huts were as quiet as when I had first made their acquaintance. Not a sound came up to the top of the little precipice save the rustling of the wind in the palms at its foot. It seemed difficult to believe that there had been such a tumult on the spot so short a time before.

Again with infinite care we crept down to the buildings, this time, however, without encountering a soul. The first was empty, so was the second, and so was the third. This result was quite unexpected, and rendered the situation even more mysterious than before.

By the time we had thoroughly explored the plateau and its surroundings it was nearly daylight, and still we had discovered no trace of the missing man. Just as the sun rose above the sea line we descended the hill again and commenced a second search along the beach, with no better luck, however, than on the previous occasion. Wetherell and our assailants seemed to have completely disappeared from the island.

About six o'clock, thoroughly worn out, we returned to the spot where the boat was waiting for us. What was to be done? We could not for obvious reasons leave the island and abandon the old gentleman to his fate, and yet it seemed useless to remain there looking for him, when he might have been spirited away elsewhere.

Suddenly one of the crew, who had been loitering behind, came into view waving something in his hand. As he approached we could see that it was a sheet of paper, and when he gave it into my hands I read as follows

If you cross the island to the north beach you will find a small cliff in which is a large cave, a little above high-water mark. There you will discover the man for whom you are searching.

There was no signature to this epistle, and the writing was quite unfamiliar to me, but I had no reason to doubt its authenticity.

'Where did you discover this?' I enquired of the man who had brought it.

'Fastened to one of them prickly bushes up on the beach there, sir,' he answered.

'Well, the only thing for us to do now is to set off to the north shore and hunt for the cave. Two of you had better take the boat back to the yacht and ask the captain to follow us round.'

As soon as the boat was under weigh we picked up our rifles and set off for the north beach. It was swelteringly hot by this time, and, as may be imagined, we were all dead tired after our long night's work. However, the men knew they would be amply rewarded if we could effect the rescue of the man for whom we had been searching, so they pushed on.

At last we turned the cape and entered the bay which constituted the north end of the island. It was not a large beach on this side, but it had, at its western end, a curious line of small cliffs, in the centre of which a small black spot could be discerned looking remarkably like the entrance to a cave. Towards this we pressed, forgetting our weariness in the excitement of the search.

It *was* a cave, and a large one. So far the letter was correct. Preparing ourselves, in case of surprise, we approached the entrance, calling Mr Wetherell's name. As our shouts died away a voice came out in answer, and thereupon we rushed in.

A remarkable sight met our eyes. In the centre of the cave was a stout upright post, some six or eight feet in height, and securely tied to this was the Colonial Secretary of New South Wales.

In less time almost than it takes to tell, we had cast loose the ropes which bound him, and led him, for he was too weak to stand alone, out into the open air. While he was resting he enquired after his daughter, and having learned that she was safe, gave us the following explanation. Addressing himself to me, he said: 'When you cried "Make for the boats", I ran up the hill with the others as fast as I could go; but I'm an old man and could not get along as quickly as I wanted to, and for this reason was soon left far behind. I must have been half-way down the hill when a tall man, dressed in white, stepped out from behind a bush, and raising a rifle bade me come to a standstill. Having no time to lift my own weapon I was obliged to do as he ordered me, and he thereupon told me to lay down my weapon and right-about face. In this fashion I was marched back to the huts we had just left, and then, another man having joined my captor, was conducted across the island to this beach, where a boat was in waiting. In it I was pulled out to a small schooner lying at anchor in the bay and ordered to board her; five minutes later I was conducted to the saloon, where two or three persons were collected.

' "Good-evening, Mr Wetherell. This is indeed a pleasure," said a man sitting at the further end of the table. He was playing with a big black cat, and directly I heard his voice I knew that I was in the presence of Dr Nikola.

' "And how do you think I am going to punish you, my friend, for giving me all this trouble?" he said when I made no reply to his first remark.

' "You dare not do anything to me," I answered. "I demand that you let me go this instant. I have a big score to settle with you."

' "If you will be warned by me you will cease to demand," he answered, his eyes the while burning like coals. "You are an obstinate man, but though you have put me to so much trouble and expense I will forgive you and come to terms with you. Now listen to me. If you will give me – "

'At that moment the little vessel gave a heavy roll, and in trying to keep my footing on the sloping deck I fell over upon the table. As I did so the little Chinese stick slipped out of my pocket and went rolling along directly into Nikola's hands. He sprang forward and seized it, and you may imagine his delight. With a cry of triumph that made the cat leap from his shoulder, he turned to a tall man by his side and said: "I've got it at last! Now let a boat's crew take this man ashore and tie him to the stake in the cave. Then devise some means of acquainting his friends of his whereabouts. Be quick, for we sail in an hour."

'Having given these orders he turned to me again and said: "Mr Wetherell, this is the last transaction we shall probably ever have together. All things considered, you are lucky in escaping so easily. It would have saved you a good deal if you had complied with my request at first. However, all's well that ends well, and I congratulate you upon your charming daughter. Now, goodbye; in an hour I am off to effect a *coup* with this stick, the magnitude of which you would never dream. One last word of advice: pause a second time, I entreat, before you think of baulking Dr Nikola."

'I was going to reply, when I was twisted round and led up on deck, where that scoundrel Baxter had the impudence to make me a low bow. In less than a quarter of an hour I was fastened to the post in that cave. The rest you know. Now let us get on board; I see the boat is approaching.'

As soon as the surf-boat had drawn up on the beach we embarked and were pulled out to the yacht. In a few moments we were on deck, and Phyllis was in her father's arms again. Over that meeting, with its rapturous embraces and general congratulations, I must draw a curtain. Suffice it that by midday the island had disappeared under the sea line, and by nightfall we were well on our way back to Sydney. That evening, after dinner, Phyllis and I patrolled the deck together, and finally came to a standstill aft. It was as beautiful an evening as any man or woman could desire. All round us was the glassy sea, rising and falling as if asleep, while overhead the tropic stars shone down with their wonderful brilliance.

'Phyllis,' I said, taking my darling's hand in mine and looking into her face, 'what a series of adventures we have both passed through since that afternoon I first saw you in the Domain! Do you know that your father has at last consented to our marriage?'

'I do. And as it is to you, Dick, I owe my rescue,' she said, coming a little closer to me, 'he could do nothing else; you have a perfect right to me.'

'I have, and I mean to assert it!' I answered. 'If I had not found you, I should never have been happy again.'

'But, Dick, there is one thing I don't at all understand. At dinner this evening the captain addressed you as Sir Richard. What does that mean?'

'Why, of course you have not heard!' I cried. 'Well, I think it means that though I cannot make you a marchioness, I can make you a baronet's wife. It remains with you to say whether you will be Lady Hatteras or not.'

'But are you a baronet, Dick? How did that come about?'

'It's a long story, but do you remember my describing to you the strange call I paid, when in England, on my only two relatives in the world?'

'The old man and his daughter in the New Forest? Yes, I re-member.'

'Well, they are both dead, and, as the next-of-kin, I have inherited the title and estates. What do you think of that?'

Her only reply was to kiss me softly on the cheek.

She had scarcely done so before her father and Beckenham came along the deck.

'Now, Phyllis,' said the former, leading her to a seat, 'supposing you give us the history of your adventures. Remember we have heard nothing yet.'

'Very well. Where shall I begin? At the moment I left the house for the ball? Very good. Well, you must know that when I arrived at Government House I met Mrs Mayford – the lady who had promised to chaperone me – in the cloakroom, and we passed into the ballroom together. I danced the first dance with Captain Hackworth, one of the *aides*, and engaged myself for the fourth to the Marquis of Beckenham.'

'The sham Marquis, unfortunately,' put in the real one.

'It proved to be unfortunate for me also,' continued Phyllis. 'As it was a square we sat it out in the ante-room leading off the drawing-room, and while we were there the young gentleman did me the honour of proposing to me. It was terribly embarrassing for me, but I allowed him to see, as unmistakably as possible, that I could give him no encouragement, and, as the introduction to the next waltz started, we parted the best of friends. About half an hour later, just as I was going to dance the lancers, Mrs Mayford came towards me and drew me into the drawing-room. Mr Baxter, his lordship's tutor, was with her, and I noticed that they both looked supernaturally grave.

' "What is the matter?" I asked, becoming alarmed by her face.

' "My dear," said she, "you must be brave. I have come to tell you that your father has been taken ill, and has sent for you."

' "Papa ill!" I cried. "Oh, I must go home to him at once."

' "I have taken the liberty of facilitating that," said Mr Baxter, "by ordering the servants to call up your carriage, which is now waiting for you at the door. If you will allow me, I will conduct you to it?"

'I apologised to my partner for being compelled to leave him, and then went to the cloakroom. As soon as I was ready I accompanied Mr Baxter to the door, where the brougham was waiting. Without looking at the coachman I got in, at the same time thanking my escort for his kindness. He shut the door and cried "Home" to the coachman. Next moment we were spinning down the drive.

'As I was far too much occupied thinking of you, papa, I did not notice the direction we were taking, and it was not until the carriage stopped before a house in a back street that I realised that something was wrong. Then the door was opened and a gentleman in evening dress begged me to alight. I did so, almost without thinking what I was doing.

' "I am sorry to say your father is not at all well, Miss Wetherell," said the person who helped me out. "If you will be good enough to step into my house I will let the nurse take you to him."

'Like a person in a dream I followed him into the dwelling, and, as soon as I was inside, the door was shut upon me.

' "Where is my father? And how is it that he is here?" I cried, beginning to get frightened.

' "You will know all when you see him," said my companion, throwing open the door of a bedroom. I went in, and that door was also shut upon me. Then I turned and faced the man.'

'What was he like?' cried Wetherell.

'He was the man you were telling us about at dinner – Dr Nikola.'

'Ah! And then?'

'He politely but firmly informed me that I was his prisoner, and that until you gave up something he had for years been trying to obtain he would be compelled to detain me. I threatened, entreated, and finally wept, but he was not to be moved. He promised that no effort should be spared to make me comfortable, but he could not let me go until you had complied with his request. So I was kept there until late one night, when I was informed that I must be ready to leave the house. A brougham was at the door, and in this, securely guarded, I was conducted to the harbour, where a boat was in waiting. In this we were rowed out to a schooner, and I was placed on board her. A comfortably furnished cabin was allotted to me, and everything I could possibly want was given me. But though the greatest consideration in all other matters was shown me I could gather nothing of where we were going or what my fate was to be, nor could I discover any means of communicating with the shore. About midnight we got under weigh and commenced our voyage. Our destination was the island where you found me.'

'And how did Nikola treat you during the voyage and your stay on Pipa Lannu?' I asked.

'With invariable courtesy,' she replied. 'A more admirable host no one could desire. I had but to express a wish and it was instantly gratified. When we were clear of the land I was allowed on deck; my meals were served to me in a cabin adjoining my own, and a stewardess had been specially engaged to wait upon me. As far as my own personal treatment went I have nothing to complain of. But oh, you can't tell how thankful I was to get away; I had begun to imagine all sorts of horrors.'

'Well, God be thanked, it's all done with now,' I said earnestly.

'And what is more,' said Wetherell, 'you have won one of the best husbands in the world. Mr Hatteras, your hand, sir; Phyllis, my darling, yours! God bless you both.'

Now what more is there to tell? A week later the eventful voyage was over and we were back in Sydney again.

Then came our marriage. But, with your kind permission, I will only give you a very bare description of that. It took place at the cathedral, the Primate officiating. The Marquis of Beckenham was kind enough to act as my best man, while the Colonial Secretary, of course, gave his daughter away.

But now I come to think of it, there is one point I must touch upon in connection with that happy occasion, and that was the arrival of an important present on the evening prior to the event.

We were sitting in the drawing-room when the butler brought in a square parcel on a salver and handed it to Phyllis.

'Another present, I expect,' she said, and began to untie the string that bound it.

When the first cover was removed a layer of tissue paper revealed itself, and after that a large Russia leather case came into view. On pressing the spring the cover lifted and revealed a superb *collet* – as I believe it is called – of diamonds, and resting against the lid a small card bearing this inscription:

> *With heartiest congratulations and best wishes to Lady Hatteras, in memory of an unfortunate detention and a voyage to the Southern Seas.*
> *From her sincere admirer,*
>   DR NIKOLA

What do you think of that?

Well, to bring my long story to a close, the Great Event passed off with much *éclat*. We spent our honeymoon in the Blue Mountains, and a fortnight later sailed once more for England in the *Orizaba*. Both Mr Wetherell – who has now resigned office – and the Marquis of Beckenham, who is as manly a fellow as you would meet anywhere in England, accompanied us home, and it was to the latter's seaside residence that we went immediately on our arrival in the mother country. My own New Forest residence is being thoroughly renovated, and will be ready for occupation in the spring.

And now as to the other persons who have figured most prominently in my narrative. Of Nikola, Baxter, Eastover, or Prendergast I have never heard since. What gigantic coup the first-named intends to accomplish with the little Chinese stick, the possession of which proved so fatal to Wetherell, is beyond my power to tell. I am only too thankful, however, that I am able to say that I am not in the least concerned in it. I am afraid of Nikola and I confess it. And with this honest expression of my feelings, and my thanks for your attention and forbearance, I will beg your permission to ring the curtain down upon the narrative of my BID FOR FORTUNE.

THE END

DOCTOR NIKOLA

INTRODUCTION

My dear William George Craigie –

I have no doubt as to your surprise at receiving this letter, after so long and unjustifiable a period of silence, from one whom you must have come to consider either a dead man or at least a permanent refugee. When last we met it was on the deck of Tremorden's yacht, in the harbour of Honolulu. I had been down to Kauai, I remember, and the day following, you, you lucky dog, were going off to England by the Royal Mail to be married to the girl of your heart. Since then I have heard, quite by chance, that you have settled down to a country life, as if to the manner born; that you take an absorbing interest in mangel-wurzels, and, while you strike terror into the hearts of poachers and other rustic evil-doers, have the reputation of making your wife the very best of husbands. Consequently you are to be envied and considered one of the happiest of men.

While, however, things have been behaving thus prosperously with you, I am afraid I cannot truthfully say that they have fared so well with me. At the termination of our pleasant South Sea cruise, just referred to, when our party dismembered itself in the Sandwich Islands, I crossed to Sydney, passed up inside the Barrier Reef to Cooktown, where I remained three months in order to try my luck upon the Palmer Gold Fields. This proving unsatisfactory I returned to the coast and continued my journey north to Thursday Island. From the last-named little spot I visited New Guinea, gave it my patronage for the better part of six months, and received in return a bad attack of fever, after recovering from which I migrated to Borneo, to bring up finally, as you will suppose, in my beloved China.

Do you remember how in the old days, when we both held positions of more or less importance in Hong-Kong, you used to rally me about my fondness for the Celestial character and my absurd liking for going *fantee* into the queerest company and places? How little did I imagine then to what straits that craze would ultimately conduct me! But we never know what the future has in store for us, do we? And perhaps it is as well.

You will observe, my dear Craigie, that it is the record of my visit to China on this particular occasion that constitutes this book; and you must also understand that it is because of our long friendship for each other, and by reason of our queer researches into the occult world together, that you find your name placed so conspicuously upon the forefront of it.

A word now as to my present existence and abode. My location I cannot reveal even to you. And believe me I make this reservation for the strongest reasons. Suffice it that I own a farm, of close upon five thousand acres, in a country such as would gladden your heart, if matrimony and continued well-being have not spoilt your eyes for richness of soil. It is shut in on all sides by precipitous mountain ranges, on the western peaks of which at this moment, as I sit in my verandah writing to you, a quantity of cloud, tinted a rose pink by the setting sun, is gathering. A quieter spot, and one more remote from the rush and bustle of civilisation, it would be difficult to find. Once every six months my stores are brought up to me on mule-back by a trusted retainer who has never spoken a word of English in his life, and once every six weeks I send to, and receive from, my post office, four hundred miles distant, my mails. In the intervals I imitate the patriarchal life and character; that is to say, I hoe and reap my corn, live in harmony with my neighbour, who is two hundred odd miles away, and, figuratively speaking, enjoy life beneath my own vine and fig-tree.

Perhaps when the cool west wind blows in the long grass, the wild duck whistle upon the lagoons, or a newspaper filled with gossip of the outer world finds its way in to me, I am a little restless, but at other times I can safely say I have few regrets. I have done with the world, and to make my exile easier I have been permitted that greatest of all blessings, a good wife. Who she is and how I won her you will discover when you have perused this narrative, the compiling of which has been my principal and, I might almost say, only recreation all through our more than tedious winter. But now the snow has departed, spring is upon us, clad in its mantle of luscious grass and accompanied by the twitterings of birds and the music of innumerable small waterfalls, and I am a new man. All nature is busy, the swallows are working overtime beneath the eaves, and tomorrow, in proof of my remembrance, this book goes off to you.

Whether I shall ever again see Dr Nikola, the principal character in it, is more than I can tell you. But I sincerely trust not. It is for the sake of circumstances brought about by that extraordinary man that I have doomed myself to perpetual exile; still I have no desire that he should know of my sacrifice. Sometimes when I lie awake in the quiet watches of the night I can hardly believe that the events of the last two years are real. The horror of that time still presses heavily upon me, and if I live to be a hundred I doubt if I shall outgrow it. When I tell you that even the things, I mean the mysteries and weird experiences, into which we thrust our impertinent noses in bygone days were absolutely as nothing compared with those I have passed through since in Nikola's company, you will at first feel inclined to believe that I am romancing. But I know this, that by the time you have got my curious story by heart all doubt on that score will have been swept away.

One last entreaty. Having read this book, do not attempt to find me, or to set my position right with the world. Take my word for it, it is better as it is.

And now, without further preamble, let us come to the story itself. God bless you, and give you every happiness. Speak kindly of me to your wife, and believe me until death finishes my career, if it does such a thing, which Dr Nikola would have me doubt,

Your affectionate friend,
WILFRED BRUCE

CHAPTER ONE

How I came to meet Dr Nikola

It was Saturday afternoon, about a quarter-past four o'clock if my memory serves me, and the road, known as the Maloo, leading to the Bubbling Well, that single breathing place of Shanghai, was crowded. Fashionable barouches, C-spring buggies, spider-wheel dogcarts, to say nothing of every species of 'rickshaw, bicycle, and pony, were following each other in one long procession towards the Well. All the European portion of Shanghai, and a considerable percentage of the native, had turned out to witness the finish of the paper hunt, which, though not exciting in itself, was important as being the only amusement the settlement boasted that afternoon.

I had walked as far as the Horse Bazaar myself, and had taken a 'rickshaw thence, more from pride than because I could afford it. To tell the truth, which will pop out sooner or later, however much I may try to prevent it, I was keeping up appearances, and though I lay back in my vehicle and smoked my cheroot with a princely air, I was painfully conscious of the fact that when the ride should be paid for the exchequer would scarcely survive the shock.

Since my arrival in Shanghai I had been more than usually unfortunate. I had tried for every billet then vacant, from those choice pickings at the top of the tree among the high gods, to the secretary-ship of a Eurasian hub of communistical tendencies located somewhere on the confines of the native city, but always without success. For the one I had not the necessary influence, for the other I lacked that peculiar gift of obsequiousness which is so essential to prosperity in that particular line of business.

In the meantime my expenditure was going remorselessly on, and I very soon saw that unless something happened, and that quickly too, I had every prospect of finding myself deprived of my belongings, sleeping on the Bund, and finally figuring in that Mixed Court in the Magistrate's Yamen, which is so justly dreaded by every Englishman, as the debtor of a Cochin China Jew. The position was not a cheerful one, look at it in whatever light I would, but I had experienced it a good many times before, and had always come out of it, if not with an increased amount of self-respect, certainly without any very great degree of personal embarrassment.

Arriving at the Well, I paid off my coolie and took up a position near 'the last jump', which I noticed was a prepared fence and ditch of considerable awkwardness. I was only just in time, for a moment later the horses came at it with a rush; some cleared it, some refused it, while others, adopting a middle course, jumped on the top of it, blundered over, and finally sent their riders spinning over their heads into the mud at the feet of their fairest friends. It was not exactly an aesthetic picture, but it was certainly a very amusing one.

When the last horse had landed, imagining the sport to be over for the day, I was in the act of moving away when there was a shout to stand clear, and wheeling round again, I was just in time to see a last horseman come dashing at the fence. Though he rode with consid- erable determination, and was evidently bent on putting a good finish to his day's amusement, it was plain that his horse was not of the same way of thinking, for, when he was distant about half a dozen yards from the fence, he broke his stride, stuck his feet into the mud, and endeavoured to come to a standstill. The result was not at all what he expected; he slid towards the fence, received his rider's *quirt*, viciously administered, round his flank, made up his mind to jump too late, hit the top rail with his forehead, turned a complete somer- sault, and landed with a crash at my feet. His rider fell into the arms of the ditch, out of which I presently dragged him. When I got him on the bank he did not look a pretty sight, but, on the other hand, that did not prevent him from recognising me.

'Wilfred Bruce, by all that's glorious!' he cried, at the same time rising to his feet and mopping his streaming face with a very muddy pocket-handkerchief. 'This is a fortunate encounter, for do you know, I spent two hours this morning looking for you?'

'I am very sorry you should have had so much trouble,' I answered; 'but are you sure you are not hurt?'

'Not in the least,' he answered, and when he had scraped off as much mud as possible, turned to his horse, which had struggled to his feet and was gazing stupidly about him.

'Let me first send this clumsy brute home,' he said, 'then I'll find my cart, and if you'll permit me I'll take you back to town with me.'

We saw the horse led away, and, when we had discovered his dog- cart among the crowd of vehicles waiting for their owners, mounted to our seats and set off – after a few preliminary antics on the part of the leader – on our return to the settlement.

Once comfortably on our way George Barkston, whom, I might mention here, I had known for more than ten years, placed his whip in the bucket and turned to me.

'Look here, Bruce,' he said, flushing a little in anticipation of what he was about to say, 'I'm not going to mince matters with you, so let us come straight to the point; we are old friends, and though we've not seen as much of each other during this visit to Shanghai as we used to do in the old days when you were deputy-commissioner of whatever it was, and I was your graceless subordinate, I think I am pretty well conversant with your present condition. I don't want you to consider me impertinent, but I *do* want you to let me help you if I can.'

'That's very good of you,' I answered, not without a little tremor, however, as he shaved a well-built American buggy by a hair's breadth. 'To tell the honest truth, I want to get something to do pretty badly. There's a serious deficit in the exchequer, my boy. And though I'm a fairly old hand at the game of poverty, I've still a sort of pride left, and I have no desire to figure in the Mixed Court next Wednesday on a charge of inability to pay my landlord twenty dollars for board and lodging.'

'Of course you don't,' said Barkston warmly; 'and so, if you'll let me help you, I've an idea that I can put you on to the right track to something. The fact is, there was a chap in the smoking-room at the club the other night with whom I got into conversation. He interested me more than I can tell you, for he was one of the most curious beings who, I should imagine, has ever visited the East. I never saw such an odd-looking fellow in my life. Talk about eyes – well, his were – augh! Why, he looked you through and through. You know old Benwell, of the revenue-cutter *Y-chang*? Well, while I was talking to this fellow, after a game of pool, in he came.

' "Hallo! Barkston," he said, as he brought up alongside the table, "I thought you were shooting with Jimmy Woodrough up the river? I'm glad to find you're not, for I – " He had got as far as this before he became aware of my companion. Then his jaw dropped; he looked hard at him, said something under his breath, and, shaking me by the hand, made a feeble excuse, and fled the room. Not being able to make it out at all, I went after him and found him looking for his hat in the hall. "Come, I say, Benwell," I cried; "what's up? What on earth made you bolt like that? Have I offended you?" He led me on one side, so that the servants should not hear, and having done so said confidentially: "Barkston, I am not a coward; in my time I've tackled Europeans, Zulus, Somalis, Malays, Japanese, and Chinese, to say nothing of Manilla and Solomon boys, and what's more, I don't mind facing them all again; but when I find myself face to face with Dr Nikola, well, I tell you I don't think twice, I bolt! Take my tip and do the same." As he might just as well have talked to me in low Dutch for all I should have understood, I tried to question him, but I might have spared myself the trouble, for I could get nothing satisfactory out of him. He simply shook me by the hand, told the boy in the hall to call him a 'rickshaw, and as soon as it drew up at the steps jumped into it and departed. When I got back to the billiard-room Nikola was still there, practising losing hazards of extraordinary difficulty.

' "I've an opinion I've seen your friend before," he said, as I sat down to watch him. "He is Benwell of the *Y-chang*, and if I mistake not Benwell of the *Y-chang* remembers me."

' "He seems to know you," I said with a laugh.

' "Yes," Nikola continued after a little pause; "I have had the pleasure of being in Mr Benwell's company once before. It was in Haiphong." Then with peculiar emphasis: "I don't know what he thinks of the place, of course, but somehow I have an idea your friend will not willingly go near Haiphong again." After he had said this he remained silent for a little while, then he took a letter from his pocket, read it carefully, examined the envelope, and having made up his mind on a certain point turned to me again.

' "I want to ask you a question," he said, putting the cue he had been using back into the rack. "You know a person named Bruce, don't you? a man who used to be in the Civil Service, and who has the reputation of being able to disguise himself so like a Chinaman that even Li Chang Tung would not know him for a European?"

' "I do," I answered; "he is an old friend of mine; and what is more, he is in Shanghai at the present moment. It was only this morning I heard of him."

' "Bring him to me," said Nikola quickly. "I am told he wants a billet, and if he sees me before twelve tomorrow night I think I can put him in the way of obtaining a good one." Now there you are, Bruce, my boy. I have done my best for you.'

'And I am sincerely grateful to you,' I answered. 'But who is this man Nikola, and what sort of a billet do you think he can find me?'

'Who he is I can no more tell you than I can fly. But if he is not the first cousin of the Old Gentleman himself, well, all I can say is, I'm no hand at finding relationships.'

'I am afraid that doesn't tell me very much,' I answered. 'What's he like to look at?'

'Well, in appearance he might be described as tall, though you must not run away with the idea that he's what you would call a big man. On the contrary, he is most slenderly built. Anything like the symmetry of his figure, however, I don't remember to have met with before. His face is clean shaven, and is always deadly pale, a sort of toad-skin pallor, that strikes you directly when you see him and the remembrance of which never leaves you again. His eyes and hair are as black as night, and he is as neat and natty as a new pin. When he is watching you he seems to be looking through the back of your head into the wall behind, and when he speaks you've just got to pay attention, whether you want to or not. All things considered, the less I see of him the better I shall like him.'

'You don't give me a very encouraging report of my new employer. What on earth can he want with me?'

'He's Apollyon himself,' laughed Barkston, 'and wants a *maître d'hotel*. I suppose he imagines you'll suit.'

By this time we had left the Maloo and were entering the town.

'Where shall I find this extraordinary man?' I asked, as we drew near the place where I intended to alight.

'We'll drive to the club and see if he's there,' said Barkston, whipping up his horses. 'But, putting all joking aside, he really seemed most anxious to find you, and as he knew I was going to look for you I don't doubt that he will have left some message for one of us there.'

Having reached the Wanderers' Club, which is too well known to need any description here, Barkston went inside, leaving me to look after the horses. Five minutes later he emerged again, carrying a letter in his hand.

'Nikola was here until ten minutes ago,' he said, with a disappointed expression upon his handsome face; 'unfortunately he's gone home now, but has left this note for me. If I find you he begs that I will send you on to his bungalow without delay. I have discovered that it is Fere's old place in the French Concession, Rue de la Fayette; you know it, the third house on the right hand side, just past where that renegade French marquis shot his wife. If you would care about it I'll give you a note to him, and you can dine, think it over quietly, and then take it on yourself this evening or not, as pleases you best.'

'That would be the better plan,' I said. 'I should like to have a little time to collect my thoughts before seeing him.'

Thereupon Barkston went back into the building, and when he returned, which was in something under a quarter of an hour, he brought the letter he had promised me in his hand. He jumped up and took the reins, the Chinese groom sprang out of the way, and we were off.

'Can I drive you round to where you are staying?' he asked.

'I don't think you can,' I answered, 'and for reasons which would be sure to commend themselves to you if I were to tell them. But I am very much obliged to you all the same. As to Nikola, I'll think the whole matter carefully out this evening, and, if I approve, after dinner I'll walk over and present this letter personally.'

I thereupon descended from the dogcart at the corner of the road, and having again thanked my friend for the kindness he had shown me, bade him goodbye and took myself off.

Reaching the Bund I sat myself down on a seat beneath a tree and dispassionately reviewed the situation. All things considered it was a pretty complicated one. Though I had not revealed as much to Barkston, who had derived such happiness from his position of guide, philosopher, and friend, this was not the first time I had heard of Nikola. Such a strange personality as his could not expect to go unremarked in a gossip-loving community such as the East, and all sorts of stories had accordingly been circulated concerning him. Though I knew my fellow-man too well to place credence in half of what I had heard, it was impossible for me to prevent myself from feeling a considerable amount of curiosity about the man.

Leaving the Bund I returned to my lodgings, had my tea, and about eight o'clock donned my hat again and set off in the direction of the French Concession. It was not a pleasant night, being unusually dark and inclined towards showery. The wind blew in fitful gusts, and drove the dust like hail against one's face. Though I stood a good chance of obtaining what I wanted so much – employment, I cannot affirm with any degree of truth that I felt easy in my mind. Was I not seeking to become connected with a man who was almost universally feared, and whose reputation was not such as would make most people desire a closer acquaintance with him? This thought in itself was not of a reassuring nature. But in the face of my poverty I could not afford to be too squeamish. So leaving the Rue de la Paix on my left hand I turned into the Rue de la Fayette, where Nikola's bungalow was situated, and having picked it out from its fellows, made my way towards it.

The compound and the house itself were in total darkness, but after I had twice knocked at the door a light came slowly down the passage towards me. The door was opened, and a China boy stood before me holding a candle in his hand.

'Does Dr Nikola live here?' I enquired, in very much the same tone as our boyhood's hero, Jack of Beanstalk climbing fame, might have used when he asked to be admitted to the residence of the giant Fee-fo-fum. The boy nodded, whereupon I handed him my letter, and ordered him to convey it to his master without delay. With such celerity did he accomplish his mission that in less than two minutes he had returned and was beckoning me to follow him. Accordingly I accompanied him down the passage towards a small room on the left hand side. When I had entered it the door was immediately closed behind me. There was no one in the apartment, and I was thus permitted an opportunity of examining it to my satisfaction, and drawing my own conclusions before Dr Nikola should enter.

As I have said, it was not large, nor was its furniture, with a few exceptions, in any way extraordinary. The greater part of it was of the usual bungalow type, neither better nor worse. On the left hand as one entered was a window, which I observed was heavily barred and shuttered; between that and the door stood a tall bookshelf, filled with works, standard and otherwise, on almost every conceivable subject, from the elementary principles of Bimetallism to abstract Confucianism. A thick matting covered the floor and a heavy curtain sheltered a doorway on the side opposite to that by which I had entered. On the walls were several fine engravings, but I noticed that they were all based on uncommon subjects, such as the visit of Saul to the Witch of Endor, a performance of the magicians before Pharaoh, and the converting of the dry bones into men in the desert. A clock ticked on the bookcase, but with that exception there was nothing to disturb the silence of the room.

I suppose I must have waited fully five minutes before my ears caught the sound of a soft footstep in an adjoining apartment, then the second door opened, the curtain which covered it was drawn slowly aside, and a man, who could have been none other than Dr Nikola, made his appearance. His description was exactly what Barkston had given me, even to the peculiar eyes and, what proved to be an apt illustration, the white toad-coloured skin. He was attired in faultless evening dress, and its deep black harmonised well with his dark eyes and hair. What his age might have been I could not possibly tell, but I afterwards discovered that he was barely thirty-eight. He crossed the room to where I stood, holding out his hand as he did so and saying – 'Mr Wilfred Bruce?'

'That is my name,' I answered, 'and I believe you are Dr Nikola?'

'Exactly,' he said, 'I am Dr Nikola; and now that we know each other, shall we proceed to business?'

As he spoke he moved with that peculiar grace which always characterised him across to the door by which he had entered, and having opened it, signed to me to pass through. I did so, and found myself in another large room, possibly forty feet long by twenty wide. At the further end was a lofty window, containing some good stained glass; the walls were hung with Japanese tapestry, and were ornamented with swords, battle-axes, two or three specimens of Rajput armour, books galore, and a quantity of exceedingly valuable china. The apartment was lit by three hanging lamps of rare workmanship and design, while scattered about the room were numberless cushioned chairs and divans, beside one of which I noticed a beautifully inlaid huqa of a certain shape and make that I had never before seen out of Istamboul.

'Pray sit down,' said Dr Nikola, and as he spoke he signed me to a chair at the further end. I seated myself and wondered what would come next.

'This is not your first visit to China, I am given to understand,' he continued, as he seated himself in a chair opposite mine, and regarded me steadfastly with his extraordinary eyes.

'It is not,' I answered. 'I am an old resident in the East, and I think I may say I know China as well as any living Englishman.'

'Quite so. You were present at the meeting at Quong Sha's house in the Wanhsien on the 23rd August, 1907, if I remember aright, and you assisted Mah Poo to evade capture by the mandarins the week following.'

'How on earth did you know that?' I asked, my surprise quite getting the better of me, for I had always been convinced that no other soul, save the man himself, was aware of my participation in that affair.

'One becomes aware of many strange things in the East,' said Nikola, hugging his knee and looking at me over the top of it, 'and yet that little circumstance I have just referred to is apt to teach one how much one might know, and how small after all our knowledge is of each other's lives. One could almost expect as much from brute beasts.'

'I am afraid I don't quite follow you,' I said simply.

'Don't you?' he answered. 'And yet it is very simple after all. Let me give you a practical illustration of my meaning. If you see anything in it other than I intend, the blame must be upon your own head.'

Upon a table close to his chair lay a large sheet of white paper. This he placed upon the floor. He then took a stick of charcoal in his hand and presently uttered a long and very peculiar whistle. Next moment, without any warning, an enormous cat, black as his master's coat, leapt down from somewhere on to the floor, and stood swishing his tail before us.

'There are some people in the world,' said Nikola calmly, at the same time stroking the great beast's soft back, 'who would endeavour to convince you that this cat is my familiar spirit, and that, with his assistance, I work all sorts of extraordinary magic. You, of course, would not be so silly as to believe such idle tales. But to bear out what I was saying just now let us try an experiment with his assistance. It is just possible I may be able to tell you something more of your life.'

Here he stooped and wrote a number of figures up to ten with the charcoal upon the paper, duplicating them in a line below. He then took the cat upon his knee, stroked it carefully, and finally whispered something in its ear. Instantly the brute sprang down, placed its right fore-paw on one of the numerals of the top row, while, whether by chance or magic I cannot say, it performed a similar action with its left on the row below.

'Twenty-four,' said Nikola, with one of his peculiar smiles.

Then taking the piece of charcoal once more in his hand, and turning the paper over, he wrote upon it the names of the different months of the year. Placing it on the floor he again said something to the cat, who this time stood upon June. The alphabet followed, and letter by letter the uncanny beast spelt out 'Apia'.

'On the 24th June,' said Nikola, 'of a year undetermined you were in Apia. Let us see if we can discover the year.'

Again he wrote the numerals up to ten, and immediately the cat, with fiendish precision, worked out 1895.

'Is that correct?' asked this extraordinary person when the brute had finished its performance.

It was quite correct, and I told him so.

'I'm glad of that. And now do you want to know any more?' he asked. 'If you wish it I might perhaps be able to tell you your business there.'

I did not want to know. And I can only ask you to believe that I had very good reasons for not doing so. Nikola laughed softly, and pressed the tips of his long white fingers together as he looked at me.

'Now tell me truthfully what you think of my cat?' said he.

'One might be excused if one endowed him with Satanic attributes,' I answered.

'And yet, though you think it so wonderful, it is only because I have subjected him to a curious form of education. There is a power latent in animals, and particularly in cats, which few of us suspect. And if animals have this power, how much more may men be expected to possess it. Do you know, Mr Bruce, I should be very interested to find out exactly how far you think the human intelligence can go; that is to say, how far you think it can penetrate into the regions of what is generally called the occult?'

'Again I must make the excuse,' I said, 'that I do not follow you.'

'Well, then, let me place it before you in a rather simpler form. If I may put it so bluntly, where should you be inclined to say this world begins and ends?'

'I should say,' I replied – this time without hesitation – 'that it begins with birth and ends with death.'

'And after death?'

'Well, what happens then is a question of theology, and one for the parsons to decide.'

'You have no individual opinion?'

'I have the remnants of what I learned as a boy.'

'I see; in that case you believe that as soon as the breath has forsaken this mortal body a certain indescribable part of us, which for the sake of argument we will denominate soul, leaves this mundane sphere and enters upon a new existence in one or other of two places?'

'That is certainly what I was taught,' I answered.

'Quite so; that was the teaching you received in the parish of High Walcombe, Somersetshire, and might be taken as a very good type of what your class thinks throughout the world, from the Archbishop of Canterbury down to the farm labourer's child who walks three miles every seventh day to attend Sunday school. But in that self-same village, if I remember rightly, there was a little man of portly build whose adherents numbered precisely forty-five souls; he was called Father O'Rorke, and I have not the slightest doubt, if you had asked him, he would have given you quite a different account of what becomes of that soul, or essence, if we may so call it, after it has left this mortal body. Tobias Smallcombe, who preaches in a spasmodic,

windy way on the green to a congregation made up of a few enthus-
iasts, a dozen small boys, and a handful of donkeys and goats, will
give you yet another, and so on through numberless varieties of
creeds to the end of the chapter. Each will claim the privilege of
being right, and each will want you to believe exactly as he does. But
at the same time we must remember, provided we would be quite
fair, that there are not wanting scientists, admittedly the cleverest
men of the day, who assert that, while all our friends are agreed that
there is a life after death – a spirit world, in fact – they are all wrong.
If you will allow me to give you my own idea of what you think, I
should say that your opinion is, that when you've done with the solid
flesh that makes up Wilfred Bruce it doesn't much matter what
happens. But let us suppose that Wilfred Bruce, or his mind, shall we
say? – that part of him at any rate which is anxious, which thinks and
which suffers – is destined to exist afterwards through endless aeons,
a prey to continual remorse for all misdeeds: how would he regard
death then?'

'But before you can expect an answer to that question it is necessary that you should prove that he does so continue to exist,' I said.

'That's exactly what I desire and intend to do,' said Nikola, 'and it
is to that end I have sought you out, and we are arguing in this
fashion now. Is your time very fully occupied at present?'

I smiled.

'I quite understand,' he said. 'Well, I have got a proposition to
make to you, if you will listen to me. Years ago and quite by chance,
when the subject we are now discussing, and in which I am more
interested than you can imagine, was first brought properly under
my notice, I fell into the company of a most extraordinary man. He
was originally an Oxford don, but for some reason he went wrong,
and was afterwards shot by Balmaceda at Santiago during the Chilean
war. Among other places, he had lived for many years in North-
Western China. He possessed one of the queerest personalities, but
he told me some wonderful things, and what was more to the point,
he backed them with proofs. You would probably have called them
clever conjuring tricks. So did I then, but I don't now. Nor do I think
will you when I have done with you. It was from that man and an old
Buddhist priest, with whom I spent some time in Ceylon, that I
learnt the tiny fact which put me on the trail of what I am now
following up. I have tracked it clue by clue, carefully and laboriously,
with varying success for eight long years, and at last I am in the
position to say that I believe I have my thumb upon the key-note. If I

can press it down and obtain the result I want, I can put myself in possession of information the magnitude of which the world – I mean the European world, of course – has not the slightest conception. I am a courageous man, but I will confess that the prospect of what I am about to attempt almost frightens me. It is neither more nor less than to penetrate, with the help of certain Chinese secret societies, into the most extraordinary seat of learning that you or any other men ever heard of, and when there to beg, borrow, or steal the marvellous secrets they possess. I cannot go alone, for a hundred reasons, therefore I must find a man to accompany me; that man must be one in a thousand, and he must also necessarily be a consummate Chinese scholar. He must be plucky beyond the average, he must be capable of disguising himself so that his nationality shall never for a moment be suspected, and he must go fully convinced in his own mind that he will never return. If he is prepared to undertake so much I am prepared to be generous. I will pay him £5,000 down before we start and £5,000 when we return, if return we do. What do you say to that?'

I didn't know what to say. The magnitude of the proposal, to leave the value of the honorarium out of the question, completely staggered me. I wanted money more than I had ever done in my life before, and this was a sum beyond even my wildest dreams; I also had no objection to adventure, but at the same time I must confess this seemed too foolhardy an undertaking altogether.

'What can I say?' I answered. 'It's such an extraordinary proposition.'

'So it is,' he said. 'But as I take it, we are both extraordinary men. Had you been one of life's rank and file I should not be discussing it with you now. I would think twice before I refused if I were you; Shanghai is such an unpleasant place to get into trouble in, and besides that, you know, next Wednesday will see the end of your money, even if you do sell your watch and chain, as you proposed to yourself tonight.'

He said this with such an air of innocence that for the moment it did not strike me to wonder how he had become acquainted with the state of my finances.

'Come,' he said, 'you had better say yes.'

'I should like a little more time to think it over,' I answered. 'I cannot pledge myself to so much without giving it thorough consideration. Even if it were not folly on my part it would scarcely be fair to you.'

'Very good then. Go home and think about it. Come and see me tomorrow night at this time and let me have your decision. In the meantime if I were you I would say nothing about our conversation to anyone.'

I assured him I would not, and then he rose, and I understood that our interview was at an end. I followed him into the hall, the black cat marching sedately at our heels. In the verandah he stopped and held out his hand, saying with an indescribable sweetness of tone – 'I hope, Mr Bruce, you will believe that I am most anxious for your companionship. I don't flatter you, I simply state the truth when I affirm that you are the only man in China whose co-operation I would ask. Now good-night. I hope you will come to me with a favourable answer tomorrow.'

As he spoke, and as if to emphasise his request, the black cat, which up to that time had been standing beside him, now came over and began to rub its head, accompanying its action with a soft, purring noise, against my leg.

'I will let you know without fail by this time tomorrow evening,' I said. 'Good-night.'

After I had bidden Dr Nikola good-night in the verandah of his house, I consulted my watch, and discovering that it was not yet eleven o'clock, set off for a long walk through the city in order to consider my position. There were many things to be reckoned for and against his offer. To begin with, as a point in its favour, I remembered the fact that I was alone in the world. My father and mother had been dead some years, and as I was their only child, I had neither brother nor sister dependent upon my exertions, or to mourn my loss if by ill-chance anything desperate should befall me. In the second place, I had been a traveller in strange lands from my youth up, and was therefore the more accustomed to hard living. This will be better understood when I say that I had run away from home at the age of fifteen to go to sea; had spent three years in the roughest life before the mast any man could dream of or desire; had got through another five, scarcely less savage, as an Australian bushman on the borders of the Great Desert; another two in a detachment of the Cape Mounted Police; I had also held a fair appointment in Hong-Kong, and had drifted in and out of many other employments, good, bad, and indifferent. I was thirty-five years of age, had never, with the exception of my attack of fever in New Guinea, known what it was to be really sick or sorry, and, if the information is of any use to the world, weighed thirteen stone, stood close upon six feet in my stockings, had grey eyes and dark-brown hair, and, if you will not deem me conceited for saying so, had the reputation of being passably good-looking.

My position at that moment, financially and otherwise, was certainly precarious in the extreme. It was true, if I looked long enough I might find something to do, but, on the other hand, it was equally probable that I should not, for, as I knew to my cost, there were dozens of men in Shanghai at that moment, also on the lookout for employment, who would snap up anything that offered at a moment's notice. Only that morning I had been assured by a well-known merchant, upon whom I had waited in the hope of obtaining a cashiership he had vacant in his office, that he could have filled it a hundred times over before my arrival. This being so, I told myself that I had no right to neglect any opportunity which might come in my way of bettering my position. I therefore resolved not to reject Nikola's offer without the most careful consideration. Unfortunately, a love of adventure formed an integral part of my constitution, and when a temptation such as the present offered, it was difficult for me to resist it. Indeed, this particular form of adventure appealed to me with a voice of more than usual strength. What was still more to the point, Nikola was such a born leader of men that the mysterious fascination of his manner seemed to compel me to give him my co-operation, whether I would or would not. That the enterprise was one involving the chance of death was its most unpleasant feature; but still, I told myself, I had to die some time or other, while if my luck held good, and I came out of it alive, £10,000 would render me independent for the rest of my existence. As the thought of this large sum came into my mind, the sinister form of my half-caste landlord rose before my mind's eye, and the memory of his ill-written and worse-spelled account, which I should certainly receive upon the morrow, chilled me like a cold douche. Yes, my mind was made up, I *would* go; and having come to this decision, I went home.

But when I woke next morning Prudence sat by my bedside. My dreams had not been good ones. I had seen myself poisoned in Chinese monasteries, dismembered by almond-eyed headsmen before city gates, and tortured in a thousand terrible ways and places. Though these nightmares were only the natural outcome of my anxiety, yet I could not disabuse my mind of the knowledge that every one was within the sphere of probability. Directly I should have changed into Celestial dress, stained my face and sewn on my pigtail, I would be a Chinaman pure and simple, amenable to Chinese laws and liable to Chinese penalties. Then there was another point to be considered. What sort of travelling companion would Nikola prove? Would I be able to trust him in moments of danger and difficulty? Would he stand by me as one comrade should by another? And if by any chance we should get into a scrape and there should be an opportunity of escape for one only, would Nikola, by virtue of being my employer, seize that chance and leave me to brave the upshot, whatever it might be? In that case my £5,000 in the Shanghai Bank and the £5,000 which was to be paid to me on my return would be a little less useful than a worn-out tobacco pouch. And this suggested to my mind another question: Was Nikola sufficiently rich to be able to pay £10,000 to a man to accompany him on such a harebrained errand? These were all matters of importance, and they were also questions that had to be satisfactorily answered before I could come to any real decision. Though Barkston had informed me that Nikola was so well known throughout the East, though Benwell, of the Chinese Revenue Service, had shown himself so frightened when he had met him face to face in the club, and though I myself had heard all sorts of queer stories about him in Saigon and the Manillas, they were none of them sufficiently definite to be any guarantee to me of his monetary stability. To set my mind at rest, I determined to make enquiries about Nikola from some unbiased person. But who was that person to be? I reviewed all my acquaintances in turn, but without pitching upon any who would be at all likely to be able to help me in my dilemma. Then, while I was dressing, I remembered a man, a merchant, owning one of the largest hongs along the Bund, who was supposed to know more about people in general, and queer folk in particular, than any man in China.

I ate my breakfast, such as it was, received my account from my landlord with the lordly air of one who has £10,000 reposing at his banker's, lit an excellent cigar in the verandah and then sauntered down town.

Arriving at the Bund, I walked along until I discovered my friend's office. It overlooked the river, and was as fine a building as any in Shanghai. In the main hall I had the good fortune to discover the merchant's chief *comprador*, who, having learned that his master was disengaged, conducted me forthwith to his presence.

Alexander McAndrew hailed from north of the Tweed – this fact the least observant would have noticed before he had been five minutes in his company. His father had been a night watchman at one of the Glasgow banks, and his own early youth was spent as a ragged, barefooted boy in the streets of that extraordinary city. Of his humble origin McAndrew, however, was prouder than any De la Zouch could have been of friendship with the Conqueror; indeed, he was wont, when he entertained friends at his princely bungalow in the English Concession, to recall and dwell with delight upon the sordid circumstances that brought about the happy chance which, one biting winter's morning, led him to seek fame and fortune in the East.

'Why, Mr Bruce,' he cried, rising from his chair and shaking me warmly by the hand, 'this is a most unexpected pleasure! How long have you been in Shanghai?'

'Longer than I care to remember,' I answered, taking the seat he offered me.

'And all that time you have never once been to see me. That's hardly fair treatment of an old friend, is it?'

'I must ask your pardon for my remissness,' I said, 'but somehow things have not gone well with me in Shanghai this time, and so I've not been to see anybody. You observe that I am candid with you.'

'I am sorry to hear that you are in trouble,' he said. 'I don't want to appear impertinent, but if I can be of any service to you I sincerely hope you will command me.'

'Thank you,' I answered. 'I have already determined to do so. Indeed, it is to consult you that I have taken the liberty of calling upon you now.'

'I am glad of that. Upon what subject do you want my advice?'

'Well, to begin with, let me tell you that I have been offered a billet which is to bring me in £10,000.'

'Why, I thought you said things were not prospering with you?' cried my friend. 'This doesn't look as if there is much wrong. What is the billet?'

'That, I am sorry to say, I am not at liberty to reveal to anyone.'

'Then in what way can I be of use to you?'

'First, I want to know if you can give me any information about my employer?'

'Tell me his name and I'll see what I can do,' the merchant answered, not without a show of pride. 'I think I know nine out of every ten men of any importance in the East.'

'Well,' I said, 'this man's name is Nikola.'

'Nikola!' he cried in complete astonishment, wheeling round to face me. 'What possible business can you have with Nikola that is to bring you in £10,000?'

'Business of the very utmost importance,' I answered, 'involving almost life and death. But it is evident you know him?'

In reply the old man leant over the table and sank his voice almost to a whisper.

'Bruce,' he said, 'I know more of that man than I dare tell you, and if you will take my advice you will back out while you have time. If you can't, why, be more than careful what arrangements you make with him.'

'You frighten me,' I said, more impressed by his earnestness than I cared to own. 'Is he not good for the money, then?'

'Oh, as for the money, I don't doubt that he could pay it a dozen times over if he wanted to,' the worthy merchant replied. 'In point of fact, between ourselves, he has the power to draw upon me up to the extent of £50,000.'

'He's a rich man, then?'

'Immensely!'

'But where on earth does his money come from?'

'Ah! that's a good deal more than I can tell you,' he replied. 'But wherever he gets it, take my advice and think twice before you put yourself into his power. Personally, and I can say it with truth, I don't fear many men, but I *do* fear Nikola, and that I'm not the only man in the world who does I will prove to you by this letter.'

As he spoke he opened a drawer in his writing-table and took out a couple of sheets of notepaper. Spreading them upon the table before him, he smoothed the page and began to read.

'This letter, you must understand,' he said, 'is from the late Colonial Secretary of New South Wales, the Hon. Sylvester Wetherell, a personal friend of mine. I will skip the commencement, which is mainly private, and come to the main issue. He says:

. . . Since I wrote to you in June last, from London, I have been passing through a time of terrible trouble. As I told you in a letter some years ago, I was brought, quite against my will, into dealings with a most peculiar person named Nikola. Some few years since I defended a man known as China Pete, in our Central Criminal Court, against a charge of murder, and, what was more, got him off. When he died, being unable to pay me, he made me a present of all he had to leave, a peculiar little stick, covered with carved Chinese characters, about which he told me a mad rigmarole, but which has since nearly proved my undoing. For some inscrutable reason this man Nikola wanted to obtain possession of this stick, and because I refused to let him have it has subjected me to such continuous persecution these few years past as to nearly drive me into a lunatic asylum. Every method that a man could possibly adopt or a demoniacal brain invent to compel me to surrender the curio he tried. You will gather something of what I mean when I tell you that my house was twice broken into by Chinese burglars, that I was garrotted within a hundred yards of my own front door, that my wife and daughter were intimidated by innumerable threatening letters, and that I was at length brought to such a pitch of nervousness that after my wife died I fled to England to escape him. Nikola followed me, drew into the plot he was weaving about me the Duke of Glenbarth, his son, the Marquis of Beckenham, Sir Richard Hatteras, who has since married my daughter, our late Governor, the Earl of Amberley, and at least a dozen other persons. Through his agency Beckenham and Hatteras were decoyed into a house in Port Said and locked up for three weeks, while a spurious nobleman was sent on in his lordship's place to Sydney to become acquainted with my daughter, and finally to solicit her hand in marriage. Fortunately, however, Sir Richard Hatteras and his friend managed to make their escape from custody in time to follow the scoundrels to Sydney, and to warn me of the plot that was hatching against me. The result was disastrous. Foiled in his endeavours to revenge himself upon me by marrying my daughter to an impostor, Nikola had the audacity to abduct my girl from a ball at Government House and to convey her on a yacht to an island in the South Pacific, whence a month later we rescued her. Whether we should have been permitted to do so if the stick referred to, which was demanded as ransom, had not fallen, quite by chance, into Nikola's possession, I cannot say. But the stick *did* become his property, and now we are free. Since then my daughter has married Sir Richard Hatteras, and at the present moment they are living on his estate in England. I expect you will be wondering why I have not prosecuted this man Nikola, but to tell you the honest truth, McAndrew, I have such a wholesome dread of him that since I have got my girl back, and have only lost the curio, which has always been a trouble to me, I am quite content to say no more about the matter. Besides, I must confess, he has worked with such devilish cunning that, trained in the law as I am, I cannot see that we should stand any chance of bringing him to book.

'Now, Bruce, that you have heard the letter, what do you think of Dr Nikola?'

'It puts rather a different complexion on affairs, doesn't it?' I said. 'But still, if Nikola will play fair by me, £10,000 is £10,000. I've been twenty years in this world trying to make money, and this is the sum total of my wealth.'

As I spoke I took out of my pocket all the money I had in the world, which comprised half a dozen coins, amounting in English to a total of 6s. 10d. I turned to the merchant.

'I don't know what you will think, but my own opinion is that Nikola's character will have to be a very outrageous one to outweigh 10,000 golden sovereigns.'

'I am afraid you are a little bit reckless, aren't you, Bruce?' said the cautious McAndrew. 'If you will take my advice I should say try for something else, and what is more, I'll help you to do so. There is a billet now open in my old friend Webster's office, the salary is a good one and the duties are light. When I saw him this morning it was still unfilled. Why not try for it? If you like I'll give you a letter of introduction to him, and will tell him at the same time that I shall consider it a personal favour if he will take you into his employ.'

'I'm sure I'm very much obliged to you,' I answered warmly. 'Yes, I think I will try for it before I give Nikola a reply. May I have the letter now?'

'With pleasure,' he said. 'I will write it at once.'

Thereupon he dipped his pen in the ink and composed the epistle. When it was written and I had taken it, I thanked him warmly for his kindness, and bade him goodbye.

Mr Webster's *hong* was at the far end of the Bund, and was another fine building. As soon as I had gained admittance I enquired for the merchant, and after a brief wait was conducted to his office. He proved to be Mr McAndrew's opposite in every way. He was tall, portly, and intensely solemn. He seldom laughed, and when he did his mirth was hard and cheerless like his own exterior. He read my letter carefully, and then said – 'I am exceedingly sorry, Mr Bruce, that you should have had all this trouble. I should have been only too glad for my friend McAndrew's sake to have taken you into my employ; unfortunately, however, the position in question was filled less than an hour ago.'

'I regret to hear that,' I said, with a little sigh of disappointment. 'I really am most unfortunate; this makes the thirteenth post I have tried for, as you see, unsuccessfully, since I arrived in Shanghai.'

'Your luck does not seem propitious,' was the reply. 'But if you would like to put your applications up to an even number I will place you in the way of another. I understand that the Red and Yellow Funnel Steamer Company have a vacancy in their office, and if you would care to come along with me at once I'll take you up and introduce you to the manager myself. In that case he will probably do all he can for you.'

I thanked him for his courtesy, and when he had donned his *topee* we accordingly set off for the office in question. But another disappointment was in store for me. As in Mr Webster's own case the vacant post had just been filled, and when we passed out of the manager's sanctum into the main office the newly-appointed clerk was already seated upon his high stool making entries in a ledger.

On leaving the building I bade my companion goodbye on the pavement, and then with a heavy heart returned to my abode. I had not been there ten minutes before my landlord entered the room, and without preface, and with the smallest modicum of civility, requested that I would make it convenient to discharge my account that very day. As I was quite unable to comply with his request, I was compelled to tell him so, and when he left the room there was a decidedly unpleasant coolness between us. For some considerable time after I was alone again, I sat wrapped in anxious thought. What was I to do? Every walk of life seemed closed against me; my very living was in jeopardy; and though, if I remained in Shanghai, I might hear of other billets, still I had no sort of guarantee that I should be any more successful in obtaining one of them than I had hitherto been. In the meantime I had to live, and what was more, to pay my bill. I could not go away and leave things to take care of themselves, for the reason that I had not the necessary capital for travelling, while if I remained and did not pay, I should find myself in the Mixed Court before many days were over.

Such being the desperate condition of my affairs, to accept Dr Nikola's offer was the only thing open to me. But I was not going to do so without driving a bargain. If he would deposit, as he said, £5,000 to my credit in the bank I should not only be saved, but I should then have a substantial guarantee of his solvency. If not, well, I had better bring matters to a climax at once. Leaving the house I returned to the Bund, and seating myself in a shady spot carefully reviewed the whole matter. By the time darkness fell my mind was made up – *I would go to Nikola*.

Exactly at eight o'clock I reached his house and rang the bell. In answer to my peal the native boy, the same who had admitted me on the previous occasion, opened the door and informed me that his master was at home and expecting me. Having entered I was conducted to the apartment in which I had waited for him on the preceding evening. Again for nearly five minutes I was left to myself and my own thoughts, then the door opened and Dr Nikola walked into the room.

'Good evening, Mr Bruce,' he said. 'You are very punctual, and that is not only a pleasant trait in your character, but it is also a good omen, I hope. Shall we go into the next room? We can talk better there.'

I followed him into the adjoining apartment, and at his invitation seated myself in the chair I had occupied on the previous night. We had not been there half a minute before the black cat made his appearance, and recognising me as an old friend rubbed his head against my leg.

'You see even the cat is anxious to conciliate you,' said Nikola, with a queer little smile. 'I don't suppose there are five other men in the world with whom he would be as friendly as that on so short an acquaintance. Now let me hear your decision. Will you come with me, or have you resolved to decline my offer?'

'Under certain conditions I have made up my mind to accompany you,' I said. 'But I think it only fair to tell you that those conditions are rather stringent.'

'Let me hear them,' said Nikola, with that gracious affability he could sometimes assume. 'Even if they are overpowering, I think it will go hard with me if I cannot effect some sort of a compromise with you.'

'Well, to begin with,' I answered, 'I shall require you to pay into a bank here the sum of £5,000. If you will do that, and will give me a bill at a year for the rest of the money, I'm your man, and you may count upon my doing everything in my power to serve you.'

'My dear fellow, is that all?' said Nikola quickly. 'I will make it £10,000 with pleasure to secure your co-operation. I had no idea it would be the money that would stop you. Excuse me one moment.'

He rose from his chair and went across to a table at the other end of the room. Having seated himself he wrote for two or three moments; then returning handed me a small slip of paper, which I discovered was a cheque for £10,000.

'There is your money,' he said. 'You can present it as soon as you like, and the bank will cash it on sight. I think that should satisfy you as to the genuineness of my motives. Now I suppose you are prepared to throw in your lot with me?'

'Wait one moment,' I said. 'That is not all. You have treated me very generously, and it is only fair that I should behave in a similar manner to you.'

'Thank you,' answered Nikola. 'What is it you have to say to me now?'

'Do you know a man named Wetherell?'

'Perfectly,' replied Nikola. 'He was Colonial Secretary of New South Wales until about six months ago. I have very good reasons for knowing him. I had the honour of abducting his daughter in Sydney, and I imprisoned his son-in-law in Port Said. Of course I know him. You see I am also candid with you.'

'Vastly. But pardon the expression, was it altogether a nice transaction?'

'It all depends upon what you consider a nice transaction,' he said. 'To you, for instance, who have your own notions of what is right and what is wrong, it might seem a little peculiar. I am in a different case, however. Whatever I do I consider right. What you might do, in nine cases out of ten, I should consider wrong. Wetherell might have saved himself all that trouble by selling me the stick which China Pete gave him, and about which he wrote to McAndrew, who read the letter to you this morning!'

'How do you know he did?'

'How do I know anything?' enquired Nikola, with an airy wave of his hand. 'He *did* read it, and if you will look at me fixedly for a moment I will tell you the exact purport of the rest of your conversation.'

'I don't know that it is necessary,' I replied.

'Nor do I,' said Nikola quietly, and then lit a cigarette. 'Are you satisfied with my explanation?'

'Was it an explanation?' I asked.

Nikola only answered with a smile, and lifted the cat on to his knee. He stroked its fur with his long white fingers, at the same time looking at me from under his half-closed eyelids.

'Do you know, I like you,' he said after a while. 'There's something so confoundedly matter-of-fact about you. You give me the impression every time you begin to speak that you are going to say something out of the common.'

'Thank you.'

'I was going to add that the rest of your sentence invariably shatters that impression.'

'You evidently have a very poor impression of my cleverness.'

'Not at all. I am the one who has to say the smart things; you will have to do them. It is an equal distribution of labour. Now, are we going together or are we not?'

'Yes, I will go with you,' I answered.

'I am delighted,' said Nikola, holding out his hand. 'Let us shake hands on it.'

We shook hands, and as we did so he looked me fairly in the face.

'Let me tell you once and for all,' he said, 'if you play fair by me I will stand by you, come what may; but if you shirk one atom of your responsibility – well, you will only have yourself to blame for what happens. That's a fair warning, isn't it?'

'Perfectly,' I answered. 'Now may I know something of the scheme itself, and when you propose to start?'

CHAPTER THREE
Nikola's scheme

'By all means,' said Dr Nikola, settling himself down comfortably in his chair and lighting a cigarette. 'As you have thrown in your lot with me it is only right I should give you the information you seek. I need not ask you to keep what I tell you to yourself. Your own common-sense will commend that course to you. It is also just possible you may think I overestimate the importance of my subject, but let me say this, if once it became known to certain folk in this town that I have obtained possession of that stick mentioned in Wetherell's letter, my life, even in Shanghai, would not be worth five minutes' purchase. Let me briefly review the circumstances of the case connected with this mysterious society. Remember I have gone into the matter most thoroughly. It is not the hobby of an hour, nor the amusement of an idle moment, but the object of research and the concentrated study of a lifetime. To obtain certain information of which I stood in need, I have tracked people all over the world. When I began my preparations for inducing Wetherell to relinquish possession of what I wanted, I had followed a man as far as Cuyaba, on the Bolivian frontier of Brazil. During the earlier part of his career this person had been a merchant buying gold-leaf in Western China, and in this capacity he chanced to hear a curious story connected with the doings of a certain sect, whose monastery is in the mountains on the way up to Thibet. It cost me six months' continuous travel and nearly a thousand pounds in hard cash to find that man, and when I did his story did not exceed a dozen sentences; in other words, I paid him fully £10 per word for a bit of information that you would not, in all probability, have given him tenpence for. But I knew its value. I followed another man as far as Monte Video for the description of an obscure Chinese village; another to the Gold Coast for the name of a certain Buddhist priest, and a Russian Jew as far as Nijni Novgorod for a symbol he wore upon his watch-chain, and of the value of which he had not the slightest conception.

The information I thus obtained personally I added to the store I had gathered by correspondence, and having accumulated it all I drafted a complete history of my researches up to that time. When that was done I think I may say without boasting that, with the exception of three men – who, by the way, are not at liberty to divulge anything, and who, I doubt very much, are even aware that a world exists at all beyond their own monastery walls – I know at least six times as much about the society in question as any man living. Now, having prefaced my remarks in this fashion, let me give you a complete summary of the case. As far as I can gather, in or about the year 288 B.C., in fact at the time that Devenipiatissa was planting the sacred Bo tree at Anuradhapura, in Ceylon, three priests, noted for their extreme piety, and for the extent of their scientific researches, migrated from what is now the island of Ceylon, across to the mainland of Asia. Having passed through the country at present called Burmah, and after innumerable vicissitudes and constant necessary changes of quarters, they brought up in the centre of the country we now call Thibet. Here two of the original trio died, while the remaining one and his new confrères built themselves a monastery, set to work to gather about them a number of peculiar devotees, and to continue their researches. Though the utmost secrecy was observed, within a few years the fame of their doings had spread itself abroad. That this was so we know, for we find constant mention made of them by numerous Chinese historians. One I will quote you.'

Dr Nikola rose from his chair and crossed the room to an old cabinet standing against the further wall. From this he took a large book, looking suspiciously like a scrap-album, in which were pasted innumerable cuttings and manuscripts. He brought it across to his chair and sat down again. Then, having turned the leaves and found what he wanted, he prepared to read.

'It may interest you to know,' he said, looking up at me before he began, 'that the paragraph I am about to read to you, which was translated from the original with the utmost care by myself, was written the same year and month that William the Conqueror landed in England. It runs as follows: "And of this vast sect, and of the peculiar powers with which they are invested, it is with some diffidence that I speak. It is affirmed by those credulous in such matters that their skill in healing is greater than that of all other living men, also that their power in witchcraft surpasses that of any others the world has known. It is said, moreover, that they possess the power of restoring the dead to life, and of prolonging beyond the ordinary span the days of man. But of these things I can only write to you as they have been told to me." '

Dr Nikola turned to another page.

'After skipping five hundred years,' he said, 'we find further mention made of them; this time the writer is Feng Lao Lan, a well-known Chinese historian who flourished about the year 1500. He describes them as making themselves a source of trouble to the kingdom in general. From being a collection of a few simple monks, installed in a lonely monastery in the centre of Thibet, they have now become one of the largest secret societies in the East, though the mystic powers supposed to be held by them are still limited to the three headmen, or principal brothers. Towards the end of the sixteenth century it is certain that they exercised such a formidable influence in political affairs as to warrant the Government in issuing orders for their extermination. Indeed, I am inclined to believe that the all-powerful Triad Society, with its motto, "Hoan Cheng Hok Beng", which, as you know, exercised such an enormous influence in China until quite recently, was only an offshoot of the society which I am so eager to explore. That the sect does possess the scientific and occult knowledge that has been attributed to it for over two thousand years I feel convinced, and if there is any power which can assist me in penetrating their secrets I intend to employ it. In our own and other countries which we are accustomed to call "civilised" it has long been the habit to ridicule any belief in what cannot be readily seen and understood by the least educated. To the average Englishman there is no occult world. But see what a contradictory creature he is when all is said and done. For if he be devout, he tells you that he firmly believes that when the body dies the soul goes to Heaven, which is equivalent to Olympus, Elysium, Arcadia, Garden of Hesperides, Valhalla, Walhalla, Paradise, or Nirvana, as the case may be. He has no notion, or rather, I think, he will not be able to give you any description, of what sort of place his Heaven is likely to be. He has all sorts of vague ideas about it, but though it is part of his religion to believe beyond question that there is such a place, it is all wrapped in shadow of more or less impenetrable depth. To sum it all up, he believes that while, in his opinion, such a thing as – shall we say Theosophy? – is arrant nonsense, and unworthy of a thought, the vital essence of man has a second and greater being after death. In other words, to put my meaning a little more plainly, it is pretty certain that if you were to laugh at him, as he laughs at the

Theosophist and Spiritualist, he would consider that he had very good grounds to consider his intelligence insulted. And yet he himself is simply a contradiction contradicted. You may wonder towards what all this rigmarole is leading. But if I were to describe to you the curious things I have myself seen in different parts of the East, and the extraordinary information I have collected first hand from others, I venture to think you would believe me either a wizard myself or an absurdly credulous person. I tell you, Bruce, I have witnessed things that would seem to upset every known law of nature. Though there was occasionally trickery in the performance I am convinced in the majority of cases the phenomena were genuine. And that brings us to another stumbling-block – the meaning of the expression "trickery". What I should probably call "trick" you would, in nine cases out of ten, consider blackest magic. But enough talking. Let me give you an illustration of my meaning.'

As he spoke he went across to a sideboard and from it he took an ordinary glass tumbler and a carafe of water, which he placed upon the table at his elbow. Then seating himself again in his chair he filled the glass to overflowing. I watched him carefully, wondering what was coming next.

'Examine the glass for yourself,' he said. 'You observe that it is quite full of water. I want you to be very sure of that.'

I examined the glass and discovered that it was so full that it would be impossible to move it without spilling some of its contents. Having done so I told him that I was convinced it was fully charged.

'Very well,' he said; 'in that case I will give you an example of what I might call "Mind *versus* Matter". That glass is quite full, as you have seen for yourself; now watch me.'

From a tray by his side he took a match, lit a wax candle, and when the flame had burnt up well, held it above the water so that one drop of wax might fall into the liquid.

'Now,' he said, 'I want you to watch that wax intently from where you are while I count twenty.'

I did as he ordered me, keeping my eyes firmly fixed upon the little globule floating on the surface of the water. Then as I looked, slowly, and to the accompaniment of Nikola's monotonous counting, the water sank lower and lower, until the tumbler was completely empty.

'Get up and look for yourself, but don't touch the glass,' said my host. 'Be perfectly sure, however, that it is empty, for I shall require your affidavit upon that point directly.'

I examined the glass most carefully, and stated that, to the best of my belief, there was not a drop of water in it.

'Very well,' said Nikola. 'Now be so good as to sit down and watch it once more.'

This time he counted backwards, and as he did so the water rose again in the glass until it was full to overflowing, and still the wax was floating on the surface.

For a moment we were both silent. Then Nikola poured the water back into the jug, and having done so handed the glass to me.

'Examine it carefully,' he said, 'or you may imagine it has been made by a London conjuring firm on purpose for the trick. Convince yourself of this, and when you have made sure give me your explanation of the mystery.'

I examined the glass with the most searching scrutiny, but no sign of any preparation or mechanism could I discover.

'I cannot understand it at all,' I said; 'and I'm sure I can give you no explanation.'

'And yet you are not thoroughly convinced in your mind that I have not performed a clever conjuring trick, such as you might see at Maskelyne and Devant's. Let me give you two more examples before I finish. Look me intently in the face until that clock on the mantelpiece, which is now standing at twenty-eight minutes past nine, shall strike the half-hour.'

I did as I was ordered, and anything like the concentrated intensify of his gaze I never remember to have experienced before. I have often heard men say that when persons gifted with the mesmeric power have looked at them (some women have this power too) they have felt as if they had no backs to their heads. In this case I can only say that I not only felt as if I had no back to my head, but as if I had no head at all.

The two minutes seemed like two hours, then the clock struck, and Nikola said: 'Pull up your left shirt cuff, and examine your arm.'

I did as he ordered me, and there in red spots I saw an exact reproduction of my own signature. As I looked at it it faded away again, until, in about half a minute from my first seeing it, it was quite gone.

'That is what I call a trick; in other words, it is neither more nor less than hypnotism. But you will wonder why I have put myself to so much trouble. In the first place the water did not go out of the glass, as you supposed, but remained exactly as when you first saw it. I simply willed that you should imagine it did go, and your imagination complied with the demand made upon it. In the last experiment you had a second proof of the first subject. Of course both are very easily explained, even by one who has dabbled in the occult as little as yourself. But though you call it hypnotism in this airy fashion, can you give me an explanation of what you mean by that ambiguous term?'

'Simply that your mind,' I answered, 'is stronger than mine, and for this reason is able to dominate it."

'That is the popular theory, I grant you,' he answered; 'but it is hardly a correct one, I fancy. Even if it were stronger, how could it be possible for me to transmit thoughts which are in my brain to yours?'

'That I cannot attempt in any way to explain,' I answered. 'But isn't it classified under the general head of thought transference?'

'Precisely – I am prepared to admit so much; but your description, hypnotism, though as involved, is quite as correct a term. But let me tell you that both these illustrations were given to lead up to another, which will bring us nearer than we have yet come to the conclusion I am endeavouring to arrive at. Try and give me your complete attention again; above all, watch my finger.'

As he spoke he began to wave his first finger in the air. It moved this way and that, describing figures of eight, and I followed each movement so carefully with my eyes that presently a small blue flame seemed to flicker at the end of it. Then, after perhaps a minute, I saw, or thought I saw, what might have been a tiny cloud settling in the further corner of the room. It was near the floor when I first noticed it, then it rose to about the height of a yard, and came slowly across the apartment towards me. Little by little it increased in size. Then it assumed definite proportions, became taller, until I thought I detected the outline of a human figure. This resemblance rapidly increased, until I could definitely distinguish the head and body of a man. He was tall and well-proportioned; his head was thrown back, and his eyes met mine with an eager, though somewhat strained, glance. Every detail was perfect, even to a ring upon his little finger; indeed, if I had met the man in the street next day I am certain I should have known him again. A strange orange-coloured light almost enveloped him, but in less than a minute he had become merged in the cloud once more; this gradually fell back into the corner, grew smaller and smaller, and finally disappeared altogether. I gave a little shiver, as if I were waking from some unpleasant dream, and turned to Nikola, who was watching me with half-closed eyes.

After I had quite recovered my wits, he took an album from the table and handed it to me.

'See if you can find in that book,' he said, 'the photograph of the man whose image you have just seen.'

I unfastened the clasp, and turned the pages eagerly. Near the middle I discovered an exact reproduction of the vision I had seen. The figure and face, the very attitude and expression, were the same in every particular, and even the ring I had noticed was upon the little finger. I was completely nonplussed.

'What do you think of my experiment?' asked Nikola.

'It was most wonderful and most mysterious,' I said.

'But how do you account for it?' he asked.

'I can't account for it at all,' I answered. 'I can only suppose, since you owned to it before, that it must also have been hypnotism.'

'Exactly,' said Nikola. 'But you will see in this case that, without any disc or passes, I not only produced the wish that you should see what I was thinking of, but also the exact expression worn by the person in the photograph. The test was successful in every way. And yet, how did I transfer the image that was in my mind to the retina of your eyes? You were positively certain you saw the water decrease in the glass just now; you would have pledged your word of honour that you saw your name printed upon your arm; and under other circumstances you would, in all probability, have ridiculed any assertion on my part that you did not see the vision of the man whose photograph is in that book. Very good. That much decided, do you feel equal to doubting that, though not present in the room, I could wake you in the night, and make you see the image of some friend, whom you knew to be long dead, standing by your bedside. Shall I make myself float in mid-air? Shall I transport you out of this room, and take you to the bottom of the Pacific Ocean? Shall I lift you up into heaven, or conduct you to the uttermost parts of hell? You have only to say what you desire to see and I will show it to you as surely and as perfectly as you saw those other things. But remember, all I have done is only what I call trickery, for it was done by hypnotism, which is to my mind, though you think it so mysterious, neither more nor less than making people believe what you will by the peculiar power of your own mind. But answer me this: if hypnotism is only the very smallest beginning of the knowledge possessed by the sect I am trying to discover, what must their greatest secret be? Believe me when I tell you that what I have shown you this evening is as a molehill to a mountain compared with what you will learn if we can only penetrate into that place of which I have told you. I pledge you my word on it. Now answer me this question: is it worth trying for, or not?'

'It is worth it,' I cried enthusiastically. 'I will go with you, and I will give you my best service; if you will play fair by me, I will do the same by you. But there is one further question I must ask you: has that stick you obtained from Mr Wetherell anything at all to do with the work in hand?'

'More than anything,' he answered. 'It is the key to everything. Originally, you must understand, there were only three of these sticks in existence. One belongs, or rather did belong, to each of the three heads of the sect. In pursuit of some particular information one of the trio left the monastery, and came out into the world. He died in a mysterious manner, and the stick fell into the possession of the abbot of the Yung Ho Kung, in Pekin, from whom it was stolen by an Englishman in my employ, known as China Pete, who risked his life, disguised as a Thibetan monk, to get it. Having stolen it, he eluded me, and fled to Australia, not knowing the real value of his treasure. The society became cognisant of its loss, and sent men after him. In attempting to obtain possession of it one of the Chinamen was killed off the coast of Queensland, and China Pete was arrested in Sydney on a charge of having murdered him. Wetherell defended him, and got him off; and, not being able to pay for his services, the latter made him a present of the stick. A month later I reached Sydney in search of it, but the Chinese were there before me. We both tried to obtain possession of it, but, owing to Wetherell's obstinacy, neither of us was successful. I offered Wetherell his own price for it; he refused to give it up. I pleaded with him, argued, entreated, but in vain. Then I set myself to get it from him at any hazard. How I succeeded you know. All that occurred six months ago. As soon as it was in my possession I returned here with the intention of penetrating into the interior, and endeavouring to find out what I so much wanted to know.'

'And where is the stick now?' I asked.

'In my own keeping,' he answered. 'If you would care to see it, I shall have very much pleasure in showing it to you.'

'I should like to see it immensely,' I answered.

With that he left the room, to return in about five minutes. Then, seating himself before me, he took from his pocket a small case, out of which he drew a tiny stick, at most not more than three inches long. It was a commonplace little affair, a deep black in colour, and covered with Chinese hieroglyphics in dead gold. A piece of frayed gold ribbon, much tarnished, and showing evident signs of having passed through many hands, was attached to it at one end.

He handed it to me, and I examined it carefully.

'But if this stick were originally stolen,' I said, 'you will surely not be so imprudent as to place yourself in the power of the society with it in your possession? It would mean certain death.'

'If it were all plain sailing, and there were no risk to be run, I doubt very much if I should pay you £10,000 for the benefit of your company,' he answered. 'It is because there is a great risk, and because I must have assistance, though I am extremely doubtful whether we shall ever come out of it alive, that I am taking you with me. I intend to discover their secret if possible, and I also intend that this stick, which undoubtedly is the key of the outer gate, so to speak, shall help me in my endeavours. If you are afraid to accompany me, having heard all, I will allow you to forego your promise and turn back while there is time.'

'I have not the slightest intention of turning back,' I answered. 'I don't know that I am a braver man than most, but if you are willing to go on I am ready to accompany you.'

'And so you shall, and there's my hand on it,' he cried, giving me his hand as he spoke.

'Now tell me what you intend to do,' I said. 'How do you mean to begin?'

'Well, in the first place,' said Nikola, 'I shall wait here until the arrival of a certain man from Pekin. He is one of the lay brethren of the society who has fallen under my influence, and as soon as he puts in an appearance and I have got his information we shall disguise ourselves, myself as an official of one of the coast provinces, you as my secretary, and together we shall set out for the capital. Arriving there we will penetrate the Llamaserai, the most anti-European monastery in all China, and, by some means or another, extract from the chief priest sufficient information to take the next step upon our journey. After that we shall proceed as circumstances dictate.'

'And when do you intend that we shall start?'

'As soon as the man arrives, perhaps tonight, probably tomorrow morning.'

'And as to our disguises?'

'I have in my possession everything we can possibly need.'

'In that case I suppose there is nothing to be done until the messenger arrives?'

'Nothing, I think.'

'Then if you will allow me I will wish you goodbye and be off to bed. In case I do not hear from you tonight, at what hour would you like me to call tomorrow?'

'I will let you know before breakfast-time without fail. You are not afraid, are you?'

'Not in the least,' I answered.

'And you'll say nothing to anybody, even under compulsion, as to our mission?'

'I have given you my promise,' I answered, and rose from my seat.

Once more I followed him down the main passage of the bungalow into the front verandah. Arriving there we shook hands and I went down the steps into the street.

As I turned the corner and made my way in the direction of the road leading to the English Concession, I saw a man, without doubt a Chinaman, rise from a corner and follow me. For nearly a quarter of a mile he remained about a hundred yards behind me, then he was joined by a second, who presently left his companion at a cross street and continued the march. Whether their espionage was only accidental, or whether I was really the object of their attention, I was for some time at a loss to conjecture, but when I saw the second give place to a third, and the third begin to decrease the distance that separated us, I must own I was not altogether comfortable in my mind. Arriving at a more crowded thoroughfare I hastened my steps, and having proceeded about fifty yards along it, dodged down a side lane. This lane conveyed me into another, which eventually brought me out within half a dozen paces of the house I wanted.

That the occupants of the dwelling had not yet retired to bed was evident from the lights I could see moving about inside. In response to my knock someone left the room upon the right hand of the passage and came towards the door where I waited. When he had opened it I discovered that it was Mr McAndrew himself.

'Why, Bruce!' he cried in surprise, as soon as he discovered who his visitor was. 'You've chosen a pretty late hour for calling; but never mind, come along in; I am glad to see you.' As he spoke he led me into the room from which he had just emerged. It was his dining-room, and was furnished in a ponderous, but luxurious, fashion. In a chair beside the long table – for Mr McAndrew has a large family, and twelve sat down to the morning and evening meal – was seated a tiny grey-haired lady, his wife, while opposite her, engaged upon some fancy work, was a pretty girl of sixteen, his youngest daughter and pet, as I remembered. That the lateness of my visit also occasioned them some surprise I could see by their faces; but after a few commonplace remarks they bade me good-night and went out of the room, leaving me alone with the head of the house.

'I suppose you have some very good reason for this visit, or you wouldn't be here,' the latter said, as he handed me a box of cigars. 'Have you heard of a new billet, or has your innocent friend Nikola commenced to blackmail you?'

'Neither of these things has happened,' I answered with a laugh.' 'But as I am in all probability leaving Shanghai tomorrow morning before banking hours, I have come to see if I may so far tax your kindness as to ask you to take charge of a cheque for me.' I thereupon produced Nikola's draft and handed it to him. He took it, glanced at it, looked up at me, returned his eyes to it once more, and then whistled.

'This looks like business,' he said.

'Doesn't it,' I answered. 'I can hardly believe that I am worth £10,000.'

'You are to be congratulated. And now what do you want me to do with it?' enquired McAndrew, turning the paper over and over in his hand as if it were some uncanny talisman which might suddenly catch him up and convert him into a camel or an octopus before he could look round.

'I want you to keep it for me if you will,' I answered 'To put it on deposit in your bank if you have no objection. I am going away, certainly for six months, possibly for a year, and when I return to Shanghai I will come and claim it. That's if I do return.'

'And if not?'

'In that case I will leave it all to you. In the meantime I want you to advance me £20 if you will; you can repay yourself out of the amount. Do you mind doing it?'

'Not in the very least,' he answered; 'but we had better have it all in writing, so that there may be no mistake.'

He thereupon produced from a drawer in a side table a sheet of notepaper. Having written a few lines on it he gave it to me to sign, at the same time calling in one of his sons to witness my signature. This formality completed he handed me £20 in notes and English gold, and our business was concluded. I rose to go.

'Bruce,' said the old gentleman in his usual kindly fashion, putting his hand upon my shoulder as he spoke, 'I don't know what you are up to, and I don't suppose it will do for me to enquire, but I am aware that you have been in pretty straitened circumstances lately, and I am afraid you are embarking on some foolishness or other now. For Heaven's sake weigh carefully the pros and cons before you commit yourself. Remember always that one moment's folly may wreck your whole after-life.'

'You need have no fear on that score,' I answered. 'I am going into this business with my eyes open. All the same I am obliged to you for your warning and for what you have done for me. Good-night and goodbye.'

I shook hands with him, and then passing into the verandah left the bungalow.

I was not fifty yards from the gate when a noise behind me induced me to look round. A man had been sitting in the shadow on the other side of the road. He had risen now and was beginning to follow me. That it was the same individual who had accompanied me to McAndrew's house I had not the slightest doubt. I turned to my right hand down a side street in order to see if he would pursue me; he also turned. I doubled again; he did the same. I proceeded across a piece of open ground instead of keeping on in the straight line I had hitherto been following; he imitated my example. This espionage was growing alarming, so I quickened my pace, and having found a side street with a high fence on one side, followed the palisading along till I came to the gate. Through this I dashed, and as soon as I was in, stooped down in the shadow. Half a minute later I heard the man coming along on the other side. When he could no longer see me ahead of him he came to a halt within half a dozen paces of where I crouched. Then having made up his mind that I must have crossed the road and gone down a dark lane opposite, he too crossed, and in a few seconds was out of sight.

As soon as I had convinced myself that I had got rid of him I passed out into the street again and made my way as quickly as possible back to my abode.

But I was not to lose my mysterious pursuer after all, for just as I was entering my own compound he put in an appearance. Seeing that I had the advantage I ran up the steps of the verandah and went inside. From a window I watched him come up the street and stand looking about him. Then he returned by the way he had come, and, for the time being, that was the last I saw of him. In less than a quarter of an hour I was in bed and asleep, dreaming of Nikola, and imagining that I was being turned into an elephant by his uncanny powers.

How long I remained snoozing I cannot say, but I was suddenly awakened by the feeling that somebody was in my room. Nor was I mistaken. A man was sitting by my bedside, and in the dim moonlight I could see that he was a Chinaman.

'What are you doing here?' I cried, sitting up in bed.

'Be silent!' my visitor whispered in Chinese. 'If you speak it will cost you your life.'

Without another word I thrust my hand under the pillow intending to produce the revolver I had placed there when I went to bed. But it was gone. Whether my visitor had stolen it or I had imagined that I had put it there and forgotten to do so, it was beyond my powers to tell. At any rate the weapon, upon which it would seem my life depended, was gone.

'What is your business with me?' I asked, resolved to bring my visitor to his bearings without loss of time.

'Not so loud,' he answered. 'I am sent by Dr Nikola to request your honourable presence. He desires that you will come to him without a moment's delay.'

'But I've only just left him,' I said. 'Why does he send for me again?'

'I cannot say, but it is possible that something important has occurred,' was the man's answer. 'He bade me tell you to come at once.'

With that I got up and dressed myself as quickly as possible. It was evident that the expected messenger from Pekin had arrived, and in that case we should probably be setting off for the capital before morning. At any rate I did not waste a moment, and as soon as I was ready went out into the verandah, where the man who had come to fetch me was sitting. He led me across the compound into the street and pointed to a chair which with its bearers was in waiting for me.

'Your friend is in a hurry,' said the man who had called me, by way of explanation, 'and he bade me not lose a moment.'

'In that case you may go along as hard as you like,' I answered; 'I am quite ready.'

I took my place in the chair, which was immediately lifted by the bearers, and within a minute of my leaving the house we were proceeding down the street at a comparatively fast pace. At that hour the town was very quiet; indeed, with the exception of an occasional Sikh policeman and a belated 'rickshaw coolie or two, we met no one. At the end of a quarter of an hour it was evident that we had arrived at our destination, for the chair came to a standstill and the bearers set me down. I sprang out and looked about me. To my surprise, however, it was not the house I expected to see that I found before me. We had pulled up at the entrance to a much larger bungalow, standing in a compound of fair size. While I waited my messenger went into the house, to presently return with the information that, if I would be pleased to follow him, Dr Nikola would see me at once.

The house was in total darkness and as silent as the grave. I passed into the main hall, and was about to proceed down it towards a door at the further end, when I was, without warning, caught by the back of the neck, a gag of some sort was placed in my mouth, and my hands were securely fastened behind me. Next moment I was lifted into the air and borne into a room whence a bright light suddenly streamed forth. Here three Chinamen were seated, clad in heavy figured silk, and wearing enormous tortoiseshell spectacles upon their noses. They received me with a grunt of welcome, and bade my captors remove the gag from my mouth. This done the elder of the trio said quietly – but it seemed to me somewhat inconsequently: 'We hope that your honourable self is enjoying good health?'

I answered, with as much calmness as I could possibly assume at so short a notice, that 'for such an utterly insignificant personage I was in the enjoyment of the best of health.' Whereupon I was requested to say how it came about that I was now in China, and what my business there might be. When I had answered this the man on the right leant a little forward and said: 'You are not telling us the honourable truth. What business have you with Dr Nikola?'

I summoned all my wits to my assistance.

'Who is Dr Nikola?' I asked.

'The person whom you have visited two nights in succession,' said the man who had first spoken. 'Tell us what mischief you and he are hatching together.'

Seeing that it would be useless attempting to deny my association with Nikola I insinuated that we were interested in the purchase of Chinese silk together, but this assertion was received with a scornful grunt of disapproval.

'We must have the truth,' said the man in the biggest spectacles.

'I can tell you no more,' I answered.

'In that case we have no option,' he said, 'but to extract the information by other means.'

With that he made a sign to one of the attendants, who immediately left the room, to return a few moments later with a roll of chain, and some oddly-shaped wooden bars. A heavy sweat rose upon my forehead. I had seen a good deal of Chinese torture in my time, and now it looked as if I were about to have a taste of it.

'What do you know of Dr Nikola?' repeated the man who had first spoken, and who was evidently the principal of the trio.

'I have already told you,' I repeated, this time with unusual emphasis.

Again he asked the same question without change of tone.

But I only repeated my previous answer.

'For the last time, what do you know of Dr Nikola?'

'I have told you,' I answered, my heart sinking like lead. Thereupon he raised his hand a little and made a sign to the men near the door. Instantly I was caught and thrown on my back upon the floor. Before I could expostulate or struggle a curious wooden collar was clasped round my neck, and a screw was turned in it until another revolution would have choked me. Once more I heard the old man say monotonously.

'What do you know of Dr Nikola?'

I tried to repeat my former assertion, but owing to the tightness of the collar I found a difficulty in speaking. Then the man in the centre rose and came over to where I lay; instantly the collar was relaxed, my arms were released, and a voice said: 'Get up, Mr Bruce. You need have no further fear; we shall not hurt you.'

It was Dr Nikola!

CHAPTER FOUR

We set out for Tientsin

I could scarcely believe the evidence of my senses. Nikola's disguise was so perfect that it would have required almost superhuman cleverness to penetrate it. In every particular he was a true Celestial. His accent was without a flaw, his deportment exactly what that of a Chinaman of high rank would be, while his general demeanour and manner of sustaining his assumed character could not have been found fault with by the most fastidious critic. I felt that if he could so easily hoodwink me there could be little doubt that he would pass muster under less exacting scrutiny. So as soon as I was released I sprang to my feet and warmly congratulated him, not a little relieved, you may be sure, to find that I was with friends, and was not to be tortured, as I had at first supposed.

'You must forgive the rough treatment to which you have been subjected,' said Nikola. 'But I wanted to test you very thoroughly. Now what do you think of my disguise?'

'It is perfect,' I answered. 'Considering your decided personality, I had no idea it could possibly be so good. But where are we?'

'In a bungalow I have taken for the time being,' he replied. 'And now let us get to business. The man whom you saw on my right was Laohwan, the messenger whom I told you I expected from Pekin. He arrived half an hour after you had left me this evening, gave me the information I wanted, and now I am ready to start as soon as you are.'

'Let me go home and put one or two things together,' I answered, 'and then I'm your man.'

'Certainly,' said Nikola. 'One of my servants shall accompany you to carry your bag, and to bring you back here as soon as your work is completed.'

With that I set off for my abode, followed by one of Nikola's boys. When we reached it I left him to wait for me outside, and let myself in to my bedroom by the window. Having lit a candle, I hastened to put together the few little odds and ends I wished to take with me on my journey. This finished I locked my trunks, wrote a letter to my landlord, enclosing the amount I owed him, and then another to Barkston, asking him to be good enough to send for, and take charge of, my trunks until I returned from a trip into the interior. This done I passed out of the house again, joined the boy who was waiting for me at the gate, and returned to the bungalow in which I had been so surprised by Nikola an hour or so before. It was long after midnight by the time I reached it, but I had no thought of fatigue. The excitement of our departure prevented my thinking of aught else. We were plunging into an unknown life bristling with dangers, and though I did not share Nikola's belief as to the result we should achieve, I had the certain knowledge that I should be well repaid for the risk I ran.

When I entered the house I found my employer awaiting my coming in the room where I had been hoaxed that evening. He was still in Chinese dress, and once again as I looked at him I felt it difficult to believe that this portly, sedate-looking Chinaman could be the slim European known to the world as Dr Nikola.

'You have not been long, Mr Bruce,' he said, 'and I am glad of it. Now if you will accompany me to the next room I will introduce you to your things. I have purchased for you everything that you can possibly require, and as I am well acquainted with your power of disguise, I have no fear at all as to the result.'

On reaching the adjoining room I divested myself of my European habiliments, and set to work to don those which were spread out for my inspection. Then with some mixture from a bottle which I found upon the table, I stained my face, neck, and arms, after which my pig-tail, which was made on a cleverly contrived scalp wig, was attached, and a large pair of tortoiseshell glasses of a similar pattern to those worn by Nikola, were placed upon my nose. My feet were encased in sandals, a stiff round hat of the ordinary Chinese pattern was placed upon my head, and this, taken with my thickly-padded robe of yellow silk, gave me a most dignified appearance.

When Nikola returned to the room he examined me carefully, and expressed himself as highly pleased with the result; indeed, when we greeted each other in the Chinese fashion and language he would have been a sharp man who could have detected that we were not what we pretended to be.

'Now,' said Nikola, 'if you are ready we will test the efficiency of our disguises. In half an hour's time there is a meeting at the house of a man named Lo Ting. The folk we shall meet there are members of a secret society aiming at the overthrow of the Manchu dynasty. Laohwan has gone on ahead, and, being a member of the society, will report to them the arrival of two distinguished merchants from the interior, who are also members. I have got the passwords, and I know the general idea of their aims, so, with your permission, we will set off at once. When we get there I will explain my intentions more fully.'

'But you are surely not going to attend a meeting of a secret society tonight?' I said, astonished at the coolness with which he proposed to run such a risk. 'Wouldn't it be wiser to wait until we are a little more accustomed to our dresses?'

'By no means,' answered Nikola. 'I consider this will be a very good test. If we are detected by the folk we shall see tonight we shall know where the fault lies, and we can remedy it before it is too late. Besides, there is to be a man present who knows something of the inner working of the society, and from him I hope to derive some important information to help us on our way. Come along.'

He passed into the passage and led the way through the house out into the compound, where we found a couple of chairs, with their attendant coolies, awaiting us. We stepped into them, and were presently being borne in a sedate fashion down the street.

In something under twenty minutes our bearers stopped and set us down again; we alighted, and after the coolies had disappeared Nikola whispered that the password was 'Liberty', and that as one said it it was necessary to place the fingers of the right hand in the palm of the left. If I should be asked any questions I was to trust to my mother wit to answer them satisfactorily.

We approached the door, which was at the end of a small alley, and when we reached it I noticed that Nikola rapped upon it twice with a large ring he wore upon the first finger of his right hand. In answer a small and peculiar sort of grille was opened, and a voice within said in Chinese: 'Who is it that disturbs honest people at this unseemly hour?'

'Two merchants from Szechuen who have come to Shanghai in search of liberty,' said my companion, holding up his hands in the manner described above.

Immediately the door was opened and I followed Nikola into the house. The passage was in darkness and terribly close. As soon as we had entered, the front gate was shut behind us, and we were told to walk straight forward. A moment later another door at the further end opened, and a bright light streamed forth. Our conductor signed to us to enter, and assuming an air of humility, and folding our hands in the prescribed fashion before us, we passed into a large apartment in which were seated possibly twenty men. Without addressing a word to one of them we crossed and took up our positions on a sort of divan at the further end. Pipes were handed to us, and for what must have been nearly five minutes we continued solemnly to puff out smoke, without a word being uttered in the room. If I were to say that I felt at my ease during this long silence it would hardly be the truth; but I flatter myself that, whatever my feelings may have been, I did not permit a sign of my embarrassment to escape me. Then an elderly Chinaman, who sat a little to our right, and who was, without doubt, the chief person present, turned to Nikola and questioned him as to his visit to Shanghai. Nikola answered slowly and gravely, after the Celestial fashion, deprecating any idea of personal advantage, and asserting that it was only to have the honour of saying he had been in Shanghai that he had come at all. When he had finished, the same question was addressed to me. I answered in similar terms, and then another silence fell upon us all. Indeed, it was not until we had been in the room nearly half an hour that any attempt at business was made. Then such a flow of gabble ensued that I could scarcely make head or tail of what I heard. Nikola was to the fore throughout. He invented plots for the overthrowing of dynasties, each of which had a peculiar merit of its own; he theoretically assassinated at least a dozen persons in high places, and, what was more, disposed of their bodies afterwards. To my thinking he out-heroded Herod in his zeal. One thing, however, was quite certain, before he had been an hour in the place he was at the head of affairs, and, had he so desired, could have obtained just what he wanted from those present. I did my best to second his efforts, but my co-operation was quite unnecessary. Three o'clock had passed before the meeting broke up. Then one by one the members left the room, until only Laohwan, the old man who had first addressed us, Nikola and myself remained in occupation.

Then little by little, with infinite tact, Nikola led the conversation round into the channel he wanted. How he had learnt that the old man knew anything at all of the matter was more than I could understand. But that he did know something, and that, with a little persuasion, he might be induced to give us the benefit of his knowledge, soon became evident.

'But these things are not for everyone,' he said, after a brief recital of the tales he had heard. 'If my honourable friend will be guided by one who has had experience, he will not seek to penetrate further.'

'The sea of knowledge is for all who desire to swim in it,' answered Nikola, puffing solemnly at his pipe. 'I have heard these things before, and I would convince myself of their truth. Can you help me to such enquiries? I ask in the name of the Light of Heaven.'

As he spoke he took from a pocket under his upper coat the small stick he had obtained from Wetherell. The old man no sooner saw it than his whole demeanour changed; he knelt humbly at Nikola's feet and implored his pardon.

'If my lord had spoken before,' he said tremblingly, 'I would have answered truthfully. All that I have is my lord's, and I will withhold nothing from him.'

'I want nothing,' said Nikola, 'save what has been arranged. That I must have at once.'

'My lord shall be obeyed,' said the old man.

'It is well,' Nikola answered. 'Let there be no delay, and permit no word to pass your lips. Send it to this address, so that I may receive it at once.'

He handed the other a card and then rose to go; five minutes later we were back in our respective chairs being borne down the street again. When we reached the house from which we had started Nikola called me into the room where I had dressed.

'You have had an opportunity now of seeing the power of that stick,' he said. 'It was Laohwan who discovered that the man was a member of the society. All that talk of overthrowing the Manchu dynasty was simply balderdash, partly real, but in a greater measure meant to deceive. Now if all goes well the old fellow will open the first gate to us, and then we shall be able to go ahead. Let us change our clothes and get back to my own house. If I mistake not we shall have to be off up the coast before breakfast-time.'

With that we set to work, and as soon as we were dressed in European habiliments, left the house and returned to the bungalow where I had first called upon Nikola. By this time day was breaking, and already a stir of life was discernible in the streets. Making our way into the house we proceeded direct to Nikola's study, where his servants had prepared a meal for us. We sat down to it, and were in the act of falling to work upon a cold pie, when a boy entered with the announcement that a Chinaman was in the hall and desired to speak with us. It was Laohwan.

'Well,' said Nikola, 'what message does the old man send?'

In reply Loahwan, who I soon found was not prodigal of speech, took from his sleeve a slip of paper on which were some words written in Chinese characters. Nikola glanced at them, and when he had mastered their purport handed it across the table to me. The message was as follows.

> In the house of Quong Sha, in the Street of a Hundred Tribulations, Tientsin.

That was all.

Nikola turned to Laohwan.

'At what time does the North China boat sail?' he asked.

'At half-past six,' answered Laohwan promptly.

Nikola looked at his watch, thought for a moment, and then said: 'Go on ahead. Book your passage and get aboard as soon as you can; we will join her later. But remember: until we get to Tientsin you must act as if you have never set eyes on either of us before.'

Laohwan bowed and left the room.

'At this point,' said Nikola, pouring himself out a cup of black coffee, 'the real adventure commences. It is a quarter to five now; we will take it easy for half an hour and then set off to the harbour and get aboard.'

Accordingly, as soon as we had finished our meal, we seated ourselves in lounge chairs and lit cigars. For half an hour we discussed the events of the evening, speculated as to the future, and, exactly as the clock struck a quarter-past five, rose to our feet again. Nikola rang a bell and his principal boy entered.

'I am going away,' said Nikola. 'I don't know when I shall be back. It may be a week, it may be a year. In the meantime you will take care of this house; you will not let one thing be stolen; and if when I come back I find a window broken or as much as a pin missing I'll saddle you with ten million devils. Mr McAndrew will pay your wages and look after you. If you want anything go to him. Do you understand?'

The boy nodded.

'That will do,' said Nikola. 'You can go.'

As the servant left the room my curious friend gave a strange whistle. Next moment the black cat came trotting in, sprang on her master's knee and crawled up onto his shoulder. Nikola looked at me and smiled.

'He will not forget me if I am away five years,' he said. 'What wife would be so constant?'

I laughed; the idea of Nikola and matrimony somehow did not harmonise very well. He lifted the cat down and placed him on the table.

'Apollyon,' said he, with the only touch of regret I saw him show throughout the trip, 'we have to part for a year. Goodbye, old cat, goodbye.'

Then having stroked the animal gently once or twice he turned briskly to me.

'Come along,' he said; 'let us be off. Time presses.'

The cat sat on the table watching him and appearing to understand every word he uttered. Nikola stroked its fur for the last time, and then walked out of the room. I followed at his heels and together we passed into the compound. By this time the streets were crowded. A new day had begun in Shanghai, and we had no difficulty in obtaining 'rickshaws.

'The *Vectis Queen*,' said Nikola, as soon as we were seated. The coolies immediately started off at a run, and in something under a quarter of an hour we had reached the wharf side of the Hwang-Pu River. The boat we were in search of lay well out in the stream, and for this reason it was necessary that we should charter a sampan to reach her.

Arriving on board we interviewed the purser, and, after we had paid our fares, were conducted to our cabins. The *Vectis Queen*, as all the East knows, is not a large steamer, and her accommodation is, well, to say the least of it, limited. But at this particular time of year there were not a great many people travelling, consequently we were not overcrowded. As soon as I had arranged my baggage, I left my cabin and went on deck. Small is the world! Hardly had I stepped out of the companion-ladder before I was accosted by a man with whom I had been well acquainted on the Australian coastal service, but whom I thought at the other end of the earth.

'Why, Wilfred Bruce!' he cried. 'Who'd have thought of seeing you here!'

'Jim Downing!' I cried, not best pleased, as you may suppose, at seeing him. 'How long have you been in China?'

'Getting on for a year,' he answered, 'I came up with one of our boats, had a row with the skipper, and left her in Hong-Kong. After that I joined this line. But though I don't think much of the Chinkies, I am fairly well satisfied. You're looking pretty well, old man; but it seems to me you've got precious sunburnt since I saw you last.'

'It's the effect of too much rice,' I said with a smile.

He laughed with the spontaneous gaiety of a man who is ready to be amused by anything, however simple, and then we walked up the deck together. As we turned to retrace our steps, Nikola emerged from the companion-hatch and joined us. I introduced Downing to him, and in five minutes you would have supposed them friends of years' standing. Before they had been together a quarter of an hour Nikola had given him a prescription for prickly-heat, from which irritation Downing suffered considerably, and as soon as this proved successful, the young man's gratitude and admiration were boundless. By breakfast-time we were well down the river, and by midday Shanghai lay far behind us.

Throughout the voyage Nikola was in his best spirits; he joined in all the amusements, organised innumerable sports and games, and was indefatigable in his exertions to amuse. And while I am on this subject, let me say that there was one thing which struck me as being even more remarkable than anything else in the character of this extraordinary man, and that was his extreme fondness for children. There was one little boy in particular on board, a wee toddler scarcely four years old, with whom Nikola soon established himself on terms of intimacy; he would play with him for hours at a stretch, never tiring, and never for one moment allowing his attention to wander from the matter in hand. I must own that when I saw them amusing themselves together under the lee of one of the boats on the promenade deck, on the hatchways, or beneath the awning aft, I could scarcely believe my eyes. I had to ask myself if this man, whose entire interest seemed to be centred on paper boats, and pigs cut out of orange peel, could be the same Nikola from whom Wetherell, ex-Colonial Secretary of New South Wales, had fled in London as from a pestilence, and at the sight of whom Benwell, of the Chinese Revenue Service, had excused himself, and rushed out of the club in Shanghai. That, however, was just Nikola's character. If he were making a paper boat, cutting a pig out of orange peel, weaving a plot round a politician, or endeavouring to steal the secret of an all-powerful society, he would give the matter in hand his whole attention, make himself master of every detail, and never leave it till he had achieved his object, or had satisfied himself that it was useless for him to work at it any longer. In the latter case he would drop it without a second thought.

Throughout the voyage Laohwan, though we saw him repeatedly, did not for a moment allow it to be supposed that he knew us. He was located on the forward deck, and, as far as we could gather, spent his whole time playing *fantan* with half-a-dozen compatriots on the cover of the forehatch.

The voyage up the coast was not an exciting one, but at last, at sunset one evening, we reached Tientsin, which, as all the world knows, is a treaty port located at the confluence of the Yu-Ho, or Grand Canal, with the river Pei-Ho. As soon as we came along-side the jetty, we collected our baggage and went ashore. Here another thing struck me. Nikola seemed to be as well known in this place as he was in Shanghai, and as soon as we arrived on the Bund called 'rickshaws, and the coolies conveyed us, without asking a question, to the residence of a certain Mr Williams in the European Concession.

This proved to be a house of modest size, built in the fashion usual in that part of the East. As we alighted from our 'rickshaws, a tall, elderly man, with a distinctly handsome cast of countenance, came into the verandah to welcome us. Seeing Nikola, he for a moment appeared to be overcome with surprise.

'Can it be possible that I see Dr Nikola?' he cried.

'It is not only possible, but quite certain that you do,' said Nikola, who signed to the coolie to lift his bag out, and then went up the steps. 'It is two years since I had the pleasure of seeing you, Mr Williams, and now I look at you you don't seem to have changed much since we taught Mah Feng that lesson in Seoul.'

'You have not forgotten that business then, Dr Nikola?'

'No more than Mah Feng had when I saw him last in Singapore,' my companion answered with a short laugh.

'And what can I do for you now?'

'I want you to let us tax your hospitality for a few hours,' said Nikola. 'This is my friend, Mr Bruce, with whom I am engaged on an important piece of work.'

'I am delighted to make your acquaintance, sir,' said Mr Williams, and having shaken hands with me he escorted us into the house.

Ten minutes later we were quite at home in his residence, and were waiting, myself impatiently, for a communication from Laoh-wan. And here I must pay another tribute to Nikola's powers of self-concentration. Anxious as the time was, peculiar as was our position, he did not waste a moment in idle conjecture, but taking from his travelling bag an abstruse work on chemistry, which was his invariable companion, settled himself down to a study of it; even when the messenger did come he did not stop at once, but continued the calculations upon which he was engaged until they were finished, when he directed Laohwan to inform him as to the progress he had made.

'Your arrival,' said the latter, 'is expected, and though I have not been to the place, I have learned that preparations are being made for your reception.'

'In that case you had better purchase ponies and have the men in readiness, for in all probability we shall leave for Pekin tomorrow morning.'

'At what time will your Excellency visit the house?' asked Laohwan.

'Some time between half-past ten and eleven this evening,' answered Nikola; and thereupon our trusty retainer left us.

At seven o'clock our evening meal was served. After it was finished I smoked a pipe in the verandah while Nikola went into a neighbouring room for half an hour's earnest conversation with our host. When he returned he informed me that it was time for us to dress, and thereupon we went to our respective rooms and attired ourselves in our Chinese costumes. Having done this we let ourselves out by a side door and set off for the native city. It was fully half-past ten before we reached it, but for an infinity of reasons we preferred to allow those who were expecting us to wait rather than we should betray any appearance of hurry.

Anyone who has had experience of Tientsin will bear me out when I say that of all the dirty and pestilential holes this earth of ours possesses, there are very few to equal it, and scarcely one that can surpass it. Narrow, irregular streets, but little wider than an average country lane in England, run in and out, and twist and twine in every conceivable direction. Overhead the second stories of the houses, decorated with sign-boards, streamers and flags, almost touch each other, so that even in the middle of the day a peculiar, dim, religious light prevails. At night, as may be supposed, it is pitch dark. And both by day and night it smells abominably.

Arriving at the end of the street to which we had been directed, we left our conveyances, and proceeded for the remainder of the distance on foot. Halfway down this particular thoroughfare – which was a little wider, and certainly a degree more respectable than its neighbours – we were met by Loahwan, who conducted us to the house of which we were in search.

In outward appearance it was not unlike its fellows, was one storey high, had large overhanging eaves, a sort of trellis-shielded verandah, and a low, arched doorway. Upon this last our Chinese companion thumped with his fist, and at the third repetition the door was opened.

Laohwan said something in a low voice to the janitor, who thereupon admitted us.

'There is but one sun,' said the guardian of the gate humbly.

'But there be many stars,' said Nikola; whereupon the man led us as far as the second door in the passage. Arriving at this he muttered a few words. It was instantly opened, and we stepped inside to find another man waiting for us, holding a queer-shaped lamp in his hand. Without questioning us he intimated that we should follow him, which we did, down a long passage, to bring up finally at a curtained archway. Drawing the curtain aside, he bade us pass through, and then redrew it after us.

On the other side of the arch we found ourselves in a large room, the floor, walls, and ceiling of which were made of some dark wood, probably teak. It was unfurnished save for a few scrolled banners suspended at regular intervals upon the walls, and a few cushions in a corner. When we entered it was untenanted, but we had not long to wait before our solitude was interrupted. I had turned to speak to Nikola, who was examining a banner on the left wall, when suddenly a quiet footfall behind me attracted my attention. I wheeled quickly round to find myself confronted by a Chinaman whose age could scarcely have been less than eighty years. His face was wrinkled like a sun-dried crab-apple, his hair was almost white, and he walked with a stick. One thing struck me as particularly curious about his appearance. Though the house in which we found ourselves was by no means a small one, though it showed every sign of care, and in places even betokened the possession of considerable wealth on the part of its owner, this old man, who was undoubtedly the principal personage in it, was clad in garments that evidenced the deepest poverty. When he reached Nikola, whom he seemed to consider, as indeed did everyone else, the chief of our party, he bowed low before him, and after the invariable compliments had been exchanged, said: 'Your Excellency has been anxiously expected. All the arrangements for your progress onward have been made this week past.'

'I was detained in Tsan-Chu,' said Nikola. 'Now tell me, what has been done?'

'News has been sent on to Pekin,' said the old man, 'and the chief priest will await you in the Llamaserai. I can tell you no more.'

'I am satisfied. And now let us know what has been said about my coming.'

'It is said that they who have chosen have chosen wisely.'

'That is good,' said Nikola. 'Now leave us; I am tired and would be alone. I shall remain the night in this house and go onwards at daybreak tomorrow morning. See that I am not disturbed.'

The old man assured Nikola that his wishes should be respected, and having done so left the room. After he had gone Nikola drew me to the further end of the apartment and whispered hurriedly: 'I see it all now. Luck is playing into our hands. If I can only get hold of the two men I want to carry this business through, I'll have the society's secret or die in the attempt. Listen to me. When we arrived tonight I learnt from Williams, who knows almost as much of the under life of China as I do myself, that what I suspected has already taken place. In other words, after this long interval, there has been an election to fill the place of the man whom China Pete killed in the Llamaserai to obtain possession of that stick. The man chosen is the chief priest of the Llama temple of Hankow, a most religious and extraordinary person. He is expected in Pekin either this week or next. Misled by Laohwan, these people have mistaken me for him, and I mean that they shall continue in their error. If they find that we are hoodwinking them we are dead men that instant, but if they don't and we can keep this other man out of the way, we stand an excellent chance of getting from them all we want to know. It is a tremendous risk, but as it is an opportunity that might never come again, we must make the most of it. Now attend carefully to me. It would never do for me to leave this place tonight, but it is most imperative that I should communicate with Williams. I must write a letter to him, and you must take it. He must send two cablegrams first thing tomorrow morning.'

So saying he drew from a pocket inside his sleeve a small notebook, and, what seemed strangely incongruous, a patent American fountain pen. Seating himself upon the floor he began to write. For nearly five minutes complete silence reigned in the room, then he tore two or three leaves from the book and handed them to me.

'Take these to Williams,' he said. 'He must find out where this other man is, without losing an instant, and communicate with the folk to whom I am cabling. Come what may they must catch him before he can get here, and then carry him out to sea. Once there he must not be allowed to land again until you and I are safely back in Shanghai.'

'And who is Williams to cable to?'

'To two men in whom I have the greatest confidence. One is named Eastover, and the other Prendergast. He will send them this message.'

He handed me another slip of paper.

To Prendergast and Eastover, care Gregson, Hong-Kong –
Come Tientsin next boat. Don't delay a moment. When you arrive call on Williams.

NIKOLA

CHAPTER FIVE

I rescue a young lady

Having left the room in which Nikola had settled himself I found the same doorkeeper who had admitted us to the house, and who now preceded and ushered me into the street. Once there I discovered that the condition of the night had changed. When we had left Mr Williams' residence it was bright starlight, now black clouds covered the face of the sky, and as I passed down the street, in the direction of the English Concession, a heavy peal of thunder rumbled overhead. It was nearly eleven o'clock, and, as I could not help thinking, a curious quiet lay upon the native city. There was an air of suppressed excitement about such Chinamen as I met that puzzled me, and when I came upon knots of them at street corners, the scraps of conversation I was able to overhear did not disabuse my mind of the notion that some disturbance was in active preparation. However, I had not time to pay much attention to them. I had to find Mr Williams's house, give him the letter, and get back to Nikola with as little delay as possible.

At last I reached the Concession, passed the Consul's house, and finally arrived at the bungalow of which I was in search.

A bright light shone from one of the windows, and towards it I directed my steps. On reaching it I discovered the owner of the house seated at a large table, writing. I tapped softly upon the pane, whereupon he rose and came towards me. That he did not recognise me was evident from his reception of me.

'What do you want?' he asked in Chinese as he opened the window.

Bending a little forward, so as to reach his ear, I whispered the following sentence into it: 'I should like to ask your honourable presence one simple question.'

'This is not the time to ask questions, however simple,' he replied; 'you must come round in the morning.'

'But the morning will be too late,' I answered earnestly. 'I tell you by the spirit of your ancestors that what I have to say must be said tonight.'

'Then come in, and for mercy's sake say it,' he replied a little testily, and beckoned me into the room. I did as he desired, and seated myself on the stool before him, covering my hands with my great sleeves in the orthodox fashion. Then, remembering the Chinese love of procrastination, I began to work the conversation in and out through various channels until I saw that his patience was well-nigh exhausted. Still, however, he did not recognise me. Then leaning towards him I said: 'Is your Excellency aware that your house has been watched since sundown?'

'By whom, and for what reason?' he enquired, looking, I thought, a little uncomfortable.

'By three men, and because of two strangers who arrived by the mail boat this afternoon.'

'What strangers?' he enquired innocently. But I noticed that he looked at me rather more fixedly than before.

'The man whom we call "The man with the Devil's eyes" – but whom you call Nikola – and his companion.'

I gave Nikola's name as nearly as a Chinaman would be able to pronounce it, and then waited to see what he would say next. That he was disconcerted was plain enough, but that he did not wish to commit himself was also very evident. He endeavoured to temporise; but as this was not to my taste, I revealed my identity by saying in my natural voice and in English: 'It would seem that my disguise is a very good one, Mr Williams.'

He stared at me.

'Surely you are not Mr Bruce?' he cried.

'I am,' I answered; 'and what's more, I am here on an important errand. I have brought you a letter from Nikola, which you must read and act upon at once.'

As I spoke I produced from a pocket in my sleeve the letter Nikola had given me and handed it to him. He sat down again at the table and perused it carefully. When he had finished, he read it over again, then a third time. Having got it by heart he went across the room to a safe in the corner. This he unlocked, and having opened a drawer, carefully placed the slip of paper in it. Then he came back and took up his old seat again. I noticed that his forehead was contracted with thought, and that there was an expression of perplexity, and one might have almost said of doubt, about his mouth. At last he spoke.

'I know you are in Nikola's employment, Mr Bruce,' he said, 'but are you aware of the contents of this letter?'

'Does it refer to the man who is expected in Pekin to take up the third stick in the society?'

'Yes,' he answered slowly, stabbing at his blotting-pad with the point of a pen, 'it does. It refers to him very vitally.'

'And now you are revolving in your mind the advisability of what Nikola says about abducting him, I suppose?'

'Exactly. Can Nikola be aware, think you, that the man in question was chief priest of one of the biggest Hankow temples?'

'I have no doubt that he is. But you say "was". Has the man then resigned his appointment in order to embrace this new calling?'

'Certainly he has.'

'Well, in that case it seems to me that the difficulty is considerably lessened.'

'In one direction, perhaps; but then it is increased in another. If he is still a priest and we abduct him, then we fight the Government and the Church. On the other hand, if he is no longer a priest, and the slightest suspicion of what we are about to do leaks out, then we shall have to fight a society which is ten times as powerful as any government or priesthood in the world.'

'You have Nikola's instructions, I suppose?'

'Yes; and I confess I would rather deal with the Government of China and the millions of the society than disobey him in one single particular. But let me tell you this, Mr Bruce, if Nikola is pig-headed enough to continue his quest in the face of this awful uncertainty, I would not give a penny piece for either his life or that of the man who accompanies him. Consider for one moment what I mean. This society into whose secrets he is so anxious to penetrate – and how much better he will be when he has done so he alone knows – is without doubt the most powerful in the whole world. If rumour is to be believed, its list of members exceeds twenty millions. It has representatives in almost every town and village in the length and breadth of this great land, to say nothing of Malaysia, Australia and America; its rules are most exacting, and when you reflect for one moment that our friend is going to impersonate one of the three leaders of this gigantic force, with chances of detection menacing him at every turn, you will see for yourself what a foolhardy undertaking it is.'

'I must own I agree with you, but still he is Nikola.'

'Yes. In that you sum up everything. *He is Nikola*.'

'Then what answer am I to take back to him?'

'That I will proceed with the work at once. Stay. I will write it down, that there may be no possible mistake.'

So saying he wrote for a moment, and when his letter was completed handed it to me.

I rose to go.

'And with regard to these telegrams?' I said.

'I will dispatch them myself the very moment the office is open,' he answered. 'I have given Nikola an assurance to that effect in my letter.'

'We leave at daybreak for Pekin, so I will wish you goodbye now.'

'You have no thought of turning back, I suppose?'

'Not the very slightest.'

'You're a plucky man.'

'I suppose I must be. But there is an old saying that just meets my case.'

'And that is?'

' "Needs must when – "'

'Well, shall we say when Nikola – ?'

'Yes. "Needs must when Nikola drives." Goodbye.'

'Goodbye, and may good luck go with you.'

I shook hands with him at the front door, and then descended the steps and set off on my return to the native city. As I left the street in which the bungalow stood a clock struck twelve. The clouds, which had been so heavy when I set out, had now drawn off the sky, and it was bright starlight once more.

As I entered the city proper my first impression was in confirmation of my original feeling that something out of the common was about to happen. Nor was I deceived. Hardly had I gone a hundred yards before a tumult of angry voices broke upon my ear. The sound increased in volume, and presently an excited mob poured into the street along which I was making my way. Had it been possible I would have turned into a by-path and so escaped them, but now this was impossible. They had hemmed me in on every side, and, whether I wished it or not, I was compelled to go with them.

For nearly half a mile they carried me on in this fashion, then, leaving the thoroughfare along which they had hitherto been passing, they turned sharply to the right hand and brought up before a moderate-sized house standing at a corner. Wondering what it all might mean, I accosted a youth by my side and questioned him. His answer was brief, but to the point: '*Kueidzu*!' (devil), he cried, and picking up a stone hurled it through the nearest window.

The house, I soon discovered, was the residence of a missionary, who, I was relieved to hear, was absent from home. As I could see the mob was bent on wrecking his dwelling I left them to their work and proceeded on my way again. But though I did not know it, I had not done with adventure yet.

As I turned from the street, into another which ran at right angles to it, I heard a shrill cry for help. I immediately stopped and listened in order to discover whence it had proceeded. I had not long to wait, however, for almost at the same instant it rang out again. This time it undoubtedly came from a lane on my right. Without a second's thought I picked up my heels and ran across to it. At first I could see nothing; then at the further end I made out three figures, and towards them I hastened. When I got there I found that one was a girl, the second an old man, who was stretched upon the ground; both were English, but their assailant was an active young fellow of the coolie class. He was standing over the man's body menacing the girl with a knife. My sandals made no noise upon the stones, and as I came up on the dark side of the lane neither of the trio noticed my presence until I was close upon them. But swift as I was I was hardly quick enough, for just as I arrived the girl threw herself upon the man, who at the same instant raised his arm and plunged his knife into her shoulder. It could not have penetrated very deep, however, before my fist was in his face. He rolled over like a ninepin, and for a moment lay on the ground without moving. But he did not remain there very long. Recovering his senses he sprang to his feet and bolted down the street, yelling '*Kueidzu! kueidzu!*' at the top of his voice, in the hope of bringing the mob to his assistance.

Before he was out of sight I was kneeling by the side of the girl upon the ground. She was unconscious. Her face was deadly pale, and I saw that her left shoulder was soaked with blood. From examining her I turned to the old man. He was a fine-looking old fellow, fairly well dressed, and boasting a venerable grey beard. He lay stretched out at full length, and one glance at his face was sufficient to tell me his fate. How it had been caused I could only imagine, but there was no doubt about the fact that he was dead. When I had convinced myself of this I returned to the girl. Her eyes were now open, and as I knelt beside her she asked in English what had happened.

'You have been wounded,' I answered.

'And my father?'

There was nothing to be gained by deceiving her, so I said simply: 'I have sad news for you – I fear he is dead.'

Upon hearing this she uttered a little cry, and for a moment seemed to lose consciousness again. I did not, however, wait to revive her, but went across to where her father lay, and picking the body up in my arms, carried it across the street to a dark corner. Having placed it there, I returned to the girl, and lifting her on to my shoulder ran down the street in the direction I had come. In the distance I could hear the noise of the mob, who were still engaged wrecking the murdered man's dwelling.

Arriving at the spot where I had stood when I first heard the cry for help, I picked up my old course and proceeded along it to my destination. In something less than ten minutes I had reached the house and knocked, in the way Laohwan had done, upon the door, which was immediately opened to me. I gave the password, and was admitted with my burden. If the custodian of the door thought anything, he did not give utterance to it, and permitted me to reach the second door unmolested.

Again I knocked, and once more the door was opened. But this time I was not to be allowed to pass unchallenged. Though I had given the password correctly, the door-keeper bade me wait while he scrutinised the burden in my arms.

'What have you here?' he asked.

'Have you the right to ask?' I said, assuming a haughty air. 'His Excellency has sent for this foreign devil to question her. She has fainted with fright. Now stand aside, or there are those who will make you pay for stopping me.'

He looked a trifle disconcerted, and after a moment's hesitation signed to me to pass. I took him at his word, and proceeded into the room where I had left my chief. That Nikola was eagerly expecting me I gathered from the pleasure my appearance seemed to give him.

'You are late,' he cried, coming quickly across to me. 'I have been expecting you this hour past. But what on earth have you got there?'

'A girl,' I answered, 'the daughter of a missionary, I believe. She has been wounded, and even now is unconscious. If I had not discovered her she would have been killed by the man who murdered her father.'

'But what on earth made you bring her here?'

'What else could I do? Her father is dead, and I believe the mob has wrecked their house.'

'Put her down,' said Nikola, 'and let me look at her.'

I did as he bade me, and thereupon he set to work to examine her wound. With a deftness extraordinary, and a tenderness of which one would scarcely have believed him capable, he bathed the wound with water, which I procured from an adjoining room, then, having anointed it with some stuff from a small medicine chest he always carried about with him, he bound it up with a piece of Chinese cloth. Having finished he said: 'Lift her up while I try the effect of this upon her.'

From the chest he took a small cut-glass bottle, shaped something like that used by European ladies for carrying smelling-salts, and having opened her mouth poured a few drops of what it contained upon her tongue. Almost instantly she opened her eyes, looked about her, and seeing, as she supposed, two Chinamen bending over her, fell back with an expression of abject terror on her face. But Nikola, who was still kneeling beside her, reassured her, saying in English: 'You need have no fear. You are in safe hands. We will protect you, come what may.'

His speech seemed to recall what had happened to her remembrance.

'Oh, my poor father!' she cried. 'What have you done with him?'

'To save your life,' I answered, 'I was compelled to leave his body in the street where I had found it; but it is quite safe.'

'I must go and get it,' she said. And as she spoke she tried to rise, but Nikola put out his hand and stopped her.

'You must not move,' he said. 'Leave everything to me. I will take care that your father's body is found and protected.'

'But I must go home.'

'My poor girl,' said Nikola tenderly, 'you do not know everything. You have no home to go to. It was wrecked by the mob this evening.'

'Oh dear! oh dear! Then what is to become of me? They have killed my father and wrecked our house! And we trusted them so.'

Without discussing this point Nikola rose and left the room. Presently he returned, and again approached the girl.

'I have sent men to find your father's body,' he said. 'It will be conveyed to a safe place, and within half an hour the English Consul will be on the trail of his murderer. Now tell me how it all occurred.'

'I will tell you what I can,' she answered. 'But it seems so little to have brought about so terrible a result. My father and I left our home this evening at half-past seven to hold a service in the little church our few converts have built for us. During the course of the service it struck me repeatedly that there was something wrong, and when we came out and saw the crowd that had collected at the door this impression was confirmed. Whether they intended to attack us or not I cannot say, but just as we were leaving a shout was raised, and instantly off the mob ran, I suppose in the direction of our house. I can see that now, though we did not suspect it then. Fearing to follow in the same direction, we passed down a side street, intending to proceed home by another route. But as we left the main thoroughfare and turned into the dark lane where you found us, a man rushed out upon my father, and with a thick stick, or a bar of iron, felled him to the ground. I endeavoured to protect him and to divert his attention to myself, whereupon he drew a knife and stabbed me in the shoulder. Then you came up and drove him off.'

As she said this she placed her hand upon my arm.

'I cannot tell you how grateful I am to you,' she said.

'It was a very small service,' I answered, feeling a little confused by her action. 'I only wished I had arrived upon the scene earlier.'

'Whatever am I to do?'

'Have you any friends in Tientsin?' enquired Nikola. 'Anyone to whom you can go?'

'No, we know no one at all,' the girl replied. 'But I have a sister in Pekin, the wife of a missionary there. Could you help me to get so far?'

'Though I cannot take you myself,' said Nikola, 'if you like I will put you in the way of getting there. In the meantime you must not remain in this house. Do not be alarmed, however; I will see that you are properly taken care of.'

Again he left the room, and while he was gone I looked more closely at the girl whom I had rescued. Her age might have been anything from twenty to twenty-three, her face was a perfect oval in shape, her skin was the most delicate I had ever seen, her mouth was small, and her eyes and hair were a beautiful shade of brown. But it was her sweet expression which was the chief charm of her face, and this was destined to haunt me for many a long day to come.

I don't think I can be said to be a ladies' man (somehow or another I have never been thrown much into feminine society), but I must confess when I looked into this girl's sweet face, a thrill, such as I had never experienced before, passed over me.

'How can I ever thank you for your goodness?' she asked simply.

'By bearing your terrible trouble bravely,' I answered. 'And now, will you consider me impertinent if I ask your name?'

'Why should I? My name is Medwin – Gladys Mary Medwin. And yours?'

'It ought to be Mah Poo in this dress, oughtn't it? In reality it is Wilfred Bruce.'

'But if you are an Englishman why are you disguised in this fashion?'

'That, I am sorry to say, I cannot tell you,' I answered. 'Do you know, Miss Medwin, it is just possible that you may be the last Englishwoman I shall ever speak to in my life?'

'What do you mean?' she asked.

'Again I can only say that I cannot tell you. But I may say this much, that I am going away in a few hours' time to undertake something which, more probably than not, will cost me my life. I don't know why I should say this to you, but one cannot be prosaic at such moments as these. Besides, though our acquaintance is only an hour or so old, I seem to have known you for years. You say I have done you a service; will you do one for me?'

'What can I do?' she asked, placing her little hand upon my arm.

'This ring,' I said, at the same time drawing a plain gold circlet from my finger, 'was my poor mother's last gift to me. I dare not take it with me where I am going. Would it be too much to ask you to keep it for me? In the event of my not returning, you might promise me to wear it as a little memento of the service you say I have done you tonight. It would be pleasant to think that I have one woman friend in the world.'

As I spoke I raised the hand that lay upon my arm, and, holding it in mine, placed the ring upon her finger.

'I will keep it for you with pleasure,' she said. 'But is this work upon which you are embarking really so dangerous?'

'More so than you can imagine,' I replied. 'But be sure of this, Miss Medwin, if I do come out of it alive, I will find you out and claim that ring.'

'I will remember,' she answered, and just as she had finished speaking Nikola re-entered the room.

'My dear young lady,' he said hurriedly, 'I have made arrangements for your safe conduct to the house of a personal friend, who will do all he can for you while you remain in Tientsin. Then as soon as you can leave this place he will have you escorted carefully to your sister in Pekin. Now I think you had better be going. A conveyance is at the door, and my friend will be waiting to receive you. Mr Bruce, will you conduct Miss Medwin to the street?'

'You are very good to me.'

'Not at all. You will amply compensate me if you will grant me one favour in return.'

'How can I serve you?'

'By never referring in any way to the fact of your having met us. When I tell you that our lives will in a great measure depend upon your reticence, I feel sure you will comply with my request.'

'Not a word shall escape my lips.'

Nikola bowed, and then almost abruptly turned on his heel and walked away. Seeing that his action was meant as a signal that she should depart, I led the way down the passage into the street, where a chair was in waiting. Having placed her in it, I bade her goodbye in a whisper.

'Goodbye,' I said. 'If ever I return alive I will enquire for you at the house to which you are now going,'

'Goodbye, and may God protect you!'

She took my hand in hers, and next moment I felt something placed in the palm. Then I withdrew it; the coolies took up the poles, and presently the equipage was moving down the street.

I waited until it was out of sight, and then went back into the house, where I found Nikola pacing up and down the room, his hands behind his back and his head bowed low upon his breast. He looked up at me, and, without referring to what had happened, said quickly: 'The ponies will be at the door in an hour's time. If you want any rest you had better take it now. I am going to have an interview with the old man we saw tonight. I want to try and worm some more information for our guidance out of him. Don't leave this room until my return, and, above all, remember in your future dealings with me that I am a chief priest, and as such am entitled to the deepest reverence. Always bear in mind the fact that one little mistake may upset all our plans, and may land both our heads on the top of the nearest city gate.'

'I will remember,' I said. And he thereupon left the room.

When he had gone I put my hand into my pocket and drew out the little keepsake Miss Medwin had given me. It proved to be a small but curiously chased locket, but, to my sorrow, contained no photograph. She had evidently worn it round her neck, for a small piece of faded ribbon was still attached to it. I looked at it for a moment, and then slipped the ribbon round my own neck, for so only could I hope to prevent its being stolen from me. Then I laid myself down upon a mat in a corner, and in less time than it takes to tell fell fast asleep. When I woke it was to find Nikola shaking me by the shoulder.

'Time's up,' he said. 'The ponies are at the door, and we must be off.'

I had hardly collected my faculties and scrambled to my feet before the old man whom I had seen on the previous evening entered the room, bringing with him a meal, consisting principally of rice and small coarse cakes made of maize. We fell to work upon them, and soon had them finished, washing them down with cups of excellent tea.

Our meal at an end, Nikola led the old man aside and said something to him in an undertone, emphasising his remarks with solemn gestures. Then, with the whole retinue of the house at our heels to do us honour, we proceeded into the courtyard, where Laohwan was in waiting with five ponies. Two were laden with baggage, upon one of the others Nikola seated himself, I appropriated the second, Laohwan taking the third. Then, amid the respectful greeting of the household, the gates were opened, and we rode into the street. We had now embarked upon another stage of our adventures.

CHAPTER SIX

On the road to Pekin

As we left the last house of the native city of Tientsin behind us the sun was in the act of rising. Whatever the others may have felt I cannot say, but this I know, that there was at least one person in the party who was heartily glad to have said goodbye to the town. Though we had only been in it a short time we had passed through such a series of excitements during that brief period as would have served to disgust even such a glutton as Don Quixote himself with an adventurous life.

For the first two or three miles our route lay over a dry mud plain, where the dust, which seemed to be mainly composed of small pebbles, was driven about our ears like hail by the dawn wind. We rode in silence. Nikola, by virtue of his pretended rank, was some yards ahead, I followed next; Laohwan came behind me, and the baggage ponies and the Mafoos (or native grooms) behind him again. I don't know what Nikola was thinking about, but I'm not ashamed to confess that my own thoughts reverted continually to the girl whom I had been permitted the opportunity of rescuing on the previous evening. Her pale sweet face never left me, but monopolised my thoughts to the exclusion of everything else. Though I tried again and again to bring my mind to bear upon the enterprise on which we were embarking, it was of no use; on each occasion I came back to the consideration of a pair of dark eyes and a wealth of nut-brown hair. That I should ever meet Miss Medwin again seemed most unlikely; that I wanted to I will not deny; and while I am about it I will even go so far as to confess that, not once but several times, I found myself wishing, for the self-same reason, that I had thought twice before accepting Nikola's offer. One moment's reflection, however, was sufficient to show me that had I not fallen in with Nikola I should in all probability not only have never known her at all, but, what was more to the point, I should most likely have been in a position where love-making would not only have been foolish, but indeed quite out of the question.

When we had proceeded something like five miles Nikola turned in his saddle and beckoned me to his side.

'By this time,' he said, 'Prendergast and Eastover will have received the telegrams I requested Williams to dispatch to them. They will not lose a moment in getting on their way, and by the middle of next week they should have the priest of Hankow in their hands. It will take another three days for them to inform us of the fact, which will mean that we shall have to wait at least ten days in Pekin before presenting ourselves at the Llamaserai. This being so, we will put up at a house which has been recommended to me in the Tartar city. I shall let it be understood there that I am anxious to undertake a week's prayer and fasting in order to fit myself for the responsibilities I am about to take upon me, and that during that time I can see no one. By the end of the tenth day, I should have heard from Prendergast and know enough to penetrate into the very midst of the monks. After that it should be all plain sailing.'

'But do you think your men will be able to abduct this well-known priest without incurring suspicion?'

'They will have to,' answered Nikola. 'If they don't we shall have to pay the penalty. But there, you need have no sort of fear. I have the most perfect faith in the men. They have been well tried, and I am sure of this, if I were to tell either of them to do anything, however dangerous the task might be, they would not think twice before obeying me. By the way, Bruce, I don't know that you are looking altogether well.'

'I don't feel quite the thing,' I answered; 'my head aches consumedly, but I don't doubt it will soon pass off.'

'Well, let us push on. We must reach the rest-house tonight, and to do that we have got a forty-mile ride ahead of us.'

It is a well-known fact that though Chinese ponies do not present very picturesque outward appearances, there are few animals living that can equal them in pluck and endurance. Our whole cavalcade, harness and pack-saddles included, might have been purchased for a twenty-pound note; but I very much doubt if the most costly animals to be seen in Rotten Row, on an afternoon in the season, could have carried us half so well as those shaggy little beasts, which stood but little more than thirteen hands.

In spite of the fact that we camped for a couple of hours in the middle of the day, we were at the rest-house, half-way to Pekin, before sundown. And a wretched place it proved – a veritable Chinese inn, with small bare rooms, quite unfurnished, and surrounded by a number of equally inhospitable stables.

As soon as we arrived we dismounted and entered the building, on the threshold of which the boorish Chinese landlord received us. His personality was in keeping with his house; but observing that we were strangers of importance he condescended to depart so far from his usual custom as to show us at least the outward signs of civility. So we chose our rooms and ordered a meal to be instantly prepared. Our blankets were unpacked and spread upon the floor of our bedrooms, and almost as soon as this was done the meal was announced as ready.

It consisted, we discovered, of half a dozen almost raw eggs, two tough fowls, and a curiously cooked mess of pork. The latter dish, as everyone knows who has had anything to do with the Celestial Empire, is one of the staple diets of all but Mohammedan Chinamen.

Swarms of beggars, loathsome to a degree, infested the place, begging and whining for any trifle, however insignificant. They crawled about the courtyards and verandahs, and at last became so emboldened by success that they ventured to penetrate our rooms. This was too much of a good thing, and I saw that Nikola thought so too.

When one beggar, more impertinent than the rest, presented himself before us, after having been warned repeatedly, Nikola called Laohwan to him and bade him take the fellow outside and, with the assistance of two coolies, treat him to a supper of bamboo. Anyone who has seen this peculiar punishment will never forget it; and at last the man's cries for mercy became so appalling as to warrant my proceeding to the courtyard and bidding them let him go.

After I returned to my room, which adjoined that occupied by Nikola, we sat talking for nearly an hour, and then retired to rest.

But though I disrobed myself of my Chinese garments, and stretched myself out upon the blankets, sleep would not visit my eyelids. Possibly I was a little feverish; at any rate I began to imagine all sorts of horrible things. Strange thoughts crowded upon my brain, and the most uncanny sounds spoke from the silence of the night. Little noises from afar concentrated themselves until they seemed to fill my room. A footfall in the street would echo against the wall with a mysterious distinctness, and the sound of a dog barking in a neighbouring compound was intensified till it might have been the barking of a dozen. So completely did this nervousness possess me that I soon found myself discovering a danger in even the creaking of the boards in an adjoining room, and the chirrup of an insect in the roof.

How long I remained in this state I cannot say. But at last I could bear it no longer. I rose therefore from my bed and was about to pace the room, in the hope of tiring myself into sleeping, when the sound of a stealthy footstep in the corridor outside caught my ears. I stood rooted to the spot, trying to listen, with every pulse in my body pumping like a piston rod. Again it sounded, but this time it was nearer my door. There was a distinct difference, however; it was no longer a human step, as we are accustomed to hear it, but an equalised and heavy shuffling sound that for a moment rather puzzled me. But my mystification was of scarcely an instant's duration. I had heard that sound before in the Manillas the same night that a man in my hotel was murdered. One second's reflection told me that it was made by someone proceeding along the passage upon his hands and knees. But why was he doing it? Then I remembered that the wall on the other side of the corridor was only a foot or two high. The intruder, whoever he might be, evidently did not wish to be seen by the occupants of the rooms across the square. I drew back into a corner, took a long hunting-knife that I always carried with me, from beneath my pillow, and awaited the turn of events. Still the sound continued; but by this time it had passed my door, and as soon as I realised this, I crept towards the passage and looked out.

From where I stood I was permitted a view of the narrow corridor, but it was empty. Instinct told me that the man had entered the room next to mine. Since I had first heard him he would not have had time to get any further. The adjoining apartment was Nikola's, and after the fatigue of the day it was ten chances to one he would be asleep. That the fellow's mission was an evil one it did not require much penetration to perceive. A man does not crawl about lonely corridors, when other men are asleep, on hands and knees, for any good purpose. Therefore, if I wished to save my employer's life, I knew I must be quick about it.

A second later I had left my own room and was hastening up the passage after him. Reaching the doorway I stood irresolute, trying to discover by listening whereabouts in the room the man might be. It was not long before I heard a heavy grunt, followed by a muttered ejaculation. Then I rushed into the room, and across to where I knew Nikola had placed his bed. As I did so I came in contact with a naked body, and next moment we were both rolling and tumbling upon the floor.

It was a unique experience that fight in the dark. Over and over the man and I rolled, clinging to each other and putting forth every possible exertion to secure a victory. Then I heard Nikola spring to his feet, and run towards the door. In response to his cry there was an immediate hubbub in the building, but before lights could reach us I had got the upper hand and was seated across my foe.

Laohwan was the first to put in an appearance, and he brought a torch. Nikola took it from him and came across to us. Signing me to get off the man whom I was holding, he bent down and looked at him.

'Ho, ho!' he said quietly. 'This is not burglary then, but vengeance. So, you rogue, you wanted to repay me for the beating you got tonight, did you? It seems I have had a narrow escape.'

It was as he said. The man whom I had caught was none other than the beggar whose persistence had earned him a beating earlier in the evening.

'What will your Excellency be pleased to do with him?' asked Laohwan.

Nikola saw his opportunity. He told the man to stand up. Then looking him straight in the eyes for perhaps a minute, he said quietly: 'Open your mouth.'

The man did as he was ordered.

'It is impossible for you to shut it again,' said Nikola. 'Try.'

The poor wretch tried and tried in vain. His jaws were as securely fastened as if they had been screwed top and bottom. He struggled with them, he tried to press them together, but in vain; they were firmly fixed and defied him. In his terror he ran about the room, perspiration streaming from his face, and all the time uttering strange cries.

'Come here!' said Nikola. 'Stand before me. Now shut your mouth.'

Instantly the man closed his mouth.

'Shut your eyes.'

The man did as he was ordered.

'You are blind and dumb; you cannot open either your eyes or your mouth.'

The man tried, but with the same result as before. His mouth and eyes were firmly sealed. This time his terror was greater than any words could express, and he fell at Nikola's feet imploring him in inarticulate grunts to spare him. The crowd who had clustered at the door stood watching this strange scene open-mouthed.

'Get up!' said Nikola to the miserable wretch at his feet. 'Open your mouth and eyes. You would have murdered me, but I have spared you. Try again what you have attempted tonight, and both sight and speech will be instantly taken from you and never again restored. Now go!'

The man did not wait to be bidden twice, but fled as if for his life, parting the crowd at the doorway just as the bows of a steamer turn away the water on either side.

When only Laohwan remained, Nikola called him up.

'Are you aware,' he said, 'that but for my friend's vigilance here I should now be a dead man? You sleep at the end of the passage, and it was your duty to have taken care that nobody passed you. But you failed in your trust. Now what is your punishment to be?'

In answer the man knelt humbly at his master's feet.

'Answer my question! What is your punishment to be?' the same remorseless voice repeated. 'Am I never to place trust in you again?'

'By the graves of my ancestors I swear that I did not know that the man had passed me.'

'That is no answer,' said Nikola. 'You have failed in your duty, and that is a thing, as you know, I never forgive. But as you have been faithful in all else, I will not be too hard upon you. In an hour's time you will saddle your horse and go back to Tientsin, where you will seek out Mr Williams and tell him that you are unsatisfactory, and that I have sent you back. You will remain with him till I communicate with you again. Fail to see him or to tell him what I have said, and you will be dead in two days. Do you understand me?'

Once more the man bowed low.

'Then go!'

Without a word the fellow rose to his feet and went towards the door. In my own heart I felt sorry for him, and when he had left, I said as much to Nikola, at the same time enquiring if he thought it prudent to make an enemy of a man who held our lives in his hand.

'My friend,' he answered, 'there is a Hindu proverb which says, "A servant who cannot be trusted is as a broken lock upon the gateway of your house." As to what you say about prudence, you need have no fear. I have had many dealings with Laohwan, and he knows me. He would rather die the death of a Thousand Cuts than betray me. But while I am blaming him I am forgetting to do justice to you. One thing is very certain, but for your intervention I should not be talking to you now. I owe you my life. I can only ask you to believe that, if ever the chance occurs, you will not find me ungrateful.'

'It was fortunate,' I said, 'that I heard him pass along the passage, otherwise we might both have perished.'

'It was strange, after all the exertions of the day, that you should have been awake. I was sleeping like a top. But let me look at you. Good heavens, man! I told you this morning you were looking ill. Give me your wrist.'

He felt my pulse, then stared anxiously into my face. After this he took a small bottle from a travelling medicine-chest, poured a few drops of what it contained into a glass, filled it up from a Chinese water-bottle nearby, and then bade me drink it. Having done so I was sent back to bed, and within five minutes of arriving there was wrapped in a dreamless sleep.

When I woke it was broad daylight and nearly six o'clock. I felt considerably better than when I had gone to bed the previous night, but still I was by no means well. What was the matter with me, however, I could not tell.

At seven o'clock an equivalent for breakfast was served to us, and at half-past the ponies were saddled and we proceeded on our journey. As we left the inn I looked about to see if I could discover any signs of poor Loahwan, but as he was not there I could only suppose he had accepted Nikola's decision as final and had gone back to Tientsin.

As usual Nikola rode on ahead, and it was not difficult to see that the story of his treatment of his would-be murderer had leaked out. The awe with which he was regarded by the people with whom we came in contact was most amusing to witness. And you may be sure he fully acted up to the character which had been given him.

After halting as usual at midday we proceeded on our way until four o'clock, when a pleasurable sensation was in store for us. Rising above the monotonous level of the plain were the walls of the great city of Pekin. They seemed to stretch away as far as the eye could reach. As we approached them they grew more imposing, and presently an enormous tower, built in the usual style of Chinese architecture, and pierced with innumerable loop-holes for cannon, appeared in sight. It was not until we were within a couple of hundred yards of it, however, that we discovered that these loop-holes were only counterfeit, and that the whole tower was little more than a sham.

We entered the city by a gateway that would have been considered insignificant in a third-rate Afghan village, and, having paid the tolls demanded of us, wondered in which direction we had best proceed, in order to find the lodgings to which our friend in Tientsin had directed us.

Having pressed a smart-looking youth into our service as guide, we were conducted by a series of tortuous thoroughfares to a house in a mean quarter of the city. By the time we reached it it was quite dark, and it was only after much waiting and repeated knockings upon the door that we contrived to make those within aware of our presence. At last, however, the door opened and an enormously stout China-man stood before us.

'What do you want?' he asked of Nikola, who was nearest to him.

'That which only peace can give,' said Nikola.

The man bowed low.

'Your Excellency has been long expected,' he said. 'If you will be honourably pleased to step inside, all that my house contains is yours.'

We followed him through the dwelling into a room at the rear. Then Nikola bade him call in the chief Mafoo, and when he appeared, discharged his account and bade him be gone.'

'We are now in Pekin,' said Nikola to me as soon as we were alone, 'and it behoves us to play our cards with the utmost care. Remember, as I have so often told you, I am a man of extreme sanctity, and I shall guide my life and actions accordingly. There is, as you see, a room leading out of this. In it I shall take up my abode. You will occupy this one. It must be your business to undertake that no one sees me. And you must allow it to be understood that I spend my time almost exclusively in study and upon my devotions. Every night when dark-ness falls I shall go out and endeavour to collect the information of which we stand in need. You will have charge of the purse and must arrange our commissariat.'

Half an hour later our evening meal was served, and when we had eaten it, being tired, we went straight to bed. But I was not destined to prove of much assistance to my friend, for next morning when I woke my old sickness had returned upon me, my skin was dry and cracked, and my head ached to distraction. I could eat no breakfast, and I could see that Nikola was growing more and more concerned about my condition.

After breakfast I went for a walk. But I could not rid myself of the heaviness which had seized me, so returned to the house feeling more dead than alive. During the afternoon I lay down upon my bed, and in a few minutes lost consciousness altogether.

CHAPTER SEVEN

A serious time

It was broad daylight when I recovered consciousness, the sunshine was streaming into my room, and birds were twittering in the trees outside. But though I sat up and looked about me I could make neither head nor tail of my position; there was evidently something wrong about it. When I had fallen asleep, as I thought, my couch had been spread upon the floor, and was composed of Chinese materials. Now I lay upon an ordinary English bedstead, boasting a spring mattress, sheets, blankets, and even a counterpane. Moreover, the room itself was different. There was a carpet upon the floor, and several pretty pictures hung upon the walls. I felt certain they had not been there when I was introduced to the apartment. Being, however, too weak to examine these wonders for very long, I laid myself down upon my pillow again and closed my eyes. In a few moments I was once more asleep and did not wake until towards evening.

When I did it was to discover someone sitting by the window reading. At first I looked at her – for it was a woman – without very much interest. She seemed part of a dream from which I should presently wake to find myself back again in the Chinese house with Nikola. But I was to be disabused of this notion very speedily.

After a while the lady in the chair put down her book, rose, and came across to look at me. *Then it was that I realised a most astounding fact; she was none other than Miss Medwin, the girl I had rescued in Tientsin!* She touched my hand with her soft fingers, to see if I were feverish, I suppose, and then poured into a medicine-glass, which stood upon a table by my side, some doctor's physic. When she put it to my lips I drank it without protest and looked up at her.

'Don't leave me, Miss Medwin,' I said, half expecting that, now I was awake, she would gradually fade away and disappear from my sight altogether.

'I am not going to leave you,' she answered; 'but I am indeed rejoiced to see that you recognise me again.'

'What is the matter with me, and where am I?' I asked.

'You have been very ill,' she answered, 'but you are much better now. You are in my brother-in-law's house in Pekin.'

I was completely mystified.

'In your brother-in-law's house,' I repeated. 'But how on earth did I get here? How long have I been here? and where is Nikola?'

'You have been here twelve days tomorrow,' she answered; 'you were taken ill in the city, and as you required careful nursing, your friend Dr Nikola had you conveyed here. Where he is now I cannot tell you; we have only seen him once. For my own part I believe he has gone into the country, but in which direction, and when he will be back, I am afraid I have no idea. Now you have talked quite enough, you must try and go to sleep again.'

I was too weak to disobey her, so I closed my eyes, and in a few minutes was in the land of Nod once more.

Next day I was so much stronger that I was able to sit up and partake of more nourishing food, and, what was still more to my taste, I was able to have a longer conversation with my nurse. This did me more good than any doctor's physic, and at the end of half an hour I was a different man. The poor girl was still grieving for her father, and I noticed that the slightest reference to Tientsin flooded her eyes with tears. From what I gathered later the Consul had acted promptly and energetically, with the result that the ringleaders of the mob which had wrecked the house had been severely punished, while the man who had gone further and murdered the unfortunate missionary himself had paid the penalty of his crime with his life.

Miss Medwin spoke in heartfelt terms of the part I had played in the tragic affair, and it was easy to see that she was also most grateful to Nikola for the way in which he had behaved towards her. Acting on his employer's instructions, Williams had taken her in and had at once communicated with the Consul. Then when Mr Medwin had been buried in the English cemetery and the legal business connected with his murder was completed, trustworthy servants had been obtained, and she had journeyed to Pekin in the greatest comfort.

During the morning following she brought me some beef-tea, and, while I was drinking it, sat down beside my bed.

'I think you might get up for a little while this afternoon, Mr Bruce,' she said; 'you seem so much stronger.'

'I should like to,' I answered. 'I must do everything in my power to regain my strength. My illness has been a most unfortunate one, and I expect Nikola will be very impatient.'

At this she looked a little mortified, I thought, and an instant later I saw what a stupid thing I had said.

'I am afraid you will think me ungrateful,' I hastened to remark; 'but believe me I was looking at it from a very different standpoint. I feel more gratitude to you than I can ever express. When I said my illness was unfortunate, I meant that at such a critical period of our affairs my being incapacitated from work was most inconvenient. You do not think that I am not properly sensible of your kindness, do you?'

As I spoke I assumed possession of her hand, which was hanging down beside her chair. She blushed a little and lowered her eyes.

'I am very glad we were able to take you in,' she answered. 'I assure you my brother and sister were most anxious to do so, when they heard what a service you had rendered me. But, Mr Bruce, I want to say something to you. You talk of this critical position in your affairs. You told me in Tientsin that if you continued the work upon which you were embarking you "might never come out of it alive". Is it quite certain that you *must* go on with it – that you *must* risk your life in this way?'

'I regret to say it is. I have given my word and I cannot draw back. If you only knew how hard it is for me to say this I don't think you would try to tempt me.'

'But it seems to me so wicked to waste your life in this fashion.'

'I have always wasted my life,' I answered, rather bitterly. 'Miss Medwin, you don't know what a derelict I am. I wonder if you would think any the worse of me if I told you that when I took up this matter upon which I am now engaged I was in abject destitution, and mainly through my own folly? I am afraid I am no good for anything but getting into scrapes and wriggling my way out of them again.'

'I expect you hardly do yourself justice,' she answered. 'I cannot believe that you are as unfortunate as you say.'

As she spoke there was a knock at the door, and in response to my call 'come in', a tall handsome man entered the room. He bore the unmistakable impress of a missionary, and might have been anything from thirty to forty years of age.

'Well, Mr Bruce,' he said cheerily, as he came over to the bed and held out his hand, 'I am glad to hear from my sister that you are progressing so nicely. I should have come in to see you, but I have been away from home. You have had a sharp touch of fever, and, if you will allow me to say so, I think you are a lucky man to have got over it so satisfactorily.'

'I have to express my thanks to you,' I said, 'for taking me into your house; but for your care I cannot imagine what would have become of me.'

'Oh, you mustn't say anything about that,' answered Mr Benfleet, for such was his name. 'We English are only a small community in Pekin, and it would be indeed a sorry thing if we did not embrace chances of helping each other whenever they occur.'

As he said this I put my hand up to my head. Immediately I was confronted with a curious discovery. When I was taken ill I was dressed as a Chinaman, wore a pigtail, and had my skin stained a sort of pale mahogany. What could my kind friends have thought of my disguise?

It was not until later that I discovered that I had been brought to the house in complete European attire, and that when Nikola had called upon Mr and Mrs Benfleet to ask them to take me in he had done so clad in orthodox morning dress and wearing a solar topee upon his head.

'Gladys tells me you are going to get up this afternoon,' said Mr Benfleet. 'I expect it will do you good. If I can be of any service to you in your dressing I hope you will command me.'

I thanked him, and then, excusing himself on the plea that his presence was required at the mission-house, he bade me goodbye and left the room.

I was about to resume my conversation with Miss Medwin, but she stopped me.

'You must not talk any more,' she said with a pretty air of authority. 'I am going to read to you for half an hour, and then I shall leave you to yourself till it is time for tiffin. After that I will place your things ready for you, and you must get up.'

She procured a book, and seating herself by the window, opened it and began to read. Her voice was soft and musical, and she interpreted the author's meaning with considerable ability. I am afraid, however, I took but small interest in the story; I was far too deeply engaged watching the expressions chasing each other across her face, noting the delicate shapeliness and whiteness of the hands that held the book, and the exquisite symmetry of the little feet and ankles that peeped beneath her dress. I think she must have suspected something of the sort, for she suddenly looked up in the middle of a passage which otherwise would have monopolised her whole attention. Her heightened colour and the quick way in which the feet slipped back beneath their covering confirmed this notion. She continued her reading, it is true, but there was not the same evenness of tone as before, and once or twice I noticed that the words were rather slurred over, as if the reader were trying to think of two things at one and the same time. Presently she shut the book with a little snap and rose to her feet.

'I think I must go now and see if I can help my sister in her work,' she said hurriedly.

'Thank you so much for reading to me,' I answered. 'I have enjoyed it very much.'

Whether she believed what I said or not I could not tell, but she smiled and looked a little conscious, as if she thought there might possibly be another meaning underlying my remark. After that I was left to myself for nearly an hour. During that time I surrendered myself to my own thoughts. Some were pleasant, others were not; but there was one conclusion to which I inevitably, however much I might digress, returned. That conclusion was that of all the girls I had ever met, Miss Gladys Medwin was by far the most adorable. She seemed to possess all the graces and virtues with which women are endowed, and to have the faculty of presenting them to the best advantage. I could not help seeing that my period of convalescence was likely to prove a very pleasant one, and you will not blame me, I suspect, if I registered a vow to make the most of it. How long I should be allowed to remain with them it was impossible for me to say. Nikola, my Old Man of the Sea, might put in an appearance at any moment, and then I should be compelled to bid my friends goodbye in order to plunge once more into his mysterious affairs.

When tiffin was finished I dressed myself in the garments which had been put out for me, and as soon as my toilet was completed took Mr Benfleet's arm and proceeded to a terrace in the garden at the back of the house. Here chairs had been placed for us, and we sat down. I looked about me, half expecting to find Miss Medwin waiting for us, but she did not put in an appearance for some considerable time. When she did, she expressed herself as pleased to see me about again, and then went across to where a little Chinese dog was lying in the sunshine at the foot of a big stone figure. Whether she was always as fond of the little cur I cannot say, but the way she petted and caressed it on this particular occasion would have driven most men mad with jealousy. I don't know that I am in any way a harsh man with animals, but I am afraid if I had been alone and that dog had come anywhere near me I should have been tempted to take a stick to him, and to have treated him to one of the finest beatings he had ever enjoyed in his canine existence.

Presently she looked up, and, seeing that I was watching her, returned to where we sat, uttered a few commonplaces, more than half of which were addressed to her brother-in-law, and finally made an excuse and returned to the house. To say that I was disappointed would scarcely be the truth; to describe myself as woefully chagrined would perhaps be nearer the mark. Had I offended her, or was this the way of women? I had read in novels that it was their custom, if they thought they had been a little too prodigal of their favours whilst a man was in trouble, to become cold and almost distant to him when he was himself again. If this were so, then her action on this particular occasion was only in the ordinary course of things, and must be taken as such. That I was in love I will not attempt to deny; it was, however, the first time I had experienced the fatal passion, and, like measles caught in later life, it was doubly severe. For this reason the treatment to which I had just been subjected was not, as may be expected, of a kind calculated to make my feelings easier.

Whether Mr Benfleet thought anything I cannot say, he certainly said nothing to me upon the subject. If, however, my manner after Miss Medwin's departure did not strike him as peculiar, he could not have been the clear-headed man of the world his Pekin friends believed him. All I know is that when I returned to the house, I was about as irritable a piece of man-flesh as could have been found in that part of Asia.

But within the hour I was to be treated to another example of the strange contrariness of the feminine mind. No sooner had I arrived in the house than everything was changed. It was hoped that I had not caught a fresh cold; the most comfortable chair was set apart for my use, and an unnecessary footstool was procured and placed at my feet. Altogether I was the recipient of as many attentions and as much insinuated sympathy as I had been subjected to coldness before. I did not know what to make of it; however, under its influence, in less than half an hour I had completely thawed, and my previous ill-temper was forgotten for good and all.

Next day I was so much stronger that I was able to spend the greater part of my time in the garden. On this occasion, both Mr and Mrs Benfleet being otherwise engaged, Miss Medwin was good enough to permit me a considerable amount of her company. You may be sure I made the most of it, and we whiled the time away chatting pleasantly on various subjects.

At tiffin, to which I sat up for the first time, it was proposed that during the afternoon we should endeavour to get as far as the Great

Wall, a matter of a quarter of a mile's walk. Accordingly, as soon as the meal was over, we set off. The narrow streets were crowded with coolies, springless private carts, sedan chairs, ponies but little bigger than St Bernard dogs, and camels, some laden with coal from the Western Hills, and others bearing brick-tea from Pekin away up into the far north. Beggars in all degrees of loathsomeness, carrying the scars of almost every known ailment upon their bodies, and in nine cases out of ten not only able but desirous of presenting us with a replica of the disease, swarmed round us, and pushed and jostled us as we walked. Add to this the fact that at least once in every few yards we were assailed with scornful cries and expressions that would bring a blush to the cheek of the most blasphemous coalheaver in existence, accompanied by gestures which made my hands itch to be upon the faces of those who practised them. Mix up with all this the sights and smells of the foulest Eastern city you can imagine, add to it the knowledge that you are despised and hated by the most despicable race under the sun, fill up whatever room is left with the dust that lies on a calm day six inches deep upon the streets, and in a storm – and storms occur on an average at least three times a week – covers one from head to foot with a coating of the vilest impurity, you will have derived but the smallest impression of what it means to take a walk in the streets of Pekin. To the Englishman who has never travelled in China this denunciation may appear a little extravagant. My regret, however, is that personally I do not consider it strong enough.

Not once but a hundred times I found good reason to regret having brought Miss Medwin out. But, thank goodness, we reached the Wall at last.

Having once arrived there, we seated ourselves on a bastion, and looked down upon the city. It was an extraordinary view we had presented to us. From the Wall we could see the Chi-en-Men, or Great Gate; to the north lay the Tartar city. Just below us was a comparatively small temple, round which a multitude of foot-passengers, merchants, coolies, carts, camels, ponies, private citizens, beggars, and hawkers, pushed and struggled. Over our heads rose the two great towers, which form part of the Wall itself, while to right and left, almost as far as the eye could reach, and seeming to overlap each other in endless confusion, were the roofs of the city, covered, in almost every instance, with a quantity of decaying brown grass, and in many cases having small trees and shrubs growing out of the interstices of the stones themselves. Away in the distance we could see the red wall of the 'Forbidden City', in other words, the

Imperial Palace; on another side was the Great Bell Tower, with the Great Drum Tower near it, and farther still the roofs of the Llama-serai. The latter, as you will suppose, had a particular attraction for me, and once having seen them, I could hardly withdraw my eyes.

When we had examined the view and were beginning to contemplate making our way home again, I turned to my companion and spoke the thoughts which were in my mind.

'I suppose, now that I am well again, I shall soon have to be leaving you,' I began. 'It cannot surely be very long before I hear from Nikola.'

She was quiet for a moment, and then said: 'You mustn't be angry with me, Mr Bruce, if I tell you that I do not altogether like your friend. He frightens me.'

'Why on earth should he?' I asked, as if it were a most unusual effect for Nikola to produce. Somehow I did not care to tell her that her opinion was shared by almost as many people as knew him.

'I don't know why I fear him,' she answered, 'unless it is because he is so different from any other man I have ever met. Don't laugh at me if I tell you that I always think his eyes are like those of a snake, so cold and passionless, yet seeming to look you through and through, and hold you fascinated until he withdraws them again. I never saw such eyes in my life before, and I hope I never may again.'

'And yet he was very kind to you.'

'I can't forget that,' she answered, 'and it makes me seem so ungrateful; but one cannot help one's likes and dislikes, can one?'

Here I came a little closer to her.

'I hope, Miss Medwin, you have not conceived such a violent antipathy to me?' I said.

She began to pick at the mud between the great stones on which we were sitting.

'No, I don't think I have,' she answered softly, seeming to find a source of interest in the movements of a tiny beetle which had come out of a hole, and was now making its way towards us.

'I am glad of that,' I replied; 'I should like you to think well of me.'

'I am sure I do,' she answered. 'Think how much I owe to you. Oh, that dreadful night! I shall never be able to drive the horror of it out of my mind. Have you forgotten it?'

I saw that she was fencing with me and endeavouring to divert the conversation to a side issue. This I was not going to permit. I looked into her face, but she turned away and stared at a cloud of dun-coloured dust that was rising on the plain behind.

'Miss Medwin,' I said, 'I suppose into the life of every man there must, sooner or later, come one woman who will be all the world to him. Gladys, can you guess what I am going to say?'

Once more she did not answer; but the unfortunate beetle, who had crawled unnoticed within reach of her foot, received his death-blow. And yet at ordinary times she was one of the kindest and most gentle of her sex. This significant little action showed me more than any words could have done how perturbed her feelings were.

'I was going to say,' I continued, 'that at last a woman – the one woman, of all others – has come into *my* life. Are you glad to hear it?'

'How can I be if I do not know her?' she protested feebly.

'If *you* do not,' I said, 'then nobody else does. Gladys, *you* are that woman. I know I have no right to tell you this, seeing what my present position is, but God knows I cannot help it. You are dearer to me than all the world; I have loved you since I first saw you. Can you love me a little in return? Speak your mind freely, tell me exactly what is in your heart, and, come what may, I will abide by your decision.'

She was trembling violently, but not a word passed her lips. Her face was very pale, and she seemed to find a difficulty in breathing, but at any cost I was going to press her for an answer. I took her hand.

'What have you to say to me, Gladys?'

'What can I say?'

'Say that you love me,' I answered.

'I love you,' she answered, so softly that I could scarcely hear the words.

And then, in the face of all Pekin, I kissed her on the lips.

Once in most men's lives – and for that reason I suppose in most women's also – there comes a certain five minutes when they understand exactly what unalloyed happiness means – a five minutes in their little spans of existence when the air seems to ring with joy-bells, when time stands still, and there is no such thing as care. That was how I felt at the moment of which I am writing. I loved and was loved; but almost before I had time to realise my happiness a knowledge of my real position sprang up before my eyes, and I was cast down into the depths again. What right had I, I asked myself, to tell a girl that I loved her, when it was almost beyond the bounds of possibility that I could ever make her my wife? None at all. I had done a cruel thing, and now I must go forward into the jaws of death, leaving behind me all that could make life worth living, and with the knowledge that I had brought pain into the one life of all others I desired to be free from it. True, I did not doubt but that if I appealed to Nikola he would let me off my bargain, but would that be fair when I had given my word that I would go on with him? No, there was nothing for it but for me to carry out my promise and trust to Fate to bring me safely back again to the woman I loved.

The afternoon was fast slipping by, and it was time for us to be thinking about getting home. I was disposed to hurry, for I had no desire to take a lady through the streets of Pekin after dusk. They, the streets, were bad enough in the daytime, at night they were ten times worse. We accordingly descended from the Wall, and in about ten minutes had reached the Benfleets' bungalow once more.

By the time we entered the house I had arrived at a determination. As an honourable man there were only two courses open to me: one was to tell Mr Benfleet the state of my affections, the other to let Gladys firmly understand that, until I returned – if return I did – from the business for which I had been engaged, I should not consider her bound to me in any shape or form. Accordingly, as soon as the evening meal was finished, I asked the missionary if he could permit me five minutes' conversation alone. He readily granted my request, but not, I thought, without a little cloud upon his face. We passed into his study, which was at the other end of the building, and when we got there he bade me take a seat, saying as he did so: 'Well, Mr Bruce, what is it you have to say to me?'

Now I don't think I am a particularly nervous man, but I will confess to not feeling at my ease in this particular situation. I cast about me for a way to begin my explanation, but for the life of me I could find none that suited me.

'Mr Benfleet,' I said at last in desperation, 'you will probably be able to agree with me when I assert that you know very little about me.'

'I think I can meet you there,' said the clergyman with a smile. 'If I am to be plain with you, I will admit that I know *very* little about you.'

'I could wish that you knew more.'

'For what reason?'

'To be frank, for a very vital one. You will understand when I tell you that I proposed to your sister-in-law, Miss Medwin, this afternoon.'

'I must confess I thought you would.' he said. 'There have been signs and wonders in the land, and though Mrs Benfleet and I live in Pekin, we are still able to realise what the result is likely to be when a man is as attentive to a girl as you have been to my sister-in-law of late.'

'I trust you do not disapprove?'

'Am I to say what I think?'

'By all means. I want you to be perfectly candid.'

'Then I am afraid I must say that I *do* disapprove.'

'You have, of course, a substantial reason?'

'I don't deny it is one that time and better acquaintance might possibly remove. But first let us consider the light in which you stand to us. Until a fortnight or so ago, neither I, my wife, nor Miss Medwin were aware that there was such a person in the world. But you were ill, and we took you in, knowing nothing, remember, as to your antecedents. You will agree with me, I think, that an English gentleman who figures in Chinese costume, and does not furnish a reason for it, and who perambulates China with a man who is very generally feared, is not the sort of person one would go out of one's way to accept for the husband of a sister one loves. But I am not a bigoted man, and I know that very often when a man has been a bit wild a good woman will do him more good than ever the Archbishop of Canterbury and all his clergy could effect. If you love her you will set yourself to win her, and, in sporting parlance, this is a race that will have to be won by waiting. If you think Gladys is worth working and waiting for, you will do both, and because I like what I have seen of you I will give you every opportunity in my power of achieving your end. If you don't want to work or to wait for her, then you will probably sheer off after this conversation, in which case we shall be well rid of you. And vice versa. One thing, however, I think would be prudent, and that is that you should leave my house tomorrow morning.'

'I was going to suggest as much myself.'

'You will understand why I say that, of course.'

'Perfectly.'

'Very good then. The matter, we are agreed therefore, stands as follows: as my sister-in-law's guardian I do not absolutely forbid your engagement. But I will consent to nothing for some considerable time to come, or, in other words, until I know you better. When you are in a position to support a wife in a befitting manner, and you can come to us without any secrecy or fear, I will talk further about it with you; in the meantime we will drop the subject. I am sure my poor father-in-law would have said the same.'

'You have treated me very fairly, and I thank you for it.'

'I am glad you fall in with my views. Now a few words as to this business upon which you are engaged. I don't know its nature, but I should be glad to receive your assurance that it is nothing of which you need be ashamed.'

'I don't know that there is anything in it of which I need reproach myself,' I said. 'It is more a matter of scientific research than anything else. I am paid a large sum to risk my life in order to find out certain things. That is as much as I can tell you.'

'You are pledged to secrecy, I suppose?'

'I have given my promise to reveal nothing.'

'In that case I won't press you. Now shall we go back to the ladies?'

'On my returning to the drawing-room my sweetheart greeted me with an anxious face. I smiled to reassure her, and when, a few minutes later, kindly Mrs Benfleet made an excuse and went out of the room to speak to her husband, I was able to tell her all that had occurred at our interview.

She quite agreed with me that the course her brother-in-law had suggested was the best we could pursue. For the whole of the time that I was absent with Nikola we would not communicate in any way. By this means we should be able to find out the true state of our own minds, and whether our passion was likely to prove lasting or not.

'But oh! how I wish that I knew what you are going to do,' said Gladys, when we had discussed the matter in all its bearings save one.

'I am afraid that is a thing I cannot tell even you,' I answered. 'I am hemmed in on every side by promises. You must trust me, Gladys.'

'It isn't that I don't trust you,' she said, with almost a sob in her voice. 'I am thinking of the dangers you will run, and of the long time that will elapse before I shall hear of you or see you again.'

'I'm afraid that cannot be helped,' I said. 'If I had only met you before I embarked on this wild-goose chase things might have been arranged differently, but now I have made my bed and must lie upon it.'

'As I said this afternoon, I am so afraid of Nikola.'

'But you needn't be. I get on very well with him, and as long as I play fair by him he will play fair by me. You might tremble for my safety if we were enemies, but so long as we remain friends I assure you you need have no fear.'

'And you are to leave us tomorrow morning?'

'Yes, darling, I *must* go! As we are placed towards each other, more than friends, and yet in the eyes of the world, less than lovers, it would hardly do for me to remain here. Besides, I expect Nikola will be requiring my services. And now, before I forget it, I want you to give me the ring I gave you in Tientsin.'

She left the room to return with it in a few moments. I took it from her and, raising her hand, placed it upon her finger, kissing her as I did so.

'I will wear it always,' she said; as she spoke, Mrs Benfleet entered the room. A moment later I caught the sound of a sharp, firm footstep in the passage that was unpleasantly familiar to me. Then Nikola entered and stood before us.

CHAPTER EIGHT

How Prendergast succeeded

To say that I was surprised at Nikola's sudden entry into the Benfleets' drawing-room would be to put too tame a construction upon my feelings. Why it should have been so I cannot say, but Nikola's appearance invariably seemed to cause me astonishment. And curiously enough I was not alone in this feeling; for more than one person of my acquaintance has since owned to having experienced the same sensation. What it was about the man that produced it, it would be difficult to say. At any rate this much is certain, it would be impossible for Nikola to say or do a commonplace thing. When he addressed you, you instinctively felt that you must answer him plainly and straightforwardly, or not at all; an evasive reply was not suited to the man. It occurred to you, almost unconsciously, that he was entitled to your best service, and it is certain that whether he was worthy or not he invariably got it. I have seen Nikola take in hand one of the keenest and, at the same time, most obstinate men in China, ask of him a favour which it would have been madness to expect the fellow to grant, talk to him in his own quiet but commanding fashion, and in less than ten minutes have the matter settled and the request granted.

One other point struck me as remarkable in this curious individual's character, and that was that he always seemed to know, before you spoke, exactly what sort of answer you were going to return to his question, and as often as not he would anticipate your reply. In my own case I soon began to feel that I might spare myself the trouble of answering at all.

Having entered the room, he crossed to where Gladys was sitting and, bowing as he took her hand, wished her good-evening. Then turning to me, and accompanying his remark with one of his indescribable smiles, he said – 'My dear Bruce, I am rejoiced to see you looking so well. I had expected to find a skeleton, and to my delight I am confronted with a man. How soon do you think you will be fit to travel again?'

'I am ready as soon as you are,' I answered, but not without a sinking in my heart as I looked across to Gladys and realised that the moment had indeed come for parting.

'I am indeed glad to hear it,' he answered, 'for time presses. Do you think you can accompany me in a few minutes? You can? – that's right. Now, if he will permit me, I should like to have a little talk with Mr Benfleet, and then we must be off.'

He went out of the room, accompanied by our hostess, and for ten minutes or so Gladys and I were left alone.

I will give you no description of what happened during that last interview. Such a parting is far too sacred to be described. It is enough to say that when it was over I joined Nikola in the verandah and we left the house together. With the shutting of the front door behind us all the happiness of my life seemed to slip away from me. For nearly five minutes I walked by my companion's side in silence, wondering whether I should ever again see those to whom I had just said goodbye. Nikola must have had some notion of what was passing in my mind, for he turned to me and said confidentially – 'Cheer up, Bruce! We shall be back again before you know where you are, and remember you will then be a comparatively rich man. Miss Medwin is a girl worth waiting for, and if you will allow me to do so, I will offer you my congratulations.'

'How do you know anything about it?' I asked in surprise.

'Haven't I just seen Mr Benfleet?' he answered.

'But surely he didn't tell you?'

'It was exactly what I went in to see him about,' said Nikola. 'You are my friend, and I owe you a good turn; for that reason, I wanted to try and make things as smooth for you as I could. To tell the truth, I am glad this has happened; it will make you so much the more careful. There's nothing like love – though I am not a believer in it as a general rule – for making a man mindful of his actions.'

'It is very good of you to take so much trouble about my affairs,' I said warmly.

'Not at all,' he answered. 'There can be no question of trouble between two men situated as we are. But now let us march along as quickly as we can. I have a lot to talk to you about, and we have many preparations to make before tomorrow morning.'

'But where are we going? This is not the way back to the house in which I was taken ill.'

'Of course not,' said Nikola. 'We're going to another place – the property of an Englishman of my acquaintance. There we shall change into our Chinese dresses again.'

'This, then, will probably be our last walk in European costume?'

'For many months at any rate.'

After this we again walked some time without speaking, Nikola revolving in his mind his interminable intrigues, I suppose; I thinking of the girl I had left behind me. At last, however, we reached the house to which we had been directing our steps, and, on knocking upon the door, were at once admitted. It was a tiny place, situated in a side street leading out of a busy thoroughfare. The owner was an Englishman, whose business often necessitated his taking long journeys into the interior; he was a bachelor, and, as I gathered from Nikola, by no means particular as to his associates; nor, I believe, did he bear any too good a reputation in Pekin. Before I had been five minutes in his company I had summed the man up exactly, though I could not for the life of me understand why Nikola had chosen him. That he was afraid of Nikola was self-evident, and that Nikola intended he should be was equally certain. To cover his nervousness the fellow, whose name was Edgehill, affected a jocular familiarity which intensified rather than concealed what he was so anxious to hide.

'You're not looking quite up to the mark, Mr Bruce,' he said, when I was introduced to him; then, with a leer, he imitated a man pulling a cork and continued – 'Eyes bright, hands shaky – the old thing. I suppose?'

'I have been down with fever,' I answered.

'Too much Pekin air,' he replied. 'This beastly country would make an Egyptian mummy turn up his toes. But never fear, keep your pecker up, and you'll pull through yet.'

I thanked him for this assurance, and then turned to Nikola, who had seated himself in a long cane chair, and, with his finger-tips pressed together, was staring hard at him. Something seemed to have ruffled his feathers. When he spoke it was distinctly and very deliberately, as if he desired that every word he uttered should be accepted by the person to whom it was addressed at its full value.

'And so, Mr Edgehill, after my repeated warnings you have informed your Chinese friends that you have a visitor?'

The man stepped back as if he had received a blow, his face flushed crimson and immediately afterwards became deathly pale. He put out his hand to the wall behind him as if for support; I also noticed that he drew such deep breaths that the glasses on the sideboard beside him rattled against each other.

'Your two Chinese friends,' said Nikola slowly and distinctly, 'must have placed a peculiar value upon the information with which you were able to furnish them if they were willing to pay so high a price for it.'

The man tried to speak, but without success. All his bounce had departed; now he was only a poor trembling coward who could not withdraw his eyes from that calm but cruel face that seemed to be looking into his very heart.

Then Nikola's manner changed, and he sprang to his feet with sudden energy.

'You dog!' he cried, and the intensity of his tone cut like a knife. 'You pitiful hound! So you thought you could play Judas with me, did you? How little you know Dr Nikola after all. Now listen, and remember every word I say to you, for I shall only speak once. Tonight, at my dictation, you will write a letter to your Chinese friends, and tomorrow morning at six o'clock you will saddle your horse and set off for Tientsin. Arriving there you will go to Mr Williams, whose address you know, and will tell him that I have sent you. You will say that you are to remain in his house, as his prisoner, for one calendar month; and if you dare to communicate with one single person concerning me or my affairs during that or any other time, I'll have your throat cut within half an hour of your doing so. Can it be possible that you think so little of me as to dare to pit your wits against mine? You fool! When you get out of my sight go down on your knees, and thank Providence that I haven't killed you at once for your presumption. Do you remember Hanotat? You do? Well, then, take care my friend that I do not treat you as I did him. Like you he thought himself clever, but eventually he preferred to blow his brains out rather than fight me further. You have been warned, remember. Now go and prepare for your journey. I will communicate with Williams myself. If you are not in his house by breakfast time on Thursday morning it will save you expense, for you will never have the appetite for another meal.'

Not a word did the man utter in reply, but left the room directly he was ordered, looking like a ghost.

When he had gone I turned to Nikola, for my astonishment exceeded all bounds, and said – 'How on earth did you know that he had given any information about us?'

In reply Nikola stooped and picked up from the floor two small stubs. On examination they proved to be the remains of two Chinese cigarettes. He then went across the room to a small curtained shelf, from which he produced a brandy bottle. Three glasses, all of which had been used, stood by the bottle, which was quite empty. Having pointed out these things to me he went back to his chair and sat down.

'Edgehill,' he explained, 'doesn't drink brandy, except when he has company; even then he takes very little. Before I left the house this evening to fetch you I took the precaution to look behind the curtain. That bottle was then more than three parts full, and I am quite certain that there were no ends of Chinese cigarettes upon the floor, because I looked about. Before that I had noticed that two men were watching the house from across the way. As I went down the street I picked up the end of a cigarette one of them had been smoking. There it is; you can compare them if you like. The man's manner when he let us in added another link to the chain of evidence, and his face, when I asked him the first question, told me the rest. Of course it was all guesswork; but I have not learned to read faces for nothing. At any rate you saw for yourself how true my accusation proved.'

'But what do you think the man can have told them?' I asked. 'And who could the people have been who questioned him?'

'He can't have told them very much,' Nikola replied, 'because there wasn't much to tell; but who the men could have been I am quite unable even to conjecture. I distrust them on principle, that's all.'

'But why did you send him to Williams?'

'To keep him out of the way of further mischief until we have had a fair start; also because I wanted to teach him a lesson. I may have occasion to use him at some future date, and a little bit of discipline of this sort will do him no harm. But now let us change the subject. I have something else I want to talk to you about. First see that there is no one at the door, and then bring your chair nearer to mine.'

I tip-toed over to the door. After I had reached it I waited for a moment and then opened it suddenly. There was no one outside, so I came back again and drew my chair nearer to Nikola. He had taken a letter from his pocket, and was evidently preparing to read it to me. Before he did so, however, he said in a low voice – 'This communication is from Prendergast. It was brought to me by special messenger at midday today. If you will give me your attention I will read it to you. It is dated from Tientsin, and runs as follows.

'To dr. Nikola, Pekin

'Dear Sir – I have to inform you that on Thursday week last I received a telegram from Mr Williams of this place bidding me come to him at once in order to negotiate some important business on your behalf. I had hardly received your wire before Mr Eastover called upon me to say that he was also in receipt of a telegram to the same effect. Understanding that no time must be lost, within two hours of receiving the messages, we were on board the steamer *James Monaghan*, *en route* for Tientsin.

'That place we reached in due course, and immediately reported our arrival to your agent, Mr Williams, from whom we learned the nature of the work upon which we were to be employed. Its danger was quite apparent to us, and at first, I must confess, the difficulties that surrounded it struck me as insurmountable. The Chief Priest of the Hankow Temple is a well-known personage, and very popular. His private life may almost be said to be nil. He never moves out unless he has a troop of people about him, while to attempt to get at him in his own town would only be to bring a mob of howling devils round our ears and ruin the whole enterprise beyond redemption. I immediately placed myself in communication with Chung-Yein, who fortunately was in Hankow at the time. It was through his agency we discovered that the priest – who, as you know, has resigned his office in the temple – was in the act of setting out upon a long journey.

'As soon as I learned this I instructed Chung-Yein to endeavour to elicit the route. He did so, and informed me that the man proposed travelling by way of Hang-Chu and Fon-Ching to Tsan-Chu, thence up the Grand Canal by way of Tsing-Hai to Tientsin, whence it was said he was going to make his way on to Pekin. I examined a chart of the country very carefully, and also conferred with Mr Williams and Mr Eastover, who both agreed with me that any action which might be necessary should be contrived and carried out at Tsan-Chu, which, as you know, is a town a little below the point where the canal, running to Nans-Shing, joins the Yun-Liang-Ho river.

'This settled, the next thing to be done was to endeavour to discover how the abduction of the priest could be effected. To suit your purposes we saw that it must be arranged in such a fashion that no scandal could possibly ensue. He would have to be abducted in such a manner that his followers would suppose he had left them of his own accord. But how to do this was a problem very difficult to work out. The man is old and exceedingly suspicious. He has a reputation for trusting nobody, and he invariably acts up to it. Unless, therefore, we could invent some really plausible excuse he would be almost impossible to catch, and foreseeing this I again called in Chung-Yein to my assistance. At any cost, I told him, he must manage to get into the priest's service, and once there to begin to ingratiate himself with his master to the very best of his ability. The time was so short that we dared not wait to cultivate an opportunity, but had to work in our chances, as they rose, to suit ourselves.

'At great risk Chung-Yein managed to get himself appointed a member of the priest's travelling party. Once this was done his peculiar abilities soon brought him under his master's notice, and that end having been achieved the rest was easy.

'Within three days of his arrival the household was broken up, and the priest, with a numerous retinue, commenced his journey. By the time they had travelled a hundred miles Chung-Yein was on very familiar terms with him; he discovered many means of adding to the priest's comfort, and during the march he was so assiduous in his attentions that his master began to place more and more trust in him. When they reached Fon-Ching he was advanced to the post of secretary, and then the plot which I had arranged was ready to be put into execution.

'Little by little Chung-Yein dropped into his master's willing ears the news of a fortune which he assured him might be obtained with very little risk. The avaricious old man swallowed the bait only too readily, and when he had digested the letters which the astute Chung read him from time to time, and which were supposed to have been written by his cousin Quong-Ta, from Tsan-Chu, he was as good as caught.

'After eight days of continuous travelling the company arrived at the entrance to the canal. Eastover and I had left Tientsin by this time, and had travelled post haste down to meet them. Once they were fairly installed at the principal inn Chung-Yein came to see me. He had arranged everything most carefully, it appeared, even to the extent of having it circulated among his fellow-servants that after leaving Tsan-Chu the high priest intended dispensing with their services and going on alone. It now only remained for us to arrange a meeting with him, and to have some means prepared whereby we might convey him across country, over the forty-odd miles that separated Tsan-Chu from Chi-Kau-Ho, to where a junk was already waiting to receive him. While Eastover undertook the arrangement of this part of the business I drew up the plan which was to give us possession of the priest's person.

'Chung-Yein was to represent to him that he was the unhappy possessor of a cousin who was a noted robber. By virtue of his evil habits he had accumulated great riches, but finding himself now likely to come within reach of the finger-tips of the law he was most anxious to purchase a friend who would stand by him in case of evil happening.

'The greedy old priest, intending to ask a large share of the plunder for the favour accorded, consented to bestow his patronage upon the youth, and when he was brought to understand that his share of the transaction would amount to something like six thousand taels, his anxiety to obtain possession of the coin became more and more intense. He discussed the matter with Chung-Yein times out of number, and finally it was decided that that night they should proceed together to a certain house in the village, where he should interview the culprit and also receive his share of the gains.

'As soon as I was made conversant with what had been arranged I pushed forward my plans, arranged with one of my own men to impersonate the cousin, and by the time dusk had fallen had everything in readiness. Relays of ponies were stationed at intervals along the road to the coast, and the skipper of the junk only waited to have his passenger aboard to weigh anchor and be off.

'At eight o'clock, almost to the minute, the priest, disguised, and accompanied by Chung-Yein, appeared at the door.

'They were admitted by the counterfeit cousin, who conducted them forthwith to the back of the house. Once in the room, negotiations were commenced, and the priest lost no time in severely reprimanding the young man for the evil life he had hitherto been leading. Then, that he might the better be able to understand what a nefarious career it had been, he demanded a glimpse of the profits that had accrued from it. They included a bag of dollars, a good selection of gold leaf, a quantity of English money, and a small bag of precious stones. All of these things had been prepared at considerable cost for his inspection.

'His old eyes twinkled greedily as they fell upon this goodly store, and his enthusiasm rose as each successive bag was opened. When at last the contents of the bag of stones were spread out before him he forgot his priestly sanctity altogether in his delight and stooped to examine them. As he did so Chung-Yein sprang forward, and threw a noose over his head, a chloroformed sponge was clapped against his nose, while the spurious cousin pulled his heels from under him and threw him on his back upon the floor.

'The anaesthetic did its work well, and in a short time the old gentleman was in our power. Half an hour later he was safely tied up in a chair, and was being deported as fast as his bearers could conduct him to Chi-Kau-Ho.

'In the meantime Chung-Yein had returned to the inn, where he paid off the retinue and informed them that their master had received a sudden summons and had started up the canal for Tientsin alone. Then Eastover and myself mounted our ponies and followed the worthy priest to the sea.

'Chi-Kau-Ho, which, as you know, is a place of abject poverty, and is only visited by junks bringing millet from Tientsin to exchange for fish, was the very place for our purpose. Fortunately it was high tide, and for that reason we were able to get our burden on board the junk without very much difficulty. At other times it is impossible for a boat drawing any depth of water at all to come within seven miles of the village. The bar, as doubtless you are aware, renders this impossible.

'As soon as we had handed over the man to the skipper we returned to the shore. An hour later the vessel set sail, and by the time you receive this letter the Chief Priest of Hankow will in all probability be somewhere among the pirates of Along Bay. As his captors on board the junk have no respect for his creed, and he has no money upon his person to bribe them to set him ashore again, I think he will find it difficult to get back to the mainland. But to prevent anything of the sort occurring I have told the owner of the junk that if, on the 21st day of August, six months ahead, he conveys him to Michel Dugenne, who by that time will be in Formosa, he will receive £100 English in exchange for his person. I think this will suit your purpose.

'As to our own movements, they were as follows.

'Leaving Chi-Kau-Ho we chartered a junk and proceeded up the coast to Pea-Tang-Ho, thence making our way on pony back to Tientsin, at which place we arrived two days since. Chung-Yein I have rewarded with 2,000 dollars, and he is now on his way, as fast as he can travel, to Hong-Kong. He intends, I believe, to make for Singapore, where he will reside till all chance of trouble has blown over. I have taken the precaution to register his address in case we should require his services again. Should you desire to see either Mr Eastover or myself, we will remain in Tientsin for a fortnight longer. After that Eastover purposes crossing to Japan, while I return to Hong-Kong, where I can always be heard of at the old address.

'Trusting that the manner in which we have conducted this dangerous affair will be to your satisfaction, I have the honour to subscribe myself, your obedient servant,

'WILLIAM PRENDERGAST

'Now,' said Nikola as he folded up this precious document, 'the coast is clear, and for the future I intend to be the Chief Priest of Hankow. During the time you have been ill I have been making a number of important enquiries, and I think I know pretty well the kind of course I shall have to steer. Tomorrow morning I intend that we shall enter the Llamaserai, where it will be imperative that we have all our wits about us. A change in our dress will also be necessary, particularly in mine. The priest is an old man, and I must resemble him as nearly as possible.'

'It will be a difficult character to support for so long. Do you think you are capable of it?'

He looked at me with one of his peculiar smiles.

'There was a time in my life,' he said, 'when I used to be a little uncertain as to my powers; since then I have taught myself to believe that if a man makes up his mind there is nothing in this world he cannot do. Yes, I shall manage it. You need have no fear on that score.'

'I have no fear,' I answered truthfully. 'I have the most implicit faith in you.'

'I am glad to hear it,' said Nikola, 'for you will want it all. Now let us retire to rest. At five o'clock we must begin to dress; at six I have to see that Edgehill starts for Tientsin.'

Without more ado we procured blankets and stretched ourselves upon the floor. In less than five minutes I was asleep, dreaming that I was helping the priest of Hankow to abduct Nikola from the Llamaserai, where he had gone to deposit the stick that Wetherell had given him.

When I woke, it was to hear horse-hoofs clattering out of the yard. It was broad daylight, and on looking about me I discovered that Nikola was not in the room. Presently he entered.

'Edgehill has departed,' he said, with a queer expression upon his face. 'I have just seen him off. Somehow I think it will be a long day before he will attempt to play tricks with Dr Nikola again.'

CHAPTER NINE

The Llamaserai

'Come,' said Nikola, when the last sounds of Edgehill's departure had died away; 'there is no time to lose; let us dress.'

I followed him into an adjoining room which, though somewhat larger than that in which we had hitherto sat, was even more poorly furnished. Here a number of dresses lay about on chairs, and from these Nikola chose two.

'The first thing to be considered,' he said, as he seated himself on a chair and looked at me, 'is that we have to change the form of our disguises in almost every particular. I have been thinking the matter most carefully out, and, as I said just now, we are going to be entirely different men. I shall be the Priest of Hankow, you will be his secretary. Here are your things; I should advise you to dress as quickly as you possibly can.'

I took him at his word, and appropriating the garments he assigned to me, returned with them to the front room. At the end of a quarter of an hour I was no longer an Englishman. My dress was of the richest silk, figured and embroidered in every conceivable fashion, my shoulders were enclosed in a grey cloak of the finest texture, my pigtail was of extraordinary length and thickness, while my sandals and hat were of the most fashionable make. If my rank had been estimated by the gorgeousness of my attire and the value of the material, I might have been a Taotai of a small province, or secretary to some metropolitan dignitary. When I had dressed myself I sat down and waited for Nikola to make his appearance.

A short while later a tall gaunt Chinaman, certainly fifty years of age, upon the chin of whose weather-beaten countenance an ill-trimmed beard was beginning to show itself, came into the room, accompanied by a smaller man much bent with age. I was resolved not to be hoodwinked this time, so I said in Chinese to the man who entered first, and who I estimated was nearer Nikola's size: 'You've not been long in getting ready.'

'It would be folly to be slow,' he answered; 'we have much to do,' and then without another word led the way down the passage towards the rear of the house. Arriving at the yard we discovered a perfect cavalcade drawn up. There were several led ponies, half a dozen mounted men, and about twice that number of hangers-on.

'One word,' I said, drawing Nikola, as I thought, on one side. 'What part am I to play in this pageant?'

'Is there not some little mistake?' the man said. 'For whom do you take me?'

'For my master,' I answered.

'Then I'm afraid you have chosen the wrong man,' he returned. 'If you want Dr Nikola, there he is mounting that pony yonder.'

I could hardly believe my eyes. The second man resembled Nikola in no possible particular. He was old, thin, and nearly bent double. His face was wrinkled into a hundred lines, and his eyes were much sunken, as also were his cheeks. If this were Nikola he might have gone through the whole length and breadth of China without any fear of his identity being for one moment questioned. I went across to him, and, scarcely believing what I had been told, addressed him as follows: 'If you are Nikola,' I said – 'and I can hardly credit it – I want you to give me my instructions.'

'You don't recognise me then?' he whispered. 'I'm glad of that; I wanted to try you. I thought to myself, if he does not find me out it is scarcely likely that anyone else will. Your own disguise is most excellent; I congratulate you upon it. With regard to your position, you are of course supposed to be my secretary. But I will give you a few points as we proceed. Now let us be starting.'

'But first, who is the man whom I mistook for you?'

'He is a fellow for whom I sent to Tientsin while you were ill; and as I have taken some trouble to ensure his fidelity you need have no fear of his betraying us. He will only accompany us as far as the Llamaserai, and then, having posed as chief of my retinue, he will leave us and return to the coast. Now mount your animal and let us start.'

I went back to my pony, and when I was in the saddle we filed slowly out of the gateway, down the crowded street and through the gates towards the Yung-Ho-Kung, or the great Llama temple. This enormous building, which has the reputation of being one of the most inaccessible places in China to Europeans, is located on the outskirts of the city, nearly five miles from the quarter in which Edgehill's house was situated.

Remembering its sinister reputation, you may imagine my sens-
ations as we rode up to the first great gate. I could not help wondering
what the Fates had in store for us inside. For all I knew to the contrary
I might be destined never to see the world outside the walls again. It
was not a cheering thought, and I tried to divert my attention from it
by looking about me.

Strangely enough the first two gates were by no means hard to
pass, but at the third the real difficulty began.

It was shut in our faces, and though we knew our coming had been
observed by those inside, not a sign of any living soul presented
itself. An awe-inspiring silence reigned in the great building, and for
some time our servants hammered upon the door in vain. Then a
shaven head appeared at a small grille and enquired our business.

Whether the answer he received was satisfactory or not I could not
say, but seeing that it did not unbar the gate, Nikola rode forward
and, leaning over in his saddle, said something in a low voice. The
effect was magical: the doors flew open instantly. Then a man came
forward and assisted Nikola to alight. He signed to me to do the
same, and I accordingly dismounted beside him. As I did so a servant
approached him and, greeting him with the utmost reverence, never
daring to raise his eyes to his face, said something which I could not
hear. When he had got through with it Nikola turned to me, and
bade me pay off the men. I did so, and they immediately returned to
the city by the way they had come. Then turning to the monk who
was still waiting, Nikola said, pointing to me: 'This is my secretary.
He is necessary to my well-being, so I beg that he may be allowed to
enter with me.' The monk nodded, and then the gate being opened
wide we passed through it. Once inside we ascended, by means of a
long flight of stone steps, to a courtyard, round which were a number
of small stone rooms not unlike cells. In the centre stood an enormous wooden statue of Buddha which riveted the attention at once; the
figure was at least seventy feet high, was covered with all sorts of
beautiful ornamentation, and held an enormous flower resembling a
lotus in either hand. On its head was a gold crown, and in each
section of the latter I could discern a smaller image, reproducing the
large one in every particular.

Above the cells just described was a series of long galleries, which
were reached by stairs from the courtyard, and above them again
rose roof after roof and tower after tower. From this terrace, if
one may so call it, we passed on to another, the approach to which
was guarded by two magnificent bronze lions. Making our way

through many temples, each decorated with Chinese hangings, to say nothing of ornaments in gold, silver, ivory, bronze and enamel, we came at last to one where we were requested to wait while our guide, who was evidently a person in authority, went off in search of the High Priest.

For nearly twenty minutes we remained alone together. The place was eerie in the extreme. The wind, entering by the windows on either side, rustled the long silken hangings; there was an intolerable odour of joss-sticks; and, as if this were not enough, we had the pleasure of knowing that we were only impostors, dependent upon our wits for our lives. If but one suspicion entered the minds of those we were deceiving, we might consider ourselves as good as dead men. In such an enormous building, unvisited by foreigners, and owning hardly any allegiance – if indeed such a feeble reed could help us – to the Emperor of China, the news of our death would excite no concern, and we would be as completely lost as the bubble which rises majestically from a child's pipe, only to burst unnoticed in mid-air.

As I watched the morning light playing among the hangings and listened to the booming of a gong which came to us from some distant part of the building, I could not help thinking of the sweet girl to whom I had plighted my troth, and who at that very moment might also be thinking of me and wondering how I fared. That I did not deserve such consideration on her part was only too certain, for surely never in the history of the world had a man embarked upon a more foolish undertaking. Columbus in his lonely little ship ploughing its way across the unknown ocean in search of a continent, the existence of which at times he must almost have doubted himself, was not one whit less desperate than we were at that moment. Franklin amid the ice, unconscious whether another week might not find his vessel ground to powder between the ice floes, and himself floating in the icy water, was not one tittle nearer death than we were while we waited for an audience with the father abbot of this most awesome monastery.

At the end of the twenty minutes my ears – which of late had been preternaturally sharp – detected the pattering of sandalled feet upon the stone staircase at the further end of the room. Next moment three figures appeared, two of whom were leading a third between them. The supporters were men in the prime of life. The third must have been at least eighty years of age. One glance was sufficient to show me that he was not a pure Mongol, but had probably Thibetan blood in his veins. Both he and his monks were attired in the usual coarse dress of the Buddhist priests, their heads being as destitute of hair as a billiard ball.

Having brought the old fellow down to the bottom of the stairs, the young men left him there, and returned up the steps again. Then it was that we made the discovery that, besides being old and infirm, the High Priest of the Llamaserai was nearly blind. He stood perfectly still for a moment after he had entered, a queer trembling figure, dressed in dingy yellow. Finally, with hands outstretched, he came towards where we stood.

'I beg you to tell me,' he said, 'who you are, and how it comes about that you thus crave our hospitality?'

He put the question in a high tremulous voice, more like a woman's than a man's.

'I am the Priest of the Temple of Hankow,' said Nikola gravely. 'And I am here for reasons that are best known to those who called me.'

'If it is as you say, how shall I know you?'

'Is the moon no longer aware that there are little stars?' asked Nikola, speaking with a perfection of accent that no Chinaman living could have excelled.

'Yea, but the dawn makes all equal,' replied the old man. 'But if you be he whom we have expected these last three weeks, there are other means whereby you can assure us of the truth of what you say.'

Nikola slipped his right hand inside his long outer jacket and drew from his pocket the tiny stick he had obtained from Wetherell, and handed it to the old man. No sooner had he received it, and run his fingers over the quaint Chinese characters engraved upon it, than the old fellow's demeanour changed entirely. Dropping upon his knees he kissed the hem of Nikola's dress.

'It is sufficient. I am satisfied that my lord is one of the Masters of Life and Death. If my lord will be pleased to follow his servant, accommodation shall be found for him.'

As he spoke he fumbled his way towards the staircase by which he had entered the room. Nikola signed to me to follow, and in single file we made our way to the room above. As we went I could not help noticing the solidity of the building. The place might have withstood a siege with the greatest ease, for the walls were in many cases two feet, and in not a few nearly three feet thick.

The stairs conducted us to a long passage, on either side of which were small rooms or cubicles. Leaving these behind us, we approached another flight of steps which led to the highest floor of the building.

At the end of a long corridor was a small ante-chamber hung round with dark coloured silks, just as we had seen in the great hall below. From this we entered another nearly twice the size, which was lighted with three narrow windows. From one of these, I afterwards discovered, a good view of the city of Pekin was obtainable.

As soon as we were safely inside, the High Priest assured us, in a quavering voice, that everything we might find in his humble dwelling was at our disposal, and that we might consider his rooms our home during our stay in the monastery. Then, with another expression of his deep respect, he left us, presumably to see that some sort of meal was prepared for us. As soon as the sound of his steps had died away Nikola leaped to his feet.

'So far so good,' he cried. 'He does not suspect us you see. We have played our parts to perfection. Tomorrow, if I can only get him into the proper frame of mind, I'll have the rest of the information I want out of him before he can turn round.'

For the rest of that day we amused ourselves perambulating the building, walking slowly with dejected bearings whenever we met any of the monks, greeting the various shrines with deepest reverences, prostrating ourselves at the altars, and in every way, so far as lay in our power, creating the impression that, in the practices of our faith, we were without our equals. At five o'clock we participated in the usual evening service held in the great hall, and for the first time saw the monks assembled together. A more disreputable crew, I can unhesitatingly assert, I had never seen before. They were of all ages and all ranks, but, so far as I could tell, there was not a face amongst them that did not suggest the fact that its owner was steeped to the eyebrows in sensuality and crime. Taken altogether, I very much doubt if, for general blackguardism, their equal could have been found in the length and breadth of Asia. Also I could not help speculating as to what sort of a chance we should stand if our secret should happen to be discovered, and we were compelled to run the gauntlet of the inmates. The service was not a long one, and in something under half an hour we were back in our rooms again. Then Nikola was summoned to an interview with the High Priest, and, while he was away, I wandered downstairs and strolled about the courtyards.

It was the time of the evening meal, and those monks who had already dined, were lolling about smoking, and gossiping over the affairs of the day. What they thought of my presence there I could not tell, but from one or two remarks I heard it struck me that I was not regarded with any too much favour.

At the end of one of the courtyards, that in fact in which we had noticed the large statue of Buddha, there was a well, and round the coping were seated quite a dozen men. Their quaintly coloured garments, their shaven heads and their curiously constructed pipes, backed by the rosy glow of the sunset, constituted a most picturesque and effective group. I crossed towards them, and bowing to the party, seated myself in a place which had just been vacated.

One of those present was an accomplished story-teller, and was in the middle of a lengthy narrative bristling with gods, devils, virtuous men, and reverend ancestors, when I sat down to listen. After he had finished I applauded vigorously, and being desirous of ingratiating myself with the company, called for silence and commenced a tale myself. Fortunately it was received with considerable favour, but I could not help noticing that my success was not very palatable to the previous narrator. He had been watching me ever since I joined the circle, and it struck me as I proceeded with my story that his interest increased. Then, like a flash, the knowledge dawned upon me that I had seen him before. As I remembered the circumstance a cold sweat of fear burst out upon me, my voice shook under my emotion, and in trying to think what I had better do, I lost the thread of my narrative. I saw my listeners look up in surprise, and an expression of malignant satisfaction came into my rival's face. Instantly I pulled myself together and tried to continue as if nothing out of the common had occurred. But it was too late; I had aroused suspicion, and for some reason or another the men had come to the conclusion that all was not right. How bitterly I regretted having joined the circle at all I need not say! But it was no use crying over spilt milk, so after a while I made an excuse and left them to their own devices, returning to the rooms set apart for the use of Dr Nikola and myself. Fortunately he was alone. Not knowing, however, who might be about, I did not address him at once, but sat down near the door and waited for him to speak. He very soon did so.

'I have been wanting you,' he said rather sharply. 'What have you been doing this hour past?'

'Wandering about the building,' I answered, 'and at the same time discovering something which is the very reverse of pleasant.'

'What do you mean,' he asked, his eyes – for he had removed his spectacles – glittering like those of a snake.

'I mean that there is a man in this monastery whom I have met before,' I said, 'and under very unpleasant circumstances.'

'Do you think he recognises you?'

'I hope not,' I answered; 'but I fear he does.'

'Where did you meet him, and why do you say "unpleasant"?'

'It was in Canton,' I answered, 'and this fellow tried to break into my house. But I caught him in time, and in the fight that followed he stabbed me in the wrist. I carry the mark to this day. Look at it for yourself. He would have been executed for it had not the magistrate before whom he was brought possessed a personal grudge against me and allowed him to escape.'

'Let me look at the mark,' said Nikola.

I gave him my left hand, pulling up my sleeve as I did so, that he might have a better view of it. Half way across, a little above the wrist bone, was a long white scar. Nikola gazed at it attentively.

'This is serious,' he said. 'You will have to be very careful, or that man will carry his news to the High Priest, and then we shall be nicely caught. For the future make it your habit to walk with your hands folded beneath your sleeves, and take care who you let come up beside you.'

'I will remember,' I answered, and as I spoke the great gongs, calling the monks to the last service of the day, boomed out from the courtyard below. Being determined not to show ourselves lacking in religious zeal we descended to the large hall, which we found already filled with worshippers. Nikola, by virtue of his sanctity, took up his place in a prominent position, hard by where sat the High Priest himself. I was near the western wall, surrounded by a set of the most loathsome and blackguardly ruffians it would be possible to imagine. At first I took but little notice of them, but when a new monk came up and pushed his way in alongside me my suspicions were aroused. It was not long before they were confirmed; the man next to me was the fellow who had looked at me in such a curious fashion when we were seated round the well, and about whom I had spoken to Nikola only a few minutes before. But even if he recognised me he did not allow a sign to escape him to show that he did. Throughout the service he occupied himself completely with his devotions, turned his face neither to the right hand nor to the left, and it was not until we were about to rise from our knees that he came out in his true colours. Then, just as I was half on to my feet, he stumbled against me with such violence that I fell back again and rolled over on to the floor. Then like lightning he sprang forward, seized me by the arm, and tearing back my sleeve looked at the scar upon my wrist. As he did so he allowed a little cry of triumph to escape him. For a moment I lay where I had fallen, too confused and horror-stricken at what had happened to say or do anything, and yet I knew that unless I acted promptly we were ruined indeed.

By this time the hall was more than half empty. I could see Nikola standing at the further end talking earnestly to the High Priest. To interrupt him would be akin to sacrilege; so after I had risen, and when the man had left me and hurried out after the others, I stood at a little distance and waited for him to notice me. As soon as he looked my way I placed three fingers of my right hand upon my forehead, a sign we had agreed to use whenever danger threatened us and it was necessary to act quickly. He saw my meaning, and a moment later, making some excuse, bade the High Priest good-night, and signing to me to follow him, retired to his dormitory.

As soon as we had reached it he turned sharply upon me, his eyes, in his excitement, blazing in his head like live coals.

'What further news have you to tell me?' he asked.

'Only that I am discovered,' I answered. 'While we were at prayers downstairs the man whom I suspected this evening pushed himself in next to me. I took the precaution to keep my hands covered with my sleeves lest he should see the scar he had inflicted. I could not move away from him for obvious reasons, and when the service was over I flattered myself that I had outwitted him. But he was as sharp as I, and just as I was rising from my knees he lurched against me and pushed me down upon the floor. Naturally I put up my hands to save myself, and as I did so he seized upon my wrist.'

For some minutes Nikola did not speak. He walked up and down the room like a caged tiger.

'This will put us in a nasty fix,' he said at last; 'and one mistake at this juncture will ruin everything. He will, of course, go direct to the High Priest in order to reveal his discovery, then that worthy will come to me, and I shall be compelled to produce you. You will be found to be an Englishman, disguised, and as soon as that is discovered we'll see the gleaming of the knives. This has come at a most unfortunate time, for by tomorrow morning, if all had gone well, I should have got the information I wanted, have been told the word that would admit us to the monastery in the mountains, and we could have left this place in safety. However, there is no time to waste talking of what might have been. I must work out some scheme that will save us, and at once. You had better go into the inner apartment and leave me alone.'

As he spoke I detected the sound of footsteps on the stairs. I ran into the inner room and drew the heavy curtain across the door. A moment later the High Priest, accompanied by two or three of the principal monks and the man who had discovered me, entered the room. Looking through a hole in the curtain I saw that Nikola had dropped upon his knees and was occupied with his devotions. On observing this the High Priest and his satellites came to a dead stop. Nikola was in no hurry, but kept them waiting for at least ten minutes. Then he rose and turned towards them.

'What does this mean?' he asked sternly; 'and how is it that this rabble intrudes upon my privacy? Begone all of you!'

He waved his arm, and the men departed, but none too pleasantly;

'Now, my father,' he said to the High Priest, who had watched these proceedings with no small amount of surprise, 'what is it that you require of me?'

'Nay, my lord,' said the man he addressed, 'be not angry with thy servants. There is without doubt some mistake, which will soon be made clear. I have come to thee because it has been asserted by a young priest that he, whom you call your secretary, is not a China-man at all, but a certain barbarian Englishman, called by the heathen name of "Bruce". I cannot believe that this is so. How long has my lord known the man?'

'It is unseemly that I should be questioned in this fashion,' began Nikola angrily. 'If the man were what thou sayest, what matter is it to thee or to anyone? Yet, lest it breed mischief, I will answer. What thy servant says is false. The man is as true a countryman of thine as the Emperor himself. There is malice in this accusation, and it shall be sifted to the dregs. Let us decide the matter in this way. If it should be as thou sayest, then tomorrow morning I will have the dog out, and he shall answer for his duplicity with his barbarian life. If not, then, I will tear the tongue of that lying knave, thy priest, out of his mouth. Tonight I have to offer many prayers, and I am weary, so let it be decided between us in the great hall tomorrow morning.'

'It shall be as you say,' said the old man. 'Do not let there be hard words between us, my lord. Have no fear; if the man be all thou sayest my servant shall surely pay the penalty.'

Having said this he bowed himself before Nikola, and then departed from the room. As soon as the sound of his footsteps had ceased upon the stone stairs Nikola came in to me.

'They have gone,' he said. 'And now we have got to find a way out of this difficulty.'

'It would seem impossible,' I answered doubtfully.

'Nothing is impossible,' Nikola answered. 'I hate the word. We've got at least six hours before us in which to do something, and if we want to save our lives we had better look sharp and decide what that something is to be.'

CHAPTER TEN

An exciting night in the Llamaserai

'There are two points which we must hold in constant remembrance,' said Nikola. 'The first is that you are not a Chinaman, and the other is that if you go before the High Priest tomorrow morning and pose as one, he'll certainly find you out, and then we shall be ruined completely. If you run away I had better run too, for all the good I can get by stopping, but that I am resolved not to do. It has cost me many years' labour, to say nothing of some thousands of British sovereigns, to get as far as I have in this business, and come what may I am determined not to turn back.'

'But in what way are we to get out of the difficulty?' I asked dejectedly. 'If I can't come before them and brazen the matter out, and I can't remain away for fear of confirming what they already suspect, and I can't leave the monastery without drawing down suspicion on you, I must confess I don't see what is to be done. I suppose we couldn't bribe the man to withdraw his charge?'

'Not to be thought of,' said Nikola, with conviction. 'Our lives would then be simply dependent on his reading of the term "good faith". You ought to know what sort of trust we could place in that.'

'Could we force him to clear out, and thus let it be supposed that he had brought a false accusation against me, and was afraid to stay and face the consequences?'

'That is not possible either,' said Nikola. 'He would want to bargain with us, and, to be revenged on us, would turn traitor when we refused his demand. In that case it would be "pull devil, pull baker", and the one who could pull the longest would gain the day. No, you had better leave the situation to me. Let me tackle it, and see what is to be done.'

I did as he wished, and for nearly half an hour could hear him pacing up and down his room. I did not intrude upon him, or interrupt him in any way. At the end of the time stated he abandoned his sentry-go and came in to me.

'I think I see my way,' he said. 'But when all is said and done it is almost as desperate as either of the other remedies we thought of. You will have to carry it out, and if you fail – well, Heaven have mercy upon both of us. You have saved my life before, I am going to trust it to you now; but remember this, if you do not carry out my plan exactly as I wish, you will never see me alive again. Give me your best attention, and endeavour to recollect everything I tell you. It is now close on midnight; the gong for early service will sound at half-past five, but it will be daylight an hour before that. By hook or by crook I must get you out of this place within a quarter of an hour, and, even if you have to steal a horse to do it, you must be in Pekin before half-past one. Once there you will find the house of Yoo Laoyeh, who lives at the rear of Legation Street, near the chief gate of the Tartar city.'

'But how am I going to get into the city at all?' I asked, amazed that he should have forgotten what struck me as a most hopeless barrier – the wall. 'The gates are closed at sundown and are not opened again till sunrise.'

'You'll have to climb the wall,' he answered.

'But, as you know very well, that's altogether impossible,' I said.

'Not a bit of it,' he replied. 'I will tell you of a place where it is quite practicable. Do you remember the spot where you proposed to Miss Medwin?'

'Perfectly,' I answered with a smile. 'But how do you know it?'

'My dear fellow, I was within a hundred yards of you the whole time. No, you need not look at me like that. I was not spying upon you. After the fashion of the great Napoleon, I like to be prepared for every emergency, and, thinking I might some day want to get into the city when the gates were shut, I utilised some spare time by taking a look at the wall. You see how useful that chance visit has proved. Well, two bastions from where you were seated that day the stones are larger and more uneven than anywhere else along the whole of that side of the city. To my certain knowledge three men have been in the habit of climbing that portion of the ramparts for the last three years, between midnight and sunrise, smuggling in goods to the city in order to avoid paying the octroi duty, which, as you know, is levied during daylight. When you have got over you will find a sentry posted on the other side; to him you will pay three taels, telling him at the same time that you intend returning in an hour, and that you will pay him the same amount for the privilege of getting out. Having passed the sentry you will proceed into the town, find Yoo Laoyeh, and let him know the fix we are in. You may promise him the sum of £100 cash if he falls in with your suggestions, and you must bring him back with you, willy-nilly, as fast as you can travel. I will meet you at the southern gate. Knock four times, and as you knock, cough. That shall be the signal, and as soon as I hear it I will open the gate. All that must be guarded against inside shall be my care. Everything outside must be yours. Now let us come along, and discover by what means I can get you out.'

Together we left the room, descended the stairs, and, crossing the ante-chamber, entered the big hall. The wind which, as I have already said, came in through the narrow windows on either side rustled the long hangings till the place seemed peopled with a thousand silk-clad ghosts. Nikola crossed it swiftly and left by the southern door. I followed close at his heels, and together we passed unobserved through the great courtyard, keeping well in the shadow of the building until we reached the first gate. Fortunately for us this also was unguarded, but we could hear the monk who was supposed to be watching it, placidly snoring in the room beside it. Slipping the enormous bar aside we opened it quietly, passed through, and, crossing an open strip of green, made for the outer wall. Just, however, as we were about to turn the corner that separated us from it, a sudden sound of voices caused us to hesitate.

'This way,' whispered Nikola, seizing my wrist and dragging me to the left. 'I can find you another exit. I noticed, yesterday, a big tree growing by the side of the wall.'

Leaving the centre gate we turned to our left hand, as I have said, and followed the wall we desired to surmount until we arrived at a large tree whose higher branches more than overspread it.

'This is the very place for our purpose,' said Nikola, coming to a halt. 'You will have to climb the tree and crawl along the branches until you get on to the wall, then you must let yourself down on the other side and be off to the city as hard as you can go. Goodbye, and may good luck go with you!'

I shook him by the hand and sprang into the branches. Hitherto it had seemed as if I had been acting all this in a wonderfully vivid dream. Now, however, the rough bark of the tree roused me to the reality of my position. I climbed until I came to the level of the wall, then, choosing a thick branch, made my way along it until I stood upon the solid masonry. Once there, only a drop of about twelve feet remained between me and freedom. Bidding Nikola, who was watching me, goodbye, in a whisper, I leant over the wall as far as I was able, grasped the coping with both hands, and then let myself drop.

Once on the ground I ran across the open space towards a cluster of small dwellings. In an enclosure adjoining one of them I could dimly make out a number of ponies running loose, and knowing that if I could only secure one of these and find a saddle and bridle in the residence of its owner, I might be in Pekin in under an hour, I resolved to make the attempt.

Creeping up to the nearest of the houses, I approached the door. Inside I could hear the stertorous breathing of the occupants. A joss-stick burnt before an image near at hand, and though it was well-nigh exhausted by the time I secured it, it still gave me sufficient light to look about me. A moment later I had a saddle and bridle down from a peg and was out among the ponies again.

Securing the most likely animal I saddled him, and as soon as I had done so, mounted and set off towards Pekin as fast as he could take me. The night was dark, but the track was plain; the little beast was more than willing, and as I did not spare him, something less than three-quarters of an hour, counting from the time I had bidden Nikola goodbye, found me dismounting under the great wall of the city.

Having found a convenient spot, I tied up my pony, and when he was made secure set to work and hunted along the wall until I came to the scaling place of which Nikola had told me.

As I reached it a light wind blew from over the plain, and sent the dust eddying about me, otherwise not a sound disturbed the stillness of the night. Then, having made sure that I was unobserved, and that I had chosen the right spot, I began to climb. It was no easy task. The stones were large and uneven. Sometimes I got a good hold, but in many cases I had veritably to cling by my nails. The strain was almost too much for my strength, and when I had been climbing for five minutes, and there still remained as much of the wall ahead, I began to despair of ever getting to the top. But I was not to be beaten; and remembering how much depended upon my getting into the city, I dragged myself wearily on, and at last crawled on to the summit. When I reached it I could see the city spread out on the other side. A little to the left of where I stood was the place, to be for ever sacred in my eyes, where I had proposed to, and been accepted by, my sweet-heart, while away to the right was that quarter of the town where at that moment she was in all probability asleep, and, I hoped, dreaming of me. As soon as I recovered my breath I crossed the wall and descended by the steps on the other side.

I had scarcely reached the bottom before a man rose from a dark corner and confronted me. In the half light I could see that he was a Chinese soldier armed with a long spear. Telling him in a whisper, in answer to his enquiry, that I was a friend, I pressed the money that Nikola had given me for that purpose into his not unwilling hand, and as soon as he drew back, astonished at my munificence, sped past him and darted down the nearest street.

From the place where I had passed the sentry to the thoroughfare where Yoo Laoyeh resided was a distance of about half a mile, and to reach it quickly it was necessary that I should pass the Benfleets' abode. You may imagine what thoughts occupied my brain as I stood in the silent street and regarded it. Under that roof was sleeping the one woman who was all the world to me. I would have given anything I possessed for five minutes' conversation with her; but as that was impossible I turned on my heel and made my way through a by-lane into the street I had been sent to find. The house was not a big one, and at first glance did not strike me very favourably. But the style of building did not matter if I found there the man I wanted. I knocked upon the door – which I discovered was heavily barred – but for some minutes got no response; then, just as I was beginning to wonder in what way I could best manage to attract the attention of those inside, I heard a patter of bare feet on the stone passage, and after much fumbling the door was opened and a man appeared before me. One glance told me that he was not the person I wanted. I enquired if Yoo Laoyeh were at home, but from the answer I received I gathered that he had gone out earlier in the evening, and that he was probably at a neighbouring house playing *fantan*.

Having asked the man if he would take me to him, and at the same time offering him a considerable bribe to do so, I was immediately conducted into the street again, down one by-lane, up another, and finally brought to a standstill before one of the largest houses in that quarter. My guide was evidently well known, for when the door was opened the keeper did not attempt to bar our passage, but permitted us to pass through to a fair-sized room at the back. Here quite thirty Chinamen were busily engaged upon their favourite pastime, but though we scanned the rows of faces, the man for whom we were searching was not among the number. As soon as we were convinced of this fact we left that room and proceeded to another, where the same game was also being carried on. Once more, however, we were doomed to disappointment; Laoyeh was not there either.

Being anxious to obtain some news of him my guide interrogated one of the players, who remembered having seen our man about an hour before. He imagined he had then gone into the room we had first visited. We returned there and made further enquiries, only to elicit the fact that he had been seen to leave the house about half an hour before our arrival.

'Have no fear. I will find him for you,' said my companion, and we thereupon proceeded down the passage, past the doorkeeper, into the street again. Once more we took up the chase, trying first one house and then another, to bring up eventually in an opium den a little behind the English Legation. The outer room, or that nearest the street, was filled with customers, but our man was not among them. The inner room was not quite so crowded, and here, after all our searching, we discovered the man we wanted. But there was this drawback, he had smoked his usual number of pipes and was now fast asleep.

By this time it was hard upon two o'clock, and at most I dared not remain in the city more than another hour. At the same time it would be a most foolish, if not dangerous, proceeding to attempt to travel with my man in his present condition. If he did nothing else he would probably fall over the wall and break his neck, and then I should either have to leave him behind or remain to answer inconvenient questions; but whatever happened I knew I must carry him out of this house as quickly as possible to some place where I could endeavour to bring him back to his senses. I said as much to the man who had found him for me, and then between us we got him on to his feet, and taking him by either arm led him off to his home. By the time we got him there he had in a small measure recovered from the effects of his smoke. Then we set to work, using every means known to our experience, to bring him round, and by half-past two had so far succeeded as to warrant me in thinking I might set off on my return journey.

'But what does your Excellency require of me?' asked Laoyeh, who was still a bit mystified, though fortunately not so far gone as to be unable to recognise me.

'You are to come with me,' I answered, taking good care before I spoke that the other man was well out of hearing, 'to the Llamaserai, where Nikola wants you. There is a hundred pounds English to be earned; how, I will tell you as we go.'

As soon as he heard Nikola's name and the amount of the reward, he seemed to become himself again. We accordingly left the house and set off together for that part of the wall where I had made my descent into the city. The same soldier was still on guard, and when I had placed the money I had promised him in his hand, he immediately allowed us to pass. Within twenty minutes of leaving Yoo's house we were ready to descend the other side of the wall.

If I had found it difficult to ascend, I discovered that it was doubly difficult to descend. The night was now very dark, and it was well-nigh impossible to see what we were doing. The cracks and crannies which were to serve as resting-places for our feet seemed almost impossible to find, and right glad I was when the business was accomplished and we stood together on terra firma at the bottom.

So far my visit to the city had proved eminently successful. But time was slipping by, and there was still the long distance out to the Serai to be overcome. I went over to where the pony stood hitched to the tree, exactly as I had left him, and placed my companion upon his back. He was almost, if not quite, himself now, so urging the little animal into a canter we set off, he riding and I running beside him. In this fashion, running and walking, we came to the southern gate of the great monastery. I had carried out my share of the business, and when once I should have got Laoyeh inside, the direction of the remainder would lie with Nikola.

Having turned the pony loose, his bridle and saddle upon his back, I approached and knocked upon the door, coughing softly as I did so. Then little by little it opened, and we found Nikola standing upon the threshold. He beckoned to us to enter, and without losing a moment we did as we were ordered. Daylight was close at hand, and the unmistakable chill of dawn was in the air. It was very certain that I had returned none too soon.

Having passed through the gate, and fastened it behind us, we made for the second archway on our left. The sentry box – if one might call it by that name – was still deserted, and the guard was snoring as placidly in his little room at the side as when we had crept through nearly four hours before. This courtyard, like its predecessor, was empty; but to show the narrowness of our escape, I may say that as we crossed it we could distinctly hear the jabbering of priests in the dormitories on either hand.

At last we reached the door of the big hall. Opening it carefully we sped across the floor and then up the stairs to our own apartments. Once inside, the door was quickly shut, and we were safe. Then Nikola turned to me, and said – 'Bruce, you have saved me a second time, and I can only say, as I said before, you will not find me ungrateful. But there is no time to lose. Yoo Laoyeh, come in here.'

We passed into the inner room, and then Nikola opened a small box he had brought with his other impedimenta. Then bidding the man seat himself upon the floor, he set to work with wonderful dexterity to change his appearance. The operation lasted about a quarter of an hour, and when it was completed Nikola turned to me.

'Change clothes with him, Bruce, as quickly as you can.'

When this was done I could hardly believe my own eyes, the likeness was so wonderful. There, standing before me, was an exact reproduction of myself. In height, build, dress, and even in feature, the resemblance was most striking. But Nikola was not satisfied.

'You must be changed too,' he said. 'We must do the thing thoroughly, or not at all. Sit down.'

I did so, and he once more set to work. By the time I left his hands I was as unlike my real self as a man could well be. No one could have recognised me, and in that case it was most unlikely that our secret would be discovered.

On the way from Pekin I had clearly explained to Laoyeh the part he would be called upon to play. Now Nikola gave the final touches to his education, and then all was completed.

'But, look here,' I cried, as a thought struck me; 'we have forgotten one thing – the scar upon my arm.'

'I had omitted that,' said Nikola. 'And it is just those little bits of forgetfulness that hang people.'

Then taking a long strip of native cloth from a chair he constructed a sling, which he placed round my neck. My left arm was placed in rough splints, which he procured from his invaluable medicine chest, and after it had been bandaged I felt I might also defy detection, as far as my wrist was concerned.

Half an hour later the great gong sounded for morning worship, and in a few moments we knew that the courtyards and halls would be filled with men. Acting under Nikola's instructions I descended to the hall alone, and choosing my opportunity slipped in and mingled with the throng. I was not the only cripple, for there were half a dozen others with their arms in slings. Nor was the fact that I was a stranger likely to attract any undue attention, inasmuch as there were mendicants and people of all sorts and descriptions passing into the Serai directly the gates were opened at daylight.

I had not been in the hall very long before I saw Nikola hobble in on his stick and take his place beside the High Priest. Then the service commenced. When it was at an end it was evident that something unusual was going to take place, for the monks and their guests remained where they were, instead of leaving the hall as usual. Then the High Priest mounted the small platform at the further end and seated himself in the chair of justice. Nikola followed and took his place beside him, and presently two tall monks appeared bringing with them the man who had brought the accusation against me on the previous evening. He seemed pretty certain of being able to prove his case, and I could not help smiling as I watched his confident air. First the old High Priest, who it must be remembered was almost blind with age, addressed him. He said something in reply, and then Nikola spoke. His voice was scarcely as loud as usual, yet every word rang across the hall.

'Liar and traitor!' he said. 'You have brought this charge against my faithful servant for some devilish reason of your own. But old as I am I will meet it, and evil be upon you if it be proved that what you say is false.'

He then turned to a monk standing beside him and said something to him; the man bowed, and leaving the platform disappeared in the direction of our staircase. Presently he returned with Lao-yeh, whose head was bent, and whose hands were folded across his breast. He climbed the steps, and, when he had done so, accuser and accused confronted each other from either end of the platform.

Then it was that I saw the cleverness of Nikola's scheme. He had arranged that the trial should take place after the morning service for the reason that, at that time, the big hall would not be thoroughly lighted. As it proved, it was still wrapped in more than semi-darkness, and by the promptness with which he commenced business it was evident that he was resolved to dispose of the matter in hand before it would be possible for anyone to see too clearly.

First the man who brought the accusation against me was ordered to repeat his tale. In reply he gave a detailed description of our meeting in Canton and led up, with a few unimportant reservations, to the stab he had given me upon the wrist. He then unhesitatingly asserted the fact that I was a *kueidzu*, or foreign devil, and dared the man who was taking my place to disprove it. When he had finished, Nikola turned to the High Priest and said – 'My father, thou hast heard all that this wicked man hath said. He accuses my servant yonder – he himself being a thief and a would-be murderer by his own confession – of being one of those barbarians whom we all hate and despise. I have found my man faithful and true in all his dealings, yet if he is a foreign devil, as this fellow asserts, then he shall be punished. On the other hand, if this rogue shall be proved to be in the wrong, and to have lied for the sake of gain, then it shall be my request to thee that I be allowed to deal with him according to the powers with which thou knowest I am invested. I have no fear; judge therefore between us.'

When he had finished the old man rose and hobbled forward on his stick; he looked steadfastly from one to the other of the two men, and then, addressing Laoyeh, said – 'Come thou with me', and took him into a small room leading out of the big hall.

For nearly half an hour we sat in silence, wondering what the upshot of it all would be. I watched Nikola, who sat during the whole of the time with his chin resting on his hand, staring straight before him.

At last our period of waiting was at an end. We heard the tapping of the High Priest's stick upon the floor, and presently he ascended the platform again. Laoyeh followed him. Reaching his chair the old man signed for silence, and as soon as he had obtained it, said – 'I have examined this man, and can swear that the charge this fellow has brought against him is without truth in every particular. Let justice be done.'

Then facing Nikola he continued – 'The rogue yonder waits for thee to do with him as thou wilt.'

Nikola rose slowly from his chair and faced the unhappy man.

'Now, dog!' he cried. 'By the words of thine own High Priest I have to deal with thee. Is it for this that thou earnest into the world. Thou hast dared to malign this my servant, and thy superior has sworn to it. Draw nearer to me.'

The man approached a few paces, and it was easily seen that he was afraid. Then for nearly a minute Nikola gazed fixedly at him, and I cannot remember ever to have seen those terrible eyes look so fierce. If you can imagine a rabbit fascinated by a serpent you will have some notion of how the man faced his persecutor. Slowly, inch by inch, Nikola raised his right hand until it pointed to a spot on the wall a little above the other's head. Then it began to descend again, and as it did so the fellow's head went down also until he stood almost in a stooping posture.

'You see,' said Nikola, 'you are in my power. You cannot move unless I bid you do so.'

'I cannot move,' echoed the man almost unconsciously.

'Try how you will, you cannot stand upright,' said Nikola.

'I cannot stand upright,' repeated the man in the same monotonous voice, and as he spoke I saw large drops of perspiration fall from his face upon the floor. You may be sure that every eye in that large hall was riveted upon them, and even the High Priest craned forward in his chair in order that he might not lose a word.

'Look into my face,' said Nikola, and his words cut the air like a sharp knife.

The man lifted his eyes and did as he was ordered, but without raising his head.

'Now leave this place,' said Nikola, 'and until this time tomorrow you cannot stand upright like your fellow-men. It is my command, and you cannot disobey. Let that help you to remember that for the future my servants must be sacred. Go!'

He pointed with his right hand to the doors at the end of the hall, and, bent double, the man went down the aisle between the rows of gaping monks out into the courtyard and the streaming sunshine. The High Priest had risen to his feet, and calling up a monk who stood beside him, said – 'Follow him, and be certain that he leaves the Serai.'

Then approaching Nikola he said – 'My master, I see that, without a doubt, thou art he whom we were told to expect. In what way can thy servant prove of service to thee?'

'Grant me an interview and I will tell you,' said Nikola.

'If my lord will follow me,' said the old man, 'we can talk in private.' Next moment they disappeared into the room where the High Priest had conducted the examination of Laoyeh. Thereupon the congregation dispersed.

As soon as the hall was empty I seized my opportunity and went upstairs to our own apartment. There I discovered Laoyeh. According to Nikola's instructions we changed clothes again, and when he was himself once more, I gave him the peddler's dress which Nikola had prepared for this occasion, and also the reward which had been promised him. Then bidding him goodbye, I bade him get out of the monastery as quickly as he could.

It was nearly an hour before Nikola joined me. When he did he could hardly conceal his exultation.

'Bruce,' he said, almost forgetting his usual caution in the excitement of the moment, 'I have discovered everything! I have got the chart, and I have learnt the password. I know where the monastery is, and at daybreak tomorrow morning we'll set out in search of it.'

CHAPTER ELEVEN

En route to Thibet

Daylight was scarcely born in the sky next morning before Nikola roused me from my slumbers.

'Wake up,' he said; 'for in half an hour we must be starting. I have already given orders for the ponies to be saddled, and as we have a long stage before us we must not keep them waiting.'

Within a quarter of an hour of his calling me I was dressed and ready. A breakfast of rice was served to us by one of the monks, and when we had eaten it we descended to the great hall. The High Priest was waiting there for us, and after a short conversation with Nikola he led us down the steps into the courtyard, where, beneath the shadow of the great statue of Buddha, we took an impressive farewell of him.

Having thanked him for his hospitality, we made our way towards the outer gate, to find our ponies and servants standing ready to receive us. The gate was thrown open, and in single file we proceeded through it. Then it clanged to behind us, and when it had done so we had said goodbye to the Great Llamaserai.

During the first day's ride nothing occurred worth chronicling. We reached a small village at midday, camped there, and after a brief rest, continued our journey, arriving at the fortified town of Ho-Yang-Lo just as dusk was falling. Having been directed to the principal inn, we rode up to it, and engaged rooms for the night. Our first day's stage had been one of thirty-six miles, and we felt that we had well earned a rest.

It was not until the evening meal was eaten, and Nikola and I had retired to our own private room, that I found an opportunity of asking what he thought of the success which had attended our efforts so far.

'To tell you the truth,' he said, 'I must confess that I am surprised that we have been as successful as we have.'

'Well, that man's recognising me was unfortunate, I admit; but still – '

'Oh, I don't mean that at all,' said Nikola. 'I regard that as quite an outside chance. And after all it proved a golden opportunity in the end. What does surprise me, however, is that I should have been accepted so blindly for the Priest of Hankow.'

'That is certainly strange,' I answered. 'But there is one thing which astonishes me even more: that is, how it comes about that, as the stick was being searched for by the Chinese in Australia who knew of your intentions, it should fail to be evident to the society in China that you are the man who stole it?'

'My dear fellow,' said Nikola, laying his hand upon my arm, 'you don't surely imagine that in such a business as the present, in which I have sunk, well, if nothing else, your £10,000, I should have left anything to chance. No, Bruce. Chance and Dr Nikola do not often act in concert. When I obtained that stick from Wetherell I took care that the fact should not be known outside the circle of a few men whom I felt perfectly certain I could trust. As soon as it was in my possession I offered a large reward for it in Sydney, and I took care that the news of this reward should reach the ears of the Chinamen who were on the lookout for it. Then, on the plea that I was still searching for it, I returned to China, with what result you know. What does puzzle me, however, is the fact that the society has not yet found out that it has been deceived. It must eventually come to this conclusion, and it can't be very long before it does. Let us hope that by that time we shall be back in civilisation once more.'

I knocked the ashes out of my pipe, and rolling over on my blankets, looked Nikola straight in the face.

'By the time you have got to the end of this business,' I said, 'your information, presuming all the time that you *do* get it, will have cost you close on £40,000 – very possibly more; you will have endangered your own life, to say nothing of mine, and have run the risk of torture and all other sorts of horrors. Do you think it is worth it?'

'My dear Bruce, I would risk twice as much to attain my ends. If I did not think it worth it I should not have embarked upon it at all. You little know the value of my quest. With the knowledge I shall gain I shall revolutionise the whole science of medicine. There will be only one doctor in the world, and he will be Dr Nikola! Think of that. If I desired fame, what greater reputation could I have. If money, there is wealth untold in this scheme for me. If I wish to benefit my fellow-man, how can I do it better than by unravelling the tangled skein of Life and Death? It is also plain that you have not grasped my character yet. I tell you this, if it became necessary for me, for a purpose I had in view, to find and kill a certain fly, I would follow that fly into the utmost parts of Asia, and spend all I possessed in the world upon the chase; but one thing is very certain, *I would kill that fly*. How much more then in a matter which is as important as life itself to me?'

As I looked at him I had to confess to myself that I had not the least doubt but that he would do all he said.

'There is a proverb,' continued Nikola, 'to the effect that "Whatever is worth doing, is worth doing well." That has been my motto through life, and I hope I shall continue to live up to it. But time is getting on; let us turn in; we have a long day's ride before us tomorrow.'

We blew out the light and composed ourselves for the night, but it was hours before sleep visited my eyelids. Thoughts on almost every conceivable subject passed in and out of my brain. One moment I was in the playing-fields of my old familiar English school; the next I was *ratching* round the Horn in an ice-bound clipper, with a scurvy-ridden crew in the forecastle, and a trio of drunken miscreants upon the quarter-deck; the next I was in the southern seas, some tropic island abeam, able to hear the thunder of the surf upon the reef, and to see palm-clad hill on palm-clad hill rearing their lovely heads up to the azure sky. Then my thoughts came back to China, and as a natural sequence, to Pekin. I enacted again that half-hour on the wall, and seemed once more to feel the pressure of a certain tiny hand in mine, and to see those frank sweet eyes gazing into my face with all the love and trust imaginable. Gladys was my promised wife, and here I lay on the road to Thibet, disguised as a Chinaman, in a filthy native inn, in the company of a man who would stop at nothing and who was feared by everybody who knew him. It was long past midnight before I fell asleep, and then it seemed as if my eyes had not been closed five minutes before Nikola, who, as usual, appeared to require no sleep at all, was up and preparing to go on; indeed, the sun was hardly risen above the horizon before our breakfast was dispatched, and we were ready for the saddle.

Prior to starting Nikola went off to speak to the man who kept the inn. While he was away I amused myself by riding round to look at the other side of the house. It was of the ordinary Chinese pattern, not much dirtier and not much cleaner. A broad verandah surrounded it on two sides, and at the rear was a sort of narrow terrace, on which, as I turned the corner, two men were standing. As soon as they saw me they were for retreating into the house, but before they were able to accomplish this manoeuvre I had had a good look at them.

The taller of the pair I had never seen before, but his companion's face was somehow familiar to me. While I was wondering where I had encountered it, a *mafoo* came round the building to inform me that Nikola was ready to be off, so touching up my pony I returned to the front to find the cavalcade in the act of starting.

As usual Nikola took the lead, I followed him at a respectful distance, and the servants were behind me again. In this fashion we made our way down the track and across a stream towards the range of mountains that could just be discerned on the northern horizon. All round us the country was bare and uncultivated, with here and there a mud-hut, in colour not unlike the plain upon which it stood.

By midday we had reached the range of mountains just mentioned, and were following a well-made track through gloomy but somewhat picturesque scenery. With the exception of a few camel teams laden with coal passing down to Pekin, and here and there a travelling hawker, we met but few people. In this region the villages are far apart, and do not bear any too good a reputation.

That night we camped at an inn on the mountain top, and next morning made our descent into the valley on the other side. By the time darkness fell we had proceeded some thirty-odd miles along it. The country was quickly changing, becoming more and more rocky, and the ascents and descents more precipitous. For this reason, at the next halting-place we were compelled to part with our ponies, and to purchase in their stead half a dozen tiny, but exceedingly muscular, donkeys.

On the third night after our entry into the hills and the fourth from Pekin, we halted at a small monastery standing in an exposed position on the hill top. As we rode up to it the sun was declining behind the mountains to the westward. There was no need for any password, as we were invited to enter almost before we had knocked upon the gate. The place was occupied by an abbot and six priests, all of whom were devotees of Shamanism. The building itself was but a poor one, consisting of an outer court, a draughty central hall, and four small rooms adjoining it. At the entrance to the central hall we were received by the abbot, a villainously dirty little fellow of middle age, who conducted us to the rooms we were to occupy. They were small and mean, very much out of repair, and, as a result, exceedingly draughty. But if a view, such as would be found in few parts of the world, could compensate for physical discomfort, we should have been able to consider ourselves domiciled in luxury. From one window we could look across the range of mountains, over valley and peak, into the very eye of the setting sun. From another we could gaze down, nearly three hundred feet, sheer drop, into the valley, and perceive the track we had followed that morning, winding its way along, while through a narrow gully to our left we could distinguish the stretch of plain, nearly fifty miles distant, where we had camped two nights before.

As the sun dropped, a chilly wind sprang up and tore round the building, screaming through the cracks and crevices with a noise that might have been likened to the shrieks of a thousand souls in torment. The flame of the peculiar lamp with which our room was furnished rose and fell in unison with the blasts, throwing the strangest shadows upon the walls and ceiling. This eccentric light, combined with the stealthy movements of the coarse-robed, shaven monks, as they passed and repassed our door, did not, as may be expected, conduce to our cheerfulness, so that it may not be a matter for surprise that when I sat down with Nikola to our evening meal, it was with a greater feeling of loneliness, and a greater amount of home-sickness in my heart, than I had felt at all since the journey commenced.

When our repast was finished we lit our pipes and sat smoking for half an hour. Then, being unable to stand the silence of the room any longer – for Nikola had a fit of the blues, and was consequently but a poor companion – I left our side of the house and went out into the courtyard before the central hall. Just as I reached it a loud knocking sounded upon the outer gate. On hearing it two of the monks crossed the yard to open it, and, when they had swung the heavy doors back, a small party of men, mounted on donkeys, rode into the square. Thinking the arrival of a party of travellers would at least serve to distract my thoughts, I went down to watch them unload.

As I approached them I discovered that they were five in party, the principals numbering three, the remaining two being coolies. Their profession I was unable to guess; they were all armed, and, as far as I could tell, carried no merchandise with them. When they had dismounted the abbot came down to receive them, and after a little talk conducted them to the guest chambers on the other side of the hall opposite to our quarters.

For some time after the leaders had retired to their rooms I remained where I was, watching the coolies unharness; then, just as the last pack-saddle was placed upon the ground, one of the owners left the house and approached the group. He had come within a few paces of where I stood before he became aware of my presence; then he stooped, and, as if to excuse his visit, opened the pack-saddle lying nearest him. I noticed that he did not take anything from it, and that all the time he was examining it he did not once turn his face in my direction; therefore, when he wheeled quickly round and hurried back to the house, without speaking to either of his men, I felt that I had every right to suppose he did not wish me to become aware of his identity.

This set me thinking, and the more I thought the more desirous I became of finding out who my gentleman might be. I waited in the courtyard for nearly a quarter of an hour after the animals had been picketed, and the pack-saddles and harness had been carried away, but he did not put in another appearance. Seeing this, I returned to the buildings, and set my brain to work to try and discover what I wanted so much to know. It was a long time before I could hit on any plan; then an idea came to me and I left the room again and went round to the back of the buildings, hoping, if possible, to find a window through which I could look in upon the new arrivals as they sat at supper; but it was easier, I discovered, to talk of such a window than actually to find it.

The back of the monastery was built flush with the edge of the cliff, the rampart wall joining the building at the angle of our room. If only, therefore, I could manage to pass along the wall, and thus reach a small window which I guessed must look out on to a tiny court, situated between the rearmost wall of the central hall and that on the left of our room, I thought I might discover what I wanted to know. But to do this would necessitate a long and danger-ous climb in the dark, which I was not at all anxious to attempt until I had satisfied myself that there was no other way of obtaining the information I required.

It might very well be asked here why I was so anxious to convince myself as to the man's identity. But one instant's reflection will show that in such a situation as ours we could not afford to run a single risk. The man had allowed me to see that he did not wish me to become aware of his personality. That in itself was sufficient to excite my suspicion and to warrant my taking any steps to satisfy myself that he was not likely to prove an enemy. As I have said before, we were carrying our lives in our hands, and one little precaution neglected might ruin all.

Before venturing on the climb just mentioned, I determined to go round to the other side of the house and endeavour to look in through one of the windows there. I did so, and was relieved to find that by putting my hands on the rough stone window-sills, and bracing my feet against a buttress in the angle of the wall, I could raise myself sufficiently to catch a glimpse of the room.

I accordingly pulled myself up and looked in, but to my astonishment and chagrin, there were only two people present, and neither of them was the man I wanted.

I lowered myself to the ground again and listened, hoping to hear the sound of a third person entering the room, but though I remained there nearly twenty minutes I could not distinguish what I wanted. That the man was a member of the same party I was perfectly convinced, but why was he not with them now? This absence on his part only increased my suspicion and made me the more anxious to catch a glimpse of him.

Seating myself on the stone steps of the central hall, I roughly traced in my own mind a ground plan of the building, as far as I was familiar with it. The central hall was, of course, empty; we occupied the rooms on the right of it, the second party those on the left; of these their coolies had the front room, while the two men I have just referred to had taken possession of the rearmost one. A moment's reasoning convinced me that there must be a third, which did not look out on the open courtyard, but must have its window in the small court, formed by the angles of the wall at the rear. If, therefore, I wanted to look into it I must undertake the climb I had first projected, and, what was more, must set about it immediately, for if I did not do so his lamp would in all probability be extinguished, and in that case I might as well spare myself the trouble and the danger.

I returned to my own side of the house, and, having convinced myself that there was no one about, mounted the wall a little to the right of where I had been standing when I heard the men knock upon the gate.

If you would estimate the difficulty and danger of what I was about to attempt, you must remember that the wall at the top was scarcely more than eighteen inches wide. On one hand it had the buildings for support, the side of which rose above my head for more than a dozen feet, and permitted no sort of hold on its smooth surface, while, on the other hand, I had a sheer drop into the valley below, a fall of fully three hundred feet.

At the summit of the mountain the wind was blowing a perfect hurricane, but so long as I was behind the building I was not subjected to its full pressure; when, however, I arrived at the courtyard, where I could see the light of the window I was so anxious to reach, it was as much as I could do to keep my footing. Clinging to everything that could offer a support, and never venturing a step till I was certain that it was safe, I descended from the wall, approached the window, and looked in. This time I was not destined to be disappointed. The man I wanted was lying upon a bed-place in the corner, smoking a long pipe.

His face was turned towards me, and directly I looked at it I remembered where I had seen him. He was one of the principal, and, at the same time, one of the most interested members of the society who had visited the house to which we had been conducted by Laohwan, in Shanghai.

As I realised this fact a cold sweat came over me. This was the same man whom we had seen at the rest-house two nights before. Was he following us? That he had recognised me, in spite of my disguise, I felt certain. If so, in whose employ was he, and what was his object? I remained watching him for upwards of an hour, hoping someone would come in, and that I should overhear something that would tell me how to act. Then, just as I was about to turn away, deeming it useless to wait any longer, the taller of the pair I had seen in the other room entered and sat down.

'Success has attended us. At last we have laid our hands on them,' said the new-comer. 'They do not suspect, and by tomorrow evening we shall meet Quong Yan Miun at the ford, tell him all, and then our part of the work will be at an end.'

'But we must have the stick, come what may,' said the man upon the bed. 'It would be death for us to go back to Pekin without it.'

'We shall receive much honour if we capture it,' chuckled the other. 'And then these foreign devils will suffer torture till they die.'

'A lesson to them not to defy the Great Ones of the Mountains,' returned his friend. 'I wish that we could be there to see it!'

'It is said that they have many new ways of torture, of which we cannot even dream, up there in the mountains,' continued the first man. 'Why may we not go forward to see what befalls them?'

'Because we could not enter even if we did go on,' returned the man I had recognised; 'nor for myself do I want to. But these foreign devils have stolen the password and imitated the Priest of Hankow, and if it had not been for Laoyeh, who liked Chinese gold better than foreign devils' secrets, and so betrayed them, we should never have found them out at all.'

Then with significant emphasis he added – 'But they will die for it, and their fate will be a warning to any who shall come after them. And now tell me, where do we meet Quong Yan Miun?'

'At the crossing of the river in the mountains, at sundown to-morrow evening.'

'And is it certain that we shall know him? There may be many crossing.'

'He will be riding a camel, and sitting upon a red saddle embroidered with silver. Moreover, it is said that he has but one eye, and that his left hand, which was cut off by the mandarin Li, is still nailed to the gateway at I-chang.'

'Does he expect our coming?'

'By no means. Once in every month he is sent down by the Great Ones of the Mountains to receive messages and alms from the outside world. Our instructions are not to tarry until this letter be delivered into his hands.'

As he spoke he took from his pocket a small roll of paper carefully tied up. Having replaced it, he turned again to his companion.

'Now leave me,' he said. 'I am tired, and would sleep. Tomorrow there be great doings on hand.'

The second man left the room, and next moment the lamp was extinguished.

As soon as all was dark I crept softly across the yard, mounted the wall – not without a tremor, as I thought of what my fate would be if I should overbalance, and retraced my steps round the house. Once safely in the courtyard I made all the haste I could back to my room.

I fully expected to find Nikola asleep; my surprise, therefore, may be imagined when I discovered him seated on the floor working out Euclid's forty-third problem with a piece of charcoal upon the stones. He looked up as I entered, and, without moving a muscle of his face, said quietly: 'What have you discovered?'

I seated myself beside him and furnished him with a complete *résumé* of what I had overheard that evening.

When I had finished he sat looking at the wall. I could see, however, that he was thinking deeply. Then he changed his position, and with his piece of charcoal began to draw figure eights inside each other upon the floor. By the time the smallest was the size of a halfpenny he had arrived at a conclusion.

'It is evident that we are in a tight place,' he said coolly, 'and if I were to sacrifice you here I could probably save myself and go forward with nothing to fear. It's a funny thing that I should think so much of a man as to be willing to save his life at the expense of my own, but in this case I intend doing so. You have no desire to be tortured, I presume?'

'I have a well-founded objection to it,' I said.

'In that case we must hit upon some scheme which will enable us to avert such a catastrophe. If these fellows arrive at the ford before us they will have the first chance of doing business with the messenger. Our endeavour must be to get there before they do, and yet to send them back to Pekin satisfied that they have fulfilled their mission. How to do this is the problem we have to work out.'

'But how *are* we to do it?' I enquired.

'Let me think for a few minutes,' he answered, 'and I'll see if I can find out.'

I waited for fully five minutes. Then Nikola said: 'The problem resolves itself into this. By hook or crook we must delay this man and his party on the road for at least three hours. Then one of us must go on to the ford and meet the man from the monastery. To him must be handed the letter I received from the High Priest at the Llama-serai, and when he has been sent back with it to his superiors there must be another man, accoutred exactly like himself, to take his place. This man, who will have to be myself, will receive our friends, take their letters and dispatch them back to Pekin with a message that their warning shall be attended to. After that it will be touch-and-go with us. But I'm not afraid to go forward, and I pay you the compliment of saying that I don't believe you are!'

'Well, upon my word, Dr Nikola,' I answered candidly, quite carried away by the boldness of his scheme, 'of all the men I've ever met you're the coolest, and since you take it in this way I will go on with you and carry it through if it costs me my life.'

'I thank you,' said Nikola quietly. 'I thought I wasn't deceived in you. Now we must arrange the manner in which these different schemes are to be worked. To begin with, we must leave here at least an hour before our friends in the other rooms. Once on the way I must push forward as fast as I can go in order to secure a camel and saddle of the kind described. Then we have got to discover some means of delaying them upon the road. How can that be accomplished?'

'Couldn't we induce the villagers along the path to rise against them?'

'It would cost too much; and then there would be the chance of their turning traitor, like our friend Laoyeh. No; we must think of something else.'

He recommenced drawing eights upon the floor. By the time he had perfected the thirtieth – for I counted them – he had worked it out to his satisfaction.

'By twelve o'clock tomorrow at the very latest,' he said, 'that is, if my information be correct, we ought to be at an inn in the mountains twenty miles from here. It is the only dwelling between this place and the ford, and they must perforce call at it. I shall instruct one of my men, whom I will leave behind for that purpose, to see that their animals are watered at a certain trough. If they drink what I give him to pour in, they will go about five miles and then drop. If they don't drink I shall see that he brings about another result.'

'If you can depend on him, that should do the trick. But what about Laoyeh?'

'I shall deal with him myself,' said Nikola with grim earnestness; 'and when I've done I think he will regret having been so imprudent as to break faith with me.'

He said no more, but I could not help entertaining a feeling of satisfaction that I was not the man in question. From what I have seen of Nikola's character, I can say that I would rather quarrel with any other half dozen people in the world, whoever they might be, than risk his displeasure.

'Now,' I said, when he had finished, 'as they've turned in we shouldn't be long in following their example.'

'But before we do so,' he answered, 'I think you had better find the coolies and see that they thoroughly understand that we start at three o'clock. Moreover, bid them hold their tongues.'

I complied with his request, and half an hour later was wrapped in my blankets and fast asleep.

CHAPTER TWELVE
Through the mountains

At ten minutes to three I was out of bed, fully dressed and prepared for the start. Nikola had roused the coolies before calling me, and they were already busy with their preparations. At three precisely a bowl of rice was brought to us by one of the monks, and by a quarter past we were on our donkeys in the courtyard ready to be off.

So far the only person aroused, in addition to our own party, was the monk who cooked our breakfast; him Nikola largely rewarded, and, in return for his generosity, the gates were opened without disturbing the household. We filed out and picked our way down the rocky path into the valley. Arriving at the bottom we continued our journey, ascending and descending according to the nature of the path. Every hour the country was growing more and more mountainous, and by midday we could plainly discern snow upon the highest peaks.

At half-past twelve we reached the inn where it had been decided that one of our retinue should be left behind to hocus the animals of our pursuers. For this work we had chosen a man whom we had the best of reasons for being able to trust. A sufficient excuse was invented to satisfy his scruples, and when we said goodbye to him it was with instructions to follow us as soon as he had done the work and could discover a convenient opportunity. That the man would do his best to accomplish his errand, we had not the slightest doubt, for the reward promised him was large enough to obviate the necessity of his doing any more work as long as he should live. Therefore when we left the inn, after baiting our animals for a short time, it was to feel comparatively certain that the success of our scheme was assured.

As soon as the caravanserai was hidden by the corner of the mountain Nikola called me up to him.

'In a few moments,' he said, 'I am going to push forward to a village which I am told lies off the track a few miles to the northward.

I hear that they have camels for sale there, and it will be hard if I cannot purchase one, and with it a silver-plated red saddle, before dusk. You must continue your journey to the ford, where you will in all probability find the messenger awaiting you. Give him this letter from the High Priest of the Llamaserai, warning the Great Ones of the Mountains of my coming, and bestow upon him this tip.' Here he handed me a number of gold pieces. 'After that be sure to hasten his departure as much as you can, for we must run no risk of his meeting those who are behind us. I turn off here, so press forward yourself with all speed, and good luck go with you.'

'But when I have dispatched the messenger back to the monastery, what am I to do?'

'Wait till he is out of sight and then follow in his track for about half a mile. Having done so, find a convenient spot, camp and wait for me. Do you understand?'

I answered that I understood perfectly. Then ordering one coolie to follow him, with a wave of his hand he turned off the track and in less than five minutes was lost to my sight. For nearly three hours I rode on, turning over and over in my mind the plan I had arranged for conducting the interview that lay before me. The chief point I had to remember was that I was a courier from the Society, sent from Pekin to warn the monastery that one of the Great Three was approaching. Upon my success in carrying out this mission would very much depend the reception accorded to Nikola, therefore the story I was about to tell must necessarily be plausible in every particular.

By five o'clock, and just as the sun was sinking behind the highest peaks, the valley began to widen out, and the track became more plain. I followed it along at a medium pace, and then, having turned a corner, saw the smooth waters of the river before me.

As I did so I felt a cold chill pass over me; the success of our expedition seemed to rest upon my shoulders, to depend upon my presence of mind and the plausibility of my tale. If by any chance the man should suspect that I was not all I pretended to be, he might decide to wait, and then, with the help of such men as he might have with him, would detain me a prisoner. In that case, those behind us would catch us up, and I should be proved to be an impostor. Then, if I were not killed upon the spot, I should find myself carried on to the monastery, to become a subject for those experiments in torture, of which I had heard mention made the previous night.

When I reached it I discovered that the river at this particular ford was about eighty yards in width and scarcely more than two feet in depth. On either bank rose precipitous cliffs, reaching, even in the lowest places, to more than two hundred feet. To the right, that is, facing the north, the channel flowed between solid granite walls, but where I stood it had evenly sloping banks. I rode to the water's edge, and, seeing no one on the other side, dismounted from my donkey and seated myself upon the sand. I was relieved to find that there were no pilgrims about; but I became more anxious when I saw that the man whom I was to meet had not yet put in an appearance. If he delayed his arrival for very long I should be placed in a nasty position, for in that case our pursuers would come up, discover me, and then I should be hopelessly lost.

But I need not have worried myself, for I had not long to wait. Within half an hour of my arrival at the ford a man mounted on a camel rode out of the defile on the other side and approached the water's edge. He was tall, was dressed in some light-brown material, rode a well-bred camel, and when he turned round I could see that his saddle was red and ornamented with silver. Calling my men together I bade them wait for me where they were, and then, taking my donkey by the head, rode him into the stream.

So small was the animal that the water was well above the saddle flaps when I reached the deepest part. But in spite of much snorting and endeavours to turn back I persuaded him to go on, and we finally reached the other side in safety. The messenger from the monastery had dismounted from his camel by this time, and was pacing up and down the shore. As I came closer to him I saw that he had but one arm, and that one of his eyes was missing.

Dismounting from my donkey on the bank, I approached him, at the same time bowing low.

'I was told that I should find here a messenger from the Great Ones of the Mountains,' I said. 'Are you he whom I seek?'

'From whom come you?' he asked, answering my question by asking another.

'I come from the High Priest of the Llamaserai at Pekin,' I answered, 'and I am the bearer of important tidings. I was told that I should find a man here who would carry forward the letter I bring, without a moment's delay.'

'Let me see the letter,' said the man. 'If it is sealed with the right seal I will do what you ask, not otherwise.'

I gave him the letter and he turned it over and over, scrutinising it carefully.

'This is the High Priest's seal,' he said at last, 'and I am satisfied; but I cannot return at once, as it is my duty to remain here until dusk has fallen.'

'Of that I am quite aware,' I answered. 'But you will see that this is a special case, and to meet it I am to pay you this gold, that is provided you will go forward and warn those from whom you come of my master's approach.'

When I had given him the bribe he counted it carefully and deposited it in his pocket.

'I will remain until the shadows fall,' he said 'and if no pilgrims have arrived by that time I will set off.'

Having arranged it in this fashion, we seated ourselves on the sandy beach, and after we had lit our pipes, smoked stolidly for half an hour. During that time my feelings were not to be envied. I did not enjoy my smoke, for I was being tortured on the rack of suspense. For aught I knew our man might have failed in drugging the ponies of the pursuing party. In that case they would probably suspect us of an attempt to outwit them, and might put in an appearance at any moment.

The sun sank lower and lower behind the hill, till finally he disappeared altogether. Long shadows fell from the cliffs across the water, the evening wind sprang up and moaned among the rocks, but still there was no sign of any cavalcade upon the opposite bank. If only our rivals did not put in an appearance for another quarter of an hour we should be saved.

In addition to this suspense I had another anxiety. Supposing Nikola had not succeeded in obtaining an animal and saddle of the kind he wanted, and should be prevented from reaching the ford in time to receive the men he was expecting, what would happen then? But I would not let my mind dwell upon such a contingency. And yet for most positive reasons I dared not attempt to hurry the messenger, who was still sitting stolidly smoking. To let him think that I was anxious to get rid of him would only be to excite his suspicions, and, those once aroused, he would in all probability determine to remain at the ford. In that case I might as well walk into the river and drown myself without further waste of time.

One by one the stars came out and began to twinkle in the cloudless heavens, such stars as one never sees anywhere save in the East. The wind was rising, and in another half hour it would be too dark to see.

At last my companion rose and shook himself.

'I see no pilgrims,' he said, 'and it is cold by the water. I shall depart. Is it your pleasure to come with me or will you remain?'

'I have no will,' I answered. 'I must perforce wait here till the caravan bringing my master arrives. Then I shall follow you. Do not wait for me.'

He did not need to be bidden twice, but approaching his camel, mounted, and then with a curt nod to me set off up the path.

As soon as he had disappeared I walked down to the water's edge and called to my men to come over, which they did. When they had landed, I bade them follow me, and, forsaking the ford, we set off at a brisk pace up the path.

A hundred yards from the river the track we were following turned abruptly to the right hand and wound through a narrow gorge. This, however, we did not enter, as I deemed it wisest to settle in a sheltered spot on the left. I rode ahead, and reconnoitred, and having ascertained that it could not be seen from the path, bade them pitch our camp there. Within ten minutes of our arrival the donkeys were picketed, the tents erected, and the camp fires lighted. Then, leaving the men to the preparation of the evening meal, I returned to the track and hurried along it in the direction of the ford.

When I was within fifty yards of the turning, which I knew would bring me within full sight of the river, I heard a low whistle. Next moment a man mounted on a camel came into view, and pulled up alongside me. In spite of the half dark I could see that the rider was dressed exactly like the man to whom I had talked at the ford; he had also one arm, and his right eye was closed.

'Bear to your left hand,' he said, leaning down from his camel to speak to me; 'there you will find some big rocks, and behind them you must hide yourself. Have your revolver ready to your hand, and if anything should happen, and I should call to you for assistance, come to me at once.'

'Did you have much difficulty in procuring your camel?' I asked, hardly able to believe that the man was Nikola.

'None whatever,' he answered; 'but the clothes and saddle were a little more difficult. However, I got them at last, and now do you think I look at all like the man I am here to represent?'

'One or two things are different,' I replied; 'but you need have no fear; they'll not suspect.'

'Let us hope not,' said Nikola. 'Where are the men?'

'Camped back yonder,' I answered, 'in a little gully to the left of the gorge.'

'That's well; now creep down to the rocks and take your place. But be sure not to forget what I have told you.'

I made my way down as he ordered and little by little crept along to where three big boulders stood out upon the sands. Between these I settled myself, and to my delight found I had an almost uninterrupted view of the ford. As I looked across the water I made out a small party coming down the slope on to the sand on the other side. Without losing time they plunged in, and so quiet was the night I could even hear the splashing made by the animals and distinguish between the first noise on the bank, and the sullen thud as they advanced into deeper water. Then I heard a hoarse call, and a moment later Nikola rode across the sand on his camel.

In two or three minutes the fording party had reached the bank, scarcely more than ten paces from where I lay. So close were they indeed that I could hear the breathing of the tired animals quite distinctly and the sigh of relief with which they hailed the dismounting of their masters. The man who was in command approached Nikola and, after a little preamble, said: 'We were delayed on the road by the sickness of our animals, or we should have been here earlier. Tell us, we pray, if any other travellers have passed this way?'

'But one party,' said the spurious messenger with a chuckle; 'and by this time they are lost among the mountains. They grudged me alms and I did not tell them the true path. Ere this time tomorrow the vultures will have torn the flesh from their bones.'

'How many in number were they?' asked the man who had first spoken.

'Five,' answered Nikola; 'and may the devils of the mountains take possession of them! And now who be ye?'

'We have come from Pekin,' answered the spokesman of the party, 'and we bring letters from the High Priest of the Llamaserai to the Great Ones of the Mountains. There be two barbarians who have stolen their way into our society, murdered him who was to be one of the Three, and substituted themselves in his place. The symbol of the Three, which was stolen by a foreign devil many years ago, is in their possession; and that was the party who passed this ford on their way to the mountains, and whom thou sawest.'

'They will go no farther,' said Nikola, when they had finished, with another grim laugh; 'and the hearts that would know our secrets will be tit-bits for the young eagles. What is it that ye want of me?'

'There is this letter of warning to be carried forward,' said the man; and as he spoke he produced from his pocket the roll of paper I had seen in his possession the previous night. He handed it to Nikola, who placed it inside his wadded coat, and then proceeded towards his camel, which he mounted. When it had risen to its feet he turned to the small party who were watching him, and said: 'Turn back on your path. Camp not near the ford, for the spirits of the lost pass up and down in the still hours of the night, and it is death for those who hear them.'

His warning was not without effect, for as soon as he had ridden off I noticed with considerable satisfaction that the party lost no time in retracing their steps across the river. I watched them for some time, and only when they were dimly outlined against the stars on the brow of the hill did I move. Then, knowing that they must be making haste to be out of the valley, I slipped from my hiding-place and made my way up the path towards the gully where we had fixed our camp.

When I reached the firelight I saw that Nikola had dismounted from his camel and had entered his own tent. I found him removing his disguise and preparing to change back into his own garments.

'We have come out of that scrape very neatly,' he said; 'and I can only add, Bruce, that it is owing to your foresight and intelligence that we have done so. Had you not had the wit to try to obtain a glimpse of that man the other night, we should in all probability have been caught in a trap from which there would have been no escaping. As it is we have not only got rid of our enemy but have improved our position into the bargain. If we make as good progress in the future as we have done in the past we should be inside the monastery by tomorrow evening.'

'I hope we shall,' I answered; 'but from what we have gone through of late I am induced to think that it could be wiser not to contemplate stocking our poultry-yard before we have seen that our incubator is in good working order.'

'You are quite right, we won't.'

Half an hour later our evening meal was served, and when it was eaten we sat round the camp fire smoking and talking, the dancing flames lighting up the rocks around us, and the great stars winking grimly down at us from overhead. The night was very still; save the grunting of the picketed donkeys, the spluttering of the flames of the fire, the occasional cry of some night bird, and once the howl of a jackal among the rocks, scarcely a sound was to be heard. It cannot be considered extraordinary, therefore, if my thoughts turned to the girl I loved. I wondered if she were thinking of me, and if so, what she imagined I was doing. Our journey to the monastery was nearly at an end. How long we should remain there when we had once got inside I had not the very vaguest notion; but, if the luck which had followed us so far still held good, we ought soon to be able to complete our errand there and return with all speed to the coast. Then, I told myself, I would seek out my darling and, with her brother's permission, make her my wife. What I would do after that was for the Fates to decide. But of one thing I was convinced, and that was that as long as I lived I would never willingly set foot in China again.

Next morning, a little after daylight, we broke camp, packed the animals, mounted, and set off. For the first ten miles or so the track was a comparatively plain one, leading along a valley, the entrance to which was the gorge I had seen on the previous night. Then circling round the side of the mountain by a precipitous path we came out on to a long tableland, whence a lovely view could be obtained. The camel we had turned loose earlier in the day to roam the country, or to find its way back to its former owner, as might seem to it best. It was well that we did so, for at the elevation to which we had now ascended, travelling with it would have proved most difficult, if not altogether impossible. Not once but several times we had to dismount and clamber from rock to rock, making our way through ravines, and across chasms as best we could. On many occasions it looked as if it would be necessary for us to abandon even the sure-footed animals we had brought with us, but in each case patience and perseverance triumphed over difficulties, and we were enabled to push on with them again.

By midday we had lost sight of the track altogether; the air had become bitterly cold, and it looked as if snow might fall at any minute. At half-past three a few flakes did descend, and by the time we found a camping-place, under an overhanging cliff, the ground was completely covered.

Being provided with plenty of warm clothing ourselves we were not so badly off, but for our poor coolies, whom nothing we had been able to say or do, before we set out, would induce to provide themselves with anything different to their ordinary attire, it was a matter of serious concern. Something had to be done for them. So choosing a hollow spot in the cliff into which we could all huddle, we collected a supply of brushwood and lit a bonfire at the mouth. Into this circle of warmth we led and picketed our donkeys, hoping to be able to keep them snug so that they should have sufficient strength left to continue their journey next day.

Every moment the snow was falling faster, and by the time we turned into our blankets it was nearly four inches deep around the camp. When we woke in the morning the whole contour of the country was changed. Where it had been bare and sterile the day before, we now had before us a plain of dazzling white. Unfortunately the intense cold had proved too much for one of our donkeys, for when we went to inspect them, we found him lying dead upon the ground. One of the smaller coolies was not in a much better state. Seeing this, Nikola immediately gave him a few drops of some liquid from that marvellous medicine-chest, without which, as I have already said, he never travelled. Whatever its constituents may have been it certainly revived the man for a time, and by the time we began our march again he was able to hobble along beside us. Within an hour of setting out, however, he was down again, and in half an hour he was dead, and we had buried him beneath the snow.

Our route now, by reason of the snow, was purely a matter of conjecture, for no track of any sort could be seen. As we could not turn back, however, and it was a dangerous matter to proceed without knowing in what direction to steer, our position might have been reckoned a fairly dangerous one. By the middle of the afternoon another of our coolies dropped, and, seeing this, Nikola decided to camp.

Choosing the most sheltered spot we could discover, we cleared away the snow and erected our tents, and, when this was done, lit a fire and picketed the remaining donkeys. The sick coolie we made as comfortable as possible with all the clothing we could spare, but the trouble was of little avail, for at nightfall he too reached the end of his journey.

By this time I must confess my own spirits had sunk down to the lowest depths. Nikola, however, was still undismayed.

'The death of these men,' he said, 'is a thing much to be regretted, but we must not let it break us down altogether. What do you say if we take that fellow out and bury him in the snow at once? There is still light enough if we are quick about it.'

Having no more desire than he to spend the night in the company of the poor man's dead body, we lifted it up and carried it out to where a great drift of snow showed some fifty paces from our tent door. Here we deposited it and went back to the camp, leaving the softly falling flakes to cover him quite as effectually as we could have done. But that evening two more unpleasant facts revealed themselves to us. Our two remaining donkeys were unable to stand the rigour of the climate any longer, and were on the verge of dying. Seeing this, Nikola left the tent again, and taking his revolver with him, put an end to their sufferings. When they dropped he cut their throats, and then returned to the tent.

'What did you do that for?' I asked, at a loss to understand his last action.

'If you want an explanation,' he said quietly, 'examine the state of our larder, and then review our position. We are here on the tops of these mountains; one track is like another; where the monastery is I cannot tell you; and now, to add to our sorrows, our provisions are running short. Donkeys are not venison, but they are better than cold snow. And now you know why I shot them.'

Accordingly, next morning before we began our journey, we cut up all that was worth carrying with us of the poor beasts. It was well that we did so, for our search for the monastery was no more successful on this occasion than it had been on the previous day. To add to the hopelessness of it all I was beginning to feel ill, while the one remaining coolie staggered on after us more like a galvanised corpse than a living man.

Sometimes in my dreams I live that dreadful time over again. I see the snow-covered country with its yawning precipices, gently sloping valleys, and towering heights; I picture our weary, heart-sick trio, struggling on and on, sinking into the white shroud at every step, Nikola always in advance, myself toiling after him, and the last coolie lagging in the rear. Round us the snow whirls and eddies, and overhead some great bird soars, his pinions casting a black shadow on the otherwise speckless white. Then the dream invariably changes, and I find myself waking with a certain nameless but haunting terror upon me, for which I cannot account. But to return to my narrative.

An hour before sundown the coolie dropped, and once more we had to camp. If I live to be a hundred I shall not forget a single particular connected with that ghastly night. We were so weak by this time that it was a matter of impossibility for us to erect a tent. A drowsiness that there seemed no withstanding had laid its finger upon us. Only the coolie could keep awake, and he chattered incoherently to himself in his delirium.

'Bruce,' said Nikola about eight o'clock, coming round the fire to where I sat, 'this will never do. That poor fellow over yonder will be dead in half an hour, and if you don't mind what you are about you will soon follow suit. I'm going to set to work to keep you awake.'

So saying, this extraordinary individual produced his medicine-chest, and opened it by the fire. From inside the cover he produced a tiny draught-board and a box of men.

'May I have the pleasure of giving you a game?' he asked, as politely as if we were comparative strangers meeting in a London club. Half awake and half asleep, I nodded, and began to arrange my men. Then, when all was ready, we commenced to play, and before three moves had been executed, I had caught Nikola's enthusiasm and was wide awake.

Whether I played it well or ill I cannot remember. I only know that Nikola worked out his plans, prepared strategies and traps for me, and not only that, but executed them, too, as if he had not a thought of anything else on his mind. Only stopping to throw wood upon the fire, and once to soothe the coolie just before he died, we played on till daylight. Then, after a hasty breakfast, we abandoned everything we had, save the medicine-chest, our few remaining provisions, and such small articles as we could stow about our persons, and started off on what we both believed must certainly prove our last march.

How strange are the workings of Fate! As we left the brow of that hill, and prepared to descend into the valley, we discerned before us, on the other side of the valley, a great stone building. It was the monastery, in search of which we had come so far and braved so much.

CHAPTER THIRTEEN

The monastery

We stood and looked across the valley, hardly able to believe that we had at last arrived at the place of which we had heard so much. There it stood gaunt and lonely, on the edge of the ravine, a dark grey collection of roofs and towers, and surrounded by a lofty wall. But, though we could see it plainly enough before us, the chief question was 'How were we to reach it?' The cañon, to employ an American term, stretched to right and left of us, as far as the eye could reach, in unbroken grandeur. Certainly, on the side upon which we stood, the cliff sloped enough for an experienced mountaineer to clamber down, but across the ravine it rose a sheer precipice for fully 1,500 feet, and though I examined it carefully I could not see a single place where even a goat could find a footing.

'It would take us a week to go round,' said Nikola, when he had examined it with his usual care; 'and starving as we are we should be dead before we got half way.'

'Then what are we to do?'

'Climb down into the valley, I suppose. It's Hobson's choice.'

'It will be a terrible business,' I said.

'You will find death up here equally undesirable,' he answered. 'The worst of it is, however, I don't see how we are going to reach it when we do get down there. But as it is within the sphere of practical politics, as they say, that we may break our necks on the way down, we had better postpone further argument until we know that we have arrived at the bottom with our lives. Come along then.'

For the next ten minutes we occupied ourselves searching the cliff for the best climbing place. That once discovered we crawled over the edge and began our descent. For the first fifty yards or so it was comparatively easy work; we had nothing to do but to drop from rock to rock. Then matters became more difficult. An unbroken face of cliff, with only one small foothold in nearly forty feet, had to be negotiated. The wall at Pekin was not to be compared with it for difficulty, and, as I knew to my cost, I had found that quite difficult enough. How we were to manage this seemed to me incomprehensible. But as usual Nikola was equal to the occasion.

'Take off your coat,' he said, 'and give it to me.'

I did as he ordered me, whereupon he divested himself of his own, and then tied the sleeves of the two garments together. This done we crawled along to the opposite end of the ledge, where grew one of the stunted trees which provided the only show of vegetation to be seen along the whole face of the cliff, and tied the end of the rope he had thus made, to a long and thick root which had straggled over the face of the cliff in the hope of finding a holding place. Thus we obtained an additional three feet, making in all nearly fifteen feet, which, when we had added our own length, should carry us down to the ledge with a foot to spare.

As soon as these preparations were completed, we tossed up (strange relic of civilisation!) for the honour of going first and testing its strength, and, of course, the position fell to Nikola, whom Fate willed should be first in everything. Before setting off he carefully examined the strap by which his treasured medicine-chest was fastened round his neck, then with a nod of farewell to me knelt down upon the edge of the cliff, took the rope in his hands and began his descent. I have spent more enjoyable moments in my life than watching the strain upon that root. Of the coats themselves I had little fear; they were of the best silk, and, save where the sleeves joined the body, were woven in one piece. However the root held, and presently I heard Nikola calling to me to follow him. Not without a feeling of trepidation I lowered myself and went down hand over hand. Though the rope was a comparatively short one, it seemed centuries before I was anywhere near Nikola. Another three feet would find me on the ledge, and I was just congratulating myself on my cleverness when there was an ominous tearing noise on the cliff top, and the next moment I was falling backwards into midair. I gave myself up for lost, but fortunately the catastrophe was not as serious as it might have been, for with that presence of mind which never deserted him Nikola braced himself against the wall and clutched the rope as it slid by. The result of his action was that the force of my fall was broken, and instead of falling on to the little plateau below, and probably breaking my neck, or at least an arm or leg, I swung against the cliff and then slipped easily to the ground.

'Are you hurt?' cried Nikola from his perch above.

'More frightened than hurt,' I replied. 'Now, how are you going to get down?'

Without vouchsafing any reply Nikola turned his face to the rock, went down upon his knees once more, and then clutching at the ledge lowered himself and finally let go. He landed safely beside me, and having ascertained that his medicine-chest was uninjured, went quietly across to where our coats had fallen and disengaged them from the broken root. Then having handed me mine he donned his own and suggested that we should continue our downward journey without more ado. I believe if Nikola were to fall by accident into the pit of Tophet, and by the exercise of superhuman ingenuity succeeded in scrambling out again, he would calmly seat himself on the brink of the crater and set to work to discover of what chemical substances the scum upon his garments was composed! I can assert with truth that in the whole of my experience of him I never once saw him really disconcerted.

Our climb from the plateau to the bottom of the valley – though still sufficiently dangerous to render it necessary that we should exercise the greatest caution – was not so difficult. At last we arrived at the foot, and, having looked up at the towering heights on either side of us, began to wonder what we had better do next.

We had not long to wait, however, for it appears our arrival had been observed. The bottom of the valley was covered with soft turf, dotted here and there with enormous rocks. We had just arranged to proceed in a westerly direction, and were in the act of setting out, when our ears were assailed by a curious noise. It was more like the sound of a badly blown Alpine horn than anything else, and seemed to be echoed from side to side of the path. Then a voice coming from somewhere close to us, but whence we could not tell, said slowly: 'Who are ye who thus approach the dwelling in the cliff?'

'I am he whom ye have been told to expect,' said Nikola.

'Welcome!' said the same passionless voice. Then, after a pause: 'Go forward to yonder open space and wait.'

All the time that the voice was speaking I had been carefully listening in the hope of being able to discover whence it came, but my exertions were useless. One moment it seemed to sound from my right, the next from my left. It had also a quaint metallic ring that made it still more difficult to detect its origin. To properly explain my meaning, I might say that it was like the echo of a voice the original of which could not be heard. The effect produced was most peculiar.

When the voice had finished Nikola moved forward in the direction indicated, and I followed him.

Arriving at the place, we stood in the centre of the open space and waited. For nearly ten minutes we looked about us wondering what would happen next. There was nothing to be seen in the valley save the green grass and the big rocks, and nothing to be heard but the icy wind sighing through the grass and the occasional note of a bird. Then from among the rocks to our right appeared one of the most extraordinary figures I have ever seen in my life. He was little more than three feet in height, his shoulders were abnormally broad, his legs bowed so that he could only walk on the sides of his feet, while his head was so big as to be out of all proportion to his body. He was attired in Chinese dress, even to the extent of a pigtail and a little round hat. Waddling towards us he said in a shrill falsetto: 'Will your Excellencies be honourably pleased to follow me?'

Thereupon he turned upon his heel and preceded us up the valley for nearly a hundred yards. Then, wheeling round to see that we were close behind him, he marched towards what looked like a hole in the cliff and disappeared within. We followed to find him standing in a large cave, bowing on the sand as if in welcome. On either side in rows were at least a dozen dwarfs, dressed in exactly the same fashion, and every one as small and ugly as himself. They held torches in their hands, and as soon as they saw that we were following, they set off up the cave, headed by the little fellow who had come to meet us.

When we had penetrated into what seemed the bowels of the earth, we left the narrow passage and found ourselves confronted by a broad stone staircase which wound upwards in spiral form. The procession of dwarfs again preceded us, still without noise. It was a weird performance, and had it not been for the reek of the torches, and the fluttering of bats' wings as the brutes were disturbed by the flames and smoke, I should have been inclined to imagine it part of some extraordinary dream; indeed, more than once I felt an impulse to touch the stone wall in order to convince myself by its rough surface that I really was awake. I could see that Nikola was fully alive to all that was passing, and I noticed that he had adopted a demeanour consistent with the aged and important position he was supposed to be filling. Up and up the stairs wound, twisting and twining this way and that, till it almost made me giddy trying to remember how far we had come; indeed, my legs were nearly giving way under me, when we came to a halt before a large door at the top of the stairs. This was thrown open, and our party filed through. From the level of the doorway a dozen more steps conducted us to the floor above, and here we came to a second stop. On looking about us we discovered that we were in an enormous hall of almost cathedral proportions. The raftered roof towered up for more than a hundred feet above our heads; to right and left were arches of strange design, while at the further end was an exquisite window, the glass of which was stained blood-red. The whole place was wrapt in semi-darkness, and though it had the appearance of a place of worship, I could distinguish no altar or anything to signify that it was used for sacred purposes.

As we reached the top the dwarf, who had met us in the valley and headed the procession up the stairs, signed to his followers to fall back on either hand and then led the way to a small square of masonry at the top of two steps and placed in the centre of the hall. Arriving there, he signed to us to take up our positions upon it, and himself mounted guard beside us.

For fully ten minutes we remained standing there, looking towards the blood-red window, and waiting for what would happen next. The silence was most unpleasant, and I had to exercise all my powers of self-control to prevent myself from allowing some sign of nervousness to escape me.

Then, without any warning, a sound of softest music greeted our ears, which gradually rose from the faintest pianissimo to the crashing chords of a barbaric march. It continued for nearly five minutes, until two doors, one on either side of what might be termed the chancel, opened, and a procession of men passed out. I call them men for the reason that I have no right to presume that they were anything else, but there was nothing in their appearance to support that theory. Each was attired in a long, black gown which reached to his feet, his hands were hidden in enormous sleeves, and his head was wrapped in a thick veil, thrown back to cover the poll and shoulders, with two round holes left for the eyes.

One after another they filed out and took up their positions in regular order on either side of us, all facing towards the window.

When the last had entered, and the doors were closed again, service commenced. The semi-darkness, through which the great red window glared like an evil eye, the rows of weird, black figures, the mysterious wailing chant and the recollection of the extraordinary character I had heard given to the place and its inmates, only increased the feeling of awe that possessed me.

When for nearly a quarter of an hour the monks had knelt at their devotions, the muffled notes of a great bell broke upon our ears. Then with one accord they rose to their feet again and filed solemnly out by the doors through which they had entered. When the last had disappeared we were left alone again in the same unearthly silence.

'What on earth does all this mean?' said Nikola in a whisper. 'Why doesn't somebody come out to receive us?'

'There is a charnel-house air about the place,' I answered, 'that is the very reverse of pleasant.'

'Hush!' said Nikola; 'someone is coming.'

As he spoke, a curtain in the chancel was drawn aside, and a man, dressed in the same fashion as those we had seen at their devotions a few minutes since, came down the steps towards us. When he reached the daïs upon which we stood, he bowed, and beckoned to us with his finger to follow him. This we did, up the steps by which he had descended, and past the curtain. Here we found another flight of steps leading to a long corridor, on either side of which were many small cells. The only light obtainable came from the torch which our guide had taken from a bracket on leaving the chancel and now carried in his hand.

Without stopping, the monk led us along the whole length of the corridor, then turned to his right hand, descended three more steps, and having drawn back another curtain, beckoned to us to pass him into a narrow but lofty room. It was plainly furnished with a table, a couple of stools, and a rough bed, and was lighted by a narrow slit in the wall about three inches wide by twenty-five deep.

When we were both inside, our guide turned, and, approaching me, pointed first to myself and then to the room, as if signifying that this was for my use, then taking Nikola by the arm, he led him through another doorway in the corner to an inner apartment, which was evidently designed for his occupation. Presently he emerged again by himself, and went out still without speaking a word. A moment later Nikola appeared at his doorway and invited me to inspect his abode. It was like mine in every particular, even to the bracket for a torch upon the wall.

'We are fairly inside now,' said Nikola, 'and we shall either find out what we want to know within a very short space of time, or be sent to explore the mysteries of another world.'

'It's within the bounds of possibility that we shall do both,' I answered.

'One thing, Bruce, before we go any further,' he said, not heeding my remark, 'you must remember that this place is not like an ordinary Shamanist or Buddhist monastery where things are carried on slipshod fashion. Here every man practises the most rigid self-denial possible, and, among other things, I have no doubt the meals will prove inadequate. We shall have to reconcile ourselves to many peculiar customs, and all the time we must keep our eyes wide open so that we may make the most of every chance that offers.'

'I don't mind the customs,' I answered, 'but I am sorry to hear about the meals, for to tell you the honest truth, at the present moment I am simply starving.'

'It can't be helped,' replied Nikola. 'Even if we don't get anything till tomorrow evening we shall have to grin and bear it.'

I groaned and went back to my room. It must have been nearly midday by this time, and we had eaten nothing since daybreak. I seated myself on my bed, and tried to reconcile myself to our position. I thought for some time, then a fit of drowsiness came over me, and before very long I was fast asleep.

For nearly two hours I must have remained unconscious of what was going on around me. When I woke my hunger was even greater than before. I rose from my bed, and went in to look at Nikola, only to find that extraordinary man occupied in his favourite way – working out abstruse problems on the floor. I did not disturb him, but returned to my own apartment, and fell to pacing the floor like a caged beast. I told myself that if I did not get a meal very soon I should do something desperate.

My hunger, however, was destined to be appeased before long. Just about sundown I heard the noise of footsteps in the corridor, and presently a bare-footed monk, dressed all in black, and wearing the same terrifying head-dress we had first seen in the great hall, made his appearance, carrying a large bowl in his hands. This he conveyed through my room and placed on Nikola's table.

When he entered, he found the latter upon his knees engaged in his devotions, and I began to reproach myself for having allowed him to catch me doing anything else.

The man had hardly left again, indeed, the sound of his footsteps had not died away on the stone steps, before I was in the inner room.

'Dinner is served,' said Nikola, and went across to the bowl upon the table. To my dismay it contained little more than a pint of the thinnest soup mortal man ever set eyes on. In this ungenerous fluid floated a few grains of rice, but anything more substantial there was none. There was neither spoon nor bread, so how we were to drink it, unless we tilted the bowl up and poured it down our throats, I could not imagine. However, Nikola solved the difficulty by taking from his medicine-chest a small travelling cup, which he placed in my hand. Thereupon I set to work. Seeing that Nikola himself took scarcely more than a cupful, I remonstrated with him, but in vain. He said he did not want it, and that settled the matter. I accordingly finished what remained, and when I had done so felt as hungry as ever. If this were to be the fare of the monastery, I argued, by the time we left it, if leave it we did, I should be reduced to a skeleton.

When I had finished my meal, the long streak of light which had been under the window when we arrived, and had gradually crossed the floor, was now some feet up the opposite wall. A little later it vanished altogether. The room was soon in total darkness, and I can assure you my spirits were none of the best. I returned to Nikola's apartment not in the most cheerful of humours.

'This is very pleasant,' I said ironically. 'Are they never going to receive us properly?'

'All in good time,' he answered quietly. 'We shall have enough excitement to last us a lifetime presently, and I don't doubt that we shall be in some danger too.'

'I don't mind the danger,' I said; 'it is this awful waiting that harasses my nerves.'

'Well, you won't have long to wait. If I mistake not there is somebody coming for us now,'

'How do you know that?' I asked. 'I can't hear anybody.'

'Still they are coming,' said Nikola. 'If I were you I should go back into my room and be ready to receive them when they arrive.'

I took the hint, and returned to my apartment, where I waited with all the patience I could command.

How Nikola knew that someone was coming to fetch us I cannot tell, but this much is certain, within five minutes of his having warned me I heard a man come down the steps, then a bright light appeared upon the wall, and a moment later the same dwarf who had ushered us into the monastery entered my room carrying a torch in his hand. Seeing that he desired speech with Nikola, I held up my hand to him in warning, and then, assuming an air of the deepest reverence, signed him to remain where he was while I proceeded into the inner room. Nikola was on the alert, and bade me call the man to him. This I did, and next moment the dwarf stood before him.

'I am sent, O stranger,' said the latter, 'to summon thee to an audience with the Great Ones of the Mountains.'

'I am prepared,' said Nikola solemnly. 'Let us go.'

Thereupon the dwarf turned himself about and led the way out into the corridor. I had no desire to be left behind, so I followed close at Nikola's heels.

We ascended first a long flight of steps, threaded the same corridor by which we had entered, mounted another flight of stairs, crossed a large hall, and finally reached a small ante-chamber. Here we were told to wait while the dwarf passed through a curtain and spoke to someone within. When he emerged again he drew back the covering of the doorway and signed to us to enter. We complied with his request, to discover a rather larger apartment, which was guarded by a monk in the usual dress. He received us with a bow, and also without speaking, conducted us to another room, the door of which was guarded by yet another monk.

All this had a most depressing effect upon my nerves, and by the time we reached the last monk I was ready to jump away from my own shadow. I make these confessions, in the first place, because having set my hand to the tale, I think I have no right to withhold anything connected with my adventures, and in the second, because I don't want to pose as a more courageous man than I really was. I have faced danger as many times as most men, and I don't think my worst enemy could accuse me of cowardice, but I feel bound to confess that on this occasion I was nervous. And who would not have been?

On reaching the last ante-room Nikola passed in ahead of me, without looking to right or left, his head bent, and his whole attitude suggestive of the deepest piety. Here we were told to wait. The monk disappeared, and for nearly five minutes did not put in an appearance again. When he did he pointed to a door on the opposite side of the apartment, and requested that we would lose no time in entering.

We complied with his request to find ourselves in a large room, the hangings of which were all of the deepest black. By the light of the torches, fixed in brackets on the walls, we could distinguish two men seated in quaintly carved chairs on a sort of daïs at the further end. They were dressed after the same fashion as the monks, and for this reason it was quite impossible to discover whether they were young or old. As soon as we got inside I came stiffly to attention alongside the door, while Nikola advanced and stood before the silent couple on the daïs. For some moments no one spoke. Then the man on the right rose, and turning towards Nikola said: 'Who are ye, and by what right do ye thus brave our solitude?'

'I am He of Hankow, of whom thou hast been informed,' answered Nikola humbly, with a low reverence. 'And I have come because thou didst command.'

'What proof have we of that?' enquired the first speaker.

'There is the letter sent forward by your messenger from the High Priest of the Llamaserai in Pekin, saying that I was coming,' replied Nikola, 'and I have this symbol that ye sent to me.'

Here he exhibited the stick he had procured from Wetherell, and held it up that the other might see.

'And if this be true, what business have ye with us?'

'I am here that I may do the bidding of the living and of the dead.'

'It is well,' said the first speaker and sat down again.

For five minutes or so there was another silence, during which no one spoke, and no one moved. I stood on one side of the door, the monk who had admitted us on the other; Nikola was before the daïs, and on it, rigid and motionless, the two black figures I have before described. When the silence had lasted the time I have mentioned I began to feel that if someone did not speak soon I should have to do so myself. The suspense was terrible, and yet Nikola stood firm, never moving a muscle or showing a sign of embarrassment.

Then the man who had not yet spoken said quietly: 'Hast thou prepared thyself for the office that awaits thee?'

'If it should fall out as ye intend,' said Nikola, 'I am prepared.'

'Art thou certain that thou hast no fear?'

'Of that I am certain,' he replied.

'And what knowledge hast thou of such things as will pertain to thy office?'

To my surprise Nikola answered humbly: 'I have no knowledge, but as thou knowest I have given my mind to the study of many things which are usually hid from the brain of man.'

'It is well,' answered this second man, after the manner of the first.

There was another silence, and then the man who had first addressed Nikola said with an air of authority: 'Tomorrow night we will test thy knowledge and thy courage. For the present prepare thyself and wait.'

Thereupon the monk at the doorway beckoned to Nikola to follow him. He did so, and I passed out of the room at his heels. Then we were conducted back to our cells and left alone for the night.

As soon as our guide had departed I went in to Nikola. 'What do you think of our interview?' I enquired.

'That its successor tomorrow evening will prove of some real importance to us,' he answered. 'Our adventure begins to grow interesting.'

'But are you prepared for all the questions they will ask?'

'I cannot say,' said Nikola. 'I am remembering what I have been taught and leaving the rest to Fate. The luck which has attended us hitherto ought surely to carry us on to the end.'

'Well, let us hope nothing will go wrong,' I continued. 'But I must confess I am not happy. I have seen more cheerful places than this monastery, and as far as diet is concerned, commend me to the cheapest Whitechapel restaurant.'

'Help me through to the end, and you shall live in luxury for the rest of your days.'

We talked for a little while and then retired to bed. For one day we had surely had enough excitement!

Next day we rose early, breakfasted on a small portion of rice, received no visitors, and did not leave our rooms all day. Only the monk who had brought us our food on the previous evening visited us, and, as on that occasion, he had nothing to say for himself. Our evening meal was served at sundown, and consisted of the same meagre soup as before. Then darkness fell, and about the same time as on the previous evening the dwarf appeared to conduct us to the rendezvous.

CHAPTER FOURTEEN

An ordeal

When we left our rooms on this occasion we turned to the right hand instead of to the left, and proceeded to a long corridor running below that in which our cells were situated. Whereabouts in the monastery this particular passage was placed, and how its bearings lay with regard to the staircase by which we had ascended from the valley on the previous day, I could not discover. Like all the others, however, it was innocent of daylight, but was lighted by enormous torches, which again were upheld by iron brackets driven into the walls. Once during our march an opportunity was vouchsafed me of examining these walls for myself, when to my astonishment I discovered that they were not hewn out of the rock as I had supposed, but were built of dressed stone, of a description remarkably resembling granite. This being so, I realised, for the first time, that the cells and the corridors were built by human hands, but how long it could have taken the builders to complete such an enormous task was a calculation altogether beyond my powers. But to return to my narrative.

From the corridor just described we passed down another flight of steps, then across a narrow landing, after which came another staircase. As we reached it our ears were assailed by a noise resembling distant thunder.

'What sound is that?' asked Nikola of our guide.

The dwarf did not answer in words, but, leading us along a side passage, held his torch above his head, and bade us look.

For a moment the dancing flame prevented us from seeing anything. Then our eyes became accustomed to the light, and to our amazement we discovered that we were standing on the very brink of an enormous precipice. In the abyss, the wind, which must have come in through some passage from the open air, tore and shrieked with a most dismal noise, while across the way, not more than twelve yards distant, fell the waters of a magnificent cataract. Picture to yourself that great volume of water crashing and roaring down through the darkness into the very bowels of the earth. The fall must have been tremendous, for no spray came up to us. All we could see was a mass of black water rushing past us. We stood and looked, open-mouthed, and when our wonder and curiosity were satisfied as much as it ever would be, turned and followed our guide back to the place where we had been standing when we had first heard the noise. At the other end of this corridor or landing, whichever you may please to term it, was a large stone archway, resembling a tunnel more than anything else, and at its mouth stood a monk. The dwarf went forward to him and said something in a low voice, whereupon he took a torch from the wall at his side and signed to us to follow him. The dwarf returned to the higher regions, while we plunged deeper still below the surface of the earth. Whether we were really as far down as we imagined, or whether the dampness was caused by some leakage from the cataract we had just seen, I cannot say; at any rate, the walls and floors were all streaming wet.

The passage, or tunnel, as I have more fittingly termed it, was a long one, measuring at least fifty feet from entrance to exit. When we had passed through it we stood in the biggest cave I have yet had the good fortune to behold; indeed, so large was it that in the half-dark it was with the utmost difficulty I could see the other side. Our guide led us across the first transept into the main aisle and then left us. No sign of furniture of any kind – either stool, altar, or daïs – was to be seen, and as far as we could judge there was not a living soul within call. The only sound to be heard was the faint dripping of water, which seemed to come from every part of the cave.

'This is eerie enough to suit anyone,' I whispered to Nikola. 'I hope the performance will soon commence.'

'Hush!' he said. 'Be careful what you say, for you don't know who may overhear you.'

He had hardly spoken before the first mysterious incident of the evening occurred. We were standing facing that part of the cavern which had been on our right when we entered. The light was better in that particular spot than anywhere else, and I am prepared to swear that at that instant, to the best of my belief, there was not a human being between ourselves and the wall. Yet as we looked a shadow seemed to rise out of the ground before us; it came closer, and as it came it took human shape. The trick was a clever one and its working puzzles me to this day. Of course the man may have made his appearance from behind a pillar, specially arranged for the purpose, or he may have risen from a trap-door in the floor, though personally I consider both these things unlikely; the fact however remains, come he did.

'By your own desire, and of no force applied by human beings,' he said, addressing Nikola, 'thou art here asking that the wisdom of our order may be revealed to thee. There is still time to draw back if thou wouldst.'

'I have no desire to draw back,' Nikola answered firmly.

'So be it,' said the man. 'Then follow me.'

Nikola moved forward, and I was about to accompany him when the man ahead of us turned, and pointing to me said: 'Come no farther! It is not meet that thou shouldst see what is now to be revealed.'

Nikola faced me and said quietly, 'Remain.'

Having given this order he followed the other along the cave and presently disappeared from my sight.

For some minutes I stood where they had left me, listening to the dripping of the water in the distant parts of the cave, watching the bats as they flitted swiftly up and down the gloomy aisles, and wondering into what mysteries Nikola was about to be initiated. The silence was most oppressive, and every moment that I waited it seemed to be growing worse. To say that I was disappointed at being thus shelved at the most important point in our adventure would scarcely express my feelings. Besides, I wanted to be at Nikola's right hand should any trouble occur.

As I waited the desire to know more of what he was doing grew upon me. I felt that come what might I must be present at the interview to which he had been summoned. No one, I argued, would be any the wiser, and even if by chance they should discover that I had followed them, I felt I could trust to my own impudence and powers of invention to explain my presence there. My mind was no sooner made up than I set off down the cave in the direction in which they had disappeared. Arriving at the further end I discovered another small passage, from which led still another flight of steps. Softly I picked my way down them, at the same time trying to reason out in my own mind how deep in the mountain we were, but as usual I could come to no satisfactory conclusion.

When I arrived at the bottom of the steps, I stood in a peculiar sort of crypt, supported by pillars, and surrounded on all sides by tiers of niches, or shelves, cut, after the fashion of the Roman catacombs, in the solid rock. This dismal place was lighted by three torches, and by their assistance I was able to discern in each niche a swaddled-up human figure. Not without a feeling of awe I left the steps by which I had descended and began to hunt about among the pillars for a doorway through which I might pass into the room below, where Nikola was engaged with the Great Ones of the Mountains. But though I searched for upwards of ten minutes, not a sign of any such entrance could I discover. I was now in a curious position. I had left my station in the larger cave and, in spite of orders to the contrary, had followed to witness what was not intended for my eyes; in that case, supposing the door at the top were shut, and I could find no other exit, I should be caught like a rat in a trap. To make matters worse, I should have disobeyed the strict command of the man who had summoned Nikola, and I should also have incurred the blame of Nikola himself. Remembering how rigorously he had dealt with those who had offended him before, I resolved in my own mind to turn back while I had the chance. But just as I was about to do so, something curious about the base of one of the pillars, to the right of where I stood, caught my eye. It was either a crack magnified by the uncertain light of the torches, or it was a doorway cleverly constructed in the stonework, and which had been improperly closed. I approached it, and, inserting the blade of my knife, pulled. It opened immediately, revealing the fact that the entire pillar was hollow, and what was more important to me, that it contained a short wooden ladder which led down into yet another crypt.

In an instant my resolution to return to the upper cave was forgotten. An opportunity of discovering their business was presented to me, and come what might I was going to make the most of it. Pulling the door open to its full extent I crept in and went softly down the ladder. By the time I reached the bottom I was in total darkness. For a moment I was at a loss to understand the reason of this, as I could plainly hear voices; but by dint of feeling I discovered that the place in which I stood was a sort of ante-chamber to a room beyond, the door of which was only partially shut. My sandals made no noise on the stone floor, and I was therefore able to creep up to the entrance of the inner room without exciting attention. What a sight it was that met my eyes!

The apartment itself was not more than fifty feet long by thirty wide. But instead of being like all the other places through which I had passed, an ordinary cave, this one was floored and wainscoted with woodwork now black with age. How high it was I could not guess, for the walls went up and up until I lost them in the darkness. Of furniture the room boasted but little; there was, however, a long and queer-shaped table at the further end, another near the door, and a tripod brazier on the left-hand side. The latter contained a mass of live coal, and, as there was some sort of forced draught behind it, it roared like a blacksmith's forge.

Nikola, when I entered, was holding what looked like a phial in his left hand. The black-hooded men I had expected to find there I could not see, but standing by his side were two dressed in a totally different fashion.

The taller of the pair was a middle-aged man, almost bald, boasting a pleasant, but slightly Semitic cast of countenance, and wearing a short black beard. His companion, evidently the chief, differed from him in almost every particular. To begin with, he was the oldest man I have ever seen in my life able to move about. He was small and shrivelled almost beyond belief, his skin was as yellow as parchment, and his bones, whenever he moved, looked as if they must certainly cut through their coverings. His countenance bore unmistakable traces of having once been extremely handsome, and was now full of intellectual beauty; at the same time, however, I could not help feeling certain that it was not the face of an Asiatic. Like his companion, he also wore a beard, but in his case it was long and snow-white, which added materially to his venerable appearance.

'My son,' he was saying, addressing himself to Nikola, 'hitherto thou hast seen the extent to which the particular powers of which we have been speaking can be cultivated by a life of continual prayer and self-denial. Now thou wilt learn to what extent our sect has benefited by earthly wisdom. Remember always that from time immemorial there have been those among us who have given up their lives to the study of the frailties and imperfections of this human frame. The wonders of medicine and all the arts of healing have come down to us from years that date from before the apotheosis of the ever-blessed Buddha. Day and night, generation after generation, century after century in these caves those of our faith have been studying and adding to the knowledge which our forefathers possessed. Remote as we are from it, every fresh discovery of the Western or Eastern world is known to us, and to the implements with which our forefathers worked we have added everything helpful that man has invented since. In the whole world there are none who hold the secret of life and death in their hands as we do. Wouldst thou have an example? There is a case at present in the monastery.'

As he spoke he struck a gong hanging upon the wall, and almost before the sound had died away a monk appeared to answer it. The old fellow said something to him, and immediately he retired by the way he had come. Five minutes later he reappeared, followed by another monk. Between them they bore a stretcher, on which lay a human figure. The old man signed to them to place him in the centre of the room, which they did, and retired.

As soon as they had departed Nikola was invited to examine the person upon the stretcher. He did so, almost forgetting, in his excitement, his role of an old man.

For nearly five minutes he bent over the patient, who lay like a log, then he rose and turned to his companions.

'A complete case of paralysis,' he said.

'You are assured in your own mind that it is complete?' enquired the old man.

'Perfectly assured,' said Nikola.

'Then pay heed, for you are about to witness the power which the wisdom of all the ages has given us.'

Turning to his companion he took from his hand a small iron ladle. This he placed upon the brazier, pouring into it about a tablespoonful of the mixture contained in the phial, which, when I first looked, Nikola had been holding in his hand. As the ladle became heated, the liquid, whatever it may have been, threw off a tiny vapour, the smell of which reminded me somewhat of a mixture of sandal-wood and camphor.

By the time this potion was ready for use the second man had divested the patient of his garments. What remained of the medicine was thereupon forced into his mouth, that and his nostrils were bound up, and after he had lost consciousness, which he did in less than a minute, he was anointed from head to toe with some penetrating unguent. Just as the liquid, when heating on the brazier, had done, this ointment threw off a vapour, which hung about the body, rising into the air to the height of about three inches. For something like five minutes this exhalation continued, then it began to die away, and as soon as it had done so the unguent was again applied, after which the two men kneaded the body in somewhat the same fashion as that adopted by masseurs. So far the colour of the man's skin had been a sort of zinc white, now it gradually assumed the appearance of that of a healthy man. Once more the massage treatment was begun, and when it was finished the limbs began to twitch in a spasmodic fashion. At the end of half an hour the bandage was removed from the mouth and nostrils, also the plugs from the ears, and the man, who had hitherto lain like one asleep, opened his eyes.

'Move thy arms,' said the old man with an air of command.

The patient promptly did as he was commanded.

'Bend thy legs.'

He complied with the order.

'Stand upon thy feet.'

He rose from the stretcher and stood before them, apparently as strong and hearty a man as one could wish to see.

'Tomorrow this treatment shall be repeated, and the day following thou shalt be cured. Now go and give thanks,' said the old man with impressive sternness. Then turning to Nikola, he continued – 'Thou hast seen our powers. Could any man in the world without these walls do as much?'

'Nay, they are ignorant as earthworms,' said Nikola. 'But I praise Buddha for the man's relief.'

'Praise to whom praise is due,' answered the old fellow. 'And now, having seen so much, it is fitting that thou shouldst go further, and to do so it is necessary that we put aside the curtain that divides man's life from death. Art thou afraid?'

'Nay,' said Nikola, 'I have no fear.'

'It is well said,' remarked the elder man, and again he struck the gong.

The monk having appeared in answer he gave him an order and the man immediately withdrew. When he returned, he and his companion brought with them another stretcher, upon which was placed the dead body of a man. The monk having withdrawn, the old priest said to Nikola – 'Gaze upon this person, my son; his earthly pilgrimage is over; he died of old age today. He was one of our lay brethren, and a devout and holy man. It is meet that he should conduct thee, of whose piety we have heard so much, into our great inner land of knowledge. Examine him for thyself, and be sure that the spirit of life has really passed out of him.'

Nikola bent over the bier and did as he was requested. At the end of his examination he said quietly – 'It is even as thou sayest; the brother's life is departed from him.'

'Thou art convinced of the truth of thy words?' enquired the second man.

'I am convinced,' said Nikola.

'Then I will once more show thee what our science can do.'

With the assistance of his colleague he brought what looked like a large electric battery and placed it at the dead man's feet. The priest connected certain wires with the body, and, having taken a handle in either hand, placed himself in position, and shut his eyes. Though I craned my head round to see, I could not tell what he did. But this much is certain, after a few moments he swayed himself backwards and forwards, seemed to breathe with difficulty, and finally became almost rigid. Then came a long pause, lasting perhaps three minutes, at the end of which time he opened his eyes, raised his right arm, and pointed with his forefinger at the dead man's face. As he did so, to my horror, I saw the eyes open! Again he seemed to pray, then he pointed at the right arm, whereupon the dead man lifted it and folded it upon his breast, then at his left, which followed suit. When both the white hands were in this position he turned to Nikola and said – 'Is there aught in thy learning can give thee the power to do that?'

'There is nothing,' said Nikola, who I could see was as much amazed as I was.

'But our power does not end there,' said the old man.

'Oh, wonderful father! what further canst thou teach me?' asked Nikola. The man did not answer, but again closed his eyes for a few moments. Then, still holding the handles but pointing them towards the dead man, he cried in a loud voice – 'Ye who are dead, arise!'

And then – but I do not expect you will believe me when I tell it – that man who had been ten hours dead, rose little by little from his bier and at last stood before us. I continued to watch what happened. I saw Nikola start forward as if carried out of himself. I saw the second man extend his arm to hold him back, and then the corpse fell in a heap upon the floor. The two men instantly sprang forward, lifted it up, and placed it upon the stretcher again.

'Art thou satisfied?' enquired the old man.

'I am filled with wonder. Is it possible that I can see more?' said Nikola.

'Thou wouldst see more?' asked the chief of the Two in a sepulchral tone. 'Then, as a last proof of our power, before thou takest upon thee the final vows of our order, when all our secrets must be revealed to thee, thou shalt penetrate the Land of Shadows, and see, as far as is possible for human eyes, the dead leaders of our order, of all ages, stand before you.'

With that he took from a bag hanging round his waist a handful of what looked like dried herbs. These he threw upon the fire, and almost instantly the room was filled with a dense smoke. For some few seconds I could distinguish nothing, then it drew slowly off, and little by little I seemed to see with an extraordinary clearness.

Whether it was that I was hypnotised, and fancied I saw what I am about to describe, or whether it really happened as I say, I shall never know. One thing, however, is certain – the room was filled with the shadowy figures of men. They were of all ages, and apparently of all nations. Some were Chinese, some were Cingalese, some were Thibetans, while one or two were certainly Aryans, and for all I knew to the contrary, might have been English. The room was filled with them, but there was something plainly unsubstantial about them. They moved to and fro without sound, yet with regular movements. I watched them, and as I watched, a terror such as I had never known in my life before, came over me. I felt that if I did not get out of the room at once I should fall upon the floor in a fit. In this state I made my way towards the door by which I had entered, fled up the ladder, through the crypt, and then across the cave to the place where I had stood when Nikola had left me, and then fell fainting upon the floor.

How long I remained in this swoon I cannot tell, but when I came to myself again I was still alone.

It must have been quite an hour later when Nikola joined me. The monk who had brought us into the hall accompanied him, and led us towards the tunnel. There the dwarf received us and conducted us back to our apartments.

Once there, Nikola, without vouchsafing me a word, retired into the inner room. I was too dazed, and, I will confess, too frightened by what I had seen to feel equal to interviewing him, so I left him alone.

Presently, however, he came into my room, and crossing to where I sat on my bed, placed his hand kindly upon my shoulder. I looked up into his face, which was paler than I had ever seen it before.

'Bruce,' he said, not without a little touch of regret in his voice, 'how was it that you did not do what you were told?'

'It was my cursed curiosity,' I said bitterly. 'But do not think I am not sorry. I would give all I possess in the world not to have seen what I saw in that room.'

'But you have seen, and nothing will ever take away that knowledge from you. You will carry it with you to the grave.'

'The grave,' I answered bitterly. 'What hope is there even in the grave after what we have seen tonight? Oh, for Heaven's sake, Nikola, let us get out of this place tonight if possible.'

'So you are afraid, are you?' he answered with a strange expression on his face. 'I did not think you would turn coward, Bruce.'

'In this I am a coward,' I answered. 'Give me something to do, something human to fight, some tangible danger to face, and I am your man! But I am not fit to fight against the invisible.'

'Come, come, cheer up!' said Nikola. 'Things are progressing splendidly with us. Our identity has not been questioned; we have been received by the heads of the sect as the people we pretend to be, and tomorrow I am to be raised to the rank of one of the Three. The remaining secrets will then be revealed to me, and when I have discovered all I want to know, we will go back to civilisation once more. Think of what I may have achieved by this time tomorrow. I tell you, Bruce, such an opportunity might never come to a Western man again. It will be invaluable to me. Think of this, and then it will help your pluck to go through with it to the end!'

'If I am not asked to see such things as I saw tonight, it may,' I answered, 'but not unless.'

'You must do me the credit to remember you were not asked to see them.'

'I know that, and I have paid severely for my disobedience.'

'Then let us say no more about it. Remember, Bruce, I trust you.'

'You need have no fear,' I said, after a pause lasting a few moments. 'Even if I could get out of it, for your sake I would go through with it, come what might.'

'I thank you for that assurance. Good-night.'

So saying, Nikola retired to his room, and I laid myself down upon my bed, but, you may be sure, it was not to sleep.

CHAPTER FIFTEEN

How Nikola was installed

As soon as I woke next morning I went into Nikola's room. To my surprise he was not there. Nor did he put in an appearance until nearly an hour later. When he did, I could see that he was completely exhausted, though he tried hard not to show it.

'What have you been doing?' I asked, meeting him on the threshold with a question.

'Qualifying myself for my position by being initiated into more mysteries,' he answered. 'Bruce, if you could have seen all that I have done since midnight tonight, I verily believe it would be impossible for you ever to be a happy man again. When I tell you that what I have witnessed has even frightened me, you will realise something of what I mean.'

'What have you seen?'

'I have been shown the flesh on the mummified bodies of men who died nearly a thousand years ago made soft and healthy as that of a little child; I have seen such surgery as the greatest operator in Europe would consider impossible; I have been shown a new anaesthetic that does not deprive the patient of his senses, and yet renders him impervious to pain; and I have seen other things, such that I dare not describe them even to you.'

'And you were not tempted to draw back?'

'Only once,' answered Nikola candidly. 'For nearly a minute, I will confess, I hesitated, but eventually I forced myself to go on. That once accomplished, the rest was easy. But I must not stay talking here. Today is going to be a big day with us. I shall go and lie down in order to recoup my energies. Call me if I am wanted, but otherwise do not disturb me.'

He went into the inner room, laid himself down upon his bed, and for nearly two hours slept as peacefully as a little child. The morning meal was served soon after sunrise, but I did not wake him for it; indeed, it was not until nearly midday that he made his appearance again. When he did, we discussed our position more fully, weighed the pros and cons more carefully, and speculated still further as to what the result of our adventure would be. Somehow a vague feeling of impending disaster had taken possession of me. I could not rid myself of the belief that before the day was over we should find our success in some way reversed. I told Nikola as much, but he only laughed, and uttered his usual reply to the effect that, disaster or no disaster, he was not going to give in, but would go through with it to the bitter end, whatever the upshot might be.

About two o'clock in the afternoon a dwarf put in an appearance, and intimated that Nikola's presence was required in the great hall. He immediately left the cell, and remained away until dusk. When he returned he looked more like a ghost than a man, but even then, tired as he undoubtedly was, his iron will would not acknowledge such a thing as fatigue. Barely vouchsafing me a word he passed into the inner room, to occupy himself there until nearly eight o'clock making notes and writing up a concise account of all that he had seen. I sat on my bed watching the dancing of his torch flame upon the wall, and feeling about as miserable as it would be possible for a man to be. Why I should have been so depressed I cannot say. But it was certain that everything served to bring back to me my present position. I thought of my old English school, and wondered if I had been told then what was to happen to me in later life whether I should have believed it. I thought of Gladys, my pretty sweetheart, and asked myself if I should ever see her again; and I was just in the act of drawing the locket she had given me from beneath my robe, when my ear caught the sound of a footstep on the stones outside. Next moment the same uncanny dwarf who had summoned us on the previous evening made his appearance. Without a word he pointed to the door of the inner room. I supposed the action to signify that those in authority wished Nikola to come to them, and went in and told him so. He immediately put away his paper and pencil, and signed to me to leave his room ahead of him. The dwarf preceded us, I came next, and Nikola following me. In this fashion we made our way up one corridor and down another, ascended and descended innumerable stairs, and at last reached the tunnel of the great cavern, the same in which we had passed through such adventures on the preceding night. On this occasion the door was guarded by fully a dozen monks, who formed into two lines to let us pass.

If the cave had been bare of ornament when we visited it the previous night, it was now altogether different. Hundreds of torches flamed from brackets upon the walls, distributed their ruddy glare upon the walls and ceiling, and were reflected, as in a million diamonds, in the stalactites hanging from the roof.

At the further end of the great cavern was a large and beautifully decorated triple throne, and opposite it, but half-way down the hall, a daïs covered with a rich crimson cloth bordered with heavy bullion fringe. As we entered we were greeted with the same mysterious music we had heard on the day of our arrival. It grew louder and louder until we reached the daïs, and then, just as Nikola took up his place at the front, and I mine a little behind him, began to die slowly away again. When it had ceased to sound a great bell in the roof above our heads struck three. The noise it made was almost deafening. It seemed to fill the entire cave, then, like the music above mentioned, to die slowly away again. Once more the same number of strokes were repeated, and once more the sound died away. When it could no longer be heard, curtains at the further end were drawn back, and the monks commenced to file slowly in from either side, just as they had done at the first service after our arrival. There must have been nearly four hundred of them; they were all dressed in black and all wore the same peculiar head-covering I have described elsewhere.

When they had taken their places on either side of the daïs upon which we stood, the curtain which covered the doorway, through which I had followed Nikola down into the subterranean chamber the night before, was drawn aside and another procession entered. First came the dwarfs, to the number of thirty, each carrying a lighted torch in his hand; following them were nearly a hundred monks, in white, swinging censers, then a dozen grey-bearded priests in black, but without the head-covering, after which the two men who were the heads of this extraordinary sect.

Reaching the throne the procession divided itself into two parts, each half taking up its position in the form of a crescent on either side. The two heads seated themselves beneath the canopy, and exactly at the moment of their doing so the great bell boomed forth again. As its echo died away all the monks who had hitherto been kneeling rose to their feet and with one accord took up the hymn of their sect. Though the music and words were barbaric in the extreme, there was something about the effect produced that stirred the heart beyond description. The

hymn ceased as suddenly as it had begun, and then, from among
the white-robed monks beside the throne, a man stepped forth
with a paper in his hand. In a loud voice he proclaimed the fact
that it had pleased the two Great Ones of the Mountains to fill
the vacancy which had so long existed in the triumvirate. For
that reason they had summoned to their presence a man who
bore a reputation for wisdom and holiness second to none. Him
they now saw before them. He had rendered good service to the
Society, he had been proved to be a just man, and now it only
remained for him to state whether he was willing to take upon
himself the responsibilities of the office to which he had been
called. Having finished his speech, the man retired to his place
again. Then four of the monks in white, two from either side of
the throne, walked slowly down the aisle towards Nikola, and,
bidding him follow them, escorted him in procession to the room
behind the curtain. While he was absent from the cave no one
moved or spoke.

At the end of something like ten minutes the small procession filed
out again, Nikola coming last. He was now attired in all the grand
robes of his office. His tall, spare form and venerable disguise became them wonderfully well, and when he once more stood upon the
daïs before me I could not help thinking I had never in my life seen a
more imposing figure.

Again the great bell tolled out, and when the sound had ceased, the
man who had first spoken stepped forward and in a loud voice bade it
be known to all present that the ex-priest of Hankow was prepared to
take upon himself the duties and responsibilities of his office. As he
retired to his place again two monks came forward and escorted
Nikola up the centre aisle towards the triple throne. Arriving at the
foot the two Great Ones threw off the veils they had hitherto been
wearing, and came down to meet him. Having each extended a hand,
they were about to escort him to his place when there was a commotion at the end of the hall.

In a flash, though so far the sound only consisted of excited
whispering, all my forebodings rushed back upon me, and my heart
seemed to stand still. The Chief of the Three dropped Nikola's
hand, and, turning to one of the monks beside him, bade him
go down the hall and discover what this unseemly interruption
might mean.

The man went, and was absent for some few minutes. When he
returned it was to report that there was a stranger in the monastery

who craved immediate speech with the Two on a matter concerning the election about to take place.

He was ordered to enter, and in a few minutes a travel-stained, soiled and bedraggled Chinaman made his appearance and humbly approached the throne. His four followers remained clustered round the door at the further end.

'Who art thou, and what is thy business here?' asked the old man in a voice that rang like a trumpet call. 'Thinkest thou that thou wilt be permitted to disturb us in this unseemly fashion?'

'I humbly sue for pardon. But I have good reason, my father!' returned the man, with a reverence that nearly touched the ground.

'Let us hear it then, and be speedy. What is thy name, and whence comest thou?'

'I am the Chief Priest of the temple of Hankow, and I come asking for justice!' said the man, and as he said it a great murmur of astonishment ran through the hall. I saw Nikola step back a pace and then stand quite still. If it were the truth this man was telling we were lost beyond hope of redemption.

'Thou foolish man to come to us with so false a story!' said the elder of the Two. 'Knowest thou not that the Priest of Hankow stands before thee?'

'It is false!' said the man. 'I come to warn you that that man is an impostor. He is no priest, but a foreign devil who captured me and sent me out of the way while he took my place.'

'Then how didst thou get here?' asked the chief of the sect.

'I escaped,' said the man, 'from among those whom he paid to keep me, and made my way to Tientsin, thence to Pekin, and so on here.'

'O my father!' said Nikola, just as quietly as if nothing unusual were happening, 'wilt thou allow such a cunningly-devised tale to do me evil in thy eyes? Did I not bring with me a letter from the High Priest of the Llamaserai, making known to thee that I am he whom thou didst expect? Wilt thou then put me to shame before the world?'

The old man did not answer.

'I, too, have a letter from the High Priest,' said the new arrival eagerly. Whereupon he produced a document and handed it to the second of the Two.

'Peace! peace! We will retire and consider upon this matter,' said the old man. Then turning to the monks beside him he said sternly: 'See that neither of these men escape.' After which he retired with his colleague to the inner room, whence they had appeared at the beginning of the ceremony.

In perfect silence we awaited their return, and during the time they were absent, I noticed a curious fact that I had remarked once or twice in my life before. Though all day I had been dreading the approach of some catastrophe, when it came, and I had to look it fairly in the face, all my fears vanished like mist before the sun. My nervousness left me like a discarded cloak, and so certain seemed our fate that I found I could meet it with almost a smile.

At the end of about twenty minutes there was a stir near the door, and presently the Two returned and mounted their thrones. It was the old man who spoke.

'We have considered the letters,' he said, 'and in our wisdom we have concluded that it would be wisest to postpone our judgment for a while. This matter must be further enquired into.' Then turning to Nikola, he continued: 'Take off those vestments. If thou art innocent they shall be restored to thee, and thou shall wear them with honour to thyself and the respect of all our order; but if thou art guilty, prepare for death, for no human soul shall save thee.' Nikola immediately divested himself of his gorgeous robes, and handed them to the monks who stood ready to receive them.

'Thou wilt now,' said the old man, 'be conducted back to the cells thou hast hitherto occupied. Tonight at a later hour this matter will be considered again.'

Nikola bowed with his peculiar grace, and then came back to where I stood, after which, escorted by a double number of monks, we returned to our rooms and were left alone, not however before we had noted the fact that armed guards were placed at the gate at the top of the steps leading into the main corridor.

When I had made sure that no one was near enough to eavesdrop, I went into Nikola's room, expecting to find him cast down by the failure of his scheme. I was about to offer him my condolences, but he stopped me by holding up his hand.

'Of course,' he said, 'I regret exceedingly that our adventure should have ended like this. We must not grumble, however, for we have the satisfaction of knowing that we have played our cards like men. We have lost on the odd trick, that is all.'

'And what is the upshot of it all to be?'

'Very simple, I should say. If we don't find a way to escape we shall pay the penalty of our rashness with our lives. I don't know that I mind so much for myself, though I should very much like to have had an opportunity of putting into practice a few of the things I have learnt here; but I certainly do regret it for your sake.'

'That is very good of you.'

'Oh, make no mistake, I am thinking of that poor little girl in Pekin who believes so implicitly in you.'

'For Heaven's sake don't speak of her or I shall turn coward! Are you certain that there is no way of escape?'

'To be frank with you I do not see one. You may be sure, however, that I shall use all my ingenuity tonight to make my case good, though I have no hope that I shall be successful. This man, you see, holds all the cards, and we are playing a lone hand against the bank. But there, I suppose it is no use thinking about the matter until after the trial tonight.'

The hours wore slowly on, and every moment I expected to hear the tramp of feet upon the stones outside summoning us to the investigation. They came at last, and two monks entered my room, and bade me fetch my master. When I had done so we were marched in single file up the stairs and along the corridor, this time to a higher level instead of descending as on previous occasions.

Arriving on a broad landing we were received by an armed guard of monks. One of them ordered us to follow him, and in response we passed through a doorway and entered a large room, at the end of which two people were seated at a table; behind them and on either side were rows of monks, and between guards at the further end, the man who had brought the accusation against us.

At a signal from a monk, who was evidently in command of the guard, I was separated from Nikola, and then the trial commenced.

First the newcomer recited his tale. He described how in the village of Tsan-Chu he had been met and betrayed by two men, who, having secured his person, had carried him out to sea, and imprisoned him aboard a junk. His first captors, it was understood, were Englishmen, but he was finally delivered into the care of a Chinaman, who had conveyed him to Along Bay. From this place he managed to effect his escape, and after great hardships reached Tientsin. On arrival there he made enquiries which induced him to push on to Pekin. Making his way to the Llamaserai, and being able to convince the High Priest of his identity, he had learned to his astonishment that he was being impersonated, and that the man who was filling his place had preceded him to Thibet.

On the strength of this discovery he obtained men and donkeys, and came on to the monastery as fast as he could travel.

At the end of his evidence he was closely questioned by both of the great men, but his testimony was sound and could not be shaken. Then his attendants were called up and gave their evidence, after which Nikola was invited to make his case good.

He accepted the invitation with alacrity, and, reviewing all that his rival had said, pointed out the manifest absurdities with which it abounded, ridiculed what he called its inconsistency, implored his judges not to be led away by an artfully contrived tale, and brought his remarks to a conclusion by stating, what was perfectly true, though hardly in the manner he intended, that he had no doubt at all as to their decision. A more masterly speech it would have been difficult to imagine. His keen instinct had detected the one weak spot in his enemy's story, and his brilliant oratory helped him to make the most of it. His points told, and to my astonishment I saw that he had already influenced his judges in his favour. If only we could go on as we had begun, we might yet come successfully out of the affair. But we were reckoning without our host.

'Since thou sayest that thou art the priest of the temple of Hankow,' said the younger of the two great men, addressing Nikola, 'it is certain that thou must be well acquainted with the temple. In the first hall is a tablet presented by a Taotai of the province: what is the inscription upon it?'

' "With the gods be the decision as to what is best for man," ' said Nikola without hesitation.

I saw that the real priest was surprised beyond measure at this ready answer.

'And upon the steps that lead up to it, what is carved?'

' "Let peace be with all men!" ' said Nikola, again without stopping. The judge turned to the other man.

'There is nothing there,' he said; and my heart went down like lead.

'Now I know,' said the old man, turning to Nikola, 'that you are not what you pretend. There are no steps; therefore there can be nothing written upon them.'

Then turning to the guards about him he said – 'Convey these men back to the room whence they came. See that they be well guarded, and at daybreak tomorrow morning let them be hurled from the battlements down into the valley below.'

Nikola bowed, but said never a word. Then, escorted by our guards, we returned to our room. When we had arrived there, and the monks had left us to take up their places at the top of the steps outside, I sat myself down on my bed and covered my face with my hands. So this was what it had all come to. It was for this I had met Nikola in Shanghai: to be hurled from the battlements, the fate for which we had braved so many dangers.

CHAPTER SIXTEEN
A terrible experience

Hour after hour I sat upon my bed-place, my mind completely overwhelmed by the consideration of our terrible position. We were caught like rats in a trap, and, as far as I could see, the only thing left for us to do now was to continue our resemblance to those animals by dying game. For fear lest my pluck should give way I would not think of Gladys at all, and when I found I could no longer keep my thoughts away from her, I went into the adjoining room to see what Nikola was doing. To my surprise I found him pacing quietly up and down, just as calm and collected as if he were waiting for dinner in a London drawing-room. 'Well, Bruce,' he said, as I entered, 'it looks as if another three hours will see the curtain rung down upon our comedy.'

'Tragedy, I should call it,' I answered bitterly.

'Isn't it rather difficult to define where one begins and the other ends?' he asked, as if desirous of starting an argument. 'Plato says – '

'Oh, confound Plato!' I answered sharply. 'What I want to know is how you are going to prevent our being put to death at daybreak.'

'I have no intention that we shall be,' said Nikola.

'But how are you going to prevent it?' I enquired.

'I have not the remotest notion,' he answered, 'but all the same I *do* intend to prevent it. The unfortunate part of it is that we are left so much in the dark, and have no idea where the execution will take place. If that were once settled we could arrange things more definitely. However, do not bother yourself about it; go to bed and leave it to me.'

I went back into my own room and laid myself down upon my bed as he commanded. One thought followed another, and presently, however singular it may seem, I fell fast asleep. I dreamt that I was once more walking upon the wall in Pekin with my sweetheart. I saw her dear face looking up into mine and I felt the pressure of her little hand upon my arm. Then suddenly from over the parapet of the wall in front of us appeared the man who had discovered my identity in the Llamaserai; he was brandishing a knife, and I was in the act of springing forward to seize him when I felt my shoulder rudely shaken, and woke up to discover a man leaning over me.

One glance told me that it was one of the monks who had conducted us to the room, and on seeing that I was awake he signed to me to get up. By this time a second had brought Nikola from his room, and as soon as we were ready we were marched out into the corridor, where we found about a dozen men assembled.

'It seems a pity to have disturbed us so early,' said Nikola, as we fell into our places and began to march up the long passage, 'especially as I was just perfecting a most admirable scheme which I feel sure would have saved us.'

'You are too late now,' I answered bitterly.

'So it would appear,' said Nikola, and strode on without further comment.

To attempt to describe to you my feelings during that march through those silent corridors, would be impossible. Indeed, I hardly like to think of it myself. What the time was I had no idea, nor could I tell to what place we were being conducted. We ascended one stair and descended another, passed through large and small caves and threaded endless corridors, till I lost all count of our direction. At last, however, we came to a halt at the foot of the smallest staircase I had yet seen in the monastery. We waited for a few moments, then ascended it and arrived at a narrow landing, at the end of which was a large door. Here our procession once more halted. Finally the doors were unbarred and thrown open, and an icy blast rushed in. Outside we could see the battlements, which were built on the sheer side of the cliff. It was broad daylight, and bitterly cold. Snow lay upon the roof-tops, but the air was transparently clear; indeed when we passed outside we could plainly distinguish the mountains across the valley where we had lost our coolies and donkeys only a week or so before.

Once in the sunshine our guides beat their torches against the wall till the flames were extinguished, and then stood at attention. From their preparations it was evident that the arrival of some person of importance was momentarily expected.

All this time my heart was beating like a wheat-flail against my ribs, and, try how I would to prevent them, my teeth were chattering in my head like castanets. As our gaolers had brought us up here it was evident we were going to be thrown over the cliff, as had been first proposed. I glanced round me to see if it would be possible to make a fight for it, but one glimpse showed me how utterly futile such an attempt would be.

While I was arguing this out in my own mind our guards had somewhat relaxed their stiffness; then they came suddenly to attention, and next moment, evidently with a signal from the other side, we were marched to a spot further along the battlements.

Here the two great men of the monastery were awaiting us, and as soon as we made our appearance they signed to our guides to bring us closer to them. The old man was the first to speak.

'Men of the West! ye have heard your sentence,' he said in a low and solemn voice. 'Ye have brought it upon yourselves; have ye anything to urge why the decree should not be executed.'   .

I looked at Nikola, but he only shook his head. Hard as I tried I could not discover sufficient reason myself, so I followed his example.

'Then let it be so,' said the old man, who had noticed our hesitation; 'there is nought to be done save to carry out the work. Prepare ye for death.'

We were then ordered to stand back, and, until I heard another commotion on the stairs, I was at a loss to understand why we were not immediately disposed of. Then a second procession of monks appeared upon the battlements escorting a third prisoner. He was a tall, burly fellow, and from the way in which he was dressed and shaved I gathered had been a monk. He made his appearance with evident reluctance, and when he arrived at the top of the steps had to be dragged up to face the Two. Their interview was short, and even more to the point than our own.

'Thou hast murdered one of thy brethren,' said the old man, still in the same sepulchral tone in which he had addressed us. 'Hast thou anything to say why the sentence of death passed upon thee should not be carried into effect?'

In answer the man first blustered, then became stolid, and finally howled outright. I watched him with a curiosity which at any other time I should have deemed impossible. Then, at a signal from the old man, four stalwart monks rushed forward, and, having seized him, dragged him to the edge of the battlements. The poor wretch struggled and screamed, but he was like a child in the hands of those who held him. Closer and closer they drew to the edge. Then there was an interval of fierce struggling, a momentary pause, a wild cry, and next moment the man had disappeared over the edge, falling in a sheer drop quite fifteen hundred feet into the valley below. As he vanished from our sight my heart seemed to stand still. The poor wretch's cry still rang in my ears, and in another minute I knew it would be our turn.

I looked up at the blue sky above our heads, across which white clouds were flying before the breeze; I looked across the valley to where the snow-capped peaks showed on the other side, then at the battlements of the monastery, and last at the crowd of black figures surrounding us. In a flash all my past life seemed to rise before my eyes. I saw myself a little boy again walking in an English garden with my pretty mother, with my play-fellows at school, at sea, on the Australian gold-fields, and so on through almost every phase of my life up to the moment of our arrival at the place where we now stood. I looked at Nikola, but his pale face showed no sign of emotion. I will stake my life that he was as cool at that awful moment as when I first saw him in Shanghai. Presently the old man came forward again.

'If ye have aught to say – any last request to make – there is still time to do it,' he said.

'I have a request to make,' answered Nikola. 'Since we *must* die, is it not a waste of good material to cast us over that cliff? I have heard it said that my skull is an extraordinary one, while my companion here boasts such a body as I would give worlds to anatomise. I have no desire to die, as you may suppose; but if nothing will satisfy you save to kill us, pray let us die in the interests of science.'

Whether they had really intended to kill us, I cannot say, but this singular request of my companion's did not seem to cause as much astonishment as I had expected it would do. He consulted with his colleague, and then turned to Nikola again.

'Thou art a brave man,' he said.

'One must reconcile oneself to the inevitable,' said Nikola coolly. 'Have you any objection to urge?'

'We will give it consideration,' said the old man. 'The lives of both of you are spared for the time being.'

Thereupon our guards were called up, and we were once more marched back to our room. Arriving there, and when the monks had departed to take up their positions at the top of the staircase as before, Nikola said: 'If we escape from this place, you will never be able to assert that science has done nothing for you. At least it has saved your life.'

'But if they are going to scoop your brains out and to practise their butchery on me,' I said with an attempt at jocularity I was far from feeling, 'I must say I fail to see how it is going to benefit us.'

'Let me explain,' said Nikola. 'If they are going to use us in the manner you describe, they cannot do so before tomorrow morning, for I happen to know that their operating room is undergoing alterations, and, as I am a conscientious surgeon myself, I should be very loath to spoil my specimens by any undue hurry. So you see we have at any rate all tonight to perfect our plan of escape.'

'But have you a plan?' I asked anxiously.

'There is one maturing somewhere in the back of my head,' said Nikola.

'And you think it will come to anything?'

'That is beyond my power to tell,' he answered; 'but I will go so far as to add that the chances are in our favour.'

Nothing would induce him to say more, and presently he went back into his own room, where he began to busy himself with his precious medicine-chest, which I saw he had taken care to hide.

'My little friend,' he said, patting and fondling it as a father would do his favourite son, 'I almost thought we were destined to part company; now it remains for you to save your master's life.'

Then turning to me he bade me leave him alone, and in obedience to his wish I went back to my own room.

How we survived the anxiety of that day I cannot think; such another period of waiting I never remember. One moment I felt confident that Nikola would carry out his plan, and that we should get away to the coast in safety; the next I could not see how it could possibly succeed, the odds being so heavy against us.

Almost punctually our midday meal was served to us, then the ray of light upon the floor began to lengthen, reached the opposite wall, climbed it, and finally disappeared altogether.

About seven o'clock Nikola came in to me.

'Look here, Bruce,' he said with unusual animation, 'I've been thinking this matter out, and I believe I've hit on a plan that will save us if anything can. In half an hour the monk will arrive with our last meal. He will place the bowl upon the floor over there, and will then turn his back on you while he puts his torch in the bracket upon the wall yonder. We will have a sponge, saturated with a little anaesthetic I have here, ready for him, and directly he turns I will get him by the throat and throttle him while you clap it over his nose. Once he's unconscious you must slip on his dress, and go out again and make your way up the steps. There are two men stationed on the other side, and the door between us and them is locked. I have noticed that the man who brings us our food simply knocks upon it and it is opened. You will do as he does, thus, and as you pass out will drop this gold coin as if by accident.' (Here he gave me some money.) 'One of the men will be certain to stoop to pick it up; as he goes down you must manage by hook or crook to seize and choke the other. I shall be behind you, and I will attend to his companion.'

'It seems a desperate scheme.'

'We are desperate men!' said Nikola.

'And when we have secured them?' I asked.

'I shall put on one of their robes,' this intrepid man answered, 'and we will then make our escape as quickly as possible. Luck must do the rest for us. Are you prepared to attempt so much?'

'To get out of this place I would attempt anything,' I answered.

'Very good then,' he said. 'We must now wait for the appearance of the man. Let us hope it won't be long before he comes.'

For nearly three-quarters of an hour we waited without hearing any sound of the monk. The minutes seemed long as years, and I don't think I ever felt more relieved in my life than I did when I heard the door at the top of the stairs open, and detected the sound of sandalled feet coming down the steps.

'Are you ready?' whispered Nikola, putting the sponge down near me, and returning to his own room.

'Quite ready,' I answered.

The man came nearer, the glare of his torch preceding him. At last he entered, carrying a light in one hand and a large bowl in the other. The latter he put down upon the floor, and, having done so, turned to place the torch in the socket fastened to the wall. He had hardly lifted his arm, however, before I saw Nikola creep out of the adjoining room. Closer and closer he approached the unsuspecting monk, and then, having measured his distance, with a great spring threw himself upon the man and clutched him by the throat. I pulled his legs from under him, and down he dropped upon the floor, with Nikola's fingers still tightening on his throat. Then, when the sponge had been applied, little by little, his struggles ceased, and presently he lay in Nikola's arms as helpless as if he were dead.

'That is one man accounted for,' said Nikola quietly, as he laid the body upon the floor; 'now for the others. Slip on this fellow's dress as quickly as you can.'

I did as he bade me, and in a few seconds had placed the peculiar black covering over the upper part of my face and head, and was ready to carry out the rest of the scheme. In the face of this excitement I felt as happy as a child; it was the creepy, crawly, supernatural, business that shook my nerve. When it came to straightforward matter-of-fact fighting I was not afraid of anything.

Carrying the money in my hand as we had arranged, I left the room and proceeded up the steps, Nikola following half a dozen yards or so behind me, but keeping in the shadow. Arriving at the gate I rapped upon it with my knuckles, and it was immediately opened. Two men were leaning on either side of it, and as I passed through, I took care that the one on the right should see the money in my hand. As if by accident I dropped it, and it rolled away beyond his feet. Instantly he stooped and made a grab for it. Seeing this I wheeled round upon the other man, and before he could divine my intention had him by the throat. But though I had him at a disadvantage, he proved no easy capture. In stature he must have stood nearly six feet, was broad in proportion, and, like all the men in the place, in most perfect training. However, I held on to him for my life, and presently we were struggling upon the floor. For some strange reason, what I cannot tell, that fight seemed to be the most enjoyable three minutes I have ever spent in the whole of my existence.

Over and over we rolled upon the stone floor, my hand still fixed upon his throat to prevent him from crying out.

At last throwing my leg over him I seated myself upon his chest, and then – having nothing else to do it with – I drew back my right arm, and let him have three blows with the whole strength of my fist.

Written in black and white it looks a trifle bloodthirsty, but you must remember we were fighting for our lives, and if by any chance he gave the alarm, nothing on earth could save us from death. I had therefore to make the most of the only opportunity I possessed of silencing him.

As soon as he was unconscious, I looked round for Nikola. He was kneeling by the body of the other man who was lying, face downwards upon the floor, as if dead.

'I would give five pounds,' whispered Nikola, as he rose to his feet, 'for this man's skull. Just look at it; it goes up at the back of his head like a tom cat! It is my luck all over to come across such a specimen when I can't make use of it.'

As he spoke he ran his first finger and thumb caressingly up and down the man's poll.

'I've got a bottle in my museum in Port Said,' he said regretfully, 'which would take him beautifully.'

Then he picked up the sponge which he had used upon the last man, and went across to my adversary. For thirty seconds or thereabouts he held it upon his nose and mouth; then, throwing it into a corner, divested the man of his garments, and attired himself in them.

'Now,' he said, when he had made his toilet to his own satisfaction, 'we must be off. They change the guard at midnight, and it is already twenty minutes past eleven.'

So saying, he led the way down the corridor, I following at his heels. We had not reached the end of it, however, before Nikola bade me wait for him while he went back. When he rejoined me, I asked him in a whisper what he had been doing.

'Nothing very much,' he answered. 'I wanted to convince myself as to, a curious malformation of the occipital bone in that man's skull. I am sorry to have kept you waiting, but I might never have had another chance of examining such a complete case.'

Having given this explanation, this extraordinary votary of science condescended to continue his escape. Leaving the long corridor, now so familiar to us, we turned to our left hand, ascended a flight of steps, followed another small passage, and then came to a standstill at a spot where four roads met.

'Where on earth are we?' enquired Nikola, looking round him. 'This place reminds me of the Hampton Court maze.'

'Hark! What is that booming noise?'

We listened, and by doing so discovered that we were near the subterranean waterfall we had seen on the occasion of our first visit to the large cave.

'We are altogether out of our course,' I said.

'On the other hand,' answered Nikola, 'we are not close enough to it yet.'

'What do you mean?' I asked.

'My dear Bruce,' he said, 'tell me this: why are we in this place? Did we not come here to obtain possession of their secrets? Well, as we are saying goodbye to them tonight for good and all, do you suppose, after adventuring so much, I am going empty-handed? If you think so, you are very much in error. Why, to do that would be to have failed altogether in our journey; and though Nikola often boasts, you must admit he seldom fails to do what he undertakes. Don't say any more, but come along with me.'

Turning into a passage on his right, he led the way down some more steps. Here the torches were almost at their last flicker.

'If we don't look sharp,' said Nikola, 'we shall have to carry out our errand in the dark, and that will be undesirable for more reasons than one.'

From the place where we now stood we could hear the roar of the waterfall quite distinctly, and could just make out, further to our left, the entrance to the great cave. To our delight there were no guards to be seen, so we were able to pass in unmolested. Taking what remained of a torch from a socket near the door, we entered together. A more uncanny place than that great cave, as it revealed itself to us by the light of our solitary torch, no man can imagine. Innumerable bats fluttered about the aisles, their wings filling the air with ghostly whisperings, while dominating all was that peculiar charnel-house smell that I had noticed on the occasion of our previous visit, and which no words could properly describe.

'The entrance to the catacombs is at this end,' said Nikola, leading the way up the central aisle. 'Let us find it.'

I followed him, and together we made towards that part of the cave furthest from the doors. The entrance once found, we had only to follow the steps, and pass down into the crypt I have before described. By the light of our torch we could discern the swathed-up figures in the niches. Nikola, however, had small attention to spare for them – he was too busily occupied endeavouring to discover the spring in the central pillar to think of anything else. When he found it he pressed it, and the door opened. Then down the ladder we crept into the anteroom where I had waited on that awful night. I can tell you one thing, and it is the sober truth – I would far rather have engaged a dozen of the strongest monks in that monastery single-handed, than have followed my chief into that room. But he would not let me draw back, and so we pushed on together. All around us were the mysterious treasures of the monastery, with every sort of implement for every sort of chemistry known to the fertile brain of man. At the further end was a large wooden door, exquisitely carved. This was padlocked in three places, and looked as if it would offer a stubborn resistance to anyone who might attempt to break it. But Nikola was a man hard to beat, and he solved the difficulty in a very simple fashion. Unfastening his loose upper garment, he unstrapped his invaluable medicine-chest, and placed it on the floor; then, choosing a small but sharp surgeon's saw, he fell to work upon the wood surrounding the staple. In less than ten minutes he had cut out the padlocks, and the door swung open. Then, with all the speed we were masters of, we set to work to hunt for the things we wanted. It contained small phials, antique parchment prescriptions, a thousand sorts of drugs, and finally, in an iron coffer, a small book written in Sanscrit and most quaintly bound. This Nikola stowed away in one of his many voluminous pockets, and, as soon as he had made a selection of the other things, announced that it was time for us to turn back. Just as he came to this conclusion, the torch, which had all the time been burning lower and lower, gave a final flicker, and went out altogether. We were left in the dark in this awful cave.

'This is most unfortunate,' said Nikola. Then, after a pause, 'However, as it can't be cured, we must make the best of it.'

I answered nothing, but waited for my leader to propose some plan. At the end of a few moments the darkness seemed to make little or no difference to Nikola. He took me by the hand, and led me straight through the cave into the ante-chamber.

'Look out!' he said; 'here is the ladder.'

And, true enough, as he spoke my shins made its acquaintance. Strange is the force of habit; the pain was sharp, and though I was buried in the centre of a mountain, surrounded by the dead men of a dozen centuries, I employed exactly the same epithet to express my feelings as I should have done, had a passing taxi splashed my boots opposite the Mansion House.

Leaving the lower regions, we climbed the ladder, and reached the crypt, passed up the stairs into the great cave, made our way across that, and then, Nikola still leading, found the tunnel, and passed through it as safely as if we had been lighted by a hundred linkmen.

'Our next endeavour must be to discover how we are to get out of the building itself,' said Nikola, as we reached the four cross passages; 'and as I have no notion how the land lies, it looks rather more serious. Let us try this passage first.'

As quickly as was possible under the circumstances we made our way up the stairs indicated, passed the great waterfall, sped along two or three corridors, were several times nearly observed, and at last, after innumerable try-backs, reached the great hall where we had been received on the day of our arrival.

Almost at the same instant there was a clamour in the monastery, followed by the ringing of the deep-toned bell; then the shouting of many voices, and the tramping of hundreds of feet.

'They are after us!' said Nikola. 'Our flight has been discovered. Now, if we cannot find a way out, we are done for completely.'

The noise was every moment coming closer, and any instant we might expect our pursuers to come into view. Like rats in a strange barn, who hear the approach of a terrier, we dashed this way and that in our endeavours to discover an exit. At last we came upon the steps leading from the great hall into the valley below. Down these we flew as fast as we could go, every moment risking a fall which would inevitably break our necks. Almost too giddy to stand, we at last reached the bottom, to find the door shut, and guarded by a stalwart monk. To throw ourselves upon him was the work of an instant. He lifted his heavy staff, and aimed a blow at me; but I dodged it in time, and got in at him before he could recover. Drawing back my arm, I hit him with all the strength at my command. His head struck the floor with a crash, and he did not move again.

Nikola bent over him, and assured himself that the sleep was genuine. Then he signed to me to give him the key, and when the door was unfastened we passed through it, and closed it after us, locking it on the other side. Then down the valley we ran as fast as our legs would carry us.

CHAPTER SEVENTEEN

Conclusion

As I have said, we were no sooner through the gates than we took to our heels and fled down the valley for our lives. For my own part I was so thankful to be out of that awful place, to be once more breathing the fresh air of Heaven, that I felt as if I could go on running for ever. Fortunately the night was pitch dark, with a high wind blowing. The darkness prevented our pursuers from seeing the direction we had taken, while the noise of the wind effectually deadened any sound we might make that would otherwise have betrayed our whereabouts.

For upwards of an hour we sped along the bottom of the valley in this fashion, paying no heed where we went and caring for nothing but to put as great a distance as possible between ourselves and our pursuers. At last I could go no further, so I stopped and threw myself upon the ground. Nikola immediately came to a standstill, glanced round him suspiciously, and then sat down beside me.

'So much for our first visit to the great monastery of Thibet,' he said as casually as if he were bidding goodbye to a chance acquaintance.

'Do you think we have given them the slip?' I queried, looking anxiously up the dark valley through which we had come.

'By no means,' he answered. 'Remember we are still hemmed in by the precipices, and at most we cannot be more than five miles from their doors. We shall have to proceed very warily for the next week or so, and to do that we must make the most of every minute of darkness.'

We were both silent for a little while. I was occupied trying to recover my breath, Nikola in distributing more comfortably about his person the parchments, etc., he had brought away with him.

'Shall we be going on again?' I asked, as soon as I thought I could go on. 'I've no desire to fall into their hands, I can assure you. Which way is it to be now?'

'Straight on,' he answered, springing to his feet. 'We must follow the valley down and see where it will bring us out. It would be hopeless to attempt to scale the cliffs.'

Without further talk we set off, not to stop again until we had added another four miles or perhaps five to our flight. By this time it was close upon daybreak, the chilliest, dreariest, greyest dawn in all my experience. With the appearance of the light the wind died down, but it still moaned among the rocks and through the high grass in the most dreary and dispiriting fashion. Half an hour later the sun rose, and then Nikola once more called a halt.

'We must hide ourselves somewhere,' he said, 'and travel on again as soon as darkness falls. Look about you for a place where we shall not be likely to be seen.'

For some time it seemed as if we should be unable to discover any such spot, but at last we hit upon one that was just suited to our purpose. It was a small enclosure sheltered by big boulders and situated on a rocky plateau high up the hill-side. To this place of refuge we scrambled, and then with armfuls of grass, which we collected from the immediate neighbourhood, endeavoured to make ourselves as comfortable as possible until night should once more descend upon us. It was not a cheery camp. To make matters worse we were quite destitute of food, and already the pangs of hunger were beginning to obtrude themselves upon us.

'If we ever do get back to civilisation,' said Nikola, after we had been sitting there some time, 'I suppose this business will rank as one of the greatest exploits of your life?'

'I have no desire ever to undertake such another,' I replied truthfully. 'This trip has more than satisfied my craving for the adventurous.'

'Wait till you've been settled in a sleepy English village for a couple of years,' he said with a laugh. 'By that time I wouldn't mind wagering you'll be ready for anything that turns up. I wonder what you would think if I told you that, dangerous as this one has been, it is as nothing to another in which I was concerned about six years since. Then I was occupied trying to discover – '

I am sorry to have to confess that it is beyond my power to narrate what his adventure was, where it occurred, or indeed anything connected with it, for while he was talking I fell into a sound sleep, from which I did not wake until nearly three hours later.

When I opened my eyes the sun was still shining brightly, the wind had dropped, and the air was as quiet as the night had been noisy and tempestuous. I looked round for Nikola, but to my surprise he was not occupying the place where he had been sitting when I fell asleep, nor indeed was he inside the enclosure at all. Alarmed lest anything untoward might have befallen him, I was in the act of going in search of him when he reappeared creeping between the rocks upon his hands and knees. I was about to express my delight at his return, but he signed to me to be silent, and a moment later reached my side.

'Keep as still as you can,' he whispered; 'they're after us.'

'How close are they?' I asked, with a sudden sinking in my heart.

'Not a hundred yards away,' he answered, and as he spoke he bent his head forward to listen.

A moment later I could hear them for myself, coming along the valley to our left. Their voices sounded quite plain and distinct, and for this reason I judged that they could not have been more than fifty yards from us. Now came the great question, would they discover us or not? Under the influence of the awful suspense I scarcely breathed. One thing I was firmly resolved upon – if they did detect our hiding-place I would fight to the last gasp rather than let them capture me and carry me back to that awful monastery. The sweat stood in great beads upon my forehead as I listened. It was evident they were searching among the rocks at the base of the cliff. Not being able to find us there, would they try higher up? Fortune, however, favoured us. Either they gave us credit for greater speed than we possessed, or they did not notice the hiding-place among the rocks; at any rate, they passed on without molesting us. The change from absolute danger to comparative safety was almost overpowering, and even the stoical Nikola heaved a sigh of relief as the sound of their voices died gradually away.

That night, as soon as it was dark, we left the place where we had hidden ourselves and proceeded down the valley, keeping a watchful eye open for any sign of our foes. But our lucky star was still in the ascendant, and we saw nothing of them. Towards daylight we left the valley and entered a large basin, if it may be so described, formed by a number of lofty hills. On the bottom of the bowl thus fashioned was a considerable village. Halting on an eminence above it, Nikola looked round him.

'We shall have to find a hiding-place on the hills somewhere hereabouts,' he said; 'but before we do so we must have food.'

'And a change of dress,' I answered, for it must be remembered that we were still clad in the monkish robes we had worn when we left the monastery.

'Quite so,' he answered: 'first the food and the dress, then the hiding-place.'

Without more ado he signed to me to follow him, and together we left the hillock and proceeded towards the village. It was not a large place, nor, from all appearances, was it a very wealthy one; it contained scarcely more than fifty houses, the majority of which were of the usual Thibetan type, that is to say, built of loose stones, roofed with split pine shingles, and as draughty and leaky as it is possible for houses to be. The family reside in one room, the other – for in few cases are there more than two – being occupied by the cows, pigs, dogs, fowls, and other domestic animals.

As we approached the first house Nikola bade me remain where I was while he went forward to see what he could procure. For many reasons I did not care very much about this arrangement, but I knew him too well by this time to waste my breath arguing. He left me and crept forward. It was bitterly cold, and while he was absent and I was standing still, I felt as if I were being frozen into a solid block of ice. What our altitude could have been I am not in a position to tell, but if one could estimate it by the keenness of the air, it must have been something considerable.

Nikola was absent for nearly twenty minutes. At last, however, he returned, bringing with him a quantity of clothing, including two typical Thibetan hats, a couple of thick blankets, and, what was better than all, a quantity of food. The latter consisted of half a dozen coarse cakes, a hunk of a peculiar sort of bread, and a number of new-laid eggs, also a large bowl of milk. As to payment he informed me that he had left a small gold piece, believing that that would be the most effectual means of silencing the owner's tongue. Seating ourselves in the shelter of a large rock, we set to work to stow away as much of the food as we could possibly consume. Then dividing the clothing into two bundles we set off across the valley in an easterly direction.

By daylight we had put a considerable distance between us and the village, and were installed in a small cave, half-way up a rugged hill. Below us was a copse of mountain pines, and across the valley a cliff, not unlike that down which we had climbed to reach the monastery. We had discarded our monkish robes by this time, and, for greater security, had buried them in a safe place beneath a tree. In our new rigs, with the tall felt hats upon our heads, we might very well have passed for typical Thibetans.

Feeling that our present hiding-place was not likely to be discovered, we laid ourselves down to sleep. How long we slumbered, I

cannot say; I only know that for some reason or other I woke in a
fright to hear a noise in the valley beneath us. I listened for a few
moments to make sure, and then shook Nikola, who was still sleeping soundly.

'What is it?' he cried, as he sat up. 'Why do you wake me?'

'Because we're in danger again,' I answered. 'What is that noise in
the valley?'

He listened for a moment.

'I can hear nothing,' he said.

Then just as he was about to speak again there came a new sound
that brought us both to our feet like lightning – *the baying of
dogs*. Now, as we both knew, the only dogs in that district are of
the formidable Deggi breed, standing about as high as Shetland
ponies, as strong as mastiffs, and as fierce as they are powerful. If
our enemies were pursuing us with these brutes our case was indeed
an unenviable one.

'Get up!' cried Nikola. 'They are hunting us down with the dogs.
Up the hill for your life!'

The words were scarcely out of his mouth before we were racing
up the hill like hares. Up and up we went, scrambling from rock to
rock and bank to bank till my legs felt as if they could go no further.
Though it was but little over a hundred yards from our hiding-
place into the wood at the summit it seemed like miles. When we
reached it we threw ourselves down exhausted upon a bed of pine
needles, but only for a minute, then we were up and on our way
again as hard as ever. Through the thicket we dashed, conscious of
nothing but a desire to get away from those horrible dogs. The
wood was a thick one, but prudence told us it could offer no
possible refuge for us. Every step we took was leaving a record to
guide them, and we dared not hesitate or delay a second longer than
was absolutely necessary.

At last we reached the far side of the wood. Here, to our surprise,
the country began to slope downwards again into a second valley.
From the skirt of the timber where we stood, for nearly a mile, it was
all open, with not a bush or a rock to serve as cover. We were in a
pretty fix. To wheel round would be to meet our pursuers face to
face; to turn to either hand would be equally as bad, while to go on
would only be to show ourselves in the open, and after that to be run
to earth like foxes in the second valley. But there was no time to stop
or to think, so for good or ill we took to our heels again and set off
down the slope. We were not half-way across the open, however,

before we heard the dogs break cover behind us, and a moment later, the excited shouting of men, who had seen us ahead of them, and were encouraging the hounds to run us down.

If we had run fast before we literally flew now. The dogs were gaining on us at every stride, and unless something unexpected happened to save us we could look upon ourselves in the light of men as good as dead. Only fifty yards separated us from the cover that bounded the moor, if I may so describe it, on the other side. If the worst came to the worst, and we could reach the timber at the bottom, we could climb a tree there and sell our lives as dearly as possible with our revolvers.

Putting on a final spurt we gained the wood and plunged into the undergrowth. The nearest dog – there were three of these gigantic brutes – was scarcely twenty yards behind us. Suddenly Nikola, who was in front, stopped as if shot, threw up his arms and fell straight backwards. Seeing him do this I stopped too, but only just in the nick of time. A moment later I should have been over a precipice into the swift-flowing river that ran below. By the time I realised this the first dog was upon us. Nikola supported himself on his elbow, and, as coolly as if he were picking off a pigeon, shot him dead. The second fell to my share; the third proved somewhat more troublesome. Seeing the fate of his companions, he stopped short and crouched among the bushes, growling savagely.

'Kill him!' cried Nikola, with one of the only signs of excitement I had ever known him show. I fired again, but must have missed him, for he rushed in at me, and had I not thrown up my arm would have seized me by the throat. Then Nikola fired – I felt the bullet whiz past my ear – and before I could think the great beast had fallen back upon the ground and was twisting and twining in his death agony.

'Quick!' cried Nikola, springing to his feet once more. 'There's not a moment to be lost. Throw the dogs into the stream.'

Without wasting time we set to work, and in less than half a minute all three animals had disappeared into the river. As the last went over the side we heard the foremost of our pursuers enter the wood. Another moment and we should have been too late.

'There's nothing for it,' cried Nikola, 'but for us to follow the dogs' example. They'll hunt about wondering which way the brutes have gone, and by that time we ought to be some distance down stream.'

'Come on then,' I said, and, without more deliberation, took a header. It was a dive of at least sixty feet, but not so unpleasant as our position would have been upon the bank had we remained. Nikola followed me, and before our enemies could have gained the river side we had swept round the bend and were out of their sight. But though we had for the moment given them the slip our position was still by no means an enviable one. The water was as cold as ice and the current ran like a mill sluice, while the depth could not have been much under fifty feet, though I could only judge this by the shelving of the banks. For nearly ten minutes we swam on side by side in silence. The voices of our pursuers grew more and more faint until we could no longer hear them. The horror of that swim I must leave you to imagine. The icy coldness of the water seemed to eat into the very marrow of my bones, and every moment I expected to feel an attack of cramp. One thing soon became evident, the stream was running more and more swiftly. Suddenly Nikola turned his head and shouted, 'Make for the bank!'

I endeavoured to do so, but the whole force of the current was against me. Vainly I battled. The stream bore me further and further from my goal, till at last I was swept beyond the ford and down between two precipitous banks where landing was impossible. It was then that I realised Nikola's reason for calling to me. For a hundred yards or so ahead I could see the river, then only blue sky and white cloud. For obvious reasons it could not have come to a standstill, so this sudden break-off could have but one meaning – *a fall*! With incredible swiftness the water bore me on, now spinning me round and round like a teetotum, now carrying me this way, now that, but all the time bringing me closer to the abyss.

Ten yards further, and I could hear the sullen boom of the falling waters, and as I heard it I saw that the bank of the fall was studded with a fringe of large rocks. If I did not wish to be hurled over into eternity, I knew I must catch one of these rocks, and cling to it with all my strength. Strange to say, even in that moment of despair, my presence of mind did not desert me. I chose my rock, and concentrated all my energies upon the work of reaching it. Fortunately the current helped me, and with hardly an effort on my part, I was carried towards it. Throwing up my arms I clutched at it, but the stone was slippery, and I missed my hold. I tried again with the same result. Then, just as I was on the very brink of the precipice, my fingers caught in a projecting ledge, and I was able to stay myself. The weight of the water upon my back was terrific, but with the strength of a dozen men I clung on, and little by little lifted myself up. I was fighting for dear life, for Gladys, for all that made life worth living, and that gave me superhuman strength. At last I managed to lift myself sufficiently to get a purchase on the rock with my knees. After that it was all plain sailing, and in less time almost than it takes to tell, I was lying stretched out upon the rock, safe, but exhausted almost to the point of death.

When I had somewhat recovered my strength, I opened my eyes and looked over the edge. Such a sight I never want to see again. Picture a river, as wide as the Thames at London Bridge, walled in between two steep banks, pouring its water down into a rocky pool almost half a mile below. The thunder of the fall was deafening, while from the lake at the foot rose a dense mist, changing, where the sun caught it, to every colour of the rainbow. Fascinated by this truly awful picture, and the narrowness of my own escape from death, I could scarcely withdraw my eyes. When I did it was to look across at the right-hand bank. Nikola stood there waving to me. Cheered by his presence, I began to cast about me for a means of reaching him, but the prospect was by no means a cheerful one. Several rocks there certainly were, and near the bank they were close enough to enable an active man to jump from one to the other. Unfortunately, however, between the one on which I lay and the next was a yawning gulf of something like eight feet. To reach it seemed impossible. I dared not risk the leap, and yet if I did not jump, what was to become of me? I was just beginning to despair again, when I saw Nikola point up stream and disappear.

For something like a quarter of an hour I saw no more of him, then he reappeared a hundred yards or so further up the bank, and as he did so he pointed into mid-stream. I looked, and immediately realised his intention. He had discovered a large log and had sent it afloat in the hope that it would be of service to me. Closer and closer it came, steering directly for where I knelt. As it drew alongside I leant over, and, catching at a small branch which decorated it, attempted to drag it athwart the channel. My strength, however, was uncertain, and had the effect of bringing the current to bear on the other end. It immediately spun swiftly round, went from me like an express train, and next moment disappeared over the brink into the abyss below, nearly dragging me with it. Once more Nikola signalled to me and disappeared into the wood. Half an hour later another log made its appearance. This time I was more fortunate, and managed, with considerable manoeuvring and coaxing, to get it jammed by the current between the two rocks.

The most perilous part of the whole undertaking was now about to commence. I had to cross on this frail bridge to the next stone. With my heart in my mouth I crawled over my own rock, and then having given a final look round, and tested it as well as I was able, seated myself astride of the log. The rush of the water against my legs was tremendous, and I soon found I should have all my time taken up endeavouring to preserve my balance. But with infinite caution I continued to advance until at last I reached the opposite rock. All the time I had never dared to look over the brink; had I done so I believe my nerve would have deserted me, and I should then have lost my balance and perished for good and all.

When the journey was accomplished, and I was safely established on the second rock, I rested for a few minutes, and then, standing up, measured my distance as carefully as possible, and jumped on to the third. The rest was easy, and in a few moments I was lying quite overcome among the bracken at Nikola's feet. As soon as I was safe, my pluck, presence of mind, nerve, or whatever you like to call it, gave way completely, and I found myself trembling like a little child.

'You have had a narrow escape,' said Nikola. 'When I saw that you could not make the bank up yonder, I made up my mind it was all over with you. However, all's well that ends well, and now we've got to find out what we had better do next.'

'What do you advise?' I asked, my teeth chattering in my head like castanets.

'That we find a sheltered spot somewhere hereabouts, light a fire and dry our things, then get down to the river below the falls, construct a raft, and travel upon it till we come to a village. There, if possible, we will buy donkeys, and, if all goes well, pursue our journey to the coast by another route.'

'But don't you think our enemies will have warned the inhabitants of the villages hereabouts to be on the lookout for us?'

'We must chance that. Now let us find a place to light a fire. You are nearly frozen.'

Half a mile or so further on we discovered the spot we wanted, lit our fire and dried our things. All this time I was in agony – one moment as cold as ice, the next in a burning fever. Nikola prescribed for me from his medicine chest, which, with the things he had obtained from the monastery, he still carried with him, and then we laid ourselves down to sleep.

From that time forward I have no recollection of anything that occurred till I woke to find myself snugly ensconced in a comfortable but simply furnished bedroom. Where I was, or how I got there, I could no more tell than I could fly. I endeavoured to get up in order to look out of the window, but I found I was too weak to manage it, so I laid myself down again, and as I did so made another startling discovery – *my pigtail was gone*!

For nearly half an hour I was occupied endeavouring to puzzle this out. Then I heard a footstep in the passage outside, and a moment later a dignified priest entered the room and asked me in French how I felt. I answered that I thought I was much better, though still very weak, and went on to state that I should feel obliged if he would tell me where I was, and how I had got there.

'You are in the French mission at Ya-Chow-Fu,' he said. 'You were brought here a fortnight ago by an Englishman, who, from what we could gather, had found you higher up the river suffering from a severe attack of rheumatic fever.'

'And where is this – this Englishman now?'

'That I cannot say. He left us a week ago to proceed on a botanising excursion, I believe, further west. When he bade us farewell he gave me a sum of money which I am to devote, as soon as you are fit to move, to chartering a boat and coolies to convey you to I-chang, where you will be able to obtain a steamer for Shanghai.'

'And did he not leave any message to say whether I should see him again, and if so, where?'

'I have a note in my pocket for you now.' Thus reminded, the worthy priest produced a letter which he handed to me. I opened it as soon as he had departed, and eagerly scanned its contents. It ran as follows.

DEAR BRUCE –
By the time you receive this I hope you will be on the high road to health again. After your little experiment on the top of the falls you became seriously ill with rheumatic fever. A nice business I had conveying you downstream on a raft, but, as you see, I accomplished it, and got you into the French Mission at Ya-Chow-Fu safely. I am writing this note to bid you goodbye for the present, as I think it is better we should henceforth travel by different routes. I may, however, run across you in I-chang. One caution before I go – figure for the future as a European, and keep your eyes wide open for treachery. The society has branches everywhere, and by this time I expect they will have been warned. Remember, they will be sure to

try to get back the things we've taken, and also will attempt to punish us for our intrusion. I thank you for your companionship, and for the loyalty you have extended to me throughout our journey. I think I am paying you the greatest compliment when I say that I could have wished for no better companion.

Yours,
NIKOLA

That was all.

A week later I bade my hospitable host, who had engaged a boat and trustworthy crew for me, goodbye, and set off on my long down-river journey. I reached I-chang – where I was to abandon my boat and take a passage to Shanghai – safely, and without any further adventure.

On learning that there would not be a river steamer leaving until the following day, I went ashore, discovered an inn, and engaged a room. But though I waited all the evening, and as late as I could next day, Nikola did not put in an appearance. Accordingly at four o'clock I boarded the steamer *Kiang-Yung*, and in due course reached Shanghai.

How thankful I was to again set foot in that place, no one will ever know. I could have gone down on my knees and kissed the very ground in gratitude. Was I not back again in civilisation, free to find my sweetheart, and, if she were still of the same mind, to make her my wife? Was not my health thoroughly restored to me? and last, but not least, was there not a sum of £10,000 reposing at my bankers to my credit? That day I determined to see Barkston and McAndrew, and the next to leave for Tientsin in search of my darling. But I was not destined to make the journey after all.

Calling at the club, I enquired for George Barkston. He happened to be in the building and greeted me in the hall with all the surprise imaginable.

'By Jove, Bruce!' he cried. 'This is really most wonderful. I was only speaking of you this morning, and here you turn up like – '

' "Like a bad penny", you were going to say.'

'Not a bit of it. Like the Wandering Jew would be more to the point. But don't let us stand here. Come along with me. I'm going to take you to my bungalow to tiffin.'

'But my dear fellow, I – '

'I know all about that,' he cried. 'However, you've just got to come along with me. I've got a bit of news for you.'

As nothing would induce him to tell me what it was, we chartered 'rickshaws, and set off for his residence.

When we reached it I was ordered to wait in the hall while he went in search of his wife. Having made some enquiries, he led me to the drawing-room, opened the door, and bade me go inside. Though inwardly wondering what all this mystery might mean, I followed his instructions.

A lady was sitting in an easy chair near the window, sewing. *That lady was Gladys!*

'Wilfred!' she cried, jumping to her feet, and turning quite pale, for she could scarcely believe her eyes.

'Gladys!' I answered, taking her in my arms, and kissing her with all the enthusiasm of a long-parted lover.

'I cannot realise it yet,' she said, when the first transports were over. 'Why did you not let me know you were coming to Shanghai?'

'Because I had no notion that you were here,' I answered.

'But did you not call on Mr Williams in Tientsin? And did he not give you my letter?'

'I have not been to Tientsin, nor have I seen Mr Williams. I have come straight down the Yangtze-Kiang from the west.'

'Oh, I am so glad – so thankful to have you back. We have been separated such a long, long time.'

'And you still love me, Gladys?'

'Can you doubt it, dear? I love you more fondly than ever. Does not the warmth of my greeting now convince you of that?'

'Of course it does,' I cried. 'I only wanted to have the assurance from your own dear lips. But now tell me, how do you come to be in Shanghai, and in George Barkston's house, of all other places?'

'Well, that would make too long a story to tell *in extenso* just now. We must reserve the bulk of it. Suffice it that my brother and sister have been transferred to a new post in Japan, and while they are getting their house in Tokyo ready, I came down here to stay with Mrs Barkston, who is an old school friend. I expect them here in about a week's time to fetch me.'

'And now the most important of all questions. When are we to be married?'

She hung her pretty head and blushed so sweetly that I had to take her in my arms again and kiss her. I pressed my question, however, and it was finally agreed that we should refer the matter to her brother-in-law on his arrival the following week.

To bring my long story to a close, let me say that we were married three weeks after my return to Shanghai, in the English church, and that we ran across to Japan for our honeymoon. It may be thought that with my marriage my connection with the Chinese nation came to an end. Unfortunately that was not so. Two days after our arrival in Nagasaki two curious incidents occurred that brought in their train a host of unpleasant suspicions. My wife and I had retired to rest for the night, and were both sleeping soundly, when we were awakened by a loud cry of fire. To my horror I discovered that our room was ablaze. I forced the door, and having done so, seized my wife, threw a blanket over her, and made a rush with her outside. How the fire had originated no one could tell, but it was fortunate we were roused in time, otherwise we should certainly have both lost our lives. As it was most of our belongings perished in the flames. A kindly Englishman, resident in the neighbourhood, seeing our plight, took pity on us, and insisted that we should make use of his house until we decided on our future movements. We remained with him for two days, and it was on that following our arrival at his abode that the second circumstance occurred to cause me uneasiness.

We had been out shopping in the morning and returned just in time for tiffin, which when we arrived was already on the table. While we were washing our hands before sitting down to it, our host's little terrier, who was possessed of a thieving disposition, clambered up and helped himself. By the time we returned (the owner of the bungalow, you must understand, lunched at his office, and did not come home till evening) he had eaten half the dish and spoiled the rest. We preferred to make our meal off biscuits and butter rather than call the servants and put them to the trouble of cooking more. An hour later the dog was dead, poisoned, as we should have been had we partaken of the curry. The new cook, who we discovered later was a Chinaman, had meanwhile decamped and could not again be found.

That evening when returning home in the dusk, a knife was thrown from a window across the street, narrowly grazed my throat, and buried itself in the woodwork of the house I was passing at the time. Without more ado I booked two passages aboard a mail steamer and next day set sail with my wife for England.

Arriving in London I took a small furnished house in a quiet part of Kensington, and settled myself down while I looked about me for a small property in the country.

Now to narrate one last surprise before I say goodbye. One afternoon I went up to town to consult a land agent about a place I had seen advertised, and was walking down the Strand, when I felt a hand placed upon my shoulder. I wheeled round to *find myself face to face with Nikola*. He was dressed in frock coat and top hat, but was otherwise the same as ever.

'Dr Nikola!' I cried in amazement.

'Yes, Dr Nikola,' he answered quietly, without any show of emotion. 'Are you glad to see me?'

'Very glad indeed,' I replied; 'but at first I can hardly believe it. I thought most probably you were still in China.'

'China became too hot to hold me,' he said with a laugh. 'But I shall go out there again as soon as this trouble blows over. In the meantime I am off to St Petersburg on important business. Where are you staying? And how is your wife?'

'I am staying in Kensington,' I replied; 'and I am glad to say that my wife is in the best of health.'

'I needn't ask if you are happy; your face tells me that. Now can you spare me half an hour?'

'With every pleasure.'

'Then come along to Charing Cross; I want to talk to you. This is my taxi.'

He led me to a cab which was waiting alongside the pavement, and when I had seated myself in it, stepped in and took his place beside me.

'This is better than Thibet, is it not?' he said, as we drove along.

'Very much better,' I answered with a laugh. 'But how wonderful it seems that we should be meeting here in this prosaic fashion after all we have been through together. There is one thing I have never been able to understand: what became of you after you left me at Ya-Chow-Fu?'

'I went off on another track to divert the attention of the men who were after us.'

'You think we were followed then?'

'I am certain of it, worse luck. And what's more they are after us now. I have had six attempts made upon my life in the last three months. But they have not managed to catch me yet. Why, you will hardly believe it, *but there are two Chinamen following you down the Strand even now*. Dusk has fallen, and you might walk down a side street and thus give them the opportunity they want. That was partly why I picked you up.'

'The devil! Then my suspicions were correct after all. The hotel we stayed at in Nagasaki was fired the first night we were in it, a dish of curry intended for us was poisoned two days later, while I was nearly struck with a knife two days after that again. Yesterday I saw a Chinaman near our house in Kensington, but though I thought he appeared to be watching my house I may have been mistaken in his intentions.'

'What was he like? Was he dressed in English clothes? And was half his left ear missing?'

'You are describing the man exactly.'

'Quong Ma. Then look out. If that gentleman has his eye upon you I should advise you to leave. He'll stick to you like wax until he gets his opportunity, and then he'll strike. Be advised by me, take time by the forelock and clear out of England while you have the chance. They want the things we took, and they want revenge To get both they'll follow us to the ends of the earth.'

'And now one very important question: have the things you took proved of sufficient value to repay you for all your trouble and expense?'

'Of more than sufficient value. I'm going to see a French chemist in St Petersburg about that anaesthetic now. In less than a year I shall enlighten this old country, I think, in a fashion it will not forget. Wait and see!'

As he said this we entered the station-yard, and a minute or so later were standing alongside the Continental express. Time was almost up, and intending passengers were already being warned to take their seats. Nikola saw his baggage placed in the van and then returned to me and held out his hand.

'Goodbye, Bruce,' he said. 'We shall probably never meet again. You served me well, and I wish you every happiness. One last word of caution, however: beware of that fellow with half an ear, and don't give him a chance to strike. Farewell, and think sometimes of Dr Nikola!'

I shook hands with him, the guard fluttered his flag, the engine whistled, and the train steamed out of the station. I waved my hand in token of goodbye, and since then I have never heard or seen anything of Dr Nikola, the most extraordinary man I have ever come in contact with.

When the last carriage was out of sight, I went into the station-yard intending to get a taxi, but when I had beckoned one up a man brushed past me and appropriated it. *To my horror it was the Chinaman with half an ear I had seen outside my house the day before.*

Waiting until he had left the station-yard, I made my way down to the Embankment and took the Underground Railway for Earl's Court, driving home as fast as I could go from there. On the threshold of my residence my servant greeted me with the information that a Chinaman had just called to see me. I waited to hear no more, but packed my things, and within a couple of hours my wife and I had left London for a tiny country town in the Midlands. Here at least we thought we should be safe; but as it turned out we were no more secure there than in London or Nagasaki, for that week the hotel in which we stayed caught fire in the middle of the night, and for the second time since our wedding we only just managed to escape with our lives.

Next day we migrated to a still smaller place in Devonshire, near Torquay. Our enemies still pursued us, however, for we had not been there a month before a most daring burglary was committed in my rooms in broad daylight, and when my wife and I returned from an excursion to a neighbouring village, it was to find our trunks rifled, and our belongings strewn about our rooms. The most extraordinary part of the affair, however, was the fact that nothing, save a small Chinese knife, was missing.

The county police were soon to the fore, but the only suspicious character they could think of was a certain Celestial with half an ear, who had been observed in the hamlet the day before, and even he could not be discovered when they wanted him.

On hearing that last piece of news I had a consultation with my wife, told her of Nikola's warning, and asked her advice.

As a result we left the hotel, much to the chagrin of the proprietor, that night, and departed for Southampton, where we shipped for New York the following day. Judge of our feelings on reading in an afternoon paper, purchased on board previous to sailing, that the occupants of our bed had been found in the morning with their throats cut from ear to ear.

In New York things became even more dangerous than in England, and four distinct attempts were made upon my life. We accordingly crossed the continent to San Francisco, only to leave it in a hurry three days later for the usual reason.

Where we are now, my dear Craigie, as I said in my Introduction, I cannot even tell you. Let me tell you one thing, however, and that is, though we have been here six months, we have seen no more of the half-eared Chinaman, nor indeed any of his sinister race. We live our own lives, and have our own interests, and now that my son is born, we are as happy as any two mortals under similar circumstances can expect to be. I love and honour my wife above all living women, and for that reason, if for no other, I shall never regret the circumstances that brought about my meeting with that extraordinary individual, Dr Nikola.

Now, old friend, you know my story. It has taken a long time to tell – let us hope that you will think it worth the trouble. If you do, I am amply repaid. Goodbye!

THE END